W9-CFG-580

in a family way

Also by James Calder

Knockout Mouse

About Face

james calder

in a family way

a bill damen mystery

CHRONICLE BOOKS
SAN FRANCISCO

acknowledgments I owe great debts to Jennifer Beachey, M.D., and Mandi Clark, Ph.D., for their help and advice on this book. Many thanks, too, to Ted Conover, Andy Black, and Damion Searls for their insightful comments. Hansel Bauman, Greta Jones, Chris Emley, Zac Unger, Dr. Shirley Tsai, Dr. Monica Gandhi, Dr. Jim Hopfenbeck, Bob Hugel, and Dana Zed provided much-appreciated help. And, as always, a great deal of gratitude to Jay Schaefer. I have tried to portray the scientific and medical techniques depicted in this novel as accurately as possible. They are based on reported results or plausible expectations in their fields, although some have been realized only with animals as of this writing. Any errors are mine alone. —*James Calder*

Library of Congress Cataloging-in-Publication Data:

Calder, James, 1957–
In a family way : a Bill Damen mystery / James Calder.
p. cm.
ISBN: 0-8118-4725-X
1. Private investigators—California—Santa Clara County—Fiction.
2. Santa Clara Valley (Santa Clara County, Calif.)—Fiction. 3. Children—Crimes against—Fiction. 4. Genetic engineering—Fiction. I. Title.
PS3603.A42515 2005
813'.6—dc22

2004029785

Printed in Canada

Designed by Benjamin Shaykin
Composition by Kristen Wurz
Typeset in Miller and Nillenium

Distributed in Canada by Raincoast Books
9050 Shaughnessy Street
Vancouver, British Columbia V6P 6E5

10 9 8 7 6 5 4 3 2 1

Chronicle Books LLC
85 Second Street
San Francisco, California 94105
www.chroniclebooks.com

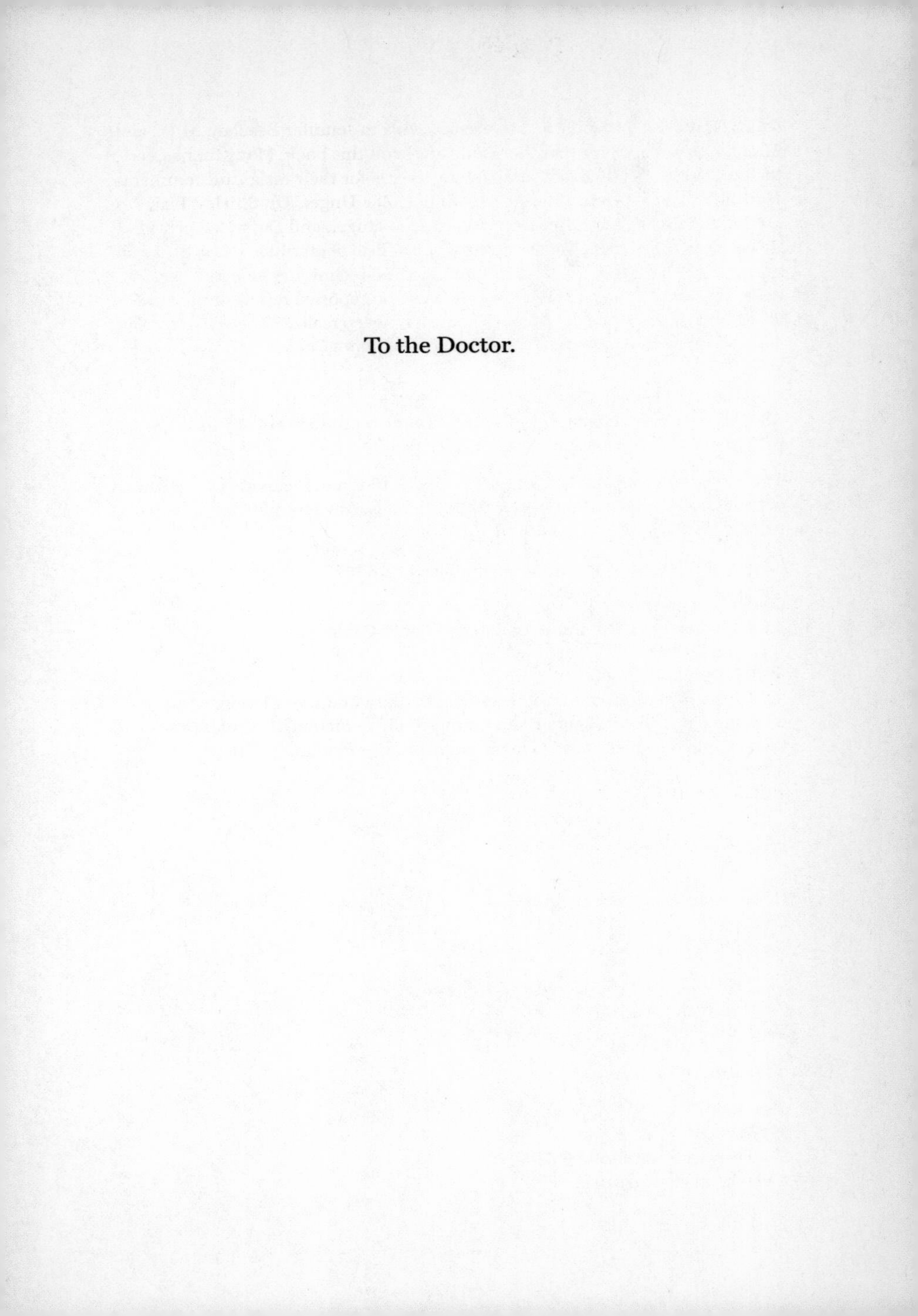

To the Doctor.

Gods who beget themselves
Solitarily from themselves
Over and over,
And yet have no idea
In the least what they are.

—Faust

1

One unbearable loss had come on top of another for Christopher and Janet Claypool, and it seemed a cruel turn that they were to be held to account for the latest. But that was before I knew of the bargains they had made and the price at which they had purchased their miracle.

Chris was my cousin and I had always counted him a lucky man. Taller than me, better looking, assured of his place in the world, settled happily with Janet. Chris was the one in the family to whom I was always compared. We were about the same age, yet I was still renting, suspiciously single, and engaged in a vaguely shady, definitely undependable line of work. Chris was married, owned a house in San Francisco's exclusive St. Francis Wood neighborhood, and was slated, someday, to take over his father's powerful construction engineering firm.

Chris called me one Sunday afternoon. This was remarkable for two reasons. First, he rarely initiated contact since we'd become adults. Second, he never, in all our lives, even in childhood, had asked for my help. That was the first sign that everything I thought I knew about him was going to change. His daughter, Margaret, was missing. But her disappearance, along with the humiliation he was about to suffer at his father's sixtieth-birthday party, was only the beginning.

» » » » »

One of the advantages of being a camera jockey was that if you had to go to a party you didn't really want to go to, your camera served as an excellent shield between you and the guests. If, on the other hand, you were at a party you did enjoy, the camera became an encumbrance.

My uncle Cole's sixtieth-birthday party was the first kind. He threw it for himself to demonstrate to the world just how powerful and successful he had become. Cole was a master of potlatch, the art of giving in order to consolidate his power. Every summer, during my childhood, I anticipated the week we spent at his "cabin"—three floors, eight bedrooms—at Lake Tahoe. The lake and the woods were the main attraction, but I was duly impressed by the private dock, the watercraft, and the multiple refrigerators filled with more steak, lobster, champagne, and beer than anyone could hope to consume in a week. My mother regarded it all with a certain sardonic humor that I would come to appreciate later in life. Cole shoveled his luxury on us to accentuate how great the chasm between our branches of the family had become, how superior his path to that of his sister. We referred to those in the clan who'd gone over to the "Cole side" the way others talked about going over to the "dark side."

The birthday party was held in an elaborate ballroom in Hillsborough, an enclave south of the city favored by San Francisco CEOs. The ballroom was decorated in blue and white bunting, the official colors of Claypool Construction Engineering. The plates were blue, the tablecloths white, and the red flower sprays added a dash of patriotism. Places were set for three hundred of Cole's best friends. The middle of the room was packed with guests drinking cocktails and plucking hors d'oeuvres from roaming trays. An ensemble on a raised platform played old standards. I recognized faces from the news—executives, former secretaries of defense, congressional representatives—as I made my way through the crowd, greeting relatives. Chris's sisters gave me careful pecks on the cheek. Amy, the younger one, wore a svelte black sheath, pearls at her throat, to catch the attention of qualified single men. Regan, the married one, looked gift-wrapped in pink crepe and a giant bow.

Chris had arrived a few minutes before me. His blond head bobbed as he worked the floor, shaking hands, forcing some hearty laughs out of himself, making sure everyone saw him. My task tonight was to run interference with his father. In his call this afternoon, Chris said that his daughter, Margaret, had been missing for two days. I found it odd that the party took priority over finding her, but Chris insisted it had to be so. He presumed Margaret's absence was simply a matter of miscommunication: His wife, Janet, had gone to Monterey to see her sister and Chris had been at work nearly the entire weekend. Ulla, the twenty-two-year-old nanny, had charge of the little girl. Ulla, most likely, had gotten the idea that she and Margy (we pronounced it with a hard *g*) ought to take a little weekend trip. Her car was gone. The only hitch was, Ulla had not answered calls to her cell phone. She'd probably just misplaced it, but Chris was a wreck. He and Janet had lost their first daughter, Helen, six years earlier. Yet anxiety about how the potential disaster would reflect on his competence as a father took precedence. Above all, he insisted that his father, Cole, know nothing about the crisis.

I dropped my birthday present off at a table in front and entered the fray. The air was rich with perfume and cigar smoke. The normal rules apparently didn't apply to his guests. My mother was sailing in the Aegean with her new boyfriend, or she would have made a dutiful appearance with me. My sister was exempt because she lived on the East Coast.

I stopped to greet an aunt, great-aunt, and ancillary relatives as I pushed my way through to the bar. I needed some fortification before I removed my small video camera from my coat pocket and took on this crowd. Kiersty, Chris's secretary, flashed me a smile. I had not failed to notice the backless green satin gown she was barely wearing. The bartender gave her a Cosmopolitan. She lifted it to a pair of glossy red lips and said, in a conspiratorial voice, "Got to go. Chris asked me to keep his dad happy."

I tossed down a glass of the house bourbon, Knob Creek, powered on the camera, and got ready to simulate nepotal affection for the man I no longer addressed as Uncle, only as Cole.

He stood at the head of a circle of his cronies. They took turns offering old-boy toasts, the ones unsuitable for mixed company at the dinner to come. It was hard not to admire the outward charm and easy humor—the expertly modulated panache evinced by all truly effective bullies—with which Cole handled his fellow alpha males.

A man with thick gray-streaked hair offered an encomium to Claypool Construction Engineering. "To the best erections in the city!" he proclaimed, raising his glass.

This elite circle, in their tailored tuxes and black shoes polished to a high gloss, cracked up at the old joke. Cole saw me and gave a wink. I came forward to offer my birthday wishes. He responded with the patented unctuous smile he reserved for my side of the family. He raised his glass at the mini-DV in my left hand.

"Here's to Bill," Cole intoned. "My nephew, the—what's the movie word?—the *auteur*."

This brought a dull murmur and a few token clinks. It was time to start shooting. Cole smirked and took a gulp of scotch, his ample stomach pushing out his cummerbund.

"You'll give me the tape, won't you, Bill?" he said. "A little birthday present, in case you forgot to bring one. Speaking of which—Amy and Regan, and even that little vixen Kiersty, have been waiting on me hand and foot, but where's that son of mine?"

"He's making sure everyone else is having a good time," I said.

"Well, he's forgotten the guest of honor. He'd better not take the old man for granted, unless it's because he's busy sealing the Jakarta deal."

Cole's eye twitched and a sneaky grin crossed his face. His glass swooped to the circle in a new toast. "To my son, Christopher! Can't blame him for acting scarce tonight. Pipsqueak's worried about my health: hale and hearty and stomping like a bull. Afraid he'll never get his chance to step into the old man's shoes. Sixty and counting, Christopher, with no retirement in sight!" Cole paused to scan the room, then lifted his voice so that it would carry. "Don't worry, son! You've got good genes! You'll be boss for plenty of years after I'm gone!"

Everyone laughed. "If you play your cards right," Cole muttered, putting the glass to his lips.

The toast had been pronounced with a kind of rough affection, and the crowd took it for good-natured ribbing. But I had Cole's face in close-up. I saw the punishing tightness of the muscles around the mouth and eyes, the ire at Chris's neglect.

As I panned the circle, I caught one man tactfully looking away, his lips pressed shut. It was Leonard Wilson, the only African-American in upper management at the firm. He was about ten years older than me, strong-shouldered, a little doughy in the cheeks and chin, with a trim mustache. He wore a perfectly tailored tux punctuated with exquisite sapphire cuff links. Wilson was impeccable on the details.

Cole saw him, too. "Here's the man that really deserves a toast," he said. "Leonard Wilson, who orchestrated this event so expertly. I don't know what I'd do without you, Leonard. You're all I could ask for. You deserve much, and you shall have it."

Wilson lifted his chin slightly, tacitly agreeing with Cole even if he'd never say so himself. "Thank you, Mr. Claypool."

The formality of his reply reminded me that to everyone but family, Cole was "Mr. Claypool." The syllables, in the halls of Claypool Construction, were intoned with a reverence reserved for deities. There was only one "Mr. Claypool." Whatever bank tellers and maître d's might call him, Chris was never more than "Chris" or "the young Mr. Claypool." Heir apparent though he might be, there was question whether he'd ever rise to the level of being anointed the next "Mr. Claypool." Cole had made that abundantly clear with the toast to Wilson. Chris had competition.

The circle around Cole began to break up. I stopped shooting. I'd seen enough to buy into Chris's rationale for not telling his father about Margaret. I went to find out how he was doing.

He was lurking behind a potted palm, staring at his cell phone.

"Hanging in there?" I asked.

He snapped the phone shut. "Did you see that stack of presents?"

I nodded. "The man who has everything just got a little more."

"Janet was supposed to get him something—but then with Margaret . . ." A new panic was in his voice. "I'm dead meat."

"I got him a GPS watch. Went in on it with my family. You can add your name to the card."

"Thanks, but he'd see right through it. Has he said anything about me?"

"He, uh, misses you."

"What was he saying about genes? People were looking at me and laughing."

"Just a joke." I nodded at the cell phone. "Any news about Margaret?"

He shook his head. "Janet told the police to go ahead and put out one of those missing-child alerts. My father won't hear about it until tomorrow."

"Janet's not coming?"

"No way."

An announcement from the band podium asked the guests to take their seats for dinner.

"I'll be at his table," Chris said. "Keep an eye out. If you see me get up, follow me."

My table was near Cole's but off to the side. Noting the others seated with me, I realized it was the table for family members who hadn't made a dent in the world the way Cole's side had. My aunt Natalie, with her husband and teenage boys, was here, along with Chris's great-aunt Henrietta and a few others from Cole's wife Regina's side. Natalie leaned over and asked me what was bothering Chris. That helped me understand his anxiety. As practiced as he was at masking his emotions, his father was bound to demand the source of his distress.

For now, though, Chris was safe. Cole was at the microphone on the podium, readying a benediction. I picked up my camera and rolled.

Cole tapped the microphone and cleared his throat. "Friends, Romans, countrymen," he began in his Jovian manner.

He stopped. His forehead curdled and his eyes became slits. Still rolling, I twisted and rose from my seat.

A pair of uniformed policemen had entered the room. They crossed the open floor and made their way through the tables. People leaned away like blades of grass bent by the wind. I eased down in my chair and the two cops grew larger in the viewfinder. Their faces were severe, with the kind of expression reserved for truly despicable felons. They filled the frame, brushed past, and marched to the head table.

Chris pushed back his chair and stepped up to meet them. "You've found her—" he began with a hint of eagerness.

The policemen flanked him. One jerked his arm behind his back. The other made the pronouncement: "Christopher Claypool, you're under arrest for the death of Margaret Claypool."

As the cops took him away, Chris shot me a piercing look, a look of anger and blame for my failure to foresee and prevent this. I'd let him down, the look said, and he'd been a fool to ask for my help in the first place.

Chris's call for help had come at one o'clock that afternoon. It surprised me because he always, always made sure you were in his debt, not the other way around. He took after his father in that he enjoyed offering me trinkets of assistance, like a tent he no longer wanted, or a computer or mountain bike. The presumption was that I was a starving artist and he was a man of means. I was no artist: At most I was a craftsman, a camera jockey, pure and simple. But because I did not work in the world of construction, finance, or software, I was considered "bohemian."

The day had started slowly. I let myself wake gradually, reading the paper, chased by water and aspirin, in bed. I'd stayed out late the night before. When people in the film trade had a chance to party, they jumped on it like it might not come along again for months. If you were lucky and got work, it wouldn't.

I dragged myself out of bed, made coffee, and faced up to the day. Late March, the sky a delicate eggshell blue, the air warm and blossom-fresh—the kind of Sunday a man should savor while he was still young(ish). Instead, I rattled around my creaky four-room Potrero Hill flat, drinking too much coffee and scrupulously ignoring the TV clicker. Part of me told myself to lace up for the local pickup basketball game or call a friend to go to the beach. But I couldn't shake the sensation that I ought to be productive. It was an especially pointless feeling, because business was dead at the moment and there was little to be done except send my reel to producers and directors I did not know and who would not respond. One of the tricks having your own business plays on you is that it doesn't let you enjoy free time when work is slack.

I'm known on my résumé as Director of Photography, or, if I'm feeling old-fashioned, Cinematographer. On location, I'm the "shooter," unless I have more responsibility, in which case I'm the "DP." I got big enough for my britches last month to rent an office down among the decaying docks and warehouses at the foot of Potrero Hill. I knew a big enough network of film hands around San Francisco that I could handle or farm out just about any project that came my way. I'd also managed to solve a couple of criminal cases and had decided to invite a new one to walk through the door. I needed to apply for an Investigator license, but so far had gotten away with connecting the cases to my film work.

I'd gone so far as to interview potential assistants. The shingle I intended to hang out would read:

DAMEN CAMERAWORK & INVESTIGATIONS

* FILMMAKING

* INVESTIGATIONS

* SECOND OPINIONS

Naturally, the work dried up about the same time the ink on the lease did. The office sat empty and the young woman I'd planned to hire as the assistant had taken off to ride waves in Baja. Exactly the kind of thing I should be doing. With her, come to think of it. Instead, I was paying for my hubris by brooding on the couch, torn between dutiful drudgery and dutiful enjoyment of the day.

I flicked some crumbs from the cushion onto the floor. The sofa, old and green and wantonly comfortable, filled the rectangular bay of the main window in my front room. With its high, pressed-tin ceiling and carved moldings, the room was meant when it was built in the 1880s to be where visitors were received on Sundays. Now half of it was occupied by a jumble of black canvas bags, my film gear, waiting to be stowed in its new place in the office, and until then blocking the path to my desk and bookshelves. In the other half were the TV, stereo, a battered oak coffee table, and the green sofa on which I lay, its seams frayed and fabric worn like an old dog losing its fur. As soon as I got more work, I could buy the furniture I needed for the office. As soon as that happened, I could move the work gear over there. As soon as it was gone, I could invite people over here again.

Camera work kept me in pretty good shape—hefting twenty pounds twelve hours a day will do that—but now that I was in my thirties, I noticed that a couple weeks' layoff caused my jeans to get smaller. I got my high-tops from the closet and pulled them on in order to burn up some calories on the court.

That was when the phone rang.

"Bill? It's Chris. Your cousin. I need your help tonight."

"Cole's birthday party. Let me guess, you want me to be the official videographer."

"No. Wait—do bring your camera. For diversion. I want you to be there with me, on call. I'm going to try to get this situation solved in the next couple of hours, but chances are I'll need you. I'll pay your full rate."

"What's going on, Chris?"

"No time. Be at my house an hour before the party. Five o'clock. If the situation gets resolved, we'll have a beer."

Typical Chris. Always in control. He'd learned from his father.

I said, "Just tell me what it is, and I'll get started now."

"Bill—" He stopped. I could almost hear him shifting gears, as if he was changing the track in his brain from Alpha Male to Human Being. "Margy's missing. We just realized it this morning."

"Oh no. How long has she been gone?"

"It was a total mix-up. Janet went to Monterey to spend a long weekend with her sister. She thought Margaret was with me. I thought Ulla had gone with them, or taken Margy to Santa Cruz. I *told* them I had no time this week. I was in meetings all frigging day, into the night. Every morning Jakarta starts ringing my mobile at six. I figured Janet knew where Ulla was. This project—it's the first time my father's put me in charge of a proposal to win a contract. I didn't have a nanosecond to think about anything until Janet came home last night and said, 'Where's Margaret?' Frigging Ulla was nowhere to be seen."

"Shit, Chris."

"Yeah, *thanks,* Bill."

"What do the police say?"

"They put out the word to pick up Ulla. And Margaret, of course, if she's with her. My father *can't* know about this."

"I think Cole would put her disappearance ahead of his birthday party."

"You . . . do . . . not . . . get . . . it." He enunciated each word as if explaining to a dense student. "Yes, he'd be concerned, even though he never sees her. But he'd rip me—Look, just do what I say."

"I'm getting the picture." I'd never heard Chris talk about his father this way. I'd seen them as a united front. I thought it'd make sense to enlist Cole and all his resources, instead of worrying about his own image, but if this was what my client wanted, this was what he'd get. His emotional defenses were obviously on red alert.

"Janet's been patrolling the streets ever since she got back from Monterey," Chris said. "I'm sure there's a simple, stupid explanation. Ulla and Margy will turn up for the party all bright-eyed and like, 'What's the big deal?'"

"Ulla should have called you."

"She probably lost her phone, or the battery ran out. She's a nice, responsible Swedish girl! What's she going to kidnap Margaret and all her health problems for?"

"At least she knows to give Margy her insulin."

A long hiss of air escaped through Chris's teeth. "This is so *fucked.* Janet should have canceled her trip to Monterey when she saw how busy I was."

"Give me some addresses. Parks, playgrounds, places Ulla took Margy."

He reeled off some locations. I knew the ones in the city. Others were farther south. "You're on the clock, Bill. I'm paying for your services."

"We'll worry about that later."

"Just keep track!" he burst out. "I've got to go. See you at five."

Click.

» » » » »

It's a sad comment on human beings (on this one, at least) that another person's misery can jerk you out of your self-pity. It no longer mattered, as I'd driven away from my flat, whether my gear got put away or my new office sat vacant and lonely. The fact that I could leave INVESTIGATIONS on my shingle was trivial. I had a purpose now. Christopher and Janet Claypool's daughter was missing. She was my three-and-a-half-year-old cousin and she'd already suffered enough for a lifetime.

Somewhere in the lower strata of the chaos on my desk, I found the Claypool family Christmas card. Margaret was front and center, smiling, as she usually, miraculously, did. I brought it with me as I drove across the Mission, then pressed the pedal to the floor to urge my old International Harvester Scout up and over Twin Peaks. The grassy flanks of the mountain radiated an eye-popping green, the result of a winter of good rain. Something about the color made me want to find the tint control. California poppies bloomed along the curb. As I crested the ridge, the Pacific scrolled out in front of me like a blue sheet. It was a welcome contrast to the hills. I liked its depth and mystery, the way the constantly shifting colors reflected the mood of some immense force beyond our conception. Right now the water was a deep, resolute cobalt blue, as if to set firm limits on the exuberance of spring.

The Scout picked up speed descending the other side, down Portola Avenue, past the compact Mediterranean-ish houses and windblown trees of West Portal. I stopped at Stern Grove, a broad ravine of a park near Chris's house, and made a circuit with my photo of Margy. No one had seen her. I had no better luck at the other parks I tried. It was still before five when I drove across Junipero Serra, into the enchanted neighborhood of undulating streets, stately Monterey pines, and tall brick houses known as St. Francis Wood. Chris and Janet's was a looming pseudo-Gothic edifice of narrow gables and dark brick chimneys. I never could figure out why they chose it, except that it was the biggest on the block.

The door chimes sounded like bells from some diminutive church. I'd begun to wonder if anyone was home when Chris swung the door open. He was haggard in a white T-shirt, floppy white socks, and sweatpants. A baseball cap hid his face and a shadow mottled his chin.

Our eyes met and for a split second I saw in them a fathomless blue abyss. I had an idea I ought to embrace and console him. There'd been little physical contact between us in the last fifteen years aside from the occasional bump on the basketball court. We'd been comrades-in-arms as kids, but growing up had meant growing apart. He'd become opaque to me, zipped up behind the neat armored package he presented to the world: close-trimmed blond hair, button-down oxford shirts, creased khakis, and well-knotted tie. His head was a squared-off oval with a forthright jaw and broad, jutting brow. It was a pleasant face, the features evenly spaced, the skin well-scrubbed. His azure eyes, capable of being both cool and intense, aristocratic and all-American, normally attracted attention from women.

He turned quickly and, leaving the door open, shambled back into the house. I followed, voicing my concern about Margaret. He mumbled that he'd be back and mounted the stairs to the second floor.

I laid my suit and camera bag on a suede sofa and waited in the medieval darkness of the living room. Chris and Janet had tried to neutralize the Goth effect of the house by enlarging some windows and painting the rooms. But the gloom still hovered. The dark maw of the brick hearth yawned in the opposite wall. A large still life hung to my right, flowers in bright bursting blossom, stems preternaturally straight. On a side table below, a forgotten bunch of real flowers drooped from their vase, stamens and pollen littering the floor. The rigidity of the stalks in the painting, the candied reds and violets and yellows of the petals, the grating perfection of the background, said more than I wanted to know about how Chris lived his life.

I took the vase into the kitchen and dumped the flowers. An open jar of peanut butter sat on the polished granite counter, along with a loaf of sliced bread, as if waiting for Margaret's imminent return. Her yellow juice cup sat on the table, along with the beaded Hello Kitty purse in which her insulin injection pens were kept. Over the back of a chair was draped her tomato-red dress with tiny white flowers, two buttons missing, a sewing basket on the seat for the mending.

It was nearly five-thirty. I climbed the main staircase from the front hall to the second floor. A voice murmured from the master bedroom. I knocked and peered in. Chris, in a chair looking out the window, turned and gave me a guilty look.

"Sorry," I said. "I didn't know you had company."

He grunted something and turned back to the window. It was a large room, with a king-size bed, walk-in closet, sitting area, and a bathroom as big as my own bedroom. The ceiling curved into a high arch, like a bishop's hat. Chris sat staring at the failing light outside.

"If we're going to go to this party, we better go," I said.

Chris dug the heels of his palms into his eyes. "Sorry. I was on the phone."

He pushed himself up from the chair and removed a thin headset. Half-dressed in a white shirt and striped boxers, he'd also pulled on a pair of dark socks that stretched to the top of his calves. He'd once let me in on the secret of these socks, his favored brand, as if they were the secret of life itself. "They don't bunch around your ankle," he'd explained. "They stay up on your leg. Bugs the crap out of me when my socks fall down."

He disappeared into the bathroom to shave. I went back downstairs to change. I was grappling with my tie in the living-room mirror when Chris came galloping down the staircase. "Let's go, Bill!" he barked.

"Hold on," I said.

"Jesus," he said, stripping my arms from my neck, yanking the knot into a chokehold. He'd snapped out of his sullen mood. "Can't you even—"

I knocked his hands away and finished the tie myself. "Quit acting like your father."

His face froze, stung, in the mirror. The fear he'd been hiding was suddenly visible. He waited for me at the door, then slammed it shut behind us. His spanking-new metallic gray Range Rover was parked in the driveway. The Scout, in all its rust-bitten, sun-faded orange glory, was planted behind the Rover. Chris stared as if he'd never seen my jeep before.

"You still drive that thing?" he demanded.

"It got you and me up to the Sierra and back a few times."

"Fifteen years ago." He paused at the door to his car. "We'll drive separately. If I have to leave, tell my dad it's a nine-one-one from Jakarta. He's been riding me about this project—'It's your big chance, let's see if you choke under pressure.' I've been elbows-and-assholes all month. Keep the camera on my father at the party. When he asks why I'm not fawning over him, make excuses. Whatever you do, make him believe everything's all right with my family. I'll keep my distance."

"Oh, that'll mollify him."

"I've got no choice! He reads me like a book. He knows what I'm feeling before I do, then uses it against me. Goddammit, why are you making me explain all this?"

"All right, all right." Chris was a chip off the old block, all right, and Cole never let him forget he was no more than a chip.

I creaked open the door of my Scout, got in, backed out, and waited for Chris to do the same. His Rover bounced out of the driveway and sped off.

I took my time driving down to the party. Chris's moods were as unpredictable as his father's, a way of keeping people off balance. In the space of a few minutes he'd transformed from a haggard, mumbling guy in his underwear into the adult Chris to which I'd become accustomed, Asshole in Charge, crisp in his charcoal Hugo Boss suit, neck stiffened by his blue silk tie. His distress about his daughter and his father made me willing, for the moment, to indulge him.

Still, I wondered: Why me? Was his half-forgotten, camera-toting cousin really his only resort? True, I was family. Maybe some memory of our childhood closeness had spurred his call. He obviously felt he couldn't go to Cole with his fears. The division between them, always couched in the jocular terms of a natural father-son rivalry, startled me, like watching a seedpod that appeared unbreakable split in two.

I suppose, in retrospect, Chris could have schemed it all ahead of time. The idea felt far-fetched: Chris had always been a man who tried, even if he didn't always succeed, to believe in fair play. This was one of the many reasons he was considered to have fallen short of his father. If Chris really had hatched a plan that put his inheritance in such jeopardy, his behavior in the days that followed was a phenomenal acting job.

» » » » »

Denial is one of those self-replicating disorders that runs through families, and Chris's had it bad. The habit had gained strength in him as he matured, tamping down any messy emotions that might jeopardize the bright and prosperous future that was his to claim. I'd been in denial myself, this afternoon, when Chris told me Margaret was missing, as if the very act of picturing her death might make it happen. Now that we knew it had, it hit me hard.

Cole denied it, too, even after it had been announced by the cops who arrested Chris. He proclaimed to the crowd gathered for his birthday party that it was all a police blunder. Cole did more than exhort the party to continue, he compelled it by force of will. When he returned to his table, he let everyone within bellowing distance know that Chris's arrest was a sick theatrical stunt perpetrated by a DA who hated Cole's guts.

I asked around to find out which police station Chris was likely to have been taken to. The ballroom was still unsettled as I left.

Chris's look of blame lingered. An irrational feeling that I could have prevented Margaret's death came over me. Chris should have called me much earlier, I thought in my own defense, even as I knew the guilt was misplaced. Everyone close to a deceased tends to feel he or she could have saved them. The feeling increases with the youth of the victim.

The station was brand new, with polished terrazzo floors, a soothing fountain, and gleaming aluminum moldings running along the walls. An equally polished young officer sat at the front desk, protected by a Plexiglas window. She was polite and said she'd tell the desk sergeant I was here.

I paced the anteroom, hoping that somehow the power of Cole's denial would alter the facts. His speech carried a near-biblical authority that almost made you believe reality would conform to his will.

A few minutes later Chris's mother, expensively fragranced and wrapped in fur, came through the door. She demanded to see her son and got the same polite reply that I did. Only then did she turn and notice me.

"Oh, hello, Bill," she said.

"Hello, Regina."

A silence followed. Regina Claypool seemed remote and preoccupied, but then, she'd been that way for as long as I could remember. She was not the kind of mom who, when Chris and I played together as kids, made us peanut butter sandwiches. A maid did that. Cole and my mother were the siblings, so I had no blood connection with Regina, and felt it. In recent years she had become remote from Cole as well—or maybe it was the other way around.

She broke the silence by saying, "I'll take care of this, Bill."

"I can stay. I'm afraid it might be more serious than Cole thinks."

She cocked her head a fraction of an inch. She'd always been thin and had grown more so with age. The slight head motion had the effect of a slicing blade. It was not an invitation to explain but an expression of doubt about what I'd just said and my judgment in general.

I said, "What's this vendetta the DA's office has against Cole?"

Her lips, vivid red against her pale skin, pursed. "*Something* must explain this outrage."

It occurred to me that her biggest concern was how her son's arrest might be talked about among her social set. She hadn't bothered to mention the possibility that Margaret really was dead.

"You can talk to him for a minute now, Mrs. Claypool," the officer said through a speaker in the window.

I started for the door. Regina held me back with a touch of her gloved fingers. "I'll do this alone, Bill. Why don't you take your little camera, go on back to the party, and let them know everything's all right?"

"Because it's not," I said.

She ignored me and went through the door the officer held open for her. I didn't hear what happened beyond it, but Mrs. Claypool reappeared three minutes later. "He wants to talk to you," she said. She never looked at me and never broke her stride on the way to the front door. It seemed pointless for Chris to remain secretive with his parents, but maybe he just wasn't ready to deal with them yet.

One of the officers who'd arrested Chris intercepted me as I came through the door. "Are you his lawyer?" His voice was flat, his words clipped at the ends, making them sound skeptical.

"No, I'm his cousin."

He eyed me. He was a beefy guy, shorter than me, with a thick brown mustache. *Officer 2582,* his badge said. "This way."

He stopped and nodded to the second arresting officer, who was guarding a door along the corridor. 2582 opened the door. Chris slumped in a chair in front of a desk sergeant and a detective, hands cuffed, head hung in a posture of defeat. All animation seemed to have left his body. The surprise, in the brief glimpse I got, was seeing a certain sympathy in the sergeant's face.

The cop grabbed my elbow. "You're coming down here."

We went into a small interrogation room. I sat in a metal chair behind a metal table. He sat across from me with a clipboard. A pad and pencil were the only objects on the table. The officer filled in my name and relation to Chris on the clipboard, then asked how I was involved. I explained tersely that Chris had called me in a state of mild panic this afternoon.

"Did you wonder why he waited so long?"

"He didn't know his daughter was missing until last night. He was tied up at work. There was a miscommunication between him and his wife."

He stared, waiting me out. I said, "Is it true that Margaret is dead?"

"Dumped like a dead kitten. We showed him a picture. He confirmed it was her. He'll get to confirm it in person, too."

"Are you *trying* to make him feel worse?"

"You need to account for your whereabouts Friday afternoon and evening."

"That's when she died? What happened?"

"Where were you?"

I told him I was at home all afternoon working. He could look up my phone records. In the evening I went to a movie with some friends. Then I said, "What makes you think Chris killed Margaret?"

"You saw his body language. That's a guilty man."

"Of course he feels guilty! He lost track of his daughter and now she's dead!"

The officer toyed with the pencil in a show of patience. "She had a lot of medical problems. Did you know he's drained his accounts paying for her health care? He and his wife live high on the hog. Margaret was bankrupting them. Now she's not."

"What that says to me is that they cared so much about Margy they were willing to spend all they had on her, even though her life expectancy was short."

"They made it real short." The cop leaned back. "People do things you'd never think. And everyone's shocked. Happens again and again."

"How did Margaret die?"

"Take a wild guess."

"She had so many ailments—she could easily have gotten lost and fallen ill. She needed regular insulin injections."

"Funny. That's just how it happened. She got 'lost,' as you say, in Montoya County Park, then turned up dead in the woods at Hobart Beach Park. Family on a picnic found her. Eight-year-old son threw a ball into the woods for their retriever. Dog dragged her body out from a patch of blackberries. She was still holding on to her blanket. Had some little medallions with horse pictures on them in the pockets of her dress. They came spilling out when the family's father lifted her up. The ants had already gotten to her eyes."

He was watching me, watching my face for flickers of recognition. Undoubtedly he'd left a crucial detail or two out of the story.

"What killed her?" I asked.

"You were on the right track before. Keep going."

"She had diabetes. If she didn't get her insulin, she could have gone into shock."

"The coroner will make the exact determination. We saw very little bruising on her wrist and arms. No signs of blunt trauma or sexual assault, nothing under her fingernails."

"What about Ulla?"

"We've got most of what we need," the cop responded cagily. "Listen, Mr. Damen, Chris is going to tell the homicide detective what happened. This is your chance. You don't need to suffer the consequences for your cousin. His wife's on the way down here, by the way. We're searching their house."

"Who's the DA around here? Cole Claypool says he's got some kind of vendetta against him."

"You're talking about Mr. Gallegos? Mike Gallegos is in Sacramento. He doesn't even know about the arrest yet."

"Is the autopsy being done tomorrow?"

"I expect so." 2582 pushed the pad and pencil at me. "Give us a statement."

I looked at the pencil and resisted the urge to write something very succinct. The officer shrugged and stood up. "Margaret was a pretty little girl. It sickens me how some of you people treat your children. Like playthings, status symbols who get passed off to a nanny who barely speaks English. These parents, they're still children themselves."

The guy genuinely seemed to believe he was doing his job right. And maybe he was. Maybe the police honestly did suspect Chris. I asked if I could talk to him. The officer laughed and said, "Sorry, you got to get your stories straight *before* the arrest."

He took me back down the corridor and opened the door to the waiting room. There, sitting in a plastic chair, was a hunched and broken figure, eyes cast down at the floor. An instant of shameful hope flashed in my mind that Janet would not look up, that I would not have to witness the raw pain in her face.

"Your turn," the cop said to Janet.

She lifted her head. The agony was there, somewhere, hidden behind a frozen mask. She was numb. I hugged her. Her return hug was limp and formal. Her eyes were blank, as if the pain was too great to show to the world. I told her how sorry I was, how it seemed impossible this could happen again.

"Anything's possible anymore," Janet said in a robotic voice.

"They're going to take Chris to identify her. I can stay here for you until he comes back."

"No," Janet said in the same monotone. "I ought to see her, too. I'm her mother. Go back to the party, Bill. Someone needs to tell Cole and the immediate family. Our lawyer is coming. He'll take care of us."

The officer took Janet away for her interview. I went to the cop at the front desk. "Are they going to file charges against Chris?" I asked.

She turned her palms up.

"Is it being treated as a homicide?" I pressed.

"I'm not—" She caught herself, then said in a low voice, "I don't think they've decided yet."

"Thanks," I said. Both her manner and the glimpse I'd had of the desk sergeant told me that not everyone at the station had prejudged Chris to be guilty. I left with that one small ray of hope.

3

I drove back to the party in the Scout, my head still spinning. That Janet and Chris had to endure this kind of loss again was beyond my grasp. Was there any way Chris had brought this on himself, or was he just a guy whom God decided to turn into a bull's-eye for no special reason?

The sense of protectiveness I felt toward my cousin was unexpected, but not completely new. Once upon a time, we'd been partners in adventure. The differences between us were clear, but in our youth we'd complemented each other. We set up funny scenes for my Instamatic camera, dressing his dog in baby clothes, posing stuffed animals in ridiculous situations. When I got a video camera, we turned to adapting characters from comic books and TV. Chris always wanted to play the superhero. I went along, but undercut it by having him enact scenes of improbable stupidity.

What bonded us the most were the times we'd rescued each other from potential disasters. At Tahoe, when we were eight, we were swimming in the lake and I swallowed some water. Chris dragged me a crucial few feet to a wooden raft. A couple of years later, when we went camping in the woods outside his parents' house, I saved him in a different way. We'd wandered a little too far and had to spend the night. We set up camp quickly, in a forested ravine, as darkness fell. Chris went to pee and discovered some rolled-up blankets, empty cans, magazines, and a piece of ragged canvas. We were sitting ducks for the presumed wayward man—or men—who would return to find us invading their site. Chris began to weep. To make us both feel better, I spun tales of our imagined hobo campmate to him. He'd arrive with newly scrounged food, which he'd cook in a coffee can. We'd drink wine and have a boisterous night of song with him. The fantasy soothed us enough to let the undertow of sleep take us away. We awoke alone and intact, but the legend of our night with the hoboes grew in our minds.

Our tastes changed, of course, as we got older, but our temperaments did not. He still wanted to emulate, I still preferred to undercut. He was the straight man and I was the jester, a fool he tolerated because we both knew who, in the end, would get the girl. And the castle. And the kingdom.

By the time Chris went to Stanford and I went to Cal, we had few things left in common. I was turning into a grungy young filmmaker, while Chris became the picture frat boy–prepster. We still talked about, and played, basketball, but the games got rougher, as if winning would prove the superiority of our individual paths. Film classes indoctrinated me to believe that the "Hollywood taste" to which he proudly adhered was an oxymoron. We couldn't even agree on what beer to drink. Both of us were right and wrong in our own ways. Later, in our twenties, we recovered enough from the post-college crucible to be able to sit around and enjoy an ice-cold Budweiser from the can, take in a game, and talk about our lives.

Now, as I pulled into the lot outside the ballroom, Chris seemed surprisingly defenseless. Defenseless against his father, against the law, and against his own emotions. The crisis seemed to be bringing us back together, a small consolation for a big loss.

Reluctantly, I trudged back into the ballroom. The party was in full swing. The band was playing and dancers were cheek to cheek on the floor. Cole presided from the head table, having himself a brandy and a cigar as well-wishers streamed by. His rotund face could be jovial one moment, as it was now, but the thick brows could turn into a thunderhead of menace instantly. His forehead was the most expressive part of him, its wrinkles a true marvel of nature. Entire weather systems, spinning vortices and low-pressure areas, seemed to pass over it.

I asked for a minute to speak privately. Cole made a gesture to Leonard Wilson, who moved people back from the table. Regina, two seats down, turned to listen in.

I told Cole the news about Margaret first. He gave a small quiver, then projected himself forward in his chair. "Little Margy? Impossible." His voice choked a little as he mashed the cigar into a plate. "How the hell did it happen?"

"They found her in a park. Chris has identified her photo. That's all I know."

Cole shot a look at Regina. "They didn't tell you this?"

"Your son wouldn't confide in us," she said. "Apparently he trusts his distant relatives more."

"The truth is, he didn't want to disrupt your party," I said. "We thought it'd just been a mix-up, that Margaret was okay. Unfortunately, we were wrong."

"What about Janet?" Cole demanded. "She didn't keep track of her own child?"

"The nanny had her," I said. "We don't know where Ulla is right now."

"I *told* them to get someone more mature," Regina said. "And legal."

"Ulla may have been a victim, too," I pointed out. "I'm so sorry to have to bring the news. Chris is still being questioned. I don't know what charges they plan to file. It seems absurd. I don't get it."

"Oh, *I* get it," Cole said. "I'm going down to the station right now."

"Janet's there already," I said. "Their lawyer's on the way. Chris is not very communicative."

Cole sat back in his chair, calculating. "Yes. He's got to learn to fight for himself, anyhow." He narrowed his eyes at me, as if I might be in on the conspiracy. "I'll tell you what, Bill, you're right. This *is* absurd. It's an outrage and it's premeditated. It's time we buried Mike Gallegos for good."

Cole raised a finger in Wilson's direction. Wilson stepped forward. "Get Harry Harvey," Cole barked. "I need him right away."

"I'm sorry it happened during your party, Cole," I said.

He looked me in the eye and gave my arm a quick squeeze. "Things happen when they happen," he said in a decisive tone. "And I've seen a lot of things happen in my time."

Wilson made his way to the table accompanied by a well-tanned man with a thick crop of white hair slicked back in even comb-rows. Cole's chair fell and rebounded on the carpet as he pushed out from the table. He motioned for Wilson and Harvey to follow him.

"Cole!" Regina said. "Aren't you going to say something to the guests?"

"Tell them what you like," Cole replied. "They'll find out soon enough. Let them have fun while they can." He gave me a good-bye nod and said, "If you'll excuse me, I'm going to speak to my attorney."

I waited to see if Regina had anything more to say. Half a cigar smoldered on a plate of cake crumbs between us. She gave me a glance and then looked away.

"Good night, Regina," I said.

She hid her eyes behind a napkin and waved me off. I slipped around the edges of the crowd, ignoring the call of my name and questions about Chris. There was something unsaid, something strange about how his family was dealing with Margaret's death. It was as if what counted was not that Margaret, in all her uniqueness, had lost her life, but that this was the second time it had happened to Chris and Janet. If Cole didn't want his guests to know about Margaret, that was his decision. Our family was already the oddballs of the clan. I didn't need to be spreading bad news.

The engine of my old Scout rumbled to life in the parking lot. All of a sudden I was looking forward to the solitude of home. Maybe it wasn't so bad living alone in my ramshackle flat, after all. There was so much less to lose.

» » » » »

I really did not want to think about the autopsy. The idea of Margaret being dissected, weighed, and analyzed was too much. But it had to be done, and I went down to the coroner's office late Monday morning to ask what had been found.

The morgue was in the basement of the county building, where the cold could stay cool. The hairs on my arm rose in a familiar chill as I descended. Cinder-block walls, thick with muted yellow paint, pressed in on me. Odors of formaldehyde and ammonia mixed unpleasantly. Fluorescent lights made everyone look just this side of alive, particularly the clerk at the front counter. She rolled on her chair, from desk to computer to filing cabinet, doing her business like an automaton for several minutes before she noticed me standing there. Trifocals hung from a chain around her neck. Her features were stark, her skin a molluscan hue. Her manner gave the impression she'd prefer if all her customers were undemandingly dead. Behind her and her filing cabinets, swinging steel doors led to the morgue and examination theater.

I asked if the autopsy on Margaret Claypool was being performed this morning. She confirmed that it was. I stretched the truth and said I was her uncle, sent by the family to observe. She said no one was allowed to observe. I sighed with secret relief and said we'd like to receive a copy of the results as soon as possible. Without looking at me, she placed a clipboard and a form on the counter.

I sat in a plastic chair with metal legs to fill out the form. The linoleum floors were spotless, but in the corners and along the edges of the walls ran inky lines of concealed grime. Not a stitch of organic life could be found in the room, not even in the vase on the counter, in which stood steel stems that terminated in flowerlike steel cups.

A man strode in wearing a lab coat that was not so much white as laundry-gray. He placed a weathered black doctor's bag on the counter and spoke to the clerk in low, authoritative tones. She replied in her steady, robotic manner. I went to the counter.

"Excuse me, are you the pathologist?" I asked.

He gave me a quick and chilling glance. His face was long, with an extended spatula of a chin and an elongated nose. Hair sprouted from his nose and ears, along with unkempt whitish wisps from his head. Thin latex gloves covered his hands. Cornstarch powdered his face, creating an eerie contrast with the red-rimmed eyes. Yet, at the center of the red, the eyes shimmered silvery-gray, like quicksilver pools.

He looked away, as if I did not exist and had not spoken. To the clerk he said, "I'm the family doctor. I want to speak to Dr. Scoponella himself." His voice had an odd inflection, vestiges of a mid-European accent. His tongue was oddly pink in contrast to his yellowed teeth.

The clerk punched an intercom button. "Oscar, come out here, please."

"I'm Margaret's uncle," I said to the doctor. "Bill Damen. I didn't catch your name."

He glanced down at my outstretched hand, then flexed his latexed fingers to let me know that he could not take it. He mumbled something like, "Can't talk," and directed his attention back to the metal doors. Clearly, being one of the family did not help me with him. But more than that, he seemed intensely focused on something beyond me. He had the air of a man for whom reality existed elsewhere, not in waiting rooms.

The swinging doors opened. A young man in surgical greens backed through them. Oscar, I assumed. He turned to the clerk, his gloved hands raised so as to avoid contact. I thought of them having just handled Margaret's tiny organs and was glad again I had not been allowed in. Still, even with his face half-hidden by a mask, Oscar's brown eyes, framed by dark brows and rich brown skin, were the first sign of human warmth I'd seen down here.

"You're not the doctor," the man at the counter said sharply.

The brown eyes flashed, as if Oscar had a notion to turn right back around. Instead, the clerk rolled over to him. She really had taken root in that chair. Oscar bent to listen to her whispered words, whispered something back, and then motioned with his head for the man to follow. The doctor grabbed his bag and, avoiding my gaze, strode around me, behind the counter, and through the swinging doors with Oscar.

I handed the clerk my form. "Who was that man you let in?"

"Didn't you say you were from the family?"

"I've never seen him. Did you verify his claim?"

She turned back to her computer. "He was allowed in at the discretion of Dr. Scoponella."

"Didn't he seem strange to you?"

"A dead body attracts all kinds of flies."

So much for decorum in dealing with the bereaved family.

"How soon can we expect to see preliminary results?"

"That's up to the pathologist, then the prosecutor's office. For now only the police have access," she replied.

"Why did you have me fill out the form, then?"

"You'll receive the report when it's released."

"I want to talk to Dr. Scoponella when the autopsy's over. I'm going to wait right here until he comes out."

She merely shrugged. The more I looked at her lacquered hair, the more convinced I became it was artificial and she herself was a flesh puppet, controlled by robotic works inside the chair.

I returned to my plastic seat. The silence in the room was made oppressive by a thick, low thrum, broken only by the death rattle of the rollers on the clerk's chair. An hour passed before it occurred to me that the staff might have another exit, one that would allow them to avoid families and their demands.

I went back down the cinder-block hall, up the stairs, out the front door, and around the side of the building. A few concrete tables were set in the shade between the building and parking lot. At the corner, a wire fence with thin wood slats hid the rear of the building from view. I leaned against the fence and surveyed the parking lot and tables, waiting for a moment when no one was nearby. Then I scrambled up and over, wedging my fingers between the slats.

The building backed up against a small hillock. At its base were a pair of large dumpsters accessed by a service road that came in from the far side of the building. Beyond them was another little lot. An ambulance was parked next to a loading dock. A smaller, locked dumpster was marked MEDICAL WASTE. I headed for the loading dock, then happened to glance up at the hillock. Directly above the dock was a little pasture of escape for the staff, a grassy area shaded by live oaks. Sitting on a concrete bench, eating something from a paper bag, was Oscar, still in his scrubs.

The oak leaves crunched under my feet as I approached. Oscar frowned at me. "I'm sorry to barge in on you," I called to him. "I'm the uncle of the little girl you were working on."

He stared at me, appearing not to have heard. I tried Spanish, which he quickly interrupted. "I heard you the first time." His jaw was square, his medium-length black hair combed back and tucked behind his ears.

I stuck out my hand and told him my name. He brushed off his own hand and shook mine cautiously. "Oscar Jemera," he said. "I can't talk about the postmortem."

"I understand that, Dr. Jemera," I answered quickly, sitting down. "I really am sorry to barge in. I have some concerns, on behalf of the family, about the autopsy. You can imagine how devastating it's been for us to lose a little girl like Margaret in the way we did."

The bag contained almonds. Oscar ate one slowly, surveying the litter of coinlike leaves on the ground. His voice was softer, but still firm. "The records on this one are sealed."

"I understand. I won't ask you to violate that. It's just that—I was concerned to see that weird character be allowed in to observe." Oscar had not liked the man, either, so I pressed. "I was hoping you could tell me who he was. The clerk was no help."

Mention of the clerk brought a brief smile to his lips. "No, she wouldn't be. Hey, I'm sorry for your family's loss. I didn't think Dr. Sabell should have been there, either, but I'm just a med student. He claimed your family sent him and that he'd treated the little girl. Scoponella seemed to know him—I'm not saying liked, but knew."

"Dr. Sabell. Do you know what hole he crawled out from?"

Oscar gave a short laugh. "You get them in this field. That wasn't what was strange about him. What really was strange was that he's not a pathologist. He's an embryologist."

"Shouldn't he be worried about birth, not death?"

"Yeah. Why he'd have treated a little girl is beyond me. He knew his stuff, though. Corrected the doctor's procedure more than once. Sabell did have a rather creepy interest in her internal organs. It didn't seem right to me, but Scoponella let him take a tissue sample."

"Is that legal?"

Oscar put up his hands quickly. "I never said it."

I put up my hand, too. "Believe me, I'm not looking to get you in trouble. You said you're a med student—UCSF?"

"Yes. I'm going into path, so I'm down here once a week. I've never done a pediatric postmortem. Must be a hard thing for your family."

I nodded. "It doesn't make it any easier to have creeps like Sabell prowling around her corpse. Do you know where he works?"

Oscar shrugged a no, then said, "I've got to get back."

"Thanks again," I said.

He held out the bag. I took an almond to be polite, then watched him go down the hill. He used a key to get back inside a door by the loading dock. I turned and went back the way I came, over the fence.

» » » » »

The call came from the lawyer, Mitch Walchuk, that Chris was being released late in the afternoon. No charges had been filed—yet. I could call Chris or stop by his house anytime after seven.

I'd spent the afternoon spinning my wheels. First I'd visited the county park, Hobart Beach, where Margaret's body had been found. The spot, a thicket of head-high blackberry bushes in the wooded margin along an open grassy area, was still marked off by yellow tape. A deputy from the sheriff's department was polite but unyielding about keeping me out while the forensics team completed their work. No forensics people were in evidence at Montoya County Park, though, where Margaret had disappeared. Nor could I find an area that had been taped off. It was a large park, and the abduction, if that's what it was, could have taken place in some remote corner. I talked to parents and nannies in the playground, but no one recognized my photo of Margaret or recalled Ulla. I would need to find Ulla herself.

An effort to see Dr. Scoponella back at the coroner's office met with predictable results. The automated clerk said he was not there and could not be reached. I went upstairs to County Records and searched for Dr. Sabell. He didn't show up in the local directories or on any 411 lists in the local area codes I called. After hearing from Mitch Walchuk, I decided to eat an early dinner before going back to the city to see Chris.

I stopped in a faux-fifties diner on El Camino, which turned out to be a bad choice. The bright lights, the forced cheer, and the gleam of chrome came off as morbid glitz. I imagined the place as a roadside autopsy theater, the meat as excised carcass tissue. I could not shake the image of the strange Dr. Sabell removing a bit of Margaret's tissue for his private collection.

The sky drained itself of color while I ate. The neon in the eatery's big windows lit up. Headlights flickered through it, creating mongrel mixes of pink and yellow. I girded myself to drive up the Peninsula to Chris's house. Grief, after a loss like this one, had a way of multiplying itself. Confronting Chris and Janet's fathomless pain would be hard. We might find some relief in determining how she died and who was responsible, but it would not bring her back. The best I could do was to be with them and sit with the pain.

If grief compounded itself like money in the bank, Chris and Janet already had a large account. I'd been abroad on a shoot and had been insulated, for the most part, from direct contact with what they'd endured after their first daughter, Helen, died of pneumonia. We knew she had cystic fibrosis, but the severity of the episode that killed her blindsided everyone. She was gone within days. The news hit me hard, too, even at a distance. Helen was six when she died, and had been a golden child, the kind of little girl who captivated everyone who met her. My mother had encouraged me to stay where I was and finish the shoot. Plenty of people were there for Chris and Janet in the short run, she said—it was after the funeral, after everyone else went back to business, that my company and comfort would be needed.

On my return, I went to their house with a mourning bouquet. Chris looked at it and said, "I am so sick of the smell of flowers." I submitted my awkward condolences. Janet accepted them silently, as an ocean accepts a drop. Chris barely reacted at all. He avoided talking about Helen's death or the aftermath. My visits and offers of support over the next two weeks were met with a grim forebearance, as if Chris was fulfilling some duty to be with me in this difficult time, not the other way around.

I tried, one night, to get to the source of his manner. "Chris," I'd asked, "do you hold it against me that I didn't come back sooner?"

"Why would I?" he said, in the matter-of-fact way he had of saying almost everything. His mouth moved, but the rest of his face remained inert. "Don't waste your time feeling guilty. You don't need to keep coming over here."

I didn't believe his answer then. But later I did. I realized that he'd long ago sealed away his emotions. He'd gone beyond seeming opaque; now he seemed stonelike. He hated the weakness of being a bereaved father, hated the fact that he'd failed to protect his child from death. A new grimness lodged in his face; a dark cloud hung over the marriage. My mother expressed her concern to Cole. He replied that Chris was "dealing with it like a man." Maybe he was, but surely the pressure was building inside him. Janet was more human in her reactions. She alternated between wild anger and puddles of tears. But with Chris, we half-expected him to be found with his brains blown out one morning.

And then Margaret had come along and everything changed. Chris sprang to life again. She was special in a different way than Helen, who was impish, charismatic, and disconcertingly bright. Margaret's radiance was more of an angelic placidity. Children often get tagged "little angels," usually a reflection of the parents' wish more than facts on the ground. But Margaret had an effortless glow that really did make her seem like she'd been formed in some higher sphere—especially in the way she dealt with her many ailments, of which the diabetes was only the start. She provided Chris with a kind of redemption.

I paid my check and went out to the Scout. As I drove up to Chris and Janet's house, I felt a stirring in my gut. Sometimes you can feel your life turning, the way that in the creeping shadow of an eclipse you perceive the rotation of the earth and it becomes clear we're just a small, wet ball spinning through empty space. What was happening now was big enough to knock the solar system of our extended clan off its axis. If Cole was the undisputed Jupiter, my side of the family were planetoids in some eccentric orbit beyond Pluto. (My father was a rogue asteroid that had long since exited the system.) I didn't yet know what my role would be, but I knew the planets were careening into in a new alignment that would send me onto a new path.

After Helen's death, I'd tried to imagine what Chris and Janet were feeling. The best I could picture was they must have felt a giant void opening up both inside of them and out, as if they were astronauts pitched into the cold depths of space. My impulse had been to grab on to them, to save them from being sucked into the vacuum. This time I did not try to imagine. No one could know. No one could save them. In the long run, no one could save anyone. The best we could do was offer a little company and warmth, a drop in the void. I thought back to how I'd been feeling sorry for myself yesterday morning, the small lift I'd gotten from the fact that Chris needed my help. You really do have to be careful what you wish for in this world.

4

The sensation of being lost in a vacuum returned to me at Chris and Janet's house. I wanted to ask about the peculiar Dr. Sabell, but the blank, stunned look on their faces told me they were still absorbing the initial shock of their daughter's death. The three of us sat silently in the vaulted gloom of the living room, suspended in a kind of purgatory before the hell to come. Chris slumped nearly horizontal in an easy chair across from me, wearing sweatpants and a sweatshirt, his wrists loose over the arms of the chair, his socked feet splayed under the coffee table. His eyes were as dull and flat as the bay under an overcast sky. A single table lamp cast long shadows across the floor.

"It's so damn quiet," Janet said after a few minutes.

Chris's body twisted, as if recoiling from an internal convulsion. "Janet, I'm so sorry!" he burst. "I'm a total—I'm such a failure. I've let you down again."

Janet gave only a small shake of the head. She was holding something in but didn't reveal what. Her legs were crossed on the sofa. She refused to look up. She wore a cashmere sweater and the same loose, ankle-length black skirt she'd worn to the police station last night. Her dark brown hair, shoulder-length, cut jauntily, with a bit of swing to it, framed her narrow chin. She had a slender nose and warm brown eyes that suggested an open, active mind. We'd always gotten along well. When I first met her, I suspected she'd prove to be a little too smart and independent for Chris. Their relationship didn't make sense to me until later on, when I heard her describe some of her previous boyfriends. She'd had her wild days, dating motorcycle mechanics, snowboarding fiends, and guys traveling through from other parts of the world, but knew that none of them were "husband material"—which, in the end, was what she decided she wanted. Chris fit the bill in the standard ways: His family had money and he was making more; he was solid and reliable; and he seemed intent on making a mark on the world, not only in business, but by having children. She was quite fond of him, too. Her choice had been about a secure environment in which to raise a family. With that secure environment shattered, her eyes had become remote.

Chris jackknifed out of his chair, knocking over a set of fireplace tools. "*What have we done to deserve this?*" he exploded, swinging an open palm into a wall. The slap resounded in the vaulted ceiling.

Janet raised her head long enough to watch him march back and forth in front of the hearth, then glanced down again, as if ashamed of Chris. As if perhaps they *did* deserve it somehow.

There was no good time to start asking questions, so I started now. I asked Chris what had happened with the police.

He stopped his pacing. "They talked to you, too," he said, suddenly on guard.

"I came down to see you and they dragged me into a room for questioning. Someone put the idea into their heads that you staged Margaret's disappearance."

He responded with a wary nod. Still pacing, he described his night with the police. After he'd gone through a booking process, a pair of detectives took him to a separate room. He was so agitated that he didn't realize at first it was an interrogation. They asked about his family life, his work, Margaret. They showed a degree of sympathy and concern. When they requested he account for his whereabouts on Friday and Saturday, the truth hit him. He told them that he'd been at work most of that time, a fact that could be substantiated by many witnesses. They took him, with little warning, to the morgue to identify Margaret. Chris went into a kind of shock. He felt he'd departed from his body, as Margaret had departed from hers. Back at the police station, the detectives ordered him to strip so they could inspect him for scratches and bruises, signs of a struggle. In his disembodied state, he barely noticed the humiliation.

Mitch Walchuk showed up and advised Chris not to talk. Chris said he'd talk all he wanted, he had nothing to hide. Walchuk left, and Chris heard him yelling at someone from the DA's office. When he came back in, he told Chris the police were keeping him under detention while the prosecutors determined what charges to file. Chris was put in a holding cell for the night. The interrogation resumed this morning. The detectives seemed to assume he'd eventually break down and admit he'd had his daughter kidnapped. All he'd done was make the inevitable happen faster, they coaxed; a jury might be sympathetic. When that produced no response, they asked why Margaret had her blanket and a pocketful of horse medallions with her when she was found. Chris explained that she collected them—silver-colored medallions embossed with images of famous horses throughout history. But Margaret hadn't taken them with her to the park, the detective said, so how did she get them? Chris, thinking Ulla must have provided this information, asked if the nanny was all right. He was told Ulla was safe, out of his reach. His request to speak to her received a knowing smirk. He'd taken the medallions and blanket to Margaret himself, to keep her quiet, the detective said, hadn't he? Chris shouted at the detectives that they were incompetent and that he was done talking to them.

"Then," Chris said, "you know what the fuckers tell me? 'You cooperate, and we'll keep a lid on this. The Claypool name doesn't have to be dragged through the slime in the news.' They said I could be charged with anything from severe child neglect to manslaughter to first-degree murder. It all depended on how much I helped them out. I asked why my lawyer hadn't been allowed to see me yet today. It turned out Mitch had been at the DA's office, applying pressure. They finally caved and let me go without charges."

"That's outrageous, Chris," I said.

"Mitch said I should consider suing." Chris heaved himself back into his chair. "I have no interest in that. I don't even blame them. That's the weird thing. Something in me wanted to plead guilty. Like I deserve punishment."

Janet shook her head hard. It was difficult to tell if it was the cops or Chris's guilt that dismayed her. He'd been inattentive, no doubt about it, but until we knew exactly what had happened to Margaret, we couldn't say if he was really at fault.

"Let's go through this hour by hour," I said. "What time did you leave for Monterey, Janet?"

"I think it was eight. Chris does the morning duties."

"I'd gotten a call from Jakarta," Chris said. "I was upstairs on the phone, then working on my laptop. I heard Ulla and Margy downstairs. Everything seemed normal."

"When did you leave the house?" I asked.

"God," he said, calculating. "It's all out of whack. When I'm talking to Indonesia the day there's already over, you know what I mean? It was, like, six in the evening their time. They were about to go home. I was wrapping things up when I got an emergency call from the office. Some meltdown with the Autocad documents. They needed me *immediately*. Normally I'd already be there."

"So you didn't have time to make a full check on Ulla and Margaret."

Chris put his head in his hands. "I mean, they seemed all right. I heard them in the kitchen a few minutes before. I gave Margy a quick kiss and rushed out the door. I said I'd be at the office and would check in later. Which I planned to do. But work was insane." His eyes welled up again. "I don't know what time I left the house. Janet was already gone."

"Did you notice if the gardener was here yet?" Janet asked, careful to keep reproach from her voice.

"Gardener?" Chris and I said at the same time.

"He comes every Friday at ten. Ulla usually takes Margaret to a park on Fridays. Or I"— she blushed—"I take her, too. Took."

"I'm not usually around then," Chris said. "I went out the back way. He could have been in the front yard."

"Give me the gardener's number," I said. "I want to talk to him. Your pediatrician, too."

Chris nodded. He and Janet glanced at each other, their faces flooded with shame. A hint of tension was in the glance, too, as each wondered if the other blamed them. It was as good a time as any to bring up Sabell.

"The coroner is keeping the autopsy results sealed. But they did let a man in to observe. Dr. Sabell. Do you know him?"

Chris froze. "No. Not anymore."

"But you did. Who is he?"

"He's irrelevant." Chris's voice was suddenly decisive.

"Not if he attended the autopsy. He'll know—"

"*Drop* it, I said." Chris had converted to full executive mode. "He tried to help Margaret once, but he can't help now. I don't want you speaking to him."

"Anybody else who could have been around, seen anything?" I said. I'd get back to Sabell later.

"Ulla, of course," Janet said, relaxing at the change of subject. Chris remained tense. "But we haven't been able to reach her at all."

"Have you checked her room? Are her belongings still there?"

"Most of them." Janet furrowed her brow. "A strange thing happened Sunday night. I came home from looking for Margaret. I parked in the garage and was coming through the backyard when I happened to look up. A light was on in Ulla's room. I thought I saw a shadow, too—not a person, just a flicker of the light. I had a distinct sense someone was in the house. I thought Ulla had come back. I rushed inside and called her name. There was no answer. I went up the back stairs to her room. The light was on but no one was there. I called for her again, then I heard a faint click. It sounded like the front door being closed. I went to our bedroom window, but I didn't see anyone, just a police car cruising by. I went back up to her room. Some of her things—a leather jacket, a pair of pants on a chair—were gone. I'm sure they'd been there before."

Chris's eyes ballooned. "So what the hell—wasn't the alarm on?"

"She's got the code," Janet said.

"The police searched your house last night," I said. "Maybe Ulla gave them her keys. She might have realized she wanted to get a few things and had them take her back again. They've got her simultaneously scared of you and scared of being charged as an accomplice. Does she have green-card issues?"

The couple glanced at each other. "It was a 'Don't ask, don't tell' situation," Janet said.

"Which means she's probably saying whatever they want to hear. Listen, Chris, I know you hired me to help find Margy when she was missing. But there's a lot more to investigate now, and the police aren't exactly on your side. I want to stay on this. I don't care about getting paid."

Chris sighed. "We'll bring in a criminal defense attorney, if it comes to that. You've done the job I asked you to. Don't feel obliged."

Janet tracked me with a steady gaze. "We appreciate your offer, Bill, but I'm afraid it's simple. We blew it. We failed to keep track of our daughter and her baby-sitter. That's all."

"My job's just beginning. We need to talk to your gardener. We need to find Ulla and get the autopsy results."

Chris stroked the arm of his chair, as if discovering its suede texture for the first time. He avoided looking at Janet and said to me, "I wouldn't mind."

"The police will clear us, eventually," Janet said. "I mean, maybe we do deserve some kind of punishment for losing track the way we did—but they'll find out what really happened."

Maybe, if they investigate this Dr. Sabell, I wanted to say. I kept that to myself. "I'm not saying the police are corrupt, but if Cole's right, there's another agenda at work here. They're being directed to approach the case from a certain angle. That angle changes what they see."

"I want to know what happened to Margaret," Chris said softly. "I do want to keep you on it, Bill. At your usual rate. Hire help if you need to. But keep this under wraps. You're family. I know you will."

"Of course. But don't worry about the money."

"Are you sure about this?" Janet asked. I couldn't tell if she was addressing me or Chris. "Wouldn't you rather be making films?"

It was a good question. Either way, you barged into people's lives and tried to get them to tell you things they'd rather not. You fit disparate shots into a coherent story. The main difference was that on a shoot, people didn't actually shoot *at* you. Or kill three-and-a-half-year-olds.

"I want to know who did what to Margaret," I said firmly.

Janet flinched, then set her jaw. Finally I'd managed to connect with her. "Thanks, Bill," she said. "If you're sure you want to be this involved. It's more complicated than—"

She was interrupted by the chime of the door. I wish she hadn't been, because I was about to get back to Dr. Sabell. Their financial situation, too, which the police cited as motive.

Neither Chris nor Janet moved, so I went to the door. Cole, cradling a flower arrangement, had already let himself in. There was a softness in his expression, though I couldn't tell whether it came from distraction or concern. The expression changed to surprise when he saw me.

"They're here, aren't they?" he said.

"Hi, Dad," Chris said in an unenthusiastic voice behind me. "Thanks for dropping those off."

Cole handed me the flowers and pushed by.

"Come here, son," he said. He spread his arms and took Chris in an awkward hug. Clearly it was not a familiar position for the two men. Chris's arms flailed a little, and Cole patted Chris's back as if he were six years old. I'd seen Cole embrace a friend or two at the party Sunday night, but they were big bear hugs, contests to squeeze the breath out of one another.

"I'm so sorry. So sorry, Christopher. A tragic ending to a life so short."

"Yeah," Chris responded, extricating himself.

Cole jerked his waist belt loose and handed me his overcoat. "Bill said you were worried about ruining my party. You know you can *always* come to me when you need me."

"Yeah."

"This is brutally unfair. It's not right for one person to have to endure this twice."

Chris turned angry. "You don't need to rub it in. I blew it. *Again.*"

"No, Christopher." Cole's gentleness took me by surprise. "You did not. It's *not* your fault. I know that worm Mike Gallegos is playing on your emotions. It's dirty pool, and he'll pay for it."

Cole headed for the living room. Janet stood to greet him. He gave her another one of his awkward hugs. She accepted it listlessly.

"Can I get you something?" she asked, fluffing a place for Cole to sit on the couch.

"No thanks, dear." He settled himself into the seat. "I'm just here to see how you two are doing. Offer my help."

Chris slumped back into his armchair. I sat across from him. Neither he nor Janet looked at Cole. The silence verged on becoming uncomfortable.

"What is it that Gallegos has against you, Cole?" I said.

A wicked, satisfied smile crossed his face. "Oh, he's got reasons to hate me. He'd be much more than DA if it wasn't for me." His mouth flattened into a righteous grimace. "That doesn't excuse this outrage. My attorney, Harry Harvey, had a talk with him today. Gallegos will regret this. Harry's staff is working on it—"

"I'll handle it myself," Chris interrupted.

This brought a curious, ruffled look from Cole. "I'm only trying to help. Harry's the best there is."

Chris's fists clenched. "She was *my* daughter. I'm handling it. Harry works for you and the company. If I need personal help, I'll tell you."

The center of Cole's forehead formed a gully of hurt. "Very well, Christopher. You may handle it your way."

A long pause ensued. One of Janet's crossed legs began to swing nervously.

"Listen," Cole said to Chris. "I've been meaning to say—you've had some tough customers to contend with on this Jakarta proposal. It's your first time being in charge, from the initial budget to closing the deal. You've done a splendid job. Wong Fen Construction doesn't have a chance against us. I was going to wait until Friday, when we send in the final proposal, to celebrate, but—you deserve praise for your work."

Chris brightened visibly, in spite of himself.

"Now," Cole went on, "you know that our rivals are connected to the triads—Chinese criminal gangs. It's more than likely that what happened to Margaret was some kind of extortion or intimidation attempt gone awry. They grabbed Margy and scared Ulla out of her wits, forcing her into hiding. What probably happened was that they didn't know about Margy's diabetes. She went and died on them before they could deliver their demands."

Janet's jaw dropped as Cole spoke. Chris stroked the bridge of his nose. Cole extended his hands in a dramatic warning gesture. "We have to be prepared. There may be more to come. Whoever did it will try to make it look like they planned Margaret's death." He glanced at Janet. "They may threaten someone else in the family."

Chris nodded grimly.

"We don't knuckle under to this, Chris. The company has ways of protecting us. Both of you. We have ways of delivering a message to these people. We're not thugs, but we're not milquetoasts, either."

Chris was limp now, his spirit deflated. "I never thought they'd go after . . ." He shook his head. "I wasn't paying attention."

"Don't do that to yourself," Cole said. "You were immersed in the deal. I didn't expect them to reach across the ocean like this, either. Listen, with these kinds of thugs, there's no way you could have stopped them. It's not your fault."

"I *would* have stopped them," Chris said stubbornly. "I can't believe that, for my own daughter, I couldn't take *ten* minutes to check on her. *Ten minutes!*" He gripped the chair, his arms trembling.

Cole put a hand on Chris's knee. His voice took on a soothing, wise tone. "Listen to me. The pain of this will never go away. I know that. But you have to realize it's also an opportunity. Margaret had a hard life, a painful life. We knew it was going to be short in any case. What we must do now is mourn her properly, and then move forward. Don't let yourself get stuck in this tragedy. You're strong, Christopher, stronger than you think. Allow yourself to grieve, but don't give up the fight. Get back on the horse. I've always said that what doesn't kill me makes me stronger."

Chris's whole body trembled now. His face turned crimson. He said in a controlled voice, "We want to be alone now."

"I understand. I'll have Wilson finish up the Jakarta deal."

"No!" Chris bolted from his chair. "I *said* I'll call if I need your help. That applies both to Margaret and Jakarta!" He stormed out of the room and up the front stairs.

Cole actually had the hint of a smile on his face. He was pleased with his son. “He’s a fighter,” Cole said. “He’ll be all right.”

Janet stood up. Her voice was stony. “I’m going to bed. Good night, Cole. Bill.”

Cole stood. “Anything I can do, Janet. Anything.”

I showed Cole to the door. “Bill, I’m very grateful that you’re here for Chris,” he said. “He needs someone his own age.”

“I’m glad to be. I wish I hadn’t been out of the country when Helen—”

I stopped myself. Why was I making excuses to this man? What was it about him that made one want to justify oneself, earn his regard? Like gravity, Cole pulled everything into himself.

Cole shrugged on his coat. “You’ve done more than your share.”

“I’ll be working with Chris full time on this,” I said. I wanted Cole to know I’d be in the picture for the foreseeable future.

“Fine. Call myself or Harry Harvey if you need help.”

“We’ll want to get our hands on any autopsy findings as soon as we can.”

“Of course.” Cole turned to me as he went out the door, his face suddenly grim. “I’m concerned for your safety, too, Bill. I’d never forgive myself if harm came to another member of our family. Help Chris as you’re able, but keep your distance from the Jakarta business. I’ve got people on that. It’s more vicious than you can imagine.”

“I’ll be careful,” I said, and watched him go down the front walk. I was used to his hard-nosed manner. It was his attempts at humanity with Chris—and me—that took me off guard.

I thought about Cole on the way home. Maybe his behavior tonight was not so unusual. I’d personally witnessed, and knew of, acts of kindness from him for which there was no visible payback or advantage to be gained. Anonymous, spontaneous acts. Someone more fair to him might say he was a man of intriguing contradictions. I was too close to him to indulge in that. I could only see the plot of potlatch at work—some kind of cosmic potlatch, where Cole never ceased to balance the ledgers and call in the accounts. Whether his concern for me and his compassion for Chris was real, or he just wanted to make sure he was still in control, was impossible to tell.

5

Dr. Nadine Tyrovsky had brown hair, straight, long, and silky. Her glasses, pushed up on her forehead, functioned as a kind of headband. She was young, with small bones and a wiry energy. We met Tuesday downtown in the library of the Mechanic's Institute, a great old San Francisco organization started in the nineteenth century. The library was a grand multitiered space with large windows.

The doctor took me to a corner where we could talk quietly. "I've been spending my lunch hours here," she explained. "Getting a paper ready for a meeting. But I always have time for Margaret." She paused to fold her hands. "I was so sad to hear what happened."

"She affected people that way."

"How are Janet and Chris doing?"

"It's rough," I said. "The DA won't give us even a hint of what the postmortem found. I wanted to ask you about a man who attended it. He called himself the 'family doctor.' His name was Sabell. Do you know him?"

Dr. Tyrovsky looked down, hesitant. The name had a similar effect on her as it had had on Chris. After a moment she said, "Do you?"

"Not before yesterday. I can't find him in any databases. I understand he's an embryologist."

She nodded, but her guarded look told me I'd have to circle back around to him. I said, "The police think Margaret died of some sort of diabetic shock."

"It's not impossible. Hyperglycemia and ketoacidosis, if she was deprived of her insulin and got dehydrated. Hypoglycemic shock, if she got too much insulin or the wrong kind. It all depends on what she ate and drank and, of course, any other substances she was given."

"Chris's father thinks foreign gangsters kidnapped her. That they didn't know about her diabetes and her death was an accident. She had several other conditions, too. Could any of them have been fatal?"

"Again, it depends on what they did with her," Tyrovsky said. "She had a heart condition, but they would have had to work at it to induce a heart attack. She suffered from seizures, too. The trauma of an abduction could have induced a seizure. She also had other metabolic disorders that might or might not have been related to the diabetes."

"How did she end up with so many medical problems?"

"It's a puzzle. Sometimes it just happens. A bad draw."

"Twice in a row, for Chris and Janet. Makes you think the deck might be stacked. Did they do prenatal tests for Margaret?"

"I'd think so, but I didn't come into the picture until later."

"The one family disease we knew about, cystic fibrosis, was the one thing Margaret never suffered from. How could that be?"

Tyrovsky shrugged. "Again, the genetic shuffle."

I made my next question quick and blunt. "What was Dr. Sabell's role?"

"I can't really say," Tyrovsky answered.

"Can't, or won't?"

"Shh," she scolded. Her pupils contracted, then flared protectively. "Don't ask me to violate my patient's confidence."

"Let's try this," I said, placing my hands on the table. "Don't speak up until I hit a wrong note. This guy, Sabell, is an embryologist. That means he could also do fertility work. Chris admitted he treated Margaret once. I keep wondering: What treatment can an embryologist give a little girl? The answer I come up with is that he 'treated' her in vitro. Through in vitro fertilization."

Dr. Tyrovsky's mouth remained set in a straight line.

I kept going. "So Margaret was an IVF child. My next question was: Why would an embryologist push his way so desperately into an autopsy? And cut out a little souvenir tissue for himself?"

Tyrovsky took in a quick breath. "What kind of souvenir?"

"I need to find out. What would you expect him to take?"

She spread her hands. "Pancreatic cells? Vitreous humor?"

"My source specifically said 'tissue.' The main reason I can think of for him to be there is that he really, really wanted to know how she died. And the main reason for that would be to cover up something. A mistake he'd made. He wanted to find out if he was responsible for her death. Or to collect evidence that he wasn't. Or to nudge the pathologist in another direction. In any case, the more firsthand information he has, the better he can cover up."

Dr. Tyrovsky kept her eyes down, watching my hands. She was trying not to let me see the stricken look on her face. "You should talk to the Claypools," she said. "And Dr. Sabell."

"Do you know how to find him?"

She shook her head and bit her lip harder. She wanted to say more but couldn't. Instead, an abbreviated sob came out. "None of this should have happened to Margaret." She stood up. "I have to go."

I stood, too. I knew what I needed to do next. "One more question. Did you know Ulla, the nanny?"

"No . . ." She hesitated, as if searching for words and holding them in at the same time. "I'm sorry I can't tell you more without the Claypools' permission. But . . ." Again she stumbled. "Keep me posted."

"Thank you, Doctor," I said, then called out a final question as she began to leave. "Can Sabell be prosecuted for taking Margaret's tissue?"

She turned. "If he did it without the Claypools' consent, yes."

"That's the answer I wanted to hear."

» » » » »

I'd taken the 15 bus downtown. Now I walked down Sutter to Market and went underground to board an M line streetcar. Rush hour hadn't begun yet. Plenty of seats were free. We rattled from the Powell station to Civic Center, Van Ness, Castro, then whistled through the belly of Twin Peaks to West Portal. I rocked from side to side as the dark tunnels and fluorescent platforms streamed by.

It was a strange thing to see Margaret in this new light. Rationally, there was no reason to view her differently because she had been made, not begotten. She'd been no less of a human being. Yet I could not shake a certain uncanny sensation. She had not sprung from the long chain that linked us to our mammal forebears. Instead, she'd been whisked up in a glass by a man who called himself the "family doctor." It made her seem separate from nature, even though I knew the notion was false. Nature did not care how its creatures were reproduced, only that they were. The history of life on earth was a long tale of mutation, adaptation, innovation. Imagine the horror with which an oviparous creature might have viewed the idea of in utero gestation and live birth.

The revelation about her genesis seemed to bear out the extended Claypool clan's view of her. They'd always spoken of her with a tragic frown, a lowering of the brows as if to ward off the misfortune that had struck the young couple, so active and full of promise, now laid low by a stumble in their segment of the genetic relay. If you heard only the somber tones in which her name was uttered, you'd expect to meet a darkly disturbed child. She wasn't. Margaret resembled her predecessor Helen physically, save for the blond hair, but while Helen liked to prance around the house, Margaret was a quiet little girl. She showed a patience and concern for others that was well beyond her years. I once spent an afternoon playing Candyland with her. She expended more energy helping me play my side than she did her own. It was important to her that the game be fair and that I not feel she was taking advantage of me. She always seemed at pains not to be too much trouble to her parents, as if she had to take care of them, not the other way around. Of course, she was a great deal of trouble, in that her special medical needs required constant doctor visits and frequent hospital stays. In spite of being the one who was sick, the one prodded and palpated and stuck with needles, her complaints were mild. A child her age was not capable of consciously choosing to be so considerate, or so we're told. But Margaret came off as an uncannily forebearing creature. There was a certain look in her eyes—a seriousness, or a resignation, as if she had a secret knowledge, an insight into the unknown that allowed her to accept her destiny.

The way her life had ended outraged me. Had her captors recognized that secret knowledge? Did the look in her eyes haunt them now? I hoped so. More likely, they simply dusted her from their hands, blaming fate or God for their bad luck in having her die on them. Something in me wanted to show them how easily they could be dusted away, too.

I got off the train at Sloat, where St. Francis Boulevard entered St. Francis Wood. Chris's sex life was the last thing I wanted to discuss. I didn't look forward to quizzing him, but I needed to know why Sabell was so eager to examine Margaret's body and where to find him.

The afternoon fog had pushed ashore. The sky was a hard gray and a chilly wind blew from the ocean. As I walked up Chris's block, I decided I'd better not just barge in on him. Generally, I avoid the phone if I need important information from someone. It so rarely gets you what you really want. But now I gave in and called him on my cell.

"It's Bill," I said. "I'm in the neighborhood. Am I interrupting?"

"Kind of." There was a pause. He was doing something else while he talked. "Can it wait?"

I'd reached his doorstep. It seemed ridiculous to stay on the phone. That was the modern world for you: Technology allowed us to be simultaneously totally connected and totally insulated. I heard my ring of the doorbell through Chris's phone. He must have moved it away from his mouth, but I still heard him say, "Shit!"

A few seconds later, the door opened. Chris's brow creased. It was not in his nature to apologize, but he did. "Sorry for being grouchy." His fists clenched and unclenched. "I'm trying to finish up the Jakarta proposal. I feel like such a, I don't know, a cad, to be doing it at a time like this."

"A regular cad, or an Autocad?"

That drew a chuckle, but only one. CAD—computer-aided design—was the primary tool in his business for creating construction drawings. Autocad was specialized software for architects and engineers.

"Janet's pissed off, too," Chris said. "She went walking on the beach. If I can just get it to a point where I'm sure we've cinched the deal, then I'll feel all right about handing it off to Leonard Wilson."

"Finish it today, if you can."

"Yeah . . ." His mind was drifting elsewhere. "I've got to make a call."

He went up the front stairs, already dialing. I followed. His home office was down the second-floor hall and around the corner. I stopped at the door to Margaret's room, then opened it.

Nothing, as far as I could tell, had been touched. Her bite-size bed had its green-and-yellow daisy quilt pulled up to the small pillow. A row of dolls and stuffed animals sat along the wall under the window, a patient audience. Many were torn or broken in ways that would bring disdain from other children. Margy had not allowed her parents to throw them out. They'd seemed to evoke a special empathy in her. The ones that could not be fixed received special love, as if she'd understood what they were going through. She applied Band-Aids and tape, and talked of the day she'd be big enough to sew, so that she could operate on them like a doctor. She would defend them fiercely when playmates dared to make fun of them.

On the opposite wall, a low table hosted a small village built from a European wood-block set. On top of the sherbet-orange dresser sat Margaret's collection of buttons, separated into little boxes by size and color. She'd loved buttons as much as she loved her horse medallions. Janet had discouraged it at first, but once Margy had proved that she knew not to put them in her mouth, she was allowed to keep them. Whenever she'd show them to me, she solemnly warned me not to swallow them.

I crept out of the room and closed the door quietly behind me. The hallway continued down to a large room that doubled as a sewing room and guest bedroom. A smaller guest room was opposite it. The hall took a right, past a bay with a small telescope pointing out the window, and ended at the room where Chris kept his home office. The door was closed. Behind it, his voice berated someone on the telephone in tones worthy of his father. It hit me, suddenly, what I'd seen in Chris's face when he opened the front door. Annoyance, yes, but anger shot out from his blue eyes, too, an anger that had been burning before I came and which made me its target for a few seconds. His lower lip had trembled and his nostrils flared. Fear lurked beneath the anger, fear and guilt. Guilt at being back at work so soon after the death of his daughter. Fear at what would happen if he didn't stay on the job and finish the Jakarta bid.

No wonder Janet had gone to the beach. It must have been unbearable to have her husband unavailable to her at this moment. I wanted to talk to Chris about Sabell and the autopsy, but only when I had his full attention. I turned to leave. Maybe phones did have a purpose after all.

» » » » »

The M line took me back to the Church Street station, from which I caught a 22 bus to Potrero Hill at the tail end of rush hour. The safety and regularity of nine-to-five looked rather cozy. I took out the notebook I kept in my jacket pocket and made a list of what I needed to do tomorrow. The first thing would be to get Chris to talk about Dr. Sabell. I also needed to find Mr. Dinh, the gardener. I'd called his number and visited his house this morning, and had gotten no answer at either.

DA Mike Gallegos, the Jakarta project, the Hong Kong triads, and above all, Ulla, needed looking into. It was time to hire an assistant.

The sun sank behind Twin Peaks as I climbed the hill from 16th Street to my flat. My Scout, parked on the street a few doors down, radiated more orange glory than usual in the sunset glow. But for all its rust-hued radiance, it gave the odd impression of having gone blind. As I approached, I saw what created that impression. The headlights had been smashed. So had both of the front windows. And the taillights. My stomach fell. Opening the front door, I discovered that something, in addition to the myriad tiny jewels of shattered glass, had been left behind on the driver's seat. It was only a sliver, about six inches long, honed to a point, with a small plug at the end. A blowgun dart. None of the items—screwdriver, pliers, wrench, maps, registration—in the glove compartment had been taken.

I gaped at the damage and thought about what it meant. My house had been broken into before, but this was more personal, more of a punch to the gut. I carried the dart by the plug end into my flat. I came back out with duct tape and cardboard, hand vacuum and brush, dustpan and paper sack. The dart, I thought as I swept the glass from the metal floor and vacuumed the crevices of the cracked vinyl seats, was an act of intimidation. But an odd one: Was I meant to think a gang of headhunters was after me? The dart could be poisoned, I supposed, with a substance used in the Amazon, or Borneo, or . . . Indonesia. Checking out Cole's theory about his company's rival for the Jakarta contract jumped to the top of my list.

I reported the crime over the phone, then called Chris. He answered in a clotted voice. I told him about the Scout and advised him to make sure his house and cars were secure. As we hung up, I realized the froggy sound in his voice was not from sleep. He'd been crying. I wondered if Janet was still out.

The quiet in my flat felt vaguely ominous. Darkness had long since fallen. I paced from one end to the other, putting away clothes, books, magazines, video and digital tapes—things that had needed stowing for weeks. It was a little hard to tell, in the mess, if my belongings had been rifled. I secured the doors and windows, kept the porch lights on, and glanced compulsively out to the street.

Eventually I forced myself to eat some leftover pizza from the refrigerator and sat down at my computer. There turned out to be a scary number of places from which you could order a blowpipe and darts. Sifting through an image search, I came upon a dart close to the type that had been left on my seat. The Dayak people of Indonesia used bamboo shaved to a deadly barbed sliver to hunt monkeys, birds, and squirrels. Their blowpipes had a range of up to 150 feet. The next question would be whether mine was tipped with poison. A job for a research assistant.

From blowpipes I surfed over to the Jobs page of the legendary San Francisco bulletin board site Craigslist.org. This was where I'd put out the call. I posted my ad under three headings: Film, Legal, and Etc.

Research assistant for films and investigations. Office in Potrero Hill, San Francisco. Vehicle required. Mediocre pay. Start immediately. Send résumé with reply.

I looked it over. The job description was meager, but that was all right. I didn't want it to sound glamorous. Still, it seemed incomplete, not quite accurate. I thought about the Scout's broken windows and smashed lights, and added to the end of it, *Dangerous.*

» » » » »

I awoke well before my alarm Wednesday morning, my mind hopping with tasks to be done and a tinge of apprehension about who or what was waiting for me. All was quiet out the front door and back. I logged on to the Internet to look up Dr. Sabell. An email was waiting. Someone named Clem had already responded to my job listing. He failed to attach a résumé but did give a phone number. I started to write it down for later, until I noticed the time of the message. Five-twenty A.M. He'd been up before me. I called him.

A woman answered. I asked for Clem. She, as it turned out, was Clem, and she was interested in the job. I proposed that we meet at Scoby's, my local café, for an interview. She agreed.

It seemed a promising start to the day. She'd responded quickly and had an intriguing voice. I found nothing on Sabell, but took care of some more email, then walked over to Scoby's in the leaden gray of an overcast dawn.

The café was quiet. I parked myself with the newspaper, a large coffee, and a pastry at a table by the window. A few minutes later, a woman opened the door. I prayed it was not her. She scanned the café. Her gaze settled on me, and my hopes sank. She wore a tawny suede jacket with leather fringe running across the back and down the arms. A flake, I feared. Below the jacket she had on low-riding jeans and cowboy boots. Clearly she had her own peculiar sense of style. The boots were beauties, black custom-stitched leather.

I stood to shake her hand. Her deep honey-tinged hazel eyes, flecked with mischief and some degree of buried pain, met mine. I offered to get coffee. She said she'd get it herself. I sat back down and watched her go to the counter. She walked with an insouciant kind of authority, not trying to impress anyone.

To my relief, she removed the jacket when she returned. I wasn't hiring Annie Oakley to ride the range. Underneath was a Western shirt with pearl buttons.

She took a healthy gulp of coffee. "So you're Bill." She said my name as if its old-fashioned, pedestrian sound amused her.

"That's right. And you're Clem. Short for Clementine?"

"Yes," she said, daring me to make a crack about it.

I accepted and said, "Oh my darling."

She batted her lashes. "Only my name doesn't rhyme with *nine*."

"Mean?"

"Queen," she said, her mouth curling into a smile. She had full lips, a strong triangle of a nose, and luminous olive skin. Her black hair covered her neck in curls. "Is this how you interview all your applicants?"

"You're the first, to be honest. Did you bring a résumé?"

"Résumé? I'm sitting right in front of you."

I sipped my coffee. We were either going to wring each other's necks or get along famously. "What makes you interested in this job?"

"The last line in your ad."

"I'm not kidding about the danger. After we talk, if you're still interested, I'll show you what happened to my car last night."

"All right. I want something that will keep me on my toes."

"There's plenty of tedium, too. Searching databases. Waiting around on sets."

She tucked her chin into her neck and regarded me with suspicion. "You think I'm flighty, don't you? That I can't stay focused."

I took in a slightly exasperated breath. An aroma of cigarettes and liquor wafted from somewhere near her. That damn jacket.

"You've been out all night," I said.

The suspicion gave way to an open-jawed, conspiratorial grin. "Congratulations, Detective. Now you know I've got stamina."

I couldn't stop myself from smiling back. The truth was, she looked like she could keep going for another eighteen hours. "Tell me about your background," I said. "Education, previous work."

"Tell me about yours."

I nearly dismissed her then and there. But something about her lips and her manner, the warm earthiness in her voice, like fresh coffee grounds, a depth in her eyes you could get lost in, made me indulge her. I gave as honest an account of myself as I could. I'd grown up in Oakland. My mother was an internist at a community hospital, my father a teacher of anthropology, although the less said about him the better. An early memory, one that defined me, was of seeing a Polaroid he'd taken of me diving to catch a Frisbee. I marveled at how the photograph captured that moment, retrieved it for us and at the same time enlarged it, made it more real than it had been in real life. It was a form of magic. I'd been in love with cameras ever since. I had an older sister who lived in New York. I went to Cal and then to the graduate film program at San Francisco State. I'd had a great cohort there; almost all of us went on to work in the business. I made a few small pieces of my own. It was the camera I loved most, though, so I worked primarily as a DP. Documentaries were my preferred genre, but I liked fiction, too, and the occasional experimental film, if the director knew what he or she was doing. Like most film workers, I paid the bills by taking industrial and corporate work when necessary. I was stupid enough to have let myself get caught up in the dot-com swell of the late nineties. Ever since it deposited me back onshore, soggy and groggy, three years ago, I'd been searching to find my way back into whatever it was I was really meant to be doing. I stumbled into detective work when a researcher named Sheila died from anaphylactic shock at my ex-girlfriend's dinner party. My most recent case had involved an engineer named Rod, who'd been murdered in the middle of a film I was making about him.

"That's very touching," Clem said with a straight face. I expected a crack, but she went on. "I like that you cared enough about these people, Sheila and Rod, to find out who killed them. You didn't know them very well, but you put yourself out for them."

"Just making a living," I said. "Now it's your turn."

"I know how to use the Internet. I read fast. I can talk most anyone into telling me most anything." She switched on a dazzling, phony smile. "I can be as charming as necessary. I'll warn you, though, what you're seeing this morning is the real me."

"Just as well. I couldn't stomach the charm. But isn't there something else you'd like to be doing in your life, something you're supporting?"

"You mean a habit? A deadbeat boyfriend?"

"Or a band, or acting, or surfing—the kind of stuff half the people our age do around here. You seem like a real San Francisco type."

"I don't know what you mean by that, but it better be good."

"Just tell me about your previous work, what interests you. Do you have any experience in film?"

She put her elbow on the table, looked down, and pressed her knuckles to her forehead for longer than was polite. When she looked up, she said, "I'm a professional busybody. How's that?"

"I'm a professional pain in the ass."

She clicked her tongue, then talked fast. "I've done serious, way too serious, academic work and burned out. I've played guitar in a cowboy-punk band. I'm a fast learner. You give me a sound gizmo, a camera gizmo, I'll bring it to its knees. Look, Bill

Damen, I can do this job. You can be smart and hire me, or you can stick to protocol. My guess is that filmmakers and PIs who stick to protocol don't get very far."

"What kind of academic work?"

She folded her hands in a manner that implied reprimand. "Does it really matter? If you've got any intelligence at all, you've got a feeling about me by now. Either you know it'll work or you don't."

The feeling I had was that it was about time to stick a fork in this one. She seemed to think she was interviewing me, not the other way around. "Are you even interested in the job? The pay is—"

"Mediocre. Use your powers of observation. I've been sitting here for forty-five minutes. If I wasn't interested, you'd be working on the crossword puzzle right now."

We stared across the table at each other. I said, "You've probably got too much experience. The position's a better fit for someone younger."

"Oh." She flinched from my gaze for half a second. I'd hit a nerve. "By position, you mean bottom. A young thing who'll look up to you and believe everything you say."

"No," I said, irritated, although to be fair, I shouldn't have implied she was too old. We were both at an age where we ought to know what we were doing with our lives. "What I mean is that, in terms of pay, it's entry level. You have a right to expect more."

"You've decoded what I expect from life but not whether I want the job?"

I broke down and laughed. I didn't know what it was—the mock-petulant tone of her rebuke, the way we both kept drinking from our coffee cups even though they were empty, or her generally ornery nature. I didn't want to part ways with her just yet.

"Let's take a walk," I said.

She stood up. The leather fringes danced as she shrugged on the jacket. "You mentioned some damage to your car," she said.

"We'll go see the Scout."

"What kind of case are you working on, anyway?"

"A very young girl. We don't know if it was murder or an accident."

We walked the few blocks to my flat in silence. Clem stifled a yawn. She didn't really care about the job. This was just a game she was playing after her night out on the town. She knew less about me than she thought, though, because when I stopped in front of the Scout, she was still looking around for my car. I told her this was it.

She focused on it. She didn't see the smashed windows. She didn't see the sightless light sockets. She saw the same beautiful, honorable, hardy piece of machinery I did. "Sweet Jesus, it *is* a Scout. An old International Harvester! It runs?"

"A little blind in the dark right now, but yeah."

She ran her hand across the IH emblem on the grille, smudged her thumb against the faded orange paint, patted the rim of the broken light well. "This is a crime. Truly a crime."

I'd been wrong. She was perfect for the job. The words slipped out of my mouth before I could stop. "You're hired."

"Good." But then, realizing how much her delight pleased me, she pulled back. "Don't you want to wait and see who else applies?"

"I don't have time. You want it or not?"

"I'll try it," she said with a shrug, as if ordering a drink.

I gestured to the Scout. "You know what the message here was?"

Clem nodded crisply. "The next body to be damaged may be your own. Who did it?"

"All I know is they left a blowgun dart on the driver's seat. My client is involved with a project in Indonesia."

"Ah. That does make a point."

"I want you to get the dart analyzed for poison."

It was a little test. She surprised me by answering, "I can do that."

"Good," I said. "You're on the clock now. I'll show you our office this afternoon. It needs a little work."

"Don't we all," she murmured. We froze, looking at each other, wondering exactly what it was we were getting into, both together and separately.

6

The lily lay crushed on the dining-room floor, its white slipper petal torn and already wilting at the edges. Dirt had exploded from the clay pot when it collided with the wall. Pot shards lay scattered over what remained of the flowers. A reddish-brown gouge marked where the plant had struck the wall.

"My mother brought it for us yesterday," Chris told me.

"So much for the Peace Lily," I said.

"It sounded like a bomb when it hit," Chris said.

After I'd left Clem with the dart, I went to Hunter's Point to have new windows put into the Scout and to buy head- and tail-light assemblies. Chris had called me in the parts store. His voice was small, barely audible, on my cell phone, as if emanating from the bottom of a well. He'd asked me to come over right away.

He pulled a chair unsteadily out from the dining table and sat. "I ran downstairs when I heard the crash," he said. "Janet was shaking. It hit me all at once, pow, like a big wave, what she was going through. Helen and Margaret had been part of her body. The loss has got to be even harder for her than it is for me. I put my arms out—and that's when she started to scream at me."

Chris squeezed his temples between the thumb and outer fingers of one hand. He was still in his bathrobe, a thick, light blue terrycloth embroidered with his initials. Janet owned one that matched. "Something about how all I really cared about was work," he went on. "I said something stupid about securing our future. Her voice went up another octave. She said, *'We don't have a future!'*"

"I'm sure she didn't mean it," I said, sitting down with him.

"Oh, she meant it." Chris's hands were trembling. "She *hated* me. It was like I was the one who killed Margaret. I tried to hold her and tell her we'd get through this, like we had before. She pushed me away, told me to go back to my Jakarta business. Then she was out the door."

"It's an emotional time. She needs to let off steam."

"Of course it's *emotional!*" he lashed out. "You don't get it—she may not come back! I'm screwing up again, Bill! *Listen* to me. A call from Indonesia woke us up before six this morning. Janet hadn't slept all week. She took a pill last night and was finally getting some rest. The frigging shrieking phone stabbed into our sleep. She went bolt upright in that middle-of-the-night panic you have, like when your child is in trouble and needs you. I saw, I knew, she was reliving the moment all over again. I knew who was calling, and I was pissed that I'd forgotten to turn the phone off. I fell all over the bedroom, cursing, and finally picked up the phone. And got drawn right into the middle of this big fuckup by our partner company in Jakarta. I yelled at them and she yelled at me to get out of the room. I went down the hall, reaming them out, and then had to make more calls before the workday ended over there. I thought Janet had gone back to sleep. I heard the shower running a little later. She looked in on me in my office and asked if I knew when Margaret's body would be released from the coroner, so that we could plan the service. I said in kind of a hurry that I'd call Mitch as soon as I could. That was my mistake, not devoting my full attention immediately."

"Then the flowerpot hit the wall," I said. "She'll be back, Chris. How soon before you can sew up the Jakarta proposal?"

Chris rapped his knuckles on the table in frustration. "I keep thinking it's almost there. Then something new comes up. Every single day I've got to hand-feed them detailed instructions."

"Tell me about your rival, Wong Fen Construction in Hong Kong. They have criminal connections?"

"Dad says they do. Did you call me last night?"

"Yes," I said, and reviewed again what had been done to the Scout.

"I'm sorry about your jeep, Bill," Chris said. "But the dart's kind of stupid. Jakarta's a modern city."

"It still gets the message across. If it's from a triad-type gang, what do they want—for CCE to pull out?"

"Or pony up a payoff to stay in. But we've gotten no threats. No demands. Why go after you?"

"Because they tried to get at you through Margaret, I suppose. Now they're warning me off investigating what happened to her. Who else would want to do that? Friends of Ulla or Dinh, maybe, if one of them was in on it."

He shrugged. "I can't believe either of them would be involved. The triad theory's the only one that makes sense."

"We'll see. Typically when they make a grab, they do it in public, with a flourish, to make sure you know who they are. It's part of the intimidation. To show they're serious, they send you the ear or finger of the abductee."

"Jesus, Bill!" His eye began to twitch. "The whole thing makes me sick." He tried to avoid touching his eyes but had to wipe a tear away. "I've been thinking about her this whole time, ever since Saturday. No matter what it looks like, I haven't stopped thinking about her. We started this little scrapbook for her, with pictures, to make a record of all her firsts. You know what I mean? The day she took her first step, there in the living room. Her first word, *buhn*. She meant button. She loved them from the day she was born. The first song she tried to sing. She had such a great voice, amazingly in tune. The first storybook she made us repeat over and over. The first time she read it herself—"

"She could read?"

Chris's forehead wrinkled. "Wait. No, I guess that was—" He gave me an embarrassed smile. "That was Helen."

I tried to smile, too. It wasn't the first time I'd been unsure if he was talking about Margaret or Helen.

"It was just—I was looking forward to Margaret growing up into that grace that Helen had," he tried to explain. "She loved music. She wanted to play the flute. I pictured her up onstage at her first school recital. The first time we'd watch *Star Wars* together—I used to do my Darth Vader imitation for her, she loved it. Her first date. Her first car. She'll never have those."

There was an awkward silence. It was unlikely Margaret would have lived long enough to do most of those things. I cleared my throat and said, "I think I told you I was at the coroner's office on Monday. They're keeping the autopsy results tight, but I'm more worried about something else right now."

I waited. I wanted Chris to ask me. "What is it?" he demanded.

"There was another person at the coroner's office. Dr. Sabell."

Chris made a visible effort to control his reaction. "What did he want?"

"You need to help me figure that out. He was desperate to get into the postmortem, and he succeeded. It's time for you to explain who he is."

Chris stood suddenly and left the table. I heard him in the bathroom, blowing his nose. When he returned, his face had become an enamel-like mask hiding his emotions.

"He took some of Margy's body tissue," I said.

He covered his ears and said, "I'm going outside!"

"You're in your bathrobe."

He went up the stairs. I waited. If this was how he dealt with his marital problems, it might be true Janet wasn't coming back.

He breezed by me a few minutes later in sweatpants, a 49ers jersey, and a baseball cap. I followed him out the back door and across the patio to the spindle on which the garden hose was wound. He screwed a nozzle to the end of the hose, dragged it across the grass to the driveway, and disappeared into the garage. A moment later, the Range Rover backed out.

"You're washing your *car?*" I said, incredulous.

He picked up the hose. "It helps me think."

A stream shot from the nozzle, then petered to nothing. He gave me a sharp look. I had control of the spigot. "Turn it on!" he commanded.

"I know about Margaret, Chris. I know about the IVF. I'm not going to tell anyone."

Chris dropped the nozzle and headed for the back door. I stepped in front of him. "I need soap," he said.

I inspected the Rover while he was gone. It was spotless.

Chris returned with a bucket of suds and a heavy sponge. "Sabell brings back bad memories," he said, turning on the water. He sprayed the car, then applied soap to the hood.

"You'll just have to deal with them. Now, it's possible he wanted the tissue for a perfectly good reason. But everything I've seen and heard about him makes me think otherwise. Did you give him permission to take it?"

Chris shook his head vehemently.

"Okay. So, unless he's working with the police, we can take action against him. I'll need your cooperation on that. But I also need to know what he did for you. Was it just IVF, or more?"

Chris scrubbed at invisible spots of dirt. "It didn't work out like it was supposed to. That's all."

"Was Helen an IVF child, too?"

He rinsed the hood, then began scrubbing the side of the Rover. "We'd tried two or three clinics before Sabell. Our first shot with him—bingo, Helen implanted. And came to term. And was an incredible child. We thought he was a miracle worker."

"So you went back to him for Margaret. But something went wrong."

Chris didn't respond. "Helen had cystic fibrosis," I went on. "That was the one thing Margaret *didn't* have. Sabell must have screened for the gene. Some kind of prenatal diagnosis that damaged the embryo. Was that it?"

Chris shook his head hard, less a "no" than an effort to contain some unruly force within. He squeezed the nozzle on full strength.

"Who else knows about Sabell?" I shouted.

He paused the spray. "Keep your voice down, goddammit. No one else knows except Nadine. And now you. Definitely not my father. Can you imagine the field day he'd have?"

"Hey, he's the one who gave you the Y chromosome."

Chris frowned, but relaxed a little. "Low motility. My guys try, they're just not good swimmers. I know that's what you were going to ask."

He wanted me to know it was not an issue of male performance but of ineffective tails.

"We've got three trillion cells in our bodies," I said. "We can't be expected to supervise them all."

"Laggards." Chris allowed himself a hint of a smile, perhaps feeling some relief at sharing his secret. He put down the hose and moved on to the tailgate with the sponge. "When we conceived Helen, I had this fear she'd be lazy or lethargic because of the sperm. I wish I was still that ignorant."

"I suppose Dr. Sabell has his own special magic he performed on them?"

"What the *hell* was he doing at the autopsy, Bill?"

"You tell me. What would he need to cover up?"

"Isn't it obvious? Mistakes. Defects. Screwups." Chris scrubbed furiously. "We cut off contact with him, but he still kept bugging us to let him see her. He said he had treatments. I didn't want him near my daughter."

"Could he have been desperate enough to kidnap her?"

Chris froze. "Maybe. Maybe he took her so that he could do whatever it was he wanted to do with her. But he wouldn't have let her die. He thought he could save her. He talked like he was the messiah of medicine."

I took a deep breath. "This is what I've been getting at. Sabell could have abducted Margaret, and things went wrong."

Chris gave the idea about a millisecond of thought, then flung the sponge into the bucket. "Forget it. He's not the kind who smashes car windows or leaves darts. Or pulls off kidnappings."

"Other people at the clinic could have. I need the phone number and address."

"I'll give them to you, but we dealt with him strictly one-on-one. He did a lot of his research at a private lab in his house."

"The work was more than IVF, wasn't it?" Chris moved around to the far side of the car, ignoring my question. "Tell me," I persisted. "In vitro's a well-established procedure. There had to be more to it."

Chris's head bowed, then snapped up in a scream. "Stop harassing me! It's over! She's gone!"

"And I'm trying to find out why!" I yelled back.

Chris turned on the hose. The spray drowned out my voice. I threw myself into an Adirondack chair on the patio. A little bit of sun burned its way through the fog. The Rover's metallic gray body managed to remain opaque.

After the wash, Chris got a chamois cloth from the garage. I let him work off his anger wiping away the water. He threw down the cloth, then sat, in a silent conciliatory gesture, in the chair next to me. His clothes were dark with moisture, his face beaded with tiny drops.

"I was worried when you asked me to come over this morning," I said quietly. "I was afraid they'd attacked your place, too."

"What a relief it was just my wife leaving me." His voice was more forlorn than acidic.

"Did something like this happen after Helen?"

He stared into the distance. "I was a wreck. God, what a wreck. Janet was solid, totally there for me. I was for her, too, I think. This time is different. It's like proof that we're cursed. That's how Janet put it after Helen—she said our union was cursed. I told her that was superstition and we were stronger than it."

"Did you two see a counselor?"

"I don't believe in that stuff. We stand on our own two feet, you know?" His chest sagged. "Except I don't know what that means anymore."

This was a startling admission from the guy whose personality was based on competence and control. He was letting his guard down a little bit more.

"There's no reason not to get help," I said. "I'll bet Janet would appreciate the effort."

"She's got her empty-cradle group. It's a grieving mothers' support circle she joined after Helen. She's got people to talk to."

I was about to ask Chris where his support was, his close friends. He and Janet used to go to, and give, plenty of parties, especially before Helen had died. Now it dawned on me that the entire extent of his support was sitting next to him. His friends were work and social connections, not men to whom he'd want to reveal weakness.

"That kind of leaves you in the cold," I said.

Chris was lost in his own thoughts. "I'd throw the whole thing away, Bill, if that's what it took. Jakarta, the whole Claypool Construction racket. Yeah, that's what I should do. Get away. Quit. Tell my father to stuff it."

Chris's path had been so marked out by Cole, Chris was so deep in his shadow, I wasn't sure what would be left if he stood naked on his own. "You could take a leave of absence," I suggested.

"Yeah." His fingers drummed furiously on the broad arm of the chair. The anger was building again. He lifted his eyes and it seared into me—not the reactive anger he'd flung at me before, but a slow, burning rage. I had a feeling it was only the tip of the iceberg. "That's what I've got to do, Bill. Leave. Screw Jakarta. It fucked up my life. It took me away from my family. It's why I lost track of Margaret."

He cut off my response. "No, it's true. If my father hadn't ridden me so frigging hard on this job, I would've had time for Margaret. He never let up. Every minute he said, 'Let Wilson do this, let Wilson do that. Wilson can expedite, Wilson has more experience'—*hounding* me, Bill, *testing* me."

"He uses Wilson to prod you. That's pretty obvious."

I was startled to have an accusing finger thrust at me. "That's it! That's exactly what my father does! Even now, Bill, *even now,* he's testing to see if I have the mettle to maintain, to work through this. It's supposed to be a trait of the men in our family. Nothing can stop us."

"He's always forcing you to prove you can fly on your own," I said. "But then he takes back the controls."

"Which makes it impossible for me to succeed! Well, I'm done with it. I *will* let Wilson finish it."

"Your father will understand you need a break," I said. "You know he plans for you to take over eventually."

The muscles in Chris's neck were taut, straining. He kept his voice low. I had to lean forward to hear what he said. "Maybe I don't want to. Maybe I want to start living for myself instead."

I nodded. For the first time since we'd been boys together, huddled in our tent in the woods, Chris was making sense to me. If only it hadn't taken so much pain to get to.

"It's weird, Chris," I said. "I've known you all these years, and I've known Cole, and until now I never fully understood how hard it was to be his son. I always thought you had it made."

Our gazes connected for a moment. His eyes went shiny and he looked away. "So did I, Bill."

» » » » »

Clem's head rested on her arms at a table inside Scoby's Café. I stopped to look at her through the window. Her eyes were closed. She shot upright when I pulled out a chair.

"I'll have a coffee!" she blurted.

"I'd be glad to get you one, if you ask nicely," I said.

She rubbed her eyes. Long corkscrews of dark hair dangled in front of her face. "Sorry. I thought you were a waiter."

"Don't worry, they won't throw you out unless you bring a pillow and alarm clock. Did you find a place that can analyze the dart?"

She nodded sleepily.

"Good," I said. "Next we need to move into the office. I've got a space in Dogpatch. Ready to check it out?"

"Coffee," she repeated.

We got ourselves cups to go and met outside the empty space I called my office. It was in a small industrial building near Islais Creek, a stream that ran at one time through the produce district, past old boatyards, and into the bay. The creek was paved over except at its mouth now, where it ebbed and flowed with the tide. The building had once housed machine shops for the shipping industry, which had pretty well departed from the city. It was a solid two-story concrete rectangle with an old welding company logo, FROYARD, painted on one side. A series of tall, arched windows faced the bay. The interior had been subdivided into studios and offices that were occupied by everyone from contractors and carpenters to tech start-ups, filmmakers, and musicians.

My cement-clad cube was on the second floor. I unlocked the door and ushered Clem in. It was a shell of a room, derelict, stripped of fixtures, lacking so much as a molding. The paint, pea-soup green, peeled from the high walls. Naked electric lines sprouted where the outlets should have been. The phone line ended in a Medusa's head of colored wires. The building had settled and the floor tilted toward the two windows on the far side of the room.

Clem went to a window. "Nice light. You've got a blank slate here." She was being kind.

"They did leave us the overhead lamp." A burgundy metal hood hung from the center of the ceiling.

"That's because it clashes so perfectly hideously with the green walls."

"The phone's the first thing," I said. "A land line and answering machine for the office."

"And a chair." Clem perched on a window ledge and folded her arms. "This place could be all right. Do I use my expense account to fix it up?" She gave me a sympathetic frown or an upside-down smile, I couldn't decide which.

"Within reason," I said. "Don't you need a little sleep before you start on all this?"

"Just give me the coffee. I'll sleep when I'm dead."

The expression brought me up short. I'd heard it plenty of times, from people for whom death was a distant prospect. Clem picked up on my change in mood. Her amusement at herself evaporated. "I'm sorry if it was someone you were close to, Bill."

"Once you get the phone arranged, I want you to make some calls. Use pay phones. We're trying to reach a woman named Ulla. She was my client's nanny, and she's hiding out."

I tore a page out of my little black notebook and copied out the contact numbers I had for Ulla. "Here's the story. You're a nanny, too. You worked for the same family she did: the Claypools, Chris, Janet, and Margaret. Margaret was less than a year old when you were there. You desperately need to talk to Ulla about them. Very private stuff. If, by some chance, you happen to get through to Ulla herself, set up a meeting. Tell her you can't talk over the phone. I'll fill you in on the rest as you need to know it."

"That's grand of you."

I slipped a copy of the office key off my ring and gave it to Clem. Her hand was warm in a pleasingly tingly way. I'd been working alone for too long. "You're the mistress of the cube. I'm going down the Peninsula to see the client's father. Take a nap, if you need it."

She stretched her arms and let rip a giant yawn. "I'll have the results on the dart this afternoon."

Closing the door, I had to admit I was impressed with Clem. But I wondered, too: How could she leap into the job so instantly? Didn't she have a life she had to take care of first? She'd materialized out of thin air and suddenly was running half my business.

I pointed the Scout down Interstate 280, which would take me to 101, Redwood City, and Claypool Construction. On my way, I called my friend Wes Garzen, a net nerd whose company had the resources to get background information fast. He listened to my description of Clem, chuckled, and agreed to do the check.

"What's so funny?" I demanded.

"You like the dangerous ones, don't you, Billy?" he said.

"They always find me. I don't know how, but they do."

Claypool Construction Engineering was headquartered in a shiny building worthy of the firm's trade. Monumental steel columns supported a frame of brushed aluminum and what seemed like acres of reflective glass. The security precautions were extreme. A tall wire fence enclosed the gated parking lot. To enter, I had to state my business to a guard at the gate, who cleared me with someone on the phone. An armed guard patrolled the building's entrance. The man at the front desk wore a uniform as well. I told him who I was. He called Cole's secretary, then badged me and sent me to the fourth floor. To my surprise, I was quickly shown to Cole's office.

It was a masculine room, redolent of fresh leather and tobacco. Intricately detailed models of the company's biggest projects were set out on a display table. An entire wall of the office was glass. A luxurious couch was positioned in a corner with a view of the bay. Cole sat behind a large mahogany desk, gut bulging into his three-piece pinstriped suit. Though his shape was portly, he'd been a wrestler in college, and still emanated that prowess. I thanked him for making time.

"Always glad to make time for you, Bill," he said, getting up from his seat. He guided me by the shoulder to the brushed calfskin couch. I sat on one end, Cole on the other. My uncle, I had to admit, just by his very presence had the uncanny ability to make you feel you were in good hands.

"How's our client?" he asked.

"He's managing. It's pretty rough, him having to sew up the Jakarta proposal at a time like this."

Cole shook his head sympathetically. "I don't know how he does it. He's made of iron. Wish I knew how to tell him how sorry I am about all this . . . you know how it is with fathers and sons. I admire the hell out of that kid."

"Does he know that?"

Cole reached into his pocket, extracted a small tin, and tucked a tiny pouch of tobacco inside his lip. A brass spittoon sat nearby. For all his airs, Cole didn't hide his habits. He worked some juice out of the tobacco and looked out the window. Whitecaps frothed on the gray-green water. "I'm sure Christopher knows it," he said. "On some level. The things you can't come out and say, sometimes they're the most true. Don't you think?"

I gave a perfunctory nod. Cole smiled his approval and said, "Is that what you came all the way down here to talk about?"

"No. My car windows got smashed last night. A blowgun dart was left on my seat. There may be a connection to the people you say kidnapped Margaret. You said the Hong Kong construction company has triad links, and I want to get specifics from you—who the gang is, where they're based, who we should work with in law enforcement."

He took in a breath the depth of which indicated both patient understanding and infinitely superior wisdom, as he hefted his left foot onto his right knee. His socks, ribbed charcoal gray, the same kind Chris wore, ran smooth and snug up his calf. "No, no, and no," he said. "You saw for yourself how the police treated Christopher. This is beyond them. I'm working with the Feds. You're a smart guy, Bill. I'm surprised you don't comprehend the danger of the situation. Do what you can do for Chris, but I'll handle what happened to Margaret. I've got people working on it now. I'm not going to help you get yourself hurt or, God forbid, killed."

I marveled at the smoothness of his condescension. It was as slippery and reflective as the glass skin covering his buildings. As the nephew on the poorer side of the family, I'd previously been worthy only of the "lite" version. Now I had some sense of what Chris was up against.

"You need to let me in on what you know," I said in an even voice. "I appreciate your protective instincts, but you've got to pass the torch."

The topography of creases and crevices on Cole's face, capable of a Shakespearean range of emotion, moved only a little, but just enough, to form the most menacing look I'd ever received in my life. Then they melted into a smile. "Chris has too much to deal with already. Don't make it worse for him. The Feds are keeping an eye on his house."

"I'd like to meet the agents. I don't want to mistake them for someone else when I'm over there."

"Right. I'll whistle them over right now." When I didn't return his smile, he said, "Seriously, if you insist, I will arrange a meeting for you. At their convenience. But don't worry, you'll be able to tell the good guys from the bad."

"All I want," I said, "is to know what you know about the triads. Is that asking too much? If they leave me alone, I'll leave them alone."

Cole let his crossed leg fall to the floor with a thump. "The construction firm is out of Hong Kong," he said, "but the men pulling the levers are in Guangdong. They're protected by the police, the Party, the whole machine over there. We have no legal means to pursue them. We have to find other ways."

"Can they really reach across the Pacific?"

"They've got people stealing Mercedes here in California and shipping them to China. DVD players, televisions, computers. Yes, they reach this far and beyond. I don't have time to give you the full briefing. I'll collect some documents for you."

"Thanks. What are these other ways you have of dealing with them?"

Cole put up a thick hand. "I've specified your role, Bill. Leave the rest to me. You're out of your league."

He was getting more blunt. That was good: It meant I was breaking through. "Here's the thing," I said. "When people intimidate you, they usually want you to have a clue who they are and what you have to do to stop it. Chris has heard nothing."

Cole looked carefully at his shoes. "As a matter of fact, we have received a transmission. I'm not going to say what was in it, but it's a clear threat."

"Targeting Chris?"

"Don't force me into this position, Bill. I don't want to burden Christopher more than he already is. I'm having our people in Jakarta deliver the message that we won't be intimidated. Now, I have recommended to Chris that he let Leonard Wilson finish the proposal. But Chris insists on doing it himself and I have to respect that. Once the deal is sealed, he can take a much-deserved vacation."

"Except that you're using Wilson to test Chris, to see how he holds up under the pressure." Almost immediately I wanted to take the statement back, in case it betrayed Chris's confidence. Certainly I wasn't going to relay what he'd said to me about quitting the project.

Cole rose slowly from the couch, his forehead creasing into a remarkably hurt look. "Frankly, I'm surprised. Is that what Christopher thinks?"

I stood up, too. "Chris is working his ass off even though his daughter has just died. He could use a little understanding."

Cole made his way to the door. My visit was over. "Thank you for your counsel," he said. "I'm listening to it. I really am."

We shook hands. I said, "I'll look forward to seeing those documents about the triads."

Cole held on to my hand. Apparently he was having second thoughts. He raised a finger and said, "One moment. I have something for you."

He went to his desk. I stayed where I was near the door. Cole waved a manila folder at me and said, "The preliminary autopsy findings."

"How'd you get them?"

"Don't feel bad, Bill." A lilt came into Cole's step. "I'm Chris's father and, more important, I've got a superb attorney. Now, I'm willing to share them with you . . ."

I was supposed to ask, *If?* I put out my hand and said, "Good."

"*If* you will leave this Hong Kong business to me. Promise you will stay out of it."

"I could lie and say I will. But truthfully, I'll butt out as soon as I'm sure the police, or FBI, are on the right track."

Cole withdrew the folder, acting disappointed. "There is so much you don't know, Bill. So much I can't tell you. For your own good."

"There are things you may not know, either. About the guy, for instance, who talked his way into the postmortem."

Cole tensed. "Who?"

I held out my hand for the folder.

He exhaled and treated me to a jovial laugh. "You win, Bill. Get yourself killed. You're an adult. I'm only your uncle."

My hand was still out. Cole made a small scene of bowing to give the folder to me. I said, "The man's name was Sabell. Do you know him?"

Cole's face was as unreadable as the surface of the moon. Maybe if I had a video that I could review frame by frame, I'd be able to decode if he knew the doctor. Instead, with a shake of his head, he tossed the question back at me. "What do you know about him?"

"Very little," I said. "Yet."

Cole's features relaxed into a bland mask. "Tell me what you find."

"Of course," I said.

The folder contained a single page. I read it sitting in the Scout in the parking lot. It was a photocopy of what appeared to be a fax of handwritten notes Cole's lawyer had scribbled. Neither Sabell nor Oscar was mentioned. What remained of the contents of Margaret's stomach indicated she'd eaten a lot of candy. She was dehydrated and her vitreous humor showed glucose and ketone levels through the roof. The cause of death was believed to be diabetic ketoacidosis. Ketamine, a powerful anesthetic, had shown up on the tox screen. Not a lot, but enough. The preliminary conclusion was that she'd died Saturday morning. The report noted in passing that her face appeared sunburned. This was odd because Janet and Ulla were very careful about protecting her skin.

I did not want to, but I had to picture the scene as I drove north. Her captors, presumably ignorant of her diabetes, had fed her the candy to keep her happy. They discovered their mistake too late and dumped the corpse. We could hope she did not experience too much pain or terror after the initial abduction. It tore at my heart to picture her in the backseat of some stranger's car, sitting quietly so as not to inconvenience her captors, gossamer strands of fair hair falling to her shoulders, her tiny cherry of a nose, her liquid, innocent, yet knowing eyes, her lips pursed in a more mature way than they should be, politely eating the candy given to her, saying nothing about her need for insulin.

» » » » »

Clem had gotten herself the world's tallest cup of coffee in lieu of a nap. She'd also managed to score a desk chair, in which she sat, and a TV tray, on top of which was placed a yellow pad and a plastic bag containing the blow dart. She turned in the chair as I came in, removed the dart, and dangled it by the plug end.

"You were right, Mr. Damen. It's the type used by the Dayak. Only this one's tipped with garden-variety arsenic, not the curare-like substance used in Borneo and Indonesia. They boil down the sap of the upas tree. Causes paralysis and cardiac failure within minutes."

"What a relief," I said, "that it would only have been arsenic introduced into my veins."

Clem swiveled in her chair, squinting at the tip of the dart. It was an ancient office chair, with a thick, rusty metal frame and a frayed yellow seat and backpad. Each time she turned, the chair made a screech that sounded something like a wild pig being torn apart.

"There wasn't enough poison to do serious damage," she said. "So the dart's semi-authentic. Until I know more about this case, Mr. Damen, there's not much more I can tell you."

"You know that I have to conduct my due diligence first. It's only fair to the client. Which lab analyzed the dart for you?"

She turned and played with the chair's screech, bringing it to an exquisitely hideous pitch. "A friend's," she said offhandedly.

I didn't have time to plumb that particular mystery, nor why she'd taken to calling me Mister. "I'm glad to see you've got the place furnished."

"There's lots of free stuff in this neighborhood, if you know where to look. Here, take this."

I put the dart back in the plastic bag while she searched for a pen in her thicket of black curls. She tore a corner of paper from her pad and wrote two phone numbers. "The first one's for our office," she said. "I cajoled the phone company into sending a technician tomorrow. The second one's the number down the hall. D&D Enterprises. They're letting me use their phone. Nice people. Damion and Danielle."

"There's a guy named Damion on our floor?"

"What about it?"

"People could get us confused."

"Not likely, Mr. Damen. He makes custom leather and fur collars, and is much better looking than you."

"If that's your taste. What about Ulla?"

"I haven't met her, but I'm sure she's better looking than you, too."

I sat, unsmiling, on the window ledge and folded my arms.

Clem took a gulp of coffee before she spoke. "Her friends are being cagey, but I've got a line on her. I might break through to actual contact tomorrow. You'll need to give me more on these Claypool people."

I eyed the coffee. She thrust it at me. I took my own gulp and filled her in a little more on the family Clem had supposedly worked for as a nanny.

She took notes on her yellow pad. "I presume I should tell them I'm scared to death of Christopher because he killed his own daughter?"

"What the hell are you talking about?"

"It was in the newspaper."

"Shit! Where?"

"Calm down. It was just a squib in the local section."

I took a deep breath and said, "Correct. Make it sound like you're scared of Chris. How are Ulla's friends going to contact you?"

"I gave them my home phone. Said I was staying with a friend."

"Good."

I handed the cup back to her, but her eyelids were descending, like a ceremonial curtain falling. Purple half moons had filled in under her eyes.

"Go on home," I said. "We'll start fresh in the morning. If you clear your background check, I'll tell all."

"Yes sir, Mr. Damen. That sounds worth getting up for," she said, then let out a large yawn.

Clem gave me her notes and the dart. We closed up the office. She went home to sleep, and I went home to follow up on her research and make some calls. Wes was meeting me for dinner in the city later in the evening. I crossed my fingers that he hadn't dug up any dirt on her. For all the week's misery, I felt unaccountably hopeful. I wasn't sure why, until I realized that it was a nice feeling to know I'd see Clem in the office tomorrow morning. It was nice she called it "our" office and that we'd soon have a phone. I liked collaboration; it was one of the reasons I'd gone into film. Clem had serious pain-in-the-ass potential, but she was resourceful. And she'd make a worthy accomplice for missions like getting behind the lines to interview Ulla, or visiting Dr. Sabell's fertility clinic and pretending we wanted to have a baby.

7

Thursday started off with a banging on my front door. Whoever it was apparently didn't believe in doorbells. It was eight-thirty and I hadn't set my alarm. I'd stayed out late with Wes telling him about the Claypool case. I was also trying to catch up on a large cache of recently misplaced sleep.

I threw on a robe and opened the door a crack. It was some white guy, late twenties. He said his name was Don. He wore a windbreaker, running shoes, and cargo pants with prominent portable-device bulges. His short hair terminated in mod sideburn bells; his baby-soft features were at once eager and peevish. The peeve derived from the fact that I hadn't replied to his response to my job post for a research assistant. I was guilty of the thing that I hated among producers and directors: not bothering to let you know if you hadn't been hired for a shoot.

"I'm sorry," I said. "I've already hired someone."

"You could at least let me in for an interview. I'm perfect for the job. I've got experience in both sound recording and the private eye business."

"Go down the block to Scoby's Café," I said. "I'll meet you there."

He agreed. I closed the door and resigned myself to talking to him. Not only did he seem qualified, there was a small matter of a prior felony arrest Clem had failed to disclose. As I woke up a little more, though, I wondered how Don had gotten my address. Maybe he meant to demonstrate his investigative skills by tracking me down, but I didn't like him just showing up at my door.

I went online. My in-box was crammed with responses to the job listing. Most of them were from younger people looking to work their way into the film business. I'd expected that. But I also knew the job required a certain savoir faire. Clem had it. Don Masterson boasted a film degree from NYU, five years of PA and sound work on various documentaries and shorts, and two years of part-time work with a New Jersey private investigator. Life was full of strange turns. If I hadn't happened to wake up so early yesterday, hadn't happened to call Clem after she'd been up all night, hadn't been impressed by her yesterday, I'd be at Scoby's with Don right now negotiating a wage. Instead, I pictured his face, cheeks puffed out with self-assurance and a sense of entitlement; and then hers, the luminous olive skin, the taunting smile, the fiendish shine in her honey-green eyes . . .

But I couldn't ignore the dirt Wes had turned up. The last thing I wanted to find myself saying to Chris, after something went terribly wrong, was, "Yes, I *did* know she had an arrest record, but . . ."

I called her at home. No answer. No way, I thought, she'd be in the office already. I blew off my morning routine, even the life-sustaining coffee, and threw on some clothes. Yes, Clem's nifty little yellow Corvair was parked in front of the Froyard Welding building. I went upstairs and found her drinking coffee from a paper cup. She swiveled in her chair. A rough desk built from an old door and cinder blocks had appeared. A phone and a laptop computer sat on the desk.

"Good morning, Mr. Damen," she said. The chair screeched its own greeting. She sat in a slouch, cowboy-booted legs crossed, dark tights showing between the top of the boots and the hem of a black skirt. I was relieved she'd left the fringe jacket on the antler rack or wherever she kept it.

"Morning, Clem. Sure you got enough sleep?"

"The phone guy said he'd be here between eight and twelve."

That took some of the punch out of my next question. "Why did you lie to me about your arrest for assault and battery?"

She bolted upright. "I never said my record was clean! Or tried to talk you out of checking up on me."

"You just hoped I wouldn't find out? Not very professional, Clem."

"I hoped you'd have the wisdom to see past it."

"You expect me to say, 'Fine, it's no problem having a potential felon representing my office in a murder investigation'?" I held back from adding that if I were her, I'd be on my knees begging forgiveness.

"If I were you, I'd ask, 'Hmm, do I want some slick guy out of film school telling me he's "got connections," or do I want a person who's lived her life and made a few mistakes?' Because I'm a shitkicker, Bill. I *am* the woman you want to have on your side."

"You're a woman of conviction, I know that much. What happened?"

She sighed, folded her arms, and looked away. "I won't bore you with the whole sad story. Let's just say I've been through a few different stages, *incarnations,* in my life. The last one was a kind of transition phase. It was about risk assessment. Playing the odds. Poker, if you must know. Started small, but I was good at it, and pretty soon I was in some expensive private games. I caught this one guy cheating. That was always my biggest risk factor—someone dealing from his sleeve. I called him on it and, not to bore you with the details, he called me by a certain part of my anatomy and I stomped a delicate part of his anatomy—his toe—with my boot heel and then smashed his nose with my knee and stepped on him. He filed charges; I pled them down to a misdemeanor and ended up with probation and community service."

I thought a minute, then said, "Well, I'm glad to know you can defend yourself. On the other hand, I can't have you doing crap like that around here."

"You might need crap like that now and then," she shot back. "I left the gambling behind that night and never looked back. The only thing I can't promise is, if I run into the guy on the street, I won't do it to him all over again. Otherwise, I'm clean as a new teapot."

I sat on the window ledge. If I'd been caught at a few things I'd done, I'd have a felony or two on my own record. "What happens if we do get mixed up in some kind of crap?" I said.

"Look, Damen, I'm getting back on my feet. You want to knock me down again? Go ahead."

"I will if I have to."

We glared at each other. She said, "Give me a probationary period."

"Done."

Clem's glare hardened. She beat me to the next shot. "I had my last meeting with my officer a month ago."

"Tell me about your other incarnations."

"It's a long story. You take me out some night. We'll have a few glasses of JD. And then I'll tell you."

I gazed out the window, thinking. She watched me for a minute, then another, and couldn't sit still. She sprang from her chair, arms spread in exasperation. "I've scrounged in Dumpsters for furniture for this place. I've analyzed your dart. I've worked my way through layers of family and friends to get a message to Ulla." She grabbed a paper sack from under the desk, shook it at me, then threw it to the floor. "I've bought phone jacks and electrical outlets. What more do you want?"

I stayed on the ledge. "Don't yell."

She threw herself back down in the chair, refusing to look at me. I looked away, too. After a minute, she reached down for the large, shapeless bag she carried with her everywhere. It was plain black leather, worn half-raw, with a thin strap. She rummaged in it, a look of concentration on her face. I had no idea what was going to come out.

It was a red tin of mints. She offered me one. There was something about the gesture—it was a peace offering, an expression of familiarity, and an insult all rolled into one. And it worked. That was the convincing thing about her, in the end. Everything she'd done so far, except the yelling, had worked.

The mints made a pleasant fire in my mouth. "I'm going to hold you to that JD," I said.

"Deal." She paused, with an inward look, and then said, "The previous phases were more . . . I guess you'd say, brainy. They burned me out. I'm just like you, Bill, trying to figure out what the fuck I'm doing with my life."

I nodded. It was close enough to an apology, and she was close enough to getting me access to Ulla, that I was willing to give her a chance.

"Faith, Mr. Damen, will be rewarded," she said. "To those who have much, much more will be given. And I'm not talking about tax cuts."

"We need to flesh out our cover story for Ulla," I said. "Something that will make her feel like she can't afford not to talk to us. Or, more likely, to you. You'll be on your own."

Clem repressed a smile. "You're right about that. The people I've contacted are extremely protective. I had to go through a family she worked for in New York to get to a sister in Sweden to get to a friend who knows a friend who's hiding her here. Ulla's very scared of someone."

"Chris, I suppose, or the triads. Unless it's all an act. I'm sure the police are keeping her in town to testify against him." I paced the room. "Tell her you didn't last long with the Claypools. Something terrible happened, you're in danger of being deported. You must talk to Ulla. You have information you can deliver only to her, personally."

I painted a fuller picture of Chris and Janet for Clem. Chris, the all-American kid who took the burden of manhood thrust upon him by his father and was in the process of becoming the world-dominating executive when the tragedies of Helen and Margaret struck. Janet, the one-time teacher and watercolorist who'd taken the comforter of security and ease offered by Chris, only to learn that no amount of money and power could fend off the wanton vicissitudes of life. I mentioned Dr. Sabell and the in vitro origin of their two daughters. Clem took it all in and we made our plan. Peace reigned again in the office. Then I remembered Don had been waiting for me at Scoby's all this time.

"I have to run up to the café," I said. "There's one more thing I want during your probation. Give me a reference. One person I can call. You materialized out of nowhere and I want to make sure you're not some kind of bizarre dream I'm having."

"You're such a gentleman to call it a dream instead of a nightmare. But yeah, sure. I'll give you a reference." She picked up the paper sack again and dumped out kits for a phone jack and electrical outlet. "On your way out, find someone who can shut off the power for us. I want to install these things."

» » » » »

Don was gone. My friends behind the register said he'd hung around for a while in an agitated state, then had stormed out. Oh well. I'd already cast my lot with Clem, which felt something like jumping into a raging river from which you knew there was no exit for miles. Don would have been easy water. Wes, unfortunately, was right. I couldn't resist the cataracts.

I got some coffee and went back to my flat. It was eleven by now. I called Chris. His voice was sluggish. He'd had a few beers last night, then found some Valium in Janet's medicine cabinet. Janet had slept in the guest bedroom. His cell phone started going off in the morning. After the third time, Janet came into the room and put the phone to his ear, to no effect. She put it on vibrate and left it cradled in Chris's arm. A man from Claypool Construction showed up around nine. She told him Chris was quite unrousable. The man left, and Janet got worried. She shook Chris and pressed a cold cloth to his face. Finally he came to. He said he'd felt half-buried, but relieved to see Janet. She'd sat in a chair near the bed and they talked. The meeting at her grieving-mothers' support group had gone late last night, she said. She apologized for throwing the plant and said work was good for him, it helped keep his mind busy. She'd had too much time to sit around the house and brood. Chris told her he was taking himself off the Jakarta project. Cole had probably put Leonard Wilson in charge already. Janet had counseled him not to act too hastily. His work would save him in the end.

That was an odd way of putting it, I thought. I started to tell him I'd gotten some preliminary autopsy results.

"My father faxed them over yesterday," Chris said. "I'll have Mitch Walchuk deal with the coroner and the prosecutors, Bill. It's outrageous they haven't released Margaret yet. The funeral is Saturday, for God's sake. You go ahead and pursue Ulla and Dinh." There was a pause. I could hear the thickness of his tongue in his mouth. "I gotta have a shower."

We signed off. I punched in the mobile number for Mr. Dinh, the gardener. I'd memorized it by now, and was so used to not getting an answer that I had to fumble the phone to my mouth when his voice came on. I asked if I could meet him to talk about a gardening job. He said he'd come to my house. We traded insistences on saving each other trouble until he finally gave an address in Seacliff where he'd be working for the next several hours.

I drove across town, through the wending ways of Seacliff, with their views of the Golden Gate and Marin, to the address Dinh had given. He stood up from his digging when he saw me. Mr. Dinh was close to seventy, thin and strong, his face deeply lined. A large brimmed cap covered his head.

He removed his gloves to shake hands. "You need gardening?" He gestured at the newly turned earth. "Springtime, time to plant."

"Actually," I said, "I need to ask you about my cousin. Christopher Claypool, in St. Francis Wood."

He took a step back. "I told the police everything."

"Good," I said, trying to set him at ease. "I just wanted to double-check a couple of things. Did you see what happened at their house on Friday?"

Dinh slapped his gloves impatiently on his thigh. "I *told* them I didn't go there on Friday."

"But someone else did. Someone worked in the garden. Do you have employees?"

"My son, sometimes. But he was out of town."

"Wasn't Friday your regular day? Why didn't you go?"

"Mrs. Claypool called and said not to. My wife took the message the day before."

"Janet Claypool called? Maybe your wife misunderstood."

"No. She wrote down the address."

"You haven't answered your phone for the past couple of days."

"We were worried." He scanned the street, left and right. "But I was losing business. I have to come back sometime."

"Did anyone else contact you about the Claypools?"

"Only the police." He took off the cap and scratched his head. "Please tell Chris and Janet—I'm sorry."

I said I would, thanked him, and left, scratching my own head. Had Janet forgotten she'd canceled when she said Chris should have seen the gardener on Friday? Nothing about Dinh made me think he wasn't telling the truth. If he'd lied about being at the Claypools', a neighbor could easily contradict him.

I was thinking about going over to my cousin's house to ask Janet about this when my cell phone rang. It was Clem.

"Guess what, Mr. Damen? You can reach me by phone at our office."

"That's good news. How's it going with Ulla?"

"Well . . ." She took a breath to make sure I was listening. "My new friends put the sob story to her. They know me as Sylvia, and oh, do they feel sorry for me. The things those Claypools did . . . Anyway, Ulla's willing to have a face-to-face. Her friends told me to sit at an outside table at Café de la Presse and wait for a call between one and three. Like I've got nothing to do but sit around and drink coffee."

"Perfect. I'll stop at home to pick up some gear."

"I'll need your mobile. I hope they don't reverse-search the number."

"I delisted it and blocked caller ID."

"Good, because they are seriously paranoid."

"No surprise. There's one more thing." I read her the number Chris had given me for Sabell's fertility clinic. "Try to get an informational interview for tomorrow. We're a couple desperately in pursuit of an in vitro baby."

"Sure we are. Only I'm sorry you prefer a jar to the real thing."

I was crazy to have hired her, but would have been crazier not to. "I'll be back at the office soon," I said. "We'll wire you there."

"Mr. Damen!"

"Relax. The only thing that'll be getting under your shirt is an MP3 recorder."

» » » » »

Café de la Presse occupied a busy corner downtown and carried a large selection of newspapers from around the world. Clem had been instructed to display a copy of *Le Monde* outside, which she appeared to be actually reading. Whoever was watching her had sight lines from both Grant Avenue and Bush Street, most obviously from the Hotel Astoria across the way. I'd taken a table on the lower of the two levels inside before she arrived. I wore glasses and a Giants cap pulled low, in case Ulla herself was watching and recognized me. I kept myself hidden behind a copy of the *Sporting News*.

The tables were small and round, faux marble, the chairs wicker. Clem looked distinctly Continental in her skirt and sweater. She'd also applied lipstick. The sky was overcast and the day not particularly warm. She showed admirable patience as Ulla's friends kept her waiting at her metal outdoor table for one hour, then most of another. More than once she was approached by lone men. Each time she sent them away laughing and shaking their heads. After she finished *Le Monde* she opened a pack of cigarettes. It carried an image of a woman going up in smoke: Gitanes. She lit up.

The call came at five minutes before three. Clem, after receiving her instructions, gave a small nod in my direction. She signaled to the waitress, paid, and stood up. I folded my paper. A guy across from me slid out of his seat at the same time I slid out of mine. He was about six-three, with sloping shoulders, and he seemed intent on getting in my way.

"You're Dave, right? Dave Simmons?" he said, sticking out a plump hand.

"No. You've mistaken me for someone else."

I sliced an arm past his shoulder to squeeze by him. He crowded me into an empty table. "I'm sure of it," he said. "I'm Wayne Orstner. Don't you remember me?"

"Out of my way!"

He prattled about some high school in Salt Lake City. I knocked him backward with a forearm. He caught himself on a chair behind him. I bounded up a couple of stairs and made for the door. If I hadn't had to dodge a busboy, I would have been out. But Wayne got a handful of my coat. I whirled, sweeping my fist in an arc. It connected with his jaw. He let out a cry. I jerked my coat away and rushed outside to the corner.

When I last saw her, Clem was crossing Bush, about to pass through the green-tiled gate to Chinatown. I went under its twin dragons and darted through the crowds on the narrow sidewalk. There was no sign of Clem's dark skirt and sweater. I went another block up Grant, checking down side streets and in storefronts. Nothing. I thought about Hong Kong construction companies and I thought about triads and I cursed myself for allowing her to be put into this position.

I returned to the gate and looked vainly up and down Bush Street. By now it was too late. There, across the street, standing outside the café, was Wayne, hands on hips, grinning a self-satisfied grin at me.

My eyes met his. Yes, he was waiting for me, challenging me. I took my time, letting the light turn green before I crossed, in order to watch him and determine whether he was the thug type or the protective boyfriend type. There was a straightness in his face; he looked pleased with himself in spite of the fact that he'd just been whacked upside the head. Still, I kept out of striking distance when I approached.

"You win, Wayne," I said. "I'll tell the police you abducted my friend."

His self-satisfaction grew. "I'm only watching out for *my* friend."

"Ulla's in danger," I said. "Why don't we sit down?"

His expression sobered. I wanted to see what I could get out of him, but I also wanted to make sure he didn't make any calls to Ulla to warn her that "Sylvia" had had a watchdog. The wait staff peered anxiously through the window as I led him to the outdoor table where Clem had been sitting. I motioned for service. The busboy came first. He wiped the table and said, "Are you making a movie?"

Wayne chuckled, then looked at me. "What's your name?"

"Call me Dave. Yours?"

"I'll stick with Wayne," he said.

I heard his accent more clearly now. Northern European. His English was excellent, though he tended to bark his sentences as if they were going out over a loudspeaker. Not Swedish, not German—given his height, I said, "Dutch, right? You didn't go to high school in Salt Lake City, Wayne."

"Ah, but I've seen Americans do this to one another." He peered at my face. "Why do they wear these baseball caps everywhere all the time?"

"Blocks the glare," I replied. He looked puzzled, and I said, "Where's Sylvia?"

"She's gone by car." He smirked again at his success.

"Who are you protecting Ulla from?"

"She's in a safe place. It is Ulla doing Sylvia the favor, is it not?"

The waitress arrived and we ordered coffees. When she left, I said, "Sylvia's very concerned about Christopher Claypool."

Wayne sat back and rolled his lips against each another. "Ulla was tricked into losing the little girl. Claypool wants to put the blame on Ulla. She went to the police first and luckily they believe her."

"What does she have to fear, then?"

"A man threatened her life if she told anyone about it." He touched the purpling patch on his jaw.

"Sorry about that," I said.

His smile was not forgiving. "Do not apologize prematurely."

"We think the men who took Margaret work for a Chinese triad."

Wayne waved a finger at me and tsked. "When Sylvia called, she said that she feared Claypool. There is a contradiction between what you say and what she said."

"Yes." I leaned back. "There are many contradictions. I just got the new information."

I left it at that. Our coffees arrived. It would be my fifth of the day and, after starting out with none, I was getting the jitters. My hand was unsteady as I lifted the cup. So was Wayne's. That made me feel there was a chance I'd see Clem again before the afternoon was over.

8

Clem returned at five. She'd been picked up in an old Toyota on Bush Street a moment after she'd received the call, then taken to Berkeley to see Ulla. Ulla's friends offered her a ride back, but Clem played it safe and took the train. She called me at the office on her way home and I went to the 16th Street station to pick her up. She looked invigorated by her adventure.

"Ulla talked to you?" I said.

"Yes." Without warning, she lifted her sweater and yanked at the first-aid tape that had pinned the MP3 recorder to her sternum, below her black bra. I pretended to gape but, for the most part, kept my eyes chivalrously on the road. "I hope this thing's waterproof," she said, settling the apparatus on her lap. "I sweated up a storm. Do you trust me to summarize or do you want to listen to the tape for yourself?"

"I'll listen later. Tell me all about it."

She rolled her neck, stretching it. "It's getting late. It's been a long day and I could use a drink."

"Sure," I agreed. "Anything but coffee."

We went down 16th to the Ramp, a dockside joint whose deck projected out over the water. The clouds had thinned and shafts of sunlight played on the bay, turning it alternately ink-blue and murk-green. We got a couple of beers and took a table by the deck railing.

"Ulla and Margaret got tricked in the park," Clem said. "Margaret was abducted, and then a man at the Claypool house threatened Ulla. She thinks—"

"That Chris is the one behind it all," I put in.

Clem scowled. "Why'd you send me on this chase if you already knew?"

"I got tackled by a Dutch friend of Ulla's on my way out of the café. We had a little chat. There's still plenty I don't know. Go on."

I didn't interrupt again. Clem, alias Sylvia, had started by telling Ulla her fairy tale of woe at the hands of the Claypool family. Chris was an ogre, Janet a witch, baby Margaret a sweet foundling who it was hard to believe had issued from them. "Sylvia" couldn't do anything right in Janet's eyes. Chris blew up at her for things that his wife had done. They withheld her pay for the first week, then the second, saying she was on "probation." (Clem winked at the word.) She finally fled in the middle of the night, after a month of work, and was never paid a cent. In fact, they threatened to turn her files over to the INS. She'd been frightened ever since. Sylvia heard that Ulla might have information that would help her.

"The Claypools will get theirs," Ulla had said in a tone of shared triumph. "The American police will charge them any day now."

Clem dramatically clamped her hands to her cheeks. "What have they done? Not little Margaret . . . ?"

Ulla nodded solemnly, her eyes welling. She proceeded with her own tale. She listed some minor infractions on the part of the

Claypools, but Clem urged her on to the main event. Ulla and Margaret had gone for a Friday outing in Montoya County Park. A man—he seemed like a rather nice old man, a bit confused—in a heavy wool coat had appealed to them to help look for his dog. He'd lost little Ricky, a Jack Russell terrier. Ricky was the apple of his eye, the light of his life—he repeated these phrases as if the dog were his son. How dreadful it was to imagine him out there lost in the woods, hungry, whimpering, possibly hurt. The story yanked on Margaret's heartstrings as powerfully as on Ulla's. Margaret had a soft spot for injured creatures.

The man led them to a steep redwood hillside where he said he'd last seen Ricky. They spread out like tines, combing through the tall trunks and dark woods, calling Ricky's name. Cresting the hill, they found themselves in a scrubby area. Ulla could no longer see the others over the bushes. She listened carefully for a minute, hearing neither Margaret's voice nor the old man's. Ulla screamed for the girl, then crashed through the bushes searching for the man, appealing to him for help. They were gone, evaporated, like phantoms, as if the earth had swallowed them. Just as the dog was. No sounds came from the bushes but the grating indifference of insects. It was then that Ulla realized the dog had been a ruse. Her mind leaped to the obvious conclusion. She collapsed in tears of despair, both for Margaret and for her own dereliction. After a few minutes of frantic searching in the bushes, screaming that a child had been taken, screaming for someone to stop the old man, Ulla herself was lost. In her panic, she could not find her way back to the playground. She scaled a wire fence and ran, face and clothes ragged, along a four-lane road back to the turnoff to the park and the lot in which she'd left the car. No one at the playground had seen

Margaret or the man. Someone offered to call 911, but Ulla, so frightened about the consequences of her mistake, said she would do it herself. She sped back to the house, hoping that by some miraculous chance the old man had returned Margaret.

A man in a large-brimmed cap, his back to her, kneeled in the front yard, working the flower beds. Mr. Dinh. Relieved to find a familiar figure, she called for his help. He didn't seem to hear. She ran to him. He spun suddenly and sprang upon her. In place of the friendly face of Mr. Dinh were hideous features distorted behind a black stocking mask. The man clamped a hand over her mouth and dragged her behind the bush near the front door. He got her down, his knee punishing her back, and came close to suffocating her before she agreed not to scream. She thought it was the end. He told her, in a horrible guttural voice, what she must do. She must give him the keys to the house. She must go away and never come back. And she must do it all without saying a word to anyone, ever. If she did, she would die. Worse, she'd cause the immediate death of the little girl, too. Ulla's visa was expired. She had no standing in the United States. "The police will blame *you,* Ulla," the man had said.

The use of her name, the knowledge of her situation, struck as much terror into her as the attack itself. Ulla nodded her understanding. The man's voice was infernal; she would never forget it. She'd been petrified into silence. The man said he would always be there, watching for her. She got up and ran to her car, then drove to Wayne's apartment. Other friends were called. They took elaborate precautions to spirit her to another friend's house, and then another. There they took turns on watch.

Ulla obsessively replayed the incidents in her mind. Her heart ached, picturing Margaret in the hands of men like the gardener. It was the parents' fault, Ulla's friends said. Chris and Janet should take the blame. It chilled her to realize that Janet's trip to Monterey and Chris's apparent preoccupation with work that same morning could have been prearranged. They'd left Ulla virtually unsupervised. She *had* to tell the police. Surely the Claypools had raised the alarm by then anyway. The authorities would be searching for Ulla. Fleeing the country would be like an admission of guilt. The blame would be laid on Ulla and the Claypools would be rid of the burden of their daughter. Who else but Chris could have told the "gardener" Ulla's name and green-card status? Ulla went to the police. They could help her friends keep her safe until she was able to return to Sweden.

The police questioned her closely about the Claypools. Things they had said began to come back to her. That very morning Chris had yelled at her to keep the damned clutter out of his way after he'd stumbled over a stuffed rabbit. Margaret was just inside the door to her room, and it seemed that by clutter he meant his daughter. A month before that, Ulla had overheard Janet say to a friend that she didn't know how much longer she could stand it. "I feel like I'm going over the edge," Janet had said. In front of Ulla, Janet had always been the loving and patient mother. But Ulla heard something else in Janet's voice that night, something that made her believe the train of events on Friday had not been coincidence.

Ulla told the police where a key was hidden and how to turn off the alarm so they could search the house. Later they escorted her back so she could pick up a few of her possessions. She ran back out to the police cruiser just as someone came home. She vowed never to return again.

Clem finished her story and took a gulp of beer.

"Poor Ulla," I said. I pictured her small round face, slightly jutting chin, and her almond-brown hair cut blunt just below the ears, bunching in a little curl at the neck. She was bright and energetic but small-boned, a bit delicate. "Now I understand the cloak-and-dagger at the café."

"Yeah," Clem agreed, "I would've been pissing in my pants, too."

"I think she's trying to lay her own feelings of guilt for losing Margaret off on Chris and Janet, though. Did she describe the man who attacked her at the house at all?"

"He was strong, burly, maybe five-seven. He had some accent she didn't recognize."

"What was your impression of Ulla? How honest was she being?"

Clem drummed her fingers on the rough wood of the table for a few seconds. The nails were bitten, the skin around them chewed. "I think she told me the story pretty straight. She was reliving it and she wanted me to relive it with her. She might have tweaked some details or left something out. She was a little too eager to hear about my misery, enjoyed it a little too much. She's got an opportunistic side. Either that or she's just young and scared."

"Maybe the two are the same thing."

"Exactly. She might help me again, especially if we could offer something in return."

I drained my beer. Clem did the same with hers. The bay had turned a deep indigo. "You did a great job, Clem," I said.

She made a sour little smile. "You say that as if you expected otherwise."

"Not at all. I have to admit, I worried when you disappeared. I didn't want to lose you."

"I knew where I was all along. But it was nice of you to be concerned." She reached into her bag on the floor, pulled out a wrinkled piece of paper, and gave it to me. "Here's my employment reference. In case you still want to check up on me."

I looked at the name and number written on the paper. "Thanks."

"I'm tired," she said. "Are we done?"

"For today." We stood and headed back out to Illinois Street.

"You still want to go to Dr. Sabell's clinic tomorrow, right?" Clem said as we parted ways. I nodded, and she said, "Good. Because I had to make myself real desperate to get us an appointment for two o'clock."

» » » » »

I got home after eight and called Chris. Janet answered. I asked how she was doing. She was hesitant at first, but then she said, "A little better, Bill. I'm so glad you're there for Chris. We've been too isolated. We can't do this alone. My sister's here from Monterey. Chris has family over tonight, too."

I asked Janet if she'd canceled Mr. Dinh's regular Friday visit last week. She was sure she hadn't. I told her there'd been a fake gardener in his place, then asked her to ask the neighbors if they'd seen the man. I heard the strain in her voice as she agreed to do so. She didn't want to be talking about this. She put Chris on as soon as she could.

"Bill," Chris said. "You called in the nick of time."

"You sound a lot better than this morning," I said.

"It's all a front. My great-aunt Henrietta is here with her husband, Fred. It's been a parade of relatives all day long. I've been drinking scotch just to deal with them." He reconsidered and said, "I did get some good news today. The DA finally allowed the coroner to release Margaret. She's being transferred to the family mortuary first thing in the morning. We can have the funeral on Saturday."

"Will the ceremony be at the funeral home?" The Claypools had a large plot in Colma going back three generations.

"No. We're having her cremated. After what Sabell did at the autopsy, I don't want to give him any more chances. I've hired a boat. We'll have a little ceremony at sea. We can only take twenty people, which is one of the reasons I want to do it this way. You're included. But Dad's so bent out of shape about it, we might have to also have a reception at the funeral home."

"I'm sure there are a lot of other people who want to come."

"Yeah, and I don't want them. It's bad enough having them troop through my house all day. I'm in the back bathroom right now so they can't hear me. My parents must have put out the word about how fucked up I was after I blew off work this morning. These people are here only out of duty. They don't want to be around the son whose life has gone rotten, because Lord knows some of it might get on them."

A combination of the scotch and last night's misery was talking. "Henrietta's nice enough," I said, "even if her brain's made of meringue."

"She's trying to take the weight of the whole thing on her shoulders. You'd think it was her own child she lost. At least she means well. You know what Cliff, our cousin, says to me? He says I need to take care of Janet. Some huge percentage of couples who lose a child break up within a few years."

"Cliff is and has always been a dolt."

"Everyone was so concerned and so consoling the first time around, with Helen. Now it's more like we did something wrong. Lightning doesn't strike twice, you know. And my mother—every day it's another plant, like I need something new to take care of. She's just going through the motions, though. I'm Cole's son, in her mind. I hate going over to their house. It's like the Ice Ages. My father's fucking Torrie at the office and everyone knows it."

I was speechless for a moment, struck more by Chris's casually acrid disclosure than by the revelation itself. I always figured Cole had someone on the side. "Any particular reason your parents stay together?"

"Stubbornness. They want the other one to give in first."

"What did Cole have to say about you going AWOL today?"

"I'm getting the silent treatment. My secretary, Kiersty, told me Leonard Wilson has taken over the Jakarta project."

"Maybe Cole doesn't want to put pressure on you."

"Believe me, if he was being nice, he'd make sure he got credit for it."

"How are things with you and Janet?" I asked.

"Oh . . ." His voice cracked. The bravura rage turned to self-pity. "Well, her sister Penny arrived today. That's improved her mood. She's acting nice, giving me little kisses, but they're just for show. She's staying in the guest room with Penny. I'm trying to spend time with her, to make things better, but she keeps coming up with reasons to get away from me. I can't figure her out. One day she's pissed because I'm distracted by work, the next because I'm paying her too much attention."

"Well . . ." I said. "From what I've heard, no one feels the loss of a child like a mother does."

Chris took a moment to answer. "Yeah," he said with a quiver in his throat. "She didn't want to have another one after Helen. She said she couldn't bear the risk of another loss. I talked her into it, and now look what I've done. God, she must hate me, Bill."

"She's probably mad at the whole world, Chris. Including herself."

"It's so wrong!" Chris burst out. "She didn't want to go through it all again—the hormones, the embryos, the implantations, the miscarriages. I can't believe I let Sabell mess with her like that again."

"Mess with Janet or the embryos?" I pictured Sabell playing three-card monte with an array of glass embryo dishes. "What did he do with the embryos?"

"Just find out what the hell happened to Margaret," Chris answered.

"We got Ulla's story today. I'll give it to you, but I want you to tell me what Sabell did. Obviously it was more than the usual in vitro procedure."

"He just made sure Margaret didn't have the same problems Helen had." Chris's voice turned steely. "Listen, Bill, *you* work for *me*. You don't withhold information. You don't demand details of my private life that you don't need to know. Got it?"

"You sound just like your father did yesterday."

"Fuck you, Bill!" he shouted. "I'd rather be talking to those idiots Henrietta and Fred right now!"

"Go on. I'll talk to you tomorrow, when you're sober."

"No, you'll tell me what Ulla said. *Now*."

I gave him a terse version of it. Chris interrupted to put me on hold. "Shit," he breathed when he came back on. "Janet said they heard me."

"At least you figured out how to get rid of them."

Chris laughed, and I relaxed the grip on my phone. I'd been pacing from the back of my flat to the front. Now I eased into my couch and finished the Ulla story. I asked if Chris had heard anything more from Mitch Walchuk.

"The inquisition continues," Chris answered. "By both the cops and the coroner's office. Now we know who their star witness is. And why I'm their favorite suspect. Can you get to Ulla personally, yourself?"

"I think so," I said. "If her story's true, it means that these weren't some low-level hoods who went after a rich family's daughter. They knew about you, your gardener, Ulla's immigration status. Cole might be right about the Hong Kong connection. Unless you think Sabell is more likely."

"I don't know . . . I just—I hate asking my father for help or information. Especially now."

"I'll ask him," I said.

"Thanks. I better go face the music. What do I say to them?"

"Nothing," I replied. "Just tell them how much you appreciate their blah blah blah, and it's time to say good night."

9

"I must say, Bill, you're putting me in touch with my femininity. Yesterday I was a battered nanny, today I'm a wannabe mom."

Clem waited by the passenger door to the Scout. "You've dressed like a lady, too, bow blouse and all," I said.

She smiled as I unlocked the door for her, then said, "And you remembered to shave for a change. But get one thing straight. None of my real clothes have bows."

The door made its metallic wail and Clem clambered in. I got us on 280 heading south to Silicon Valley and the Sabell Clinic. Clem and I rehearsed the story of our coupledom as we drove. Our eyes had met not across a room but through a camera lens. I saw her on a shoot and zoomed all the way in. She was an actress-producer, I was a director-writer, and together we were wildly successful. My shabby flat in Potrero Hill morphed into a fabulously chic loft. It was a happy, romantic story until the fly of infertility had spoiled the ointment. We'd run the fertility gauntlet: the coital timings and positions; the temperature-takings, sperm counts, and ovulation profiles; the sonograms and hormone injections and inseminations. My fortuitous meeting with Dr. Sabell at the coroner's had inspired us into taking the ultimate step in the quest for offspring.

The clinic was nestled in one of the series of pastoral valleys hidden in the layers of hills defining the western edge of Silicon Valley. We exited the freeway and followed a narrow country road up and over a wooded crest. The clinic turnoff was marked only with a five-digit address sign. We were now on a narrow lane of packed dirt. It wound up and over one small ridge after another, through groves of live oak, poplar, and sycamore, the sunlight dappling warm and cool as we passed. Every half-mile we passed a small icon sign that let us know we were on the right course. The signs gave the feeling, as the miles added up, that we were on a pilgrimage, or a treasure hunt. Each valley we passed through was its own little world, glimpses of which were revealed by the winding road: verdant meadows, brushy creeks, grazing horses, a tilled field or orchard here and there.

Several miles in, we curved over a ridge and passed a turn leading to a gated lane. The gate was crowned with a wrought-iron arch whose leaved vines spelled out A. REMLY. In the distance stood a grand estate done in the style of a Bavarian castle. Dark firs clustered around the house, but spread before it were acres of pasture, lush and emerald. Over the next ridge, another fork took off to the right, this one also gated but unnamed.

One more ascent brought us to the clinic. The clean, hard lines of the facility were startling in the rural landscape. The parking lot was soothingly smooth. We dismounted from the Scout and straightened our clothes. A flawless walkway curved through a forecourt garden to automatic glass doors. The doors whooshed open and we entered the lobby. The reception area, a small oval defined by an onyx counter, greeted us. Above, silky white material billowed softly from the ceiling, creating the sense of being inside a giant tent. Clem and I waited at the counter while the receptionist finished typing at her workstation. The bulge of her belly became visible when she turned toward us, a living advertisement for the doctor's expertise.

I said we had an appointment with Dr. Sabell. Her generous features opened into a smile. "It wouldn't be with Dr. Sabell," she said. "He's doing research today. You'll be consulting with Dr. Rosen after the nurse completes your intake." She handed us some forms and a clipboard. "Please complete these questionnaires. Would you like me to get you some tea?"

We declined and made our way into the waiting area, a maze of toile love seats arranged so that none faced the others. Large planters of palm, ficus, and fern created suitable separation between each seating area. A fountain, a small grotto of stones and maidenhair ferns, burbled along the wall. A delicate scent of jasmine soothed the nose. Mostly women occupied the seats, some well-dressed, others in loose, casual clothes, all with expensive haircuts and the complexion of wealth. Two couples were there, one younger, one closer to our age, leaning together and clasping hands. A distinguished-looking man with a lean face and salt-and-pepper hair and beard sat alone, partially hidden behind a palm, holding a brown bag carefully creased at the top. He looked worried that the bag might explode in his lap.

Clem and I found an empty couch and filled in the forms, conferring under our breath. I'd gallantly volunteered to take responsibility for our infertility. Insurance was not mentioned. Not only was the clinic highly exclusive and hard to find, it was all cash.

A nurse called our names. We followed her down one of the corridors that branched from either side of the lobby, into a small examination room. She didn't introduce herself, but her name tag said STACY HATCHER. We sat in comfortable padded chairs while Stacy stood and reviewed our forms. Clem said, "We thought our appointment was with Dr. Sabell."

Stacy kept reading as if Clem had not spoken. Her hair, blond-streaked and dark-rooted, was up in a bun. Her nose was small and her mouth and brows were straight, severe lines. The foundation caked onto her cheeks looked like wall plaster in the room's fluorescent light. A diamond ring sprouted from the fourth finger of her left hand.

"Only special cases see Sabell," Stacy said abruptly.

"Special as in wealthy?" I said.

"Special as in hopeless." She jotted notes on the questionnaire. "You've got a ways to go before you're desperate enough to have George jerk you around."

Clem and I looked at each other, stunned. "Do you not recommend his services?" I asked.

Stacy lowered the clipboard. "Why didn't you bring your medical records with you?"

"They were lost in a fire. We'd rather start from the beginning."

"You didn't fill in your sperm count, Bill."

"I don't remember it. Motility is the problem, anyway."

She glanced down at my crotch, and I got a little taste of how Chris must have felt. "We'll need to collect a semen sample today. We'll also take blood. Dr. Rosen may request a dye test and ultrasound for you, Mrs."—Stacy glanced at the form—"Willendorf. Why are your last names different?"

Returning the nurse's steady gaze, Clem said, "We're not siblings. And if the doctor doesn't mind, we may wait on the tests for me."

Stacy inspected Clem and shrugged. "You're not getting any younger."

"We came here because of Dr. Sabell's reputation," I said. "How does he jerk people around?"

"Who said that he does?" Stacy replied.

Clem and I exchanged glances again. She mouthed the word "hormones." To Stacy, she said, "He enjoys the power, huh? Having his finger on the button of creation."

"All men want that power," Stacy said. "Get up there on the scale."

I refrained from watching the scale's digital readout. "I understand Dr. Sabell has some special ways of manipulating sperm, eggs, embryos," I said.

"He can make your wife give birth to a green pig that glows in the dark, if he feels like it," Stacy said offhandedly. "Your turn."

I got up on the scale. Clem let out a low whistle. "One eighty-four. Honey, we're going on a diet."

Stacy wrote it down, then prompted us in turn to sit to have our blood pressure taken. "Most clinics don't bother with this," she explained as she wrapped the blood pressure cuff around my arm. "We're full service."

"Which will be reflected in the tab," I said.

"Good luck getting them to explain all the charges." She wrote down my numbers, then motioned Clem into the chair. Stacy stared at Clem's fingernails while the cuff tightened around her arm. "You stated on the form that you don't smoke."

Clem was taken aback. "I don't. Much."

"I see that yellow stain on your fingers." She shook her head in disgust, her lips forming a razor line across her face. "With the money you're paying, you two better decide if you're serious about this. No more drinking, no more smoking." Throwing a nod at me, she asked Clem, "He's not the type who wears tight underwear, is he?"

Clem leaned forward conspiratorially. "When he can get away with it."

Stacy looked at me. "Have you had sex in the last three days?"

"Of course not," I said. "Can I ask—do you have children?"

Stacy snorted and noted Clem's numbers.

"This isn't your favorite place to work, is it?" Clem asked.

"I *love* it here," Stacy said in an exaggerated tone that told us not to pursue the subject.

"You must have met my cousin Chris Claypool," I said. "Four, five years ago. Dr. Sabell helped Janet and Chris conceive their daughter Margaret."

"Before my time. And if I had met them," she added icily, "I wouldn't breach patient confidentiality. Dr. Rosen will see you soon. You can return to the waiting area."

We went back to our love seat. "That was bizarre," Clem said. "Is the problem that she forgot to take her medication or that she *didn't* forget?"

"The bigger question is, how does she keep her job?" I said. "She must have something on Sabell. Bad-mouthing him to new clients like that means she's got some protection, some leverage."

"If I had to guess, that snort meant she's trying to have children but hasn't succeeded yet."

"Which could explain where she gets her attitude about Sabell. I wonder what he's done to her."

The receptionist called our names again. Dr. Rosen, a short woman with short brown hair, led us down the corridor to a sitting room adjacent to her office. We ensconced ourselves in a comfortable sofa and she placed herself in an easy chair. The room had a homey feel, with tranquil landscape paintings, indirect lighting, and shelves decorated with plants and pictures of what I presumed to be her husband and two brainy-looking kids. The doctor herself had thick brows, a dimpled chin, and a warm, knowledgeable alto voice. She wore the standard white coat over an open-collared violet shirt, gray wool pants, and sensible flats.

Rosen beamed and started by asking us about our lives and work. We spun out our little fantasy of success: my documentary about Tibetan monks, Clem's work with Soderbergh. Oh yes, it was fabulous.

The doctor took it all in. "How nice to be so busy. But you're ready to have children now?"

Clem and I glanced at each other, just as a real couple would. "Our lives feel incomplete without them," she said. "We've set aside money. How much do you think it will take?"

"It all depends," Rosen said, making a note on our forms on the clipboard resting on her knee. "You've had some tests run in other clinics, but we have our own methods and trust our own lab. I'll be honest, it can run into tens of thousands of dollars. You'll want to meet with our financial counselor soon."

We nodded soberly. "It's worth it if I can have a little baby to call my own," Clem said in a dreamy voice. I hit her with a too-syrupy smile that let her know she was overdoing it.

"Our success rate is close to fifty percent, which no other clinic can touch," Rosen said. "That reduces your expense in the long run. We use the safest, most advanced procedures in assisting your conception."

"No scrambled eggs?" Clem said with a little twinkle. She'd told me about cases where clinics had mislabeled gametes, resulting in black parents having white children and vice versa.

There'd also been a scandal in Irvine where the doctors had knowingly switched eggs around.

Rosen cracked a smile. "It's never happened here. Our filing system is ironclad and we haven't had a single lawsuit. What we do have are the lowest rates of unwanted multiple births and of miscarriage of implanted embryos."

"That's encouraging," I said. "But I know a couple—Christopher and Janet Claypool—whose daughter Margaret was conceived here. She ended up having a whole lot of problems."

Rosen's forehead wrinkled. "I'm sorry to hear that. I recall the name—they were Dr. Sabell's patients, I believe. Please, I'd be glad to address any concerns you have."

"What accounts for your phenomenal success rate?" I asked. "I hear Dr. Sabell has special methods of manipulating embryos and gametes."

"Special methods and a special touch. I mean that literally. He has a way of handling these cells as if their membranes were his own skin. Watching him extract a cell from an embryo for preimplantation screening gives me, honestly, a sense of awe." She lowered her voice to let us in on a confidence. "We call him 'the egghead' because his touch is especially good with oocytes—egg cells. He's an innate genius. Not just in handling the cells, but in the sophisticated techniques and patented media he's developed to culture embryos and oocytes. He seems to have a sixth sense for which individual cells are the most robust, as if he knows them personally. On top of that, our cryogenic facilities are the equal of the best universities. So that's it. When you have an ethic, as we do, of careful attention to each and every procedure, and when you're guided by a special man like the doctor, good things happen."

"I've met him briefly," I said. "He's a little . . . odd."

Rosen chuckled. "Great minds often come in odd packages. He is, in fact, one of the most generous—and amusing—men I've ever worked with."

"That's reassuring," I said. "But the manipulations I heard about went beyond the usual in vitro things. The Claypools said he tinkered with the embryo in some way. Do you have ways of correcting a genetic mutation?"

"All of that's in the early research stage. Things have been done with animals—nuclear transfer, germ-line modification, gene targeting—but that's in the future for us humans. Perhaps your friends had PGD: preimplantation genetic diagnosis. We extract a cell from the embryo prior to the blastocyst stage and screen it for certain diseases, selecting embryos without the mutation."

"I'll have to check. What reason would Dr. Sabell have for attending the autopsy of an IVF child like Margaret?"

Dr. Rosen looked genuinely perplexed. "I can't think of one offhand. But I'm sure it was good."

"What else do you offer?" Clem asked.

"Well," Rosen said, relieved to move on to familiar ground, "let me make sure you understand the basic procedure. You start by receiving hormone injections, Mrs. Willendorf, and we induce superovulation. Your eggs are extracted and immediately fertilized, in a glass dish, with fresh sperm. The resulting zygotes are cultured for a few days into embryos. The healthiest ones are implanted in your uterus for what we hope is a normal pregnancy." She glanced at the clipboard. "We can do some more sophisticated interventions along the way, as needed. I see motility is a problem, so we might want to do an ICSI: intracytoplasmic sperm injection."

"That's similar to nuclear transfer, right?" Clem asked.

"Instead of the nucleus being replaced, a sperm is microinjected into the middle of the egg. Dr. Sabell excels at it."

I had a sudden thought. "I know your research lab is connected with the clinic. Do you use any of the embryos in the lab?"

The frequently asked question brought an indulgent smile from Rosen. "We keep a strict separation. We have the capacity to freeze and to culture oocytes and sperm, along with the embryos. If a couple chooses to donate embryos they don't plan to use, they are welcome to do so. But our contract specifies that we never move them without your consent. All this will make more sense in the context of your personal needs. Shall we review your history?"

Even the most expensive doctor did not have an infinite amount of time. Her fingers had been running nervously along the edge of the clipboard. We spent some time discussing our reproductive systems and the conception of our fictional child. Fortunately, we hadn't left the doctor much time to quiz us.

"We can get started today, if you like," she said. "I know we're assuming sperm motility is the issue, and we do find that with about a third of the cases, the problem originates with the man. A third of the time it's with the woman, but in the other third, we simply can't establish the cause. So we'll still want to develop your ovulation profile, Clem—an ultrasound for ovarian structure and normality of uterus, a pelvic laparoscopy, a falloposcopy, and a dye injection for tubal patency. Bill, for your part, are you interested in leaving a sperm sample with us?"

"He's always interested," Clem said with a straight face.

The doctor stood. "I'll buzz Stacy. You're welcome to go with him, Mrs. Willendorf, or you can have Stacy start working you up."

Clem gave me a goopy smile. "I'll come with you, honey."

"But *honey,*" I protested, "we're running short on time."

She took my arm. "It'll be so much more romantic this way."

I appealed to Dr. Rosen. "I can just bring some in next time, can't I?"

She beamed again. "Freshness is important. We'll need two samples, a month apart, so I'd recommend leaving the first one now. The room is completely private. Take as much time as you want. Stacy will get you set up."

"One last question," I said. "Do you find that parents treat their offspring any differently when conceived this way?"

"Oh yes," she answered quickly. "They're so much more special to them."

I nodded. From what I'd seen of Chris, that was true, at least with Helen. The nurse arrived with a plastic jar in hand. She led us back down the corridor to an unmarked door. Handing me the jar, she said, "Have me paged as soon as you're done. We don't want it getting cold." Her razor lips turned up in a hint of a smile, almost as if she envied us.

We went in. I found a DO NOT DISTURB sign, hung it outside, and locked the door. Clem was already exploring the room, or rather series of rooms, connected by short corridors. The first one was the biggest, with plush tiger-stripe carpeting. A velvety doublewide leopard-print couch faced a large television. Beside it kneeled a three-foot marble Aphrodite. Videotapes and DVDs were stored in a white glass-doored medicine cabinet by the TV, while a collection of magazines and "artistic" photography books were arrayed on a shelf. Behind the couch were varnished wood cabinets and an L-shaped counter.

"All tastes accommodated," Clem said, returning from her exploration. She poked into the cabinets behind the couch. I'd discovered a panel of light controls and was playing with the room's radiance and hue.

"Ah," she said with a catlike growl, "I've found the lubrication." She'd also found a box of rubber gloves, a pair of which she tossed at me.

I let them fall to the carpet. "Clem, why are you here?"

"Are you crazy? I didn't want to take my pants off for Nurse Hatcher. Besides, I've always wanted to see one of these places. It gets kinky back there. You've got a sterile room with lots of chrome, hospital fixtures, rubber tubing. A gymnastic horse. Black rubber sheets. What's your fetish, Bill?"

"I'll stick to the fur."

"I hope not. What'd you think of Dr. Rosen?"

"Sabell might be pushing the limits in his lab, but she seemed like a straight shooter."

Clem eyed the jar on the counter. I adjusted the controls to create a warm, red fuzzy feeling in the room and said, in my best Mae West, "Are you blushing, Clem, or are you just happy to see me?"

She walked over to a pair of horizontal black filing cabinets on the other side of the room. Inside was a row of vinyl cases, each with its own latch. Looking over her shoulder, I read the labels aloud: "Bestiality, Bondage, Gay, Extra Large. Isn't it bizarre that this stuff is connected with making babies?"

"One of nature's little tricks," she said, unlatching a case. "Here's one for pregnant women. Correction, *featuring* pregnant women." She closed it and showed me a magazine cover from the Bondage drawer. A big-bellied guy in a black hood was doing something or other to a young woman.

"*The Executioner's Dong,*" I read.

"Turn you on?"

"Ugh. Being naked's good enough for me."

Clem made a show of yawning. "You've *got* to have a better fetish than that. You just don't know what it is yet."

"Yeah, well, I don't intend to find out right this moment."

Clem tapped her finger on the box. "If you believe the evolutionary psychologists, nature produces in the male of the species desire for big-hipped, large-breasted, young, fertile females. So how do you explain the stick-figure women you see in the magazines today?"

"You mean the sticks without the figures? Overpopulation."

"Right," she said. "They're disconnected from reproduction. So-called 'exotic' preferences have a new survival value."

While Clem talked, I was inspecting the walls and ceilings for places where a camera could be hidden. "It's not impossible that we're being recorded," I said.

"Hmm, let's see who's in the Amateur file."

"Clem! We're here to do a job."

She peered at me over her shoulder. Her brow furrowed and a slightly evil glint came into her eye. "Want me to give you a hand?"

I sank into the plush couch. There *was* something exciting about being here. It was sexy in the way hotel rooms, with their whiff of the illicit, were: a strange place, surrounded by strangers going about their business outside, while you in your secret room do yours. The fact that we barely knew each other added to the effect. So did her undeniable sexiness, even in the bow blouse. As her employer, though, I had no intention of going there.

I said, "This is one of those moments when you should lead, follow, or get out of the way."

I meant it as a joke, but she took a step in my direction. My stomach did a little flip-flop. I wanted her to take another step, and then again I didn't.

She stopped. "What do you think the average time a couple spends in here is?"

"I think the others take it a little more seriously."

Clem cast a glance back at the videos and the black file drawer. "I'll leave you to your business. I'm going to chat up the women in the lobby and find out what they can tell me about Nurse Stacy and Dr. Sabell."

The door clicked shut behind her. I stared, from my spot on the couch, at the plastic jar. It sat on the counter in what I imagined to be an impatient and slightly accusatory manner. I'd been in some odd positions in the film business, but this one was brand new. Well, work is work.

I opened the jar and looked into its small waiting volume. The phrase Chris had used about Sabell messing with embryos came back to me. I thought again about giving the doctor a jarful of my gametes to play with. Whatever frisson I'd felt with Clem in the room evaporated. The vessel would be returned empty to Stacy. I almost looked forward to finding out what cutting remark she would have in store for me.

» » » » »

By the time we left the clinic, I had a lot more sympathy for Chris's desire to keep his fertility problems secret. There's nothing like having a woman announce, loud enough for a whole room to hear, that you didn't ejaculate. Those were Stacy's words when I returned the empty jar to her. I said the missus and I needed to talk it over some more before we shared our bodily fluids.

Stacy looked down her nose as if I wasn't worthy of reproduction. "You'll still be billed."

We slipped past the receptionist and back out to the Scout. Clem, while she was waiting, had managed to draw three women out of their isolated love seats and compare experiences at the clinic. One had a shot at Dr. Sabell himself handling her case. She'd been through two abortions of Down's-diagnosed fetuses and would do anything to avoid a third. Sabell had promised her a 100 percent defect-free take-home baby, guaranteed healthy before implantation. The other women were impressed. Clem declared they should start a support group. She collected cards from all three.

I wanted to check out the gated roads we'd passed on our way to the clinic. The lower road led to the estate of one A. Remly. It was the unmarked upper road that drew my attention. I pulled off the main road about two hundred yards down from the turnoff. I retrieved my camera from under the seat and we walked back to the gate to the upper road. The gate was electronic, activated by a card reader. We climbed over it and walked another half-mile, gradually descending, before a low building, shrouded in trees, came into sight. We'd found the research lab.

It had been built in a style similar to the clinic, but more utilitarian. The rectangular windows were long and narrow, designed to prevent both spying and break-ins. The road never came within a hundred yards of the facility; the parking lot sat some distance behind it. I snapped my camera out of its case and shot a couple of pictures, just for the record. Another dirt road climbed from the clinic to pastures and a large barn in the hills above. My long lens gave me a closer look at the barn. It was solidly built of new sheet metal, and was clearly intended for research, not agriculture. A series of tall fences divided sheep and cattle into a maze of pens.

Clem tapped my shoulder. Two men in dark pants and jackets had appeared from nowhere. They advanced on us with a sense of purpose. One of the men's jacket flapped open to reveal the strap of his holster.

I stepped forward to meet them. One man put up his hand in a stop signal. "This area is off limits to the public," he called.

I kept moving toward them, downhill. Clem was a step or two behind me. "I'm a client of Dr. Sabell's," I said. "I was told he's working here in the lab today."

We were face-to-face now. The guy started to repeat the same sentence as before. I interrupted and said, "We're not the public. Dr. Sabell violated some serious regulations at an autopsy he attended Monday morning. How happy is he going to be to find out you sent me away and the police came back in my place?"

The man eyed us, his gaze lingering on Clem's bow blouse. Apparently he decided it meant we were legit. He took our names and moved away to conduct a short conversation on a two-way radio. When he turned back to us, he said, "The doctor can spare five minutes, no more."

I nodded. The guy kept us where we were. "Sir, ma'am, I'll have to ask you both to spread your arms and legs, please. Sorry, this is standard procedure."

They patted us down. I said, "Pretty tight security just for reproductive research."

"Yes, sir. Put away your camera. Follow me."

We were led off the road, across a sloping lawn, to a spot below one of the thin horizontal windows on the first floor. The window levered open like a lid and the bald spot atop Sabell's shaggy white head appeared. He had to crane his neck, his chest pressing against the sill, to squeeze through the narrow aperture. Although his face did not give the morbid impression it had at the morgue, it still struck me as gargoylish. His awkward position created the effect of a disembodied head flanked by two sets of clawlike white knuckles.

He squinted at me. "Damen, you said?"

"Yes. Margaret Claypool's uncle."

Sabell's head made a shooing motion at the security men. They stepped back a few yards but did not leave. Clem glanced at them, then asked Sabell, "What are you doing out here with all the guards, cloning aliens?"

"We have a legitimate concern about terrorist attacks," he said.

"You're working on biological weapons?" I said.

"No!" His voice was cranky. "I'm talking about homegrown groups who oppose basic research. You know who I mean."

"People who shoot doctors and call themselves 'pro-life,'" Clem said.

"Vigilantes," Sabell confirmed.

The subject seemed to get him exercised, so I pushed it. "Amazing how much energy they put into defending cells that have never been inside a human womb and never will be, when so many children who already exist need help."

"Exactly!" Sabell barked. "Over four hundred thousand in vitro embryos are sitting in freezers in this country, yet these people would rather see them thrown away than be used for research. What does it mean to focus all your energy on a *potentiality,* something that's not yet a human being? Why is no one planting bombs so that a four-year-old in East Palo Alto will have decent schools and health care? I'll tell you why. It's because that child is already a defined individual. You can invest a zygote with your own ego and your own sense of omnipotence. That's what those people want to control. The point of creation."

"They want their own little slice of Genesis," Clem said. "Other people's slices, too."

"Oh yes. These people would prescribe how and where and when to copulate, if they could, as in the Puritan days."

"The Puritans had to control sex," I said. "They were afraid it might lead to dancing."

Sabell laughed. It was endearing, the childlike way his emotions played over his face. He lived so much inside his world of ideas, he had little skill in concealing them. We'd gotten him going. "What's also remarkable to me is how attached parents can become to a bit of miscarried protoplasm," he said. "They've been known to ask doctors to clone their 'late loved one,' leaving their other in vitro embryos in the freezer. Don't get me wrong, their grief is real. Most are not strong enough to confront nature in the raw. If you want to believe a fairy tale about your little bundle of cells going to heaven, that's okay. Just try to remember there are more where it came from."

He was hitting close to home now. "I can tell you that Chris and Janet were pretty attached to a bundle of cells named Margaret," I said.

"That proves my point. She had a face, a personality, a history. It hurt me very much when I heard what happened."

"What exactly did you do with Margaret?" I asked.

"Well, I created her."

I was dumbstruck for a moment, then the words just came out of my mouth. "Wow. I'd have thought God would make fewer mistakes."

Sabell laughed again, unexpectedly. "God, my dear boy, did much worse in his day. I'm sorry to say that he's packed it in and departed for a distant shore. He did leave his toys behind."

"So you're filling the void. Someone's got to go on creating human beings, right?"

"Do you have children?" Clem asked suddenly.

"Not in the sense you mean," Sabell said.

"What mistakes did you make with Margaret?" I said.

"Now you *are* making me think you're spying for them. Ask her parents—aren't you Chris's brother? Or is it Janet's?"

"I'm here on Chris's behalf. There are technical issues only you can clear up."

He grimaced at his uncomfortable position. "This window is killing me!"

"We'll come inside," I said.

"No, no," he replied. "It'll have to be later."

"It would be wise for you to take the time. I know what happened at Margaret's autopsy. I'd rather handle this quietly than bring in lawyers, cops, maybe the media—"

"Never mind that!" Sabell cut in. He rotated his neck with irritation, as if it was the window that had put him in this bind. "I *said* we'll talk. Give me your number."

I drew a card from my billfold. "Meet you at the front door."

"No, give it to security. And don't forget to write her name on the back! I'm liable to forget."

The head disappeared and the window closed. By the time I'd scribbled Margaret's name on the back of my card, a security man was there to take it. He escorted us way back up the road, opening the gate for us rather than forcing us to climb over. He did not return our good-bye.

Clem and I walked to the Scout in silence. She didn't speak until we reached it. "He was everything you said, and more."

"We wasted too much time with the chitchat," I said, climbing in.

"No, it was good," she said. She buckled her seat belt. "He feels we're on his side about certain things."

"We need to talk to him soon," I said. "A research facility that big, that well-protected, that secretive, tells me he's into some weird science."

"He's got a serious security force, all right," Clem noted. "Those guys are paid to do whatever's required to protect his work."

"Up to and including the abduction of a little girl," I said.

10

A mere six days ago, my cousin Christopher Claypool had called to ask my help in the matter of his missing daughter, Margaret. We'd both assumed that we'd find her, if not safe and sound, at least alive. Now on Saturday morning we were getting ready to bury her. Chris had bolted from his father's company and the blood was turning bad between them. Prosecutors might file charges against Chris any day for anything up to and including murder. Chris and Janet were barely hanging on, both together and separately.

The shock of Margaret's death still churned in my stomach. The decision to cremate her made it seem as if her parents wanted to obliterate all traces, all evidence of a life that had been misbegotten from the start. But who was I to say how Chris and Janet should wrangle with their grief? Many prescriptions have been written about the proper course of bereavement, and the only thing I knew for sure was that you could not tell another person what to feel.

The one ray of light for me had been the entry of Clem into my office. I couldn't imagine conducting this investigation without her now. When I went to bed last night I regretted our silliness in the sperm room. But I woke up in the morning reminding myself that everyone needed to let off steam. True, Clem's background was still mysterious and her moves unpredictable, but so far, most of the surprises had been good ones. I had called the reference she gave me, a woman named Anita Salisco. Though I only got voicemail, I learned she was a partner in a respected law firm. Meanwhile, Don Masterson had been bugging me, sending several new emails about setting up an interview. The moment I answered saying I didn't have time, he wrote back proposing that I give him freelance assignments. I thanked the heavens that Clem had stayed up all night, doing whatever it was she did, when I'd posted the job.

I'd made other calls last night, too, including one to Wayne to keep the contact warm and to press him to have Ulla show us where Margaret had been abducted. After that, Chris and I had our daily conversation. I didn't mention the visit to the clinic. He was too harried to talk for long. He'd been working on the arrangements for today, making sure the boat he'd hired was ready and the mortuary did its job. Just when he thought it was all taken care of, he began getting calls from his family about people for whom space on the boat just *had* to be made. Janet and her sister Penny had left the house yesterday afternoon, leaving Chris to deal with it.

I'd woken early this morning. The boat did not leave until noon, but I had the cameraman's phobia of being late. I felt a sense of ceremony about the day, a need to do things right. I took my time in the shower. I put a new blade in my razor and dug an iron from the depths of my closet to press my dark wool pants. Some slob had left them wadded in the bedroom corner. I rolled lint-removal tape over the pants and polished my shoes.

I buttoned a clean white shirt and put on my suit, taking time to knot my tie. The sky was heavy and low, in tune with the somberness of the day. I felt as though every move and every step was being observed by the universe to note whether we paid Margaret the proper honor.

How *did* you honor a person who was so young, so unformed? Sabell's question came back to me: "Why become attached to this particular bundle of cells?" For someone who spent his day in a lab hatching bundles, it might be a sensible, or necessary, logic. I wondered if she really had become something more to him than a blastocyst whose limb buds formed into arms and legs covered with the soft down of childhood—a bigger bundle of cells, with a face, but still an experiment to be autopsied and left behind. Nature had the leisure not to get overly concerned about an evolutionary experiment that withered on the vine. We did not. Sabell had turned out to be more interesting than my first impression had given him credit for, yet he still seemed to lack a sense of humility. Maybe it couldn't coexist with the ambition driving a scientist like him. But working with human cells the way he was, it *had* to.

The truth was, Margaret *did* have a personality. She had more luster and spirit than a lot of adults I knew. Even if the ocean currents carried her ashes to the four corners of the globe, even if Chris was cleared and the kidnappers locked up, even if he and Janet managed to patch up their lives, that spirit would remain. It dawned on me, as I made my preparations for the memorial service, how much I'd learned from Margy about grace under duress, courage without bravado, kindness without obligation. She'd always seemed the afterthought, the classic second-born. Helen's death was the main event: She'd been the daughter with all the promise, the charisma, the talent, the unlimited future. Margy was an alternate, somehow, from the beginning, even before all the medical problems that meant her future was likely to be short. This would be the one day when all focus would be on her, when we'd remember her not for her ailments but the goodness and wonder of her, the peculiar wisdom with which she bore her pain. I hoped it would not be the only day. Her fourth birthday would have been in September, and I'd suggested to Chris that we hold another remembrance on that day, by which time, I hoped, all the distracting questions of guilt, punishment, and family discord would be resolved. A day only for Margy.

My phone rang. It was Clem, conscientiously checking in with me before I left. She'd requested a day off to catch up on errands. I was relieved to find out she did have a life of some kind. As we talked and I assured her I didn't need her help today, Chris called my mobile in a panic. He had so many last-minute details to tend to that he couldn't pick up the urn with Margaret's ashes from the mortuary. I told him I'd do it. The whole reason I'd gotten ready early was for something like this. I signed off, grabbed my small camera, raced out to the Scout, and pushed it hard down 280 to Colma.

Mr. Dunfeld, the mortician, had the urn ready in a square cardboard box. Preparations in the reception room were under way. He assured me that all would be ready by two o'clock, when we were scheduled to return from what he tactfully referred to as our "boat trip." Technically, it was illegal to spread ashes at sea, except at a designated area off the Marin coast.

I sped back up to the St. Francis Yacht Club in the Marina. The dark-clad mourners had gathered near the gate to the docks. I parked, then went around to the passenger door for the box. It seemed tacky to bring Margaret to her final resting place in cardboard, so I lifted the simple black clay urn and cradled it in my arms. It was so light, so small. The group stared at me as if I were carrying fissionable material. Cole's girth was immediately identifiable. He wore a dark wool suit, with a fedora atop his bald head. Regina stood erect in a rather lurid black dress with some frilly detail around the neck and arms. Janet and Penny, clad in overcoats for the chilly day, kept their distance from Cole.

I looked down at my jacket, my pants, my shoes, and then at the small curved shape in my arms. Was I holding it wrong? I tried to keep up my sense of ceremony. Chris stepped forward to take the urn. His great-aunt Henrietta was right behind him, bobbing and peering over his shoulder like a long-necked fowl hunting for seed, persevering in her self-appointed role as comforter-in-chief. Regina's body language made it clear she was above it all.

Chris thanked me, then draped the urn in a wrap of purple velvet with gold fringe. We filed wordlessly through a gate and down the dock, heels resounding on the wood. The boat was a sixty-foot yacht with a well-appointed parlor on the deck. Maybe it was only my imagination, but I sensed an undercurrent of resentment among the family at Chris for forcing them on this outing. The older people took refuge in the parlor, a mahogany-paneled space with cushioned benches, stout captain's chairs, and a station dispensing coffee and tea. Flowers and a framed photo of Margaret sat on a small side table.

Cole, cousin Cliff, and the younger family members gravitated to the bow. I stuck with Chris, who handed me the urn and climbed a steep-railed stairway to the pilot house. I handed the urn up and joined him. The captain wore a white jacket with shoulder bars and a cap, an outfit I assumed came with the job and which matched his bushy white sideburns, the brass instruments, and the large, spoked wooden wheel. Chris exchanged low-key greetings with him. The captain told us we were welcome to the two fixed swivel chairs, then kept a tactful silence.

We sat down and Chris thanked me again for picking up the ashes. The captain got the boat under way. We remained quiet as we chugged under the Golden Gate Bridge. Open ocean was in front of us now. Bruised purplish-gray clouds lowered on the water the farther out we went. The dark, steely swells came at us, one after another, rising and falling as far as we could see, an endless churn. Maybe it was the nature of the outing, or my sense of ritual, that made the verse from Genesis about the spirit moving over the face of the chaotic waters come into my head.

I nodded at the bundle loosely cradled on Chris's lap and said, "What kind of ceremony do you have planned?"

"Janet has a poem that she and Penny found. Then I guess I'll just open the urn and let the ashes out."

I saw the captain wince, but he said nothing. "And you'll also bury some of her at the mortuary?" I asked.

Chris frowned. Cole had won the concession that a part of Margaret's remains would be interred under a small headstone in the family plot. "You'd think the memorial would be about what Janet and I want," Chris said, "but it seems to be more about making everyone else happy."

He stared out to sea and said, "I was there last night for the cremation. I didn't want her to go through it alone." He broke off for a minute, then went on. "It tore me up. But I felt a little better afterwards. Like she'd been purified. I wanted to stay until the urn was ready, but I thought Janet was waiting for me for dinner."

"Did you really do it because of Sabell?"

"That put me over the edge, I guess. But when I said the idea out loud, Janet and I both agreed it sounded right. I don't know why. Like maybe it'd free Margy from all the pain her body had put her through."

I left unspoken my sense that her parents might want to be freed of it themselves. Changing the subject, I said, "Did you find space on board for everyone who wanted to come?"

Chris rolled his eyes. "My mother got into one of her fits because Henrietta was the only one we invited from her side. Nobody cared until they found out space was limited."

"They may not show it very well, but I'm sure they care." Actually, I wasn't sure at all, but I wanted to keep Chris calm. "I know my mother does. She's sorry she couldn't be here."

"She left us a really nice message. But I'm telling you, Bill, it's been nothing like after Helen. That time, everybody rallied around me and Janet, asked what they could do for us. This time . . ." He shook his head. "These people are incredible. First they object to the idea of the boat, supposedly because it's not our family tradition, but really because it's inconvenient. Then, when they find out there isn't enough room for everyone, it turns into a major outrage, like they were all just dying to be out here. They're vultures is all they are, coming to pick at the bones."

Again I found it jarring to hear Chris, the scion, the prime inheritor, speak of his family this way. The solid, squared-off oval shape of his head, the pale sheen of his skin, the large, well-sculpted ears: He was so clearly one of them. It was Chris's eyes that were different now, bracketed by a new set of concentric ripples, hung with half-moons, brooding—the sort of thing you were more likely to see on my side of the family, the orphan branch, almost unrecognizable in its connection to Cole's main trunk.

We sailed on quietly. The boat rose and fell, rose and fell. My stomach heaved with it. Every so often we hit a wave off-beam and spray shot over the bow. The passengers up there had retreated to the stern or gone inside. I tried to focus on a steady horizon line, but with the land behind us, it rose and fell, too.

The captain cleared his throat. "A little rough today. Wind waves and a swell from a storm up north."

He directed our attention to the starboard side. A smaller boat, in the distance, was also fighting its way out to sea. A handful of dark figures was barely visible on deck.

"Fishing boat?" Chris asked.

"No, not outfitted for it. Don't know what they're doing out on a day like this."

A voice from the main cabin below broke our contemplation. It was Henrietta. "Christopher! Are you all right? Do you need any help?"

"We're fine. I'll come down in a minute."

"I only ask because I'm not feeling too well," she shouted back up, as if we were at the other end of the boat. "I'm not sure how long I'll last."

Chris thanked her and again rolled his eyes. "After Thursday night, she's been trying twice as hard. She's that much more convinced I need saving. She invites me to church with her and tells me I should see a minister. I almost wish I'd invited Fred along so he could keep her under control."

"At least she cares."

"You never know what's going on between her and Mom," Chris said.

Henrietta's voice came again. "Can I hold her for a minute?"

Chris crouched at the hatch and handed the bundle down to Henrietta. He turned and started to descend, his back to the scene, which was for the better. I saw it happen as I looked down into the parlor. Henrietta held the urn lengthwise in her hands, as if to make an offering. The boat hit a big wave and listed a moment before the captain righted it. Henrietta's face went green. You could see the heave building from within. She extended her arms in an effort to protect the urn by handing it off to Regina, who only stepped back in dismay. The purple bundle and a stream of grapefruit-pink vomit flew into the air at the same time. Thankfully they landed in different spots on the wood floor. But a sickening crack came from the bundle when it hit.

Chris jumped into the middle of the parlor and backed everyone away from the purple lump on the floor. Cole rushed in. So did the first mate. He told the deckhand to get a bucket and mop, then helped Henrietta, who was bent double, to the head.

"Oh, for God's sake!" Cole blurted. "You *dropped* it, Christopher?"

"Henrietta did," came Regina's icy voice.

"Dunfeld gave you a faulty urn!"

Chris knelt and gently opened the velvet cloth. The urn had broken into several large pieces. Sticky dark ash, dotted with specks of white, lay scattered in the cloth.

"I was the one who asked for it to be made of clay," Chris said. He looked up at me. "Dust to dust, I was thinking . . ."

I climbed down and knelt with him. "We didn't lose any of the ashes," I said. "We'll get another urn from Dunfeld. It'll be okay."

But I knew it wasn't. Chris stared at the shards and whispered to me, "Get them out of here."

"Everybody," I announced, "let's move out on deck. The ceremony will begin soon."

I herded them out of the parlor, voicing the false assurance that all would be well. As the crowd moved outside, I looked back at Chris, hunched over the spilled ashes of his daughter. The whole point of a ritual like this was to restore some kind of order to the universe when its fabric had been ripped, and there was no rending as terrible, as unnatural, as the death of a child before her parents. The broken urn only magnified the sense of doom that had hung over Margaret from the beginning. This morning I had thought, naively perhaps, that her miraculously sunny disposition had somehow canceled it out.

I went below to round up the rest of the passengers. The furniture in the stateroom was fine oak and the cabinets beveled glass, but right now the smell of vomit permeated. My aunt Natalie's two sons, in their twenties yet still adolescent, lolled on the carpet. I told them to go up to the deck.

"And start puking my guts out again? No thanks," one answered.

"This was the stupidest idea ever," the other said.

I found Janet and Penny in the sleeping quarters. Janet lay on a bunk and Penny sat beside her. Henrietta was in a bunk across from them, her pink-and-black shawl draped over her chest. I told Janet we were about to start, and suggested she'd feel better in the fresh air.

Penny shook her head. "She loses it as soon as she stands up. You'll have to go ahead without us. I'll stay down here."

Janet handed me a crumpled piece of paper, damp with sweat. "Here's the poem I was going to read."

"Tell Chris," Henrietta said in a shaky voice, "how sorry I am."

I touched her arm. "He understands. It's not your fault."

Penny gave me a sympathetic smile. I tucked the piece of paper in my jacket pocket and went back up to the cabin. Chris was still on the floor, knotting ends of the velvet cloth to form an improvised bag.

The captain peered down from the pilot house and said, "Anytime you're ready."

"Let's get it over with," Chris said.

A familiar bitterness had slithered back into his voice. I led the way out of the cabin to the rounded stern, where those still able to stand had gathered. The mate reported to the captain that we were ready. He came about, throttled down, and did his best to hold the boat in position. We were at the mercy of the swells now, rising and falling like a lost cork.

Chris stood at the railing on the port side. I waited for him to take the lead, but he didn't. He seemed sealed off from the rest of us. He just kept staring, with his back turned, to the western horizon. Slowly he reached into the knotted bag, brought out a handful of ash, and flung it overhand into the water, as if flinging sand at a bully. The wind picked up the finer particles and shoved them back into our faces. We all inhaled a little bit of Margaret.

"Talk about blowback," I heard Cliff murmur to Cole, who chuckled.

"Isn't anybody going to say anything?" Regina demanded. "Is there a minister or something?"

"Good-bye, Margy!" Chris screamed into the wind, flinging another handful.

I'd brought my mini-DV, but I had no intention of putting this on tape. Instead, I stepped between Chris and the rest of the crowd and announced I had a poem Janet had chosen. Cole asked me in an impatient tone to please read it, and I began: "'Margaret, are you grieving / Over Goldengrove unleaving?'"

Chris did not stop. He went on casting ashes into the sea, yelling over my voice, into the wind, "Good-bye, Margy! Good-bye, Margy! Good-bye, Margy!"

"'Ah! as the heart grows older,'" I continued, "'It will come to such sights colder.'"

Chris, with a final fling, let out a scream from the bottom of his lungs: *"Fuck you, Jakarta! Fuck you, Hong Kong!"*

I rushed to the last lines. "'It is the blight man was born for, / It is Margaret you mourn for.'"

Chris wrapped what remained inside the purple cloth. Clutching it to his chest, he pushed past us, his face streaked with tears and ash, his mouth twisted into a mixture of spite and grief.

An uneasy milling and censorious chatter followed up top. I glanced at Cole, who had removed his hat and was pressing it to his heart. Our eyes met. He gave a regretful *tsk. Poor Chris,* he seemed to be saying. But I saw what was behind it, too, the sense of humiliation for his family and the hard anger that evoked.

Then his expression shifted to something like recognition and concern. He squinted to starboard. Bobbing on the waves, closer than it had been before, was the small boat we'd seen earlier. I made out the figures now, five of them. All were clad in black, standing, watching us. Their faces appeared blank, illegible, featureless. I recalled Ulla's description of the stocking-faced man who had attacked her. Someone from our boat waved, but the others did not respond. They simply watched us, motionless, like some crew of demons who'd come to insure their curse had poisoned the proceedings through and through. It was hard not to believe that Margaret and all that was good about her had been erased from the earth.

A moment later, a shout came from the port side. I hurried over, fearing the worst. Natalie pointed and I followed her arm. It took a moment before I saw them: a school of four dolphins swimming alongside us. Their opalescent gray backs shimmered as they cut the water in perfect, broad rainbow arcs. Their leaps conveyed a kind of intrinsic joy. How lucky they are, I thought, to be cavorting in their own world, oblivious to the human one above.

At the same time, with all that had gone so wrong, I was tempted to read in their appearance a final augury of destruction. I turned it over in my mind, but the image did not fit. There was no such thing as the Four Dolphins of the Apocalypse. Instead, the idea occurred to me that they had come to the rescue. They had come to carry what was left of Margaret off to a better place, a happier shore, far from here.

11

I drove back down 280 to the cemetery. The dolphins had provided a moment of grace, but once they went off on their own course, it had been back to the dismal Claypools. No one said anything out loud. The talk was contained in private whispers and discussions, and it implied that Chris was losing it. Cole did nothing to discourage that notion.

The demon boat, as I'd come to think of it, had kept its distance on our return trip but remained visible. I shot it for a couple of minutes on my mini-DV, knowing it would come out as little more than a dark blot.

The crowd had filed sullenly off the yacht. I waited by the stairway for Chris, who'd stayed down below with Janet during the return. He emerged, after the rest were gone, with an unsteady Henrietta on his arm. Janet and Penny, looking drained, followed.

A larger crowd had already gathered in the twin reception rooms of the funeral home. More were in the garden outside. Those of us who'd been on the boat trip were buttonholed to tell the tale. The air of lingering resentment turned to gloating as word spread about what had happened. Chris may have brought it on himself, but I began to see what he meant about his relatives not taking the loss of Margaret seriously. The tone of the conversation was a little too convivial, a little too much in harmony with the scrolls and flutes and gold leaf of the Louis Quatorze decor, as if Margy had never really been part of the family.

I made a circuit through the rooms and through the small formal garden. About sixty people were here, but Chris had not arrived yet. I did spot Cole talking to Mr. Dunfeld near an upright piano in the reception room. Both men looked at their watches, presumably discussing the afternoon's service. The mortician departed tactfully as I approached.

Cole gave me a warm handshake. He had reverted to paternal mode. If you watched Cole in a seemingly unguarded moment, his face looked mild. Its manifold crevices relaxed into a round moon with a genial, contented, open appearance. It was a trap, of course, because he had no truly unguarded moments, but he'd managed, with practice, to make this his default expression.

"You did well out there, Bill," he said. "Would you mind showing me that poem you read?"

I handed him the folded piece of paper from my jacket pocket. "It was written by Gerard Manley Hopkins."

Cole shook his head sadly. "I'm sorry I couldn't hear it. I can't help but be ashamed of Christopher. But then, none of us knows what it's like to be in his position. A tragic end to a life so short."

I nodded. He'd used the phrase before. "Who was in the small boat shadowing us out there?"

Cole waved to someone across the room, then cocked his head before he answered. "I think we both can guess. Clearly a further attempt at intimidation, aimed at me this time. They've already succeeded in driving Chris off the Jakarta project."

"What have the Feds found out about them?"

“Give them time. They’re not miracle workers.”

“Meanwhile, these guys keep threatening.”

“You’re supposed to be the investigator. What have you found?”

“You promised to send me your files.”

“I’ll have it done on Monday,” Cole said.

I needed access to his information enough to give up a little of my own. I related to Cole a few salient details about what I’d learned from Ulla. Cole grunted and said, “As we thought, Ulla is the rat that Gallegos is using to corner Chris. She needs to understand the consequences of her lies about him. You know where to find her?”

That was a card I’d save for later. “My connection is indirect. Ulla’s terrified of these people. Her description of the fake gardener tallies with the guys on the boat.”

“I understand someone called Dinh to tell him not to come that Friday. We’ve only got Dinh and his wife’s word on that. Maybe he’s in on it.”

“I don’t think so. I’ve talked to him.”

“Don’t count him out. The city’s rife with Southeast Asian gangs. They could be linked to a triad.”

“I’m still looking forward to being filled in on the triads.”

Cole smiled and grasped my elbow. “Let’s not argue, Bill. Not here, not today. Let the professionals do their job.” He held my gaze for a moment, then added, “You also promised to keep me informed about this character at Margaret’s postmortem, George Sabell.”

“I thought you said you didn’t know him.” I’d never mentioned Sabell’s first name to Cole.

“Bill, Bill,” Cole sighed. “It bears repeating, there are so *many* things you don’t know.”

A sickening feeling rumbled in the pit of my stomach. "You've known about Sabell all along, haven't you?"

"Known what?"

I didn't want to be the one to say it. But the connections were clicking. "You wanted to ensure the continuation of the family line. You have two daughters, one of whom has a son. But what you want more than anything is for your son to have a son, too."

"I'm just happy if he's happy," Cole said calmly.

"What did Sabell do with Margaret?" I asked bluntly.

Cole smiled to let me know he was about to indulge me. "No one quite knows what he does in that lab. It's got private funding, you know, and the research need not be reported to anyone but Austin Remly, his benefactor."

I pressed Cole. "Gender selection? So Janet would have a boy?"

"Is that a service they offered to you and your girlfriend?"

The sick feeling got a little sicker. "You've been *spying* on me?"

Cole snorted. "Don't flatter yourself. I'm initiating action against Dr. Sabell for what he did at the autopsy. Did you see him remove tissue from Margaret yourself?"

"No, I didn't." And I wasn't about to tell him who did, not without full disclosure from Cole. "What do you know about his patron—Austin Remly?"

Cole cut me off with a hand motion. "We'll talk later," he said in a low voice, then turned to the man hovering nearby. "Sorry to keep you waiting, Leonard. Do you know my nephew, Bill Damen? This is Leonard Wilson, my VP for Special Projects."

"We've never formally met," Wilson said, stepping forward to give me a firm shake of the hand. Today he was wearing a dark Armani suit. He'd been a protégé of Cole's for several years and had ascended to his current position by conquering a string of challenges Cole had put before him. They seemed an odd pair, in that Wilson exuded integrity. But that's exactly what Cole, in his guile, needed.

"Did you need to speak to me, Leonard?" Before Wilson could answer, Cole turned back to me and said, "He's really stepped into the breach. Chris left us in an awful position when he failed to come to work Thursday, failed even to call in. Leonard saved the day. He got the proposal in on time yesterday, and it'll be a winner. Truth is, he's doing a superior job. He's qualified to take over for me one day."

Wilson looked straight ahead, as if waiting for a medical procedure to be completed. His expression, sober and quietly alert, rarely changed.

"Sorry to go on, Leonard, I'll be with you in a minute," Cole said. "Bill, I'll be frank, I'm concerned about my son. If the rumors around the DA's office are true, he's going to be charged with homicide any day now. And yet he won't let me help him. He's virtually cut off contact. Now, I know you're doing *your* best for him. The best course you can steer him on is back into the fold. All will be forgiven."

"I thought Wilson was taking charge," I said.

Wilson's attention had been drawn to the small buffet table. I followed his line of sight. Chris had arrived, and the look in his eyes was furious. Wilson turned to me, preparing his answer. "I'd be the first to welcome Chris back," he said. "But of course we all understand that at a time like this, he has to do what's best for his family."

I shook Wilson's hand and said I was glad to meet him, then held out my hand to Cole. He pulled me close and murmured, "Don't, under any circumstances, tell Chris what I've said."

The delay prevented me from intercepting Chris. He stopped near a round flower-topped marble stand about four feet away. It was Wilson he was glaring at, not Cole or me.

"What are you doing here?" Chris demanded. The question was genuine but did not hide the truculence in his voice.

"I'm very sorry about Margaret—" Wilson began.

Chris's voice became a roar. "This service is for family and friends. *My* friends."

Wilson drew back. Cole did the same. Chris advanced another step or two. Wilson stiffened. I stepped in front of Chris.

He grabbed me by the shoulders. "Out of my way, Bill."

"Good afternoon," Wilson said. He made a small bow in my direction, then to Cole, to whom he gave a glance of betrayal, and left.

The room had gone silent. Cole took the opportunity to deliver a reprimand. "I'm shocked at you, Chris. The man comes to pay his respects—"

Chris jabbed his finger over my shoulder at Cole and screamed, "*You* put him up to it. *You* invited him in order to rub my face in—"

He broke off as I told him to take it easy. I moved him back away from Cole. It seemed entirely possible that he might attack his own father.

Henrietta came fluttering to his side. "Oh, Christopher dear, everyone's here only to support you!"

I got Chris turned in the other direction, put my arm over his shoulder, and said, "Let's go sit down for a minute."

Chris hid his face in his hands as we crossed the length of the room. The crowd gaped at us. "Is he drunk?" I heard someone say.

Dunfeld, standing near a doorway that led to the next room, caught my eye. He ushered us through the door and pointed to a staircase. "We have a room where he can rest. Top of the stairs, turn left."

We climbed the narrow stairs. By now Janet and Penny had joined us. Henrietta followed. We took a left at the top and found a spare office. It was furnished with a large floral-patterned sofa, two upholstered chairs facing a desk, and a made-up cot in the corner. Dunfeld was well prepared for clients who fainted, needed a time-out, or were otherwise overcome. I tried to steer Chris to the sofa, but he pulled away. He wanted to sit behind the polished walnut desk. Its surface was empty except for a box of tissue, a pot of silk roses, and a foot-tall caryatid supporting an entablature on her head. Light simmered through a pair of half-drawn blinds.

Janet and Penny sat on the sofa, at right angles to the desk. Henrietta sat on the edge of a chair, her back straight. I sat in the other one. Chris swiveled in the desk chair, turning the caryatid over in his hands. His jaw was clenched, his teeth grinding. A faint streak of ash still ran down his right temple.

Henrietta finally spoke. "I don't think that man meant you any harm, Christopher. He's from your work, isn't he?"

Chris balanced the caryatid upside down on the desk and didn't answer.

I said to him, "Do you really think Wilson came to insult you?"

Chris exhaled deeply. "He's only doing his job, I suppose. It's the way my father plays him against me."

"So why did you go after him?"

"Because it *is* an insult! He's stealing *my* job!" Chris's jaw set harder. "If that's the way Dad wants to play it, that's the way he'll get it."

"Chris," Janet said, "you need to get away from Claypool Construction."

"What do we do then, Janet?" he burst out. "Do you think anyone else in this industry would hire Cole Claypool's son? Ha!"

She looked away, fighting to hold in her anger. Penny said gently, "You've got to consider the cost of your feud with your father to the rest of your family, Chris."

"It's Janet I'm fighting for!" he responded. "To keep what we have. Does she want me to just give in to him?"

"No!" Janet cried. "I said to *get away* from him!"

Henrietta shrank in her chair. "You shouldn't talk about Cole that way. Either of you. He's a tough man, but a good man."

Chris rubbed his eyes wearily. "Henrietta, I appreciate all you've done for us, but to be honest, you don't know what the hell you're talking about."

Henrietta's lip trembled and her hands played with her bag. She glanced down at her watch. "The service is going to begin in a few minutes."

"Thank you," Chris said. "We'll be right there."

Henrietta moved to the door. She turned before she left. "Chris, we love you," she said simply, a tear dripping down her cheek.

When she was gone, Chris let out a long, exasperated sigh. That, in turn, exasperated Janet. "Let's face it, Chris," she said, her voice sharp now, "it's your father who's driven you to this. He talked you into the Jakarta project, with the Chinese gangs and all of that, and then he drove you so hard on it that you couldn't keep track of your own daughter."

Chris leaned forward, his fists clenched. "I'm not his puppet. I made the choices. I dug this hole myself." His voice was low, not in a cathartic admission of guilt but in a tone that suggested he was winding tighter and tighter inside.

"These people were determined to kidnap Margaret," I said. "They planned it carefully. I know that from listening to Ulla. Somehow they knew her routine. They were waiting for her. Neither of you could have stopped them."

Again the room was silent. "That only proves what I'm saying," Janet said, her voice cracking.

"We should go to the service," Penny said.

Chris didn't budge. "My father insists on giving a eulogy. I don't want to hear it."

Janet drew in her shoulders and stared at the floor. Penny looked at her sister and said, "It's not only about how you feel, Chris."

Still no one moved. "They never treated Margaret as part of the family," Chris answered. "To them, she was a mistake, a misfire. I don't want to hear their phony condolences. They all secretly think it's 'for the best.' "

Penny looked from Janet to Chris and back to Janet. The hunched pain of her sister, frozen in place, gave her strength. "Maybe it *is* for the best. Have you considered what Janet's been through? She put so many chemicals into her body that she didn't know which emotions were her own anymore. The ultrasounds, the aspiration needles, the nausea, the miscarriages—do you have any idea what that does to a woman? But you pressed her and pressured her and pushed the doctor so you could have a child to replace Helen. It was like you and that doctor were hatching the baby and Janet was just some kind of hen keeping it warm. And then, after she'd been through it all, losing one child, bearing another—*then* the hard part began.

The medications, the emergency trips to the hospital, the nights staying up—"

Chris latched onto the last sentence. "So you're like the rest. Margaret was nothing more to you than a *problem*."

"Is Janet anything more to you than a *womb?*"

Chris rose, quivering, as if to strike Penny. "You *never* thought it was real! But it was! We loved each other. Helen came out of that love. She was a miracle!"

He toppled back into his chair, a stunned look on his face, as if he was just now comprehending his own words. *"Loved,"* he repeated, speaking to the desk. "My wife hates me now. Thank you for making me see what I already knew in my heart."

Penny started to answer. Janet looked up, her face wet, and put a hand on her sister's. "Stop, both of you. I don't know where we went wrong, Christopher. We never should have tried to replace Helen. We never should have tried so *hard*. It's not supposed to be that hard!"

Chris rose again. "You, too, Janet? You're glad to be rid of her?"

Janet shook her head as if trying to shake him off her back. "Why do you twist my emotions?! You have no idea how I feel! But you force the issue—the way you're acting, the things you're doing—you drive me to say these things!"

"*You* cared so much for Margaret, Chris, that you bolted for work last Friday without even checking on her," Penny said. Her voice, devastatingly quiet, froze Chris.

"Maybe we deserve the neglect charge," Janet said. "I don't know anymore. I don't want to be in the middle of this—you and Sabell, you and Cole, you and Jakarta, gangs, all of it. It's time to let her go now. Like we should have let Helen go in the first place."

"Hello?" came a timid voice from the doorway. It was Henrietta. "The service has started."

When no one responded, she grew bolder. "I wish you had heard your father, Chris. He said beautiful things about Margaret. He read a poem with her name in it—"

That was the poem Cole had pocketed from me downstairs.

"You see!" Chris blurted. "He stole it. He takes credit for what others do."

"No, dear, he mentioned it was the same one Bill read," Henrietta insisted. "He was afraid people didn't hear it the first time."

Penny squeezed Janet's hand. "Do you want to join them?"

Janet nodded, and the two sisters got to their feet.

"Oh, good. Everyone is hoping so," Henrietta said. "There's one problem . . . Mr. Dunfeld has a new urn, but there's, um, nothing in it."

Janet stood in front of the desk. "We're not going to the grave empty-handed, Chris."

Chris didn't meet her eyes. He stared at the inverted caryatid.

"I want our daughter buried," Janet said.

Chris leaned back in the swivel chair, reached into his pocket, and tossed his car keys on the desk. "It's in the back."

Janet took the keys. I stood to join the three women, expecting Chris to do the same.

"Stay with me, Bill," he said in a soft voice.

"We should go," I said.

"You go." He swiveled in the chair, showing me the back of his head.

Janet gave him one last furious look, then turned and went through the door with Penny and Henrietta.

Without turning, Chris intoned, "I said good-bye to her on the boat, Bill. I know it was messed up but—it's been messed up from the start."

I sat down again. "You need to tell me about that, Chris. You need to tell me what Sabell did and why he's still so involved."

"He crippled her before she was even born."

"Have you ever thought of suing him?"

"He'd deserve it," Chris said, "but I'm not the kind looking to blame others. I take responsibility for my choices. Besides, I don't want to relive it all. Especially if it got into the media."

"Did you sign a waiver with Sabell?"

"Sure, consent forms. But Sabell promised things he couldn't deliver."

"Do me a favor," I said. "Don't tell anyone you're not planning to sue, especially not anyone who knows Sabell."

"Are you kidding? I don't talk to those freaks. I don't know, Bill . . . Maybe Janet's right. If anyone's to blame, it's me. Maybe I should pay for what I did."

"You made a mistake last Friday, Chris. That doesn't mean Ulla wouldn't have taken Margaret to the park. Right now I want to know what Sabell was after."

Chris drummed his fingers on the desk. "He was so insistent on getting to examine Margaret again, even after I cut him off. He claimed he had some next-generation therapy for her. He was trying to justify himself, see? Trying to prove he wasn't the cause of her problems. Or maybe find out where he went wrong."

"Trying hard enough to kidnap her?"

Chris had evaded the question before, but this time he said, "Maybe. Yeah, maybe. He's a frigging ambitious guy."

"He's got a security crew that could have done the job."

"If that's the case, Bill . . ." Chris shook his head, at a loss for words. "I'll kill him."

"Let's take this one step at a time. You're the one who's been closest to the Jakarta project. How real is this threat of the triads?"

"It's plausible," Chris said. "What exactly were you talking about with Wilson and my father?"

"That smaller boat that we saw on the water. The general situation. Wilson said only good things about you."

"He's taken over Jakarta, hasn't he?"

I hesitated. Cole had asked me not to say, which seemed a good enough reason to nod and confirm Chris's suspicion.

"He didn't finish the proposal, did he?"

I hesitated again. It seemed best for Chris to let it go. But he'd be beside himself when he found out. Chris was the one I worked for, so I said, "They think the deal will be wrapped up next week."

Chris's eyes narrowed. His jaw began to grind again. "I'll never step foot in Claypool Construction Engineering again."

I didn't respond. Chris kept grinding, glaring as if I was the one who'd brought all of this about. Then his jaw set. His eyes turned a freezing blue.

"No, I'll go in first thing Monday," he said, reversing himself. "Forget that, tomorrow is Monday in Jakarta. Yes, I'll be back on the job tomorrow."

He was looking right through me now. His features had contracted like water setting into ice. That was when it occurred to me that when Cole told me not to breathe a word to Chris, he wanted me to do just the opposite.

12

Clem's day off had put her in a good mood. "Happy Sunday!" she declared to the entire café when she strode into Scoby's. She wore her cowboy boots below a flimsy black-and-white patterned skirt that ended just above a pair of robust knees. The frayed ends of the skirt had a nice swing when she walked. I wanted to ask what the fixation on fringe was about, but for all I knew, fringe was in.

"Remind me to give you another day off sometime," I said as she sat down. "It had a good effect."

She screwed her face into a lemony smile. "It's wonderful what a day with friends will do for a girl."

Hmm, *friends,* I thought. She did have a certain glow, her dark hair swinging free, her unmade-up face beaming, the sexy skirt . . . I shoved the ideas they evoked out of my mind. It was not my business, but more important, I knew from a few knotty experiences in the film world that fishing off the company pier during a job was a bad idea.

We drank coffee and nibbled on rolls while I recounted the fiasco of Margaret's memorial. Clem blanched at each new insult. "Cole wants me to help him get to Ulla," I said. "I still want to talk her into showing us where she lost Margaret in the park.

I'll only sic Cole on her if she clams up. He's supposed to turn over his files on the Hong Kong triads tomorrow. Cole also tossed out the idea that Mr. Dinh could be in league with a Vietnamese street gang. I suppose there's a speck of a chance he's the victim of some kind of extortion."

"Guilt by ethnicity," Clem said. "A popular investigative method. What do you think Cole's real aim is?"

I pondered that. "A few days ago, I would have said equally to protect Chris and make sure no harm came to Claypool Construction. Now I think he's trying to manipulate Chris to get the Jakarta deal done. It's not working, because Chris has gone out of his fucking mind. He's having his rebellious phase about twenty years too late."

"So what have we got? Blowgun darts and the Jakarta connection. Sabell, his lab, his security people. Margaret's real origins. Ulla and the park. The guys shadowing you in the boat yesterday. It's a real garden of forking paths. What about talking to the police and prosecutors?"

I gave my empty cup a few turns. "Chris's lawyer has more leverage, so I'm waiting to hear from him. Sabell's the one I want to nail today. He's got a home lab. Sunday ought to be a good day to catch him there. The way Janet and Chris talk about him—they're furious, and at the same time embarrassed, like he leads a cult they once joined. They won't say exactly what happened. It's one of those big secret family sins whose name can't be spoken."

"Incest," Clem mused. "That's what cloning always makes me think of. It seems wrong for the same reason incest is."

"Margaret and Helen were similar in some uncanny ways, but they weren't replicas. It's the aura of secrecy around Sabell that gets me. He hasn't returned my calls to set up a meeting. See, I have this personality disorder where I have to get to the bottom of things."

Clem slammed her cup down beside mine as if we were drinking whiskey at a frontier bar. "I'm with you. Let's go pin him down today."

I got up. "I need to drop in on Chris first. He's got Sabell's address, but I also want to make sure he's all right."

"I've got plenty of research to do at the office."

"Work in my flat, if you want. I've got a high-speed connection."

Clem decided to do that. We walked down 18th Street. The bay sparkled before us, and beside it the old brick industrial plants, piers, and hoists of what once was a thriving waterfront. The cranes of the port of Oakland, which drew all the container ships now, loomed in the distance like prehistoric creatures. Just north of us, the old railyards had been razed. Silvery, shimmering new buildings had arisen, including brand-new UCSF biomedical research facilities. The new technology was everywhere. I couldn't escape it.

We turned the corner and there, waiting in front of my flat, was none other than Don Masterson, wearing shorts and big sneakers. Instead of a baby-face peeve, he looked delighted with himself. He rushed up to shake my hand.

"Bill, dude, I've got the *greatest* job for you. Did you get my messages?"

"All of them, Don." He'd left about ten more yesterday, saying he had an incredible opportunity, a new documentary about the Antarctic. He wanted to put my name forward as the shooter.

"This is Clem, my research assistant," I added.

Don's grin disappeared. He looked her up and down. She did the same to him, which sent his eyes scurrying back to me. "No, listen," he said, "it's cool. But the film, man—I mean, Antarctica! Wow! The thing is, I got to know right away if you're on board."

"Don, you're turning into a grade-A pain."

"Sign of a good investigator, right? Seriously, I need an answer."

"I'll let you know tomorrow."

"Yeah, right. It's now been *four days* since you stood me up, Bill. You owe me, dude!" he said, and strode off. His tone remained triumphal, though, as if he'd proved I needed him more than he needed me.

Clem squeezed my arm. She waited for me to look at her. "Bill, how many times do you get a paid trip to the Antarctic? You should do the film."

I shook my head. "Eighty to one it's vapor. If by some miracle it's for real, I still wouldn't go. Not until we get to the bottom of what happened to Margaret."

"You really *do* have a problem. Must be in your DNA. You're a hunter-gatherer. Addicted to periods of intense pursuit, followed by long bouts of indolence and ennui. The diligent-farmer genes haven't kicked in."

An insult was in there somewhere, but I couldn't argue with her description. "You, too," I said. "It's a recipe for burnout."

"I'm afraid so."

I gave her a sideways smile, but she wasn't joking. The corners of her mouth had folded down and a small furrow of worry creased her brow. I stopped at my front stoop. "Take today off," I said. "I can go to Sabell's on my own."

She shook her head. "You know how we hunters get."

I cringed inwardly as she came into the flat. I should have remembered about the mess before I offered to let her work here. She seemed not to notice it, though. I got her situated for browsing and told her I'd be back before too long.

"You're not going to call Chris first?" she asked.

"I like to take him by surprise," I said, heading for the door. "That way I know what's really going on."

» » » » »

I killed the engine at the corner of Chris's block. I wanted to spot the federal agent supposedly keeping watch on the house. After waiting for ten minutes and seeing no motion in the vehicles parked along the curb, I cruised the street. The cars were empty. None looked like FBI-issue. A guy in a red pickup, a Ranger, passed me, also driving slow, but he looked harmless. I took a right and circled the block, then a left and did the same. Nothing.

As I headed for Chris's driveway, there, like déjà vu, was the red Ranger coming from the opposite direction.

I slowed. He'd started an arc to turn left into the driveway. I waved him in ahead of me. He motioned *no* with his hand and waved me in. I made a "Please, you first" motion. He hit the gas and swerved around me, tires whining.

I did a quick three-point and went after him. He took a left on St. Francis. The light turned red as the Ranger approached the multi-lane intersection at Junipero Serra. Good. I was a block behind but would catch him. Instead, he gunned it and ran the light. Tires screeched, horns blared. I had no choice but to stop. From my stationary position, I saw him catch a green at the big 19th Avenue crossing. I could try to run parallel with him on

Junipero Serra, but chances were he'd turn off 19th and lose me in the side streets. He was gone.

I did another three-point and went back to the house, wondering who I'd just scared away. His face had been manly-man, uncomplicated. Maybe he was FBI, working undercover as a handyman. Maybe he was doing surveillance for the kidnappers under the same cover. Or maybe he was just a guy who'd gotten lost in the neighborhood and didn't like the look of a beat-up old Scout.

Janet answered the door after I'd rung four times. She looked startled to see me. When I asked for Chris, she said he'd gone into the office.

He'd made good on his threat, I thought. Janet didn't seem bothered by that. She looked jumpy. "Is Penny with you?" I asked.

"No, she went out." Janet peered past me, to the driveway.

I worried about her being alone. "This guy in a red pickup, a Ranger, was about to turn into your driveway. He saw me and all of a sudden changed his mind. Pleasant face, soft brown hair, thinning on top, medium build, plaid shirt. Locked toolboxes in the flatbed, probably a contractor or tradesman."

She clasped her hands together and shook her head. "Maybe he was lost?"

"Lost people don't usually peel out when you do them a courtesy. Were you expecting anyone?"

She shook her head again, distracted. She seemed antsy to get rid of me. "Be on the lookout," I said. "Call me if you need help."

"I will." She eked out a smile.

I took the door handle from her as she began to close it. I checked to make sure it was going to lock behind me. Already she'd turned to go back into the house with the unmistakable gait of a woman headed for a phone.

» » » » »

I waited until I was at the front door of Claypool Construction Engineering to call Chris. He said he was too busy to see me. I told him where I was and that it would only take a minute. He came down himself to let me in. He'd put on his good blue work shirt, tie, and jacket. I remarked on the fact that he was the only one here.

"It's Sunday," Chris retorted. "Keep moving."

We took the elevator to the fourth floor. Instead of turning right to go to Chris's office, we went left, down a corridor, and into an office with Leonard Wilson's name on it. Sheaves of paper, rolled-up drawings, and a pen set were stacked on the floor, presumably by Chris. He plopped into Wilson's chair with a grunt of satisfaction. All that remained on the desk were the papers and drawings Chris was working on, his laptop, Wilson's desktop, and a large framed photograph. The photo showed Wilson's parents, his mother in a high-buttoned church dress, his father in a crisp blue policeman's uniform.

"Is Leonard hooked up?" I asked. "Girlfriend, wife?"

"Never heard of one. The guy's an android."

"Or likes his privacy." I nodded at the desktop computer, which Chris had booted.

Chris grinned, proud of his little coup. "What's he expect when he steals my job?"

I sat in a chair facing the desk. "Does Cole know you're here?"

"No one does. And you'll keep it that way."

"Are you sure you know what you're doing?"

He challenged me with a direct look. "Don't talk to me about right and wrong, Bill. No one can judge me. No one in the world knows how I feel."

"True enough," I said, but did not elaborate on how I meant it. It was precisely because Chris felt so judged, and it mattered so much, that he was overreacting so strongly. From the beginning, he'd feared that Margaret's death was the final proof of his incompetence, his shortcomings as a father and a man. Even as Chris denied it, he fled from that judgment. For a few moments last week he'd been able to dwell on his real emotions, the enormity of losing Margaret and what it meant to him and Janet. But no more. Once again, the fear had overpowered his legitimate grief.

I went on to a new subject. I described the red Ranger and asked, "Were you having any work done on your house today?"

"Of course not. We're getting out of that place. It feels like a frigging tomb now."

I held back from saying that to me, it always had. "How are you and Janet?"

"I don't know," he said, impatient to keep the conversation moving. "She didn't lift a finger to stop me from coming in today."

"Is she still going to that support group?"

"Yeah. I hate the idea of her spilling her guts to them instead of me, but it's okay for now. Until I'm done here."

"Wrapping up the Jakarta deal?"

"Like a Christmas present." The twinkle came back into his eye. He was inordinately pleased with himself. He must have come up with a way to ace out Wilson. "What do you need from me?"

"I just need to know where George Sabell lives."

"Talk to him at the clinic," Chris said.

"I tried that." I gave him a concise account of my visit—better he hear it from me than Cole. "He knows he's got to talk to me, but he's playing hard to get. You want me to find out what he did with those bits of Margaret he stole at the autopsy, don't you?"

"No. Yes. I don't know. I never want to see the man again."

"You didn't ask him to clone Helen, did you?" It was a bad time to ask, but I couldn't resist.

Chris slammed his fist on the desk. "No! Dammit, Bill, I don't have time for this now!"

"All right. Just tell me how to get to his house."

Chris savagely punched the keys on his laptop. "I've noticed how you like to show up unannounced," he said, then read out an address. I put it in my notebook. "Sabell will never let you in. He lives in a weird place on the far side of the coast range. I was one of the very few, very rare clients he invited up there."

"Thanks, Chris."

His eyes flashed revulsion at me. With unutterable bitterness in his voice, he said, "A *special* client. Get the fuck out of here, Bill."

» » » » »

Once again Clem and I drove the winding road into the hills above Silicon Valley. We'd passed the turnoff to the clinic, then climbed two thousand feet to crest the main ridge. Now we dropped into the wet side of the Santa Cruz Mountains. Dense forest carpeted the range below us, layer after layer of ridge all the way to the coast. Caskets of fog lay in the deep valley hollows, as if unwilling to let them wake. It was a place for recluses, geniuses—Neil Young lived out here—and more recently, siliconnaires.

We turned off on a small paved road that led into a side valley. A few well-spaced houses dotted the broad mouth of the valley, but as pavement gave way to gravel and the road ascended, all signs of habitation disappeared. Another turn put us on a rutted dirt lane that sidled along a ravine into the heart of the silent, dripping forest. I rolled down my window. The smells were rich here: pungent eucalyptus and laurel, mixed with fungus and the damp whiff of decay.

The rutted lane eventually leveled off. We found our way blocked by a high black metal gate. I leaned out to peer at an electronic keypad mounted on a steel post. "Looks like we walk from here," I said.

I put the Scout in reverse and found a space to pull off. The bars of the gate were too close together to squeeze through, and the edge of the road fell steeply to our right. By grabbing the gate post we were able to pivot around it to the other side. We walked on up the road, deeper into the valley. We'd entered a realm of old-growth redwoods, towering sentries that had been watching over this place for a thousand years. It was nearly soundless in here, with only the distant caw of a crow to break the crackle of our shoes on gravel. Speech seemed forbidden. Perhaps that's why neither of us said anything, even as a feeling of apprehension grew. Every snap of a twig startled us.

I looked at Clem, then into the dark woods left and right. They appeared empty. I had the distinct sense we were not alone. I wheeled. Behind us was a black dog. The prickles went up on the back of my neck. Who knew how long it had been trailing us. The dog was a full-size poodle, jet black, not trimmed like a town dog, but shaggy in the breast and tail. It was not the color or the coat, it was the way the dog regarded us that unsettled me. Its moist brown eyes had a watchful, human look. More than that, an uncanny intelligence inhabited them. I had the sense the dog was leading us, not the other way around. I took a step in its direction. It let out a vicious snarl that froze me in place.

"Let's go this way," Clem said, turning back up the road.

We went, and the dog followed us, the watchful look never leaving its face. Strains of music filtered through the forest, tremulous minor-seventh chords, lush strings, bellowing horns. We came to a house built of redwood boards and shingles. It was modest at the entrance, but increased in height and bulk in the back. A black Saab was parked in the carport. The dog bolted past us, through a small rock garden, to sit on the front porch. It gave a single bark. Most dogs have eager faces, caring very much what you think of them. If not eager, then defensive. This dog was neither. It inspected us as if deciding what to do with us.

Clem squatted, her fingertips pressing the ground. She made odd grunting noises, neither human nor animal, and hopped from side to side, inching closer to the dog. It extended its neck and narrowed its eyes. Clem stopped a few feet in front of it and stared directly into its eyes. They remained locked on each other for what seemed a very long time until the dog at last lowered its head. Clem scooted closer. The dog licked her hand, then her face. It takes a devil to charm a devil, I thought.

The front door opened. The music, opera, spilled out from behind George Sabell. Clem stood. Sabell seemed only a little startled. He wore black canvas pants and a wool sweater with large buttons. His black work shoes were well-creased.

"Dr. Sabell," I said, "Christopher Claypool sent us."

"I've got to get that gate fixed," he murmured, then looked at the dog. "What do you say, Gigi?"

Gigi's mouth came open, revealing blood-pink jaws beneath black lips.

"You haven't returned my calls," I said. "You know you have to talk to us sometime."

"Yes, yes," he replied, still talking more to himself than to us. He left the door open and disappeared down a low, dark hallway. Clem and I gave Gigi a wide berth. The strains of the opera rose as we passed through the front part of the house, which consisted of a handful of dimly lit studies and bedrooms off the narrow corridor.

"Götterdämerung," Clem said. "I saw it at the San Francisco Opera."

"Yes," Sabell called back to her, "in '99? Sublime!"

"Great crowd. All the Wagnerites in their leather chaps and studded collars."

"Hmm, well, there are certain interpretations I don't comprehend."

Somehow Gigi had gotten in front of us again. She, along with Clem and Sabell, entered a larger room with a peaked ceiling. It was furnished with a wide, comfortable couch and armchairs of ancient, cracked leather. I noticed framed diplomas on the wall in a small room along the corridor, and dropped back to read them. He'd graduated from Johns Hopkins. When I came back into the larger room, Clem was admiring a medieval tapestry. I lingered in front of a pair of Dürer prints on another wall. An ancient oak grandfather clock ticked.

"Your name again?" Sabell asked.

"Bill Damen. Margaret's uncle," I said, and introduced Clem as well.

"Yes . . ." Sabell shifted from foot to foot, as if unsure where to put us or himself. Maybe he was more in his element, or maybe Dr. Rosen's description of him as the man with the magic touch had changed my perception, but Sabell seemed less imposing here. His eyes were rimmed red under his overhanging brow, and he hadn't bothered to comb the wayward strands on his head. His shoulders slumped in the dowdy sweater. The hair sprouting from his ears and unshaven on his face gave him a shaggy trollish look. The mercury-like pools of his eyes were still.

"We need to settle some questions about her," I reminded him.

The music hit another crescendo and Sabell went to turn it down. Gigi had trotted into the next room, the kitchen, and Sabell wandered in that direction himself. We followed, past a dining table, through the well-kept country kitchen, and out a back door into the garden. The patio was paved with red bricks. A profusion of moss grew in the cracks. Beyond the patio stood what appeared to be a forest of ferns.

"You have a lab up here, don't you?" Clem asked.

Sabell smiled to himself. "Yes. A place where I can bend solitary to my subtle tasks in still nights."

He seemed to be quoting. Clem picked up on it. "'Working forgetful of family and regardless of his friends . . .' Where is it?"

The smile widened to include her for a moment. "In its secret, safe spot. We must stay hidden from the goblins of righteousness."

"Do they come after you up here?" I asked, assuming he was referring to the groups we'd talked about Friday at the clinic.

"Not yet." He looked fondly at the dog. "I have only Gigi to protect me."

"What is it in your work that they object to? IVF is well-accepted. You must be doing research on embryos. Stem cells, maybe, nuclear transfer—cloning?"

He snorted. "Cloning. Bogeyman of the popular imagination. We study nuclear transfer in mammals, but cloning, no. What's the point of repeating the past, merely creating more of what came before? The uninformed mind sees clones as doppelgängers, soulless doubles." He fluttered his fingers and made horror-film noises. "Did you know, when the first in vitro child was born in 1978, the tabloids reported incredible tales of her demonic powers? She was said to knock pictures off the wall and move furniture in her room. This little tiny infant."

"None of which she did," I said.

"Pfft. She's normal. So are most of the million-plus IVF babies now in the world. In truth, a clone is nothing but a delayed identical twin—in fact, less identical, because they share neither mitochondrial DNA nor the same womb environment. One day I predict clones will be accepted as test-tube babies are now. But it won't be me cranking them out. If a parent came to me and said he wanted a copy of himself, I'd say, 'What's so great about *you?* Is it *your*self you love in your children, or *their* unique selves?'"

"What about for treatment?" I had a sudden vision of Margaret's brain-dead twin being kept alive on machines somewhere in the depths of Sabell's lab. "You know, a clone for spare parts."

Sabell let out a heaving laugh. "Did you read that in a science fiction book? Please understand, I'm using this technology to better the human race, not keep it standing still. The only scenario in which I could see human cloning being useful is if you've engineered the original to be something special in the first place."

"But you did say to Chris that you could treat Margaret. In fact, you insisted that he let you. You told him you had some next-generation therapy."

"Pfft," he repeated. "One says such things."

Gigi had been sniffing at a small, dirty-yellow cylinder. Sabell interrupted himself to pick it up. It was a banana slug, about five inches long and spotted black, oozing along the damp red pavement near a small lettuce garden. The slug curled in his fingers as he dangled it.

"You look so good I could eat you!" Sabell said.

I thought for a moment he would put it in his mouth. Instead, he tossed it in the direction of a shallow pan full of golden fluid. Beer, I realized, used to attract slugs and snails. The pan was ringed with rock salt. The slug would either drown, starve, or shrivel.

"What treatment did you have for Margaret?" I asked.

Gigi moved onto a narrow brick path that led into the ferns. Sabell ambled after her, saying to me over his shoulder, "It's a little late to help her now. What exactly does Chris want? Reparations?"

"It depends on how forthcoming you are," I answered, falling into single file behind him, with Clem behind me. "Let's start at the beginning. What techniques did you use to create Margaret?"

"In the beginning . . ." Sabell intoned, as if from on high, then dropped his voice to a more reasonable tone. "I'm sure you have mistaken ideas about me. I want you to try to understand. My closer colleagues call me the egghead, referring both to my"— he made circular flapping motions around his ear—"personality, and also to the subject of my fascination. But they also know what it is that gives me real joy. That is when a couple in distress, suffering from a barren life—or worse, a loss, such as the Claypools did—comes to see me. I am their last hope; I take only the toughest cases. When I am able to make their dream come true, to give them that take-home baby, a continuation of themselves, that gives me joy. The great spiral of life, it goes on and up. You two, you'll have children?"

I gave an aw-shucks shrug when he glanced back at me. "We did have our first appointment with the clinic before we saw you on Friday. I guess you could say we have more than an idle interest."

Clem was right in sync. She smiled shyly and said, "I wish I'd realized earlier in my life how much I wanted one."

Sabell cocked his head, gauging whether we were serious. It was Clem's smile that won him over. "Yes, madam. This is the incredible power woman has, something every man envies in his secret heart. Use it! Blossom!"

"So you're a champion of women," Clem said, egging him on.

"They say that God created man, from dust with his own hands, on the sixth day. But we know there's more to it, don't we? There was a beginning *before the beginning*, the old deep night, Mother Chaos, the roiling face of the waters. That is the real power, usurped by the supposed Creator. We must sort out false creators from true creators."

"And now you're taking the power of creation for yourself," Clem said.

"I'm just Mother's little helper," he answered with a droll smile. "Or maybe I should say Eve's little helper."

"You should go all the way back, then, to Lillith," Clem said.

"The demonized goddess." He winked at Clem. "You've discovered my muse."

The sinuous path branched, and then branched again. I realized now that this was more than a garden, it was a labyrinth. Its walls were formed mainly by the variety of unusually tall and thick ferns Sabell grew here. Walking through them, with their prehistoric fronds, was like winding slowly back in time. Spaces between the ferns were filled by thorny vines and bushes, trimmed in curving divider rows. Along the base of every dividing hedge ran a web of nettles that prevented you from jumping to a neighboring path. I tried to keep track of the turns we took as Sabell talked on. His emotions spilled out, ungoverned, as they had before, but today, in his garden, in his element, he was looser and more impetuous.

"Women have fought to be free from social limitation for the past century," he said. "This is the next step. I am freeing women from the limitations imposed by their bodies."

"But that's not a social convention," Clem objected. "I don't like it either, but criminy, it's the way nature made us."

"There, you've hit on it. What could be more *natural* than nature? *Us!* 'Natural' is nothing more than a trick of language. Evolution is what's made us the way we are. We contend with it all the time: These brains of ours are Paleolithic, programmed to eat everything in sight and to smack down anyone who infringes on our social space. We've had to fight back those caveman impulses ever since we civilized ourselves. Stress, pent-up anger, and obesity are the result, yet everyone but the most rabid fundamentalist or savage-romantic tree-hugger would agree our present is superior to our brutal past. We shape and mold ourselves to our present needs and aspirations. This is exactly what makes us human: It's *natural* to us. So let's move from the nervous system to the reproductive system. You need not put yourself at evolution's mercy there, either."

"You talk like our minds are completely separate from our bodies," Clem said. "I've heard how male OBs talk about women—we're 'gestation environments,' 'the best heart and lung machines available.'"

This got a giggle of recognition from Sabell. "We've all had to unlearn what we were taught. But think of it this way. We've talked about the issue of choice. Men have set up society so they have nearly unlimited choice: A man can father a child in his teens, then waltz off. From his twenties to his forties, he has his pick from a fertile crop of female peers. When he moves into his fifties, sixties, seventies, then it gets really unfair. He can go back to a new crop and sire yet more offspring. That gives him *three generations* through which his genes can be fruitful and multiply. Women are limited to a couple of decades, decades that just happen to be their best years for career advancement, if they so choose. So you tell me, madam, who it is who treats women as mere gestation environments?"

By now I'd given up on keeping track of the twists and turns we took in Sabell's garden, a maze as convoluted as his brain. He was a nineteenth-century man who let his twenty-first-century mind run away with itself on tracks that conveniently diverged from the subject at hand.

"Dr. Sabell," I said placatingly, "you've convinced us that you care about your clientele. Let's talk about Chris and Janet and Margaret. Why was she born with so many medical problems?"

He fondled a frond, then turned to face us. "You can't freeze time, you know, even here, lost among these three-hundred-million-year-old plants. But we do have the power to shift it in the reproductive system—"

"Or by bringing back someone who's died," I interrupted, remembering a phrase Janet said to Chris at the funeral home. "Chris asked you to bring Helen back, didn't he?"

Sabell raised a finger and began to walk again. "I gave him a new child, as much like his lost daughter as could be—only without the genetic defect that proved so tragic. I can only work with the clay, if you will, that is given me. I saw how devastated he was by his loss of Helen and did all I could to satisfy his specifications. Not by repeating the past, as I've said—"

"You improved on it," I put in. Interrupting was the only way to keep him on track. "You said something earlier about 'engineering the original.' How did you engineer Margaret?"

He chuckled with an unpleasant amusement. "You claim to come in the spirit of negotiation. Yet all I hear are demands."

"The deal works like this. First, you tell me what you did with Margaret and what treatment you offered after she was born. In return, Chris agrees not to sue for damages, malpractice, and so on. Second, you tell me what tissue you took from the autopsy and what you've learned from it. In return, we don't press charges for your theft."

He turned with his secret smile. Again I caught a quicksilver shimmer in his eyes, mutable, plenipotent. "I admit to, ah, fiddling a bit with the embryonic genome. The techniques are well-established. You will have noted that not only did she lack the mutation causing cystic fibrosis"—Sabell could not resist bragging about his success—"but she was unusually talented musically?"

"Oh my God," I muttered, thinking back on Chris and Janet, Cole and Regina and their relatives, their inability to carry a tune, the songs they mangled at their parties. Margaret had seemed to have perfect pitch. "You knocked out the cystic fibrosis mutation, but you knocked in genes, too? How many?"

"It was all within our agreement. I share this with you freely. Chris could tell you, if he felt like it."

Yes, I thought, but Sabell couldn't pass up an opportunity to share his brilliance. He was like a sea animal that luminesces to attract mates—or prey. "Was she identical to Helen, other than the gene replacements?"

"I've told you she was not! The process is beyond your knowledge and would be time-consuming to explain. I don't care about money, except insofar as it gives me what I need to do my work. That and time are what are most precious to me."

"What instructions did Cole give you?" I sprang the question on him abruptly.

The hesitation in his shoulders, before he glanced back at me, gave Sabell away. "Cole Claypool? He was never part of our agreement."

"He is now," I said. Sabell was playing with words again, wanting me to believe he meant his agreement with Chris. That was all right, he'd already revealed what I wanted to know. "What tissues of Margaret's did you take at the autopsy?"

Another of his droll smiles crossed his lips.

"I know you took something," I said. "I have a witness up in the city at UCSF."

"Bravo," Sabell said with a clap of his hands. He turned to face us again, his eyes glittering. We'd reached an open, circular space carpeted with newly sprouted grass. I fought an urge to take him to the ground and pound the truth out of him. The dog, behind us now, prevented that, as did knowing that the only answers I'd get would be appeasing lies.

"The truth is," Sabell said, "I want to find who caused her death, too. In part to protect myself, but equally from a sense of outrage. Now that she's gone, I can no longer help her. I can no longer prove to Chris and Janet that they were wrong about me. They would have come back to me at the last moment, when her life was in the balance, when they were desperate enough to try my treatments."

"What kind of treatments were you proposing?"

"There was an element of risk, I grant," he said, "but her life was likely to be short anyway—what was to be lost? Success would have been a historic breakthrough."

"You're making me think you really did have a reason to kidnap her—in order to complete your experiment that began in vitro."

"What an imagination you have. Look at me." He drew his shoulders in, making himself look more hunched than he already was. "Look at the autopsy: The hyperglycemic shock had to have been induced deliberately for it to have killed her as quickly as it did. I'm a doctor. I never would have stuffed her with sugar or failed to give her insulin."

"Why were you at the autopsy, then?"

"She had many ailments, as you know. I wondered which, if any, contributed to her death. I needed to satisfy myself that the coroner was drawing the correct conclusion. I'm quite sure her death had nothing to do with our work."

"Except that it caused the diabetes in the first place. Are you testing the tissues you took?"

"I'm analyzing tissue from her liver, along with a vitreous humor sample. I'm wondering if, even with help from her captors inducing the coma, the diabetes was really what killed her. There, you see? I just saved you a trip to UCSF."

"And you'll contact the coroner when you have something?"

"I'd think so," he said calmly. "Or rather, why don't you? I'd rather not be in the middle of this."

Sabell had been backing into the clearing. Something about the place made me uncomfortable, but with my eyes on the doctor, I hadn't fixed on what it was until now. The center of the labyrinth was occupied by a single marble slab, familiar in its proportions and beveled edges, leaning as if a little tipsy.

"Who's in charge of your security force?" I said. "Do you run it yourself?"

Sabell gave a dismissive wave. "I hardly think about it. It's a regrettable necessity, but not my concern."

"Whose is it, then?" I asked. "Your patron, Austin Remly?"

A moment of mild surprise jumped across his face. He turned the alertness into concern. "Goodness, where did Gigi go?"

Sabell gestured at the path from which we'd entered. I turned and retreated a few steps, as did Clem, expecting to find the dog gazing at us around the bend. She wasn't.

When we came back into the clearing, Sabell was gone.

Clem stared at me and I stared at her. I put a finger to my lips. We listened. Not a whisper of a footfall could be heard. The ferns were still. The only sound was the breathing of the redwood crowns in the wind, and our own lungs.

13

Dr. Sabell could only have escaped down the path on the opposite side of the clearing. The tombstone at the center of the labyrinth stood between us and that path, and I couldn't help pausing to read it. I expected to see the name of a lost wife, or perhaps child. I was not prepared for the name I did see: GEORGE JOHAN SABELL. Below was a blank space for an epitaph, the substance of which Sabell was still striving to fulfill.

Clem and I moved quickly down the path, choosing the forks on instinct. The plants around us grew taller and more ancient, their fronds like the shaggy beards of old men watching and testing us. We stopped every few seconds to listen for Sabell. We heard nothing. We called his name. There was no response.

The plants were high enough that we could not see the house and thick enough that we could not plunge directly through them. Mist flitted through the redwoods like lost souls. Darkness was coming, oozing from the ground itself more than descending from above. I could have sworn we'd been in the garden for only an hour, but the entire day seemed to have passed. It was impossible to tell in which direction the sun had disappeared.

Clem and I looked at each other again and recognized the same thought. "Forget Sabell," she said. "We need to get out."

We set off, striding fast now, without pause. Behind me, Clem whispered the direction of each turn we took. We branched and branched again, many more times than I remembered having done with Sabell. The ferns became a blur. The moment had long since passed when I thought we should have reached the beginning.

Then, without warning, the path opened onto the patio. Clem spread her arms and inhaled a breath of relief. The slug Sabell had tossed into the ring of salt had been on a journey of its own, inching its way to the edge of the beer pan.

The mists had lowered, shrouding the upper half of the house. No light came from inside. I started toward the door to the kitchen and abruptly stopped, more from what I felt than what I saw. Guarding the door, standing erect, tail extended, was Gigi. Her stance and the disquietingly avid look on her face told us that we would have to fight to get inside. Never in my life had I feared a poodle, but for this one I made an exception.

"Can you put your spell on her again?" I asked Clem.

She looked at the dog and said softly, "No."

We went to the side of the house and found a narrow passage, scraping ourselves between the outer wall and a rock ledge. This led us to the front of the house. Sabell's Saab was still in the carport. We stood in the driveway, watching. Still no lights were on inside. Murky dusk sealed us into smaller and smaller spaces. Clem started back down the driveway. My gaze lingered on the house. A stirring in the bottom of my stomach made it impossible to stay.

Something glinted near the front door, a brief, demonic shine. It came from the eyes of the dog, who sat watching us from the porch, nearly merged with the darkness. My feet started down the driveway, almost of their own volition. I glanced over my shoulder one more time. The dog watched as if she knew exactly where to find us.

» » » » »

Clem and I stopped at a roadside tavern called the Bullshead on our way out of the hills. We needed food, a beer, and a dose of reality. The mixture of stale beer and frying grease worked as a kind of smelling salt. We asked around the bar about Sabell but got nothing. He didn't fit in with the mix of Harley dudes, relic hippies, and nouveau geeks patronizing the place.

"Bill, I give you credit," Clem said after we'd ordered. "I've seen and done a lot of weird things in my life, but George Sabell takes the cake."

"Him and his mistress, Gigi. He pretty much admitted he'd made a mistake with Margaret."

Our beers came. We lifted them for a clink.

"What did he intend to do with us after he ditched us in that maze?" Clem said.

"Just what he did. Get rid of us. He was done talking."

"On the other hand, he was pretty casual about letting us in. You think he really cares about finding out who killed Margaret?"

"Maybe, but it could be his cover story. What he didn't say is as important as what he did. He said the gene-replacement techniques he used on Margaret's embryo were well-established. He didn't mention they've only been done on animals, not humans—at least from what I've read."

"Depends when and how he did it," she said. "If her cells had differentiated, he might only have targeted genes in specific organs. That's more like somatic gene therapy, hitting only the relevant tissue, leaving the other cells alone. That could explain why he wanted to examine certain tissues postmortem."

"But if he did the tinkering in the earliest stages, say the blastocyst, when Margaret was a tiny ball of stem cells, then every cell in her body would carry the new genes. Including her germ cells. Germ-line modification therapy. He said he did the work in vitro, not in utero, didn't he?"

"You said that, not him. His wording was careful. Did you notice he said *the* embryo, not Margaret's embryo, or even Chris and Janet's embryo—as if Sabell was the one who owned it?"

"Yeah, I noticed. It made me wonder for a minute if he used DNA from someone other than Chris and Janet. But I don't think so. Margaret looked a lot like Helen, and Helen clearly came from her parents. What gave me the shivers, though, is when he mentioned Margaret's musical ability. She could carry a tune, while no one else in the family can sing two notes in a row."

Clem grabbed my wrist. "That could prove his gene-targeting technique worked. There are theories about a gene for absolute pitch. If he knocked it into Margaret and proved the theory, that would be big news. I mean, not as big as human germ-line engineering, but still . . . It's quite a fix he's got himself in—his work is groundbreaking, but he can't share it because it's so beyond the pale."

"Yeah, I feel real bad for him," I said acidly. "Remember how he talked about going back to 'before the beginning'? That's how he sees himself. The force that precedes creation. Sabell saw himself as the precondition of Margaret's existence."

"He's not alone. Plenty of parents have the same attitude toward their children. Life isn't a gift, but something that puts the children in infinite debt. The parents think that gives them permission to pound their beliefs into the child."

Clem said the last sentence with an intensity that made me think she was speaking from personal experience. The moment was interrupted by the waitress arriving with our food, hamburgers, big, juicy, and oozing over the plate. We ordered another round of beer. I stared at the wall-eyed bull mounted above the bar for a minute, then said, "Sabell is not going to be able to share his results with the rest of the world as long as someone like Chris is around to sue him for his mistakes. Here's a hypothesis. If Sabell screwed up Margaret's conception, that meant the longer she stayed around, the more likely it was that Chris and Janet might seek some kind of satisfaction from the clinic. But money and security are Austin Remly's department, not Sabell's. Maybe Remly's the one who ordered Margaret kidnapped. He would have known about her diabetes. Once she was gone, Chris could no longer blame Sabell for her death. It was the fault of Indonesian kidnappers. Remly could have sent the fake warning note to Claypool Construction."

Clem nodded. "The moment you said Remly's name was the moment Sabell disappeared. We need to find out about him."

I sighed. "That means talking to Cole again. That's all right. I've got more ammunition now."

Clem eyed her hamburger and said, "Greasy, like I like it."

We dug in. The strangeness of the afternoon began to wear off as the reassuring fat hit my taste buds. We talked about Sabell and the ferns for a while, then got into talking about places we knew in the area: We both realized that if we'd turned right instead of left coming down from Sabell's house, we could have gone to Duarte's in Pescadero and had artichoke soup. We compared our favorite places to get fresh ravioli by the box, dive bars in the Mission and the Tenderloin, the best places to shoot pool . . . I found reasons to talk about the San Francisco film world, the cast of shooters, recordists, and gaffers I knew; Rita, my producer-director collaborator, and Wes, the physics geek I'd known since college.

None of this elicited similar stories from Clem. She lived in South City, the town on the far side of San Bruno Mountain that combined old-fashioned working-class neighborhoods with the newest of the new technology parks, especially biotech. But she didn't explain how she knew so much about the field, and I didn't push it. I looked at her restive green eyes, the wild ringlets of black hair, the sensual pleasure her lips took in forming the words of her conversation. I remembered the charm she'd put on Gigi and wondered: Who the hell are you?

Not that I had anything more than a professional interest. Getting to know her was going to be like going into the labyrinth. You couldn't go straight to the center and demand the answer. It would unfold only when you allowed yourself to get lost.

» » » » »

The arrest came on Monday morning. Chris's voice had a peculiar serenity when I called at nine. He was at home, not at work, and said he did not intend to step foot into Claypool Construction Engineering again. He'd said it before, but this time he seemed to mean it. I told him I was coming over to talk about new information I'd gotten yesterday.

Janet, wearing a bathrobe, let me in. She gave me a quick greeting, told me Chris was on the back patio, and disappeared upstairs. I found him in the Adirondack chair, reading the newspaper, wearing pressed khakis and a clean shirt, his fully loaded gas barbecue and coiled hose nearby. He could have been mistaken for a picture of the happy husband.

I'd begun to describe my visit to Sabell's house when the police showed up. Janet reappeared, her uncombed hair falling in thin strings, the lines on her face etched with worry. The tone in which she said the police were at the door implied Chris might want to make an escape over the back fence. He simply said to send them out to him.

A detective in a suit and tie accompanied the two cops who'd arrested Chris the first time. He was under arrest again, they informed him, and this time charges would be filed. Severe child neglect. Chris, looking amused, folded his newspaper neatly and stood for the bracelets.

"I thought you guys would come for me at the funeral so you could make the Monday papers," he said.

"We've kept it out of the news, asshole," the senior cop said.

It was true there'd been only two short articles about Margaret's death. The fact that the prosecutor's office had kept a lid on it didn't square with Cole's vendetta theory, but maybe they were saving their bullets.

"You're doing a Martha Stewart on me, right?" Chris replied. "Trying to get me to dig a hole while I deal with a charge you have no evidence for."

"Thaaat's right," the detective said.

"You're doing a lousy job with the cuffs," Chris said, wriggling a hand free and showing it to the cop, who grabbed it, crackled the bracelets tighter on Chris's wrists, and pushed him toward the door. Chris asked Janet to call their lawyer, Mitch, and told me not to waste my time coming down to the station.

Janet called, then sat with me at the dining-room table. She placed her palms flat as if trying to hold down some chaotic force rising from it. We were at right angles from each other, and she stared past me into the kitchen. The plums in her cheeks had gone soggy and pale.

"What do we do now?" she said in a numb voice.

"I'll talk to Cole," I said. "We'll check in with Mitch. I'm sure you'll be questioned again."

"I've told them everything I can."

"Let me ask you some questions, then. I've seen a lot of Chris, but I haven't had a chance to get your side."

Janet's robe matched the one I'd seen Chris wearing, thick blue terrycloth embroidered with her initials. She cinched it a little tighter and said, "There's not much more than what I've already told you, Bill."

"You haven't been crazy about me investigating this from the beginning. Why is that?"

One of her spread hands moved in my direction, then stopped. "I didn't see the point at first. But now I'm glad you're here for Chris. To be honest, I don't know what I'd do without you. He's got no one to talk to. I can't handle all of his moods myself. You've given me time with Penny and some other people to feel what I'm feeling."

I watched her and the way she kept gazing into the kitchen as if some scene from the past was playing in there. A measure of detachment was in her voice. I asked, "Will you two be able to repair your relationship?"

She flashed anger at me, startled at my directness. "We're in an awful lot of trouble," she said evenly. "I don't know what Chris wants."

"He can't imagine life without you."

"He did seem more relaxed today, even when they arrested him. I'm glad he didn't make a scene. But he must know—"

"That you've been getting more distant. That you're angry at his behavior. He's been a maniac, I know. Credit Cole for that."

"No kidding," she said caustically. "It's become all about defying his father. I don't know if he even thinks about Margaret anymore."

"He's been trying to break free of Cole and the company so he can devote his full attention to you, and mourn Margy. I have a feeling he's finally getting there. Was he different last night, too?"

"He talked about a trip. Somewhere very far away. Fiji."

"And?"

Janet's voice broke. "It's too far! I need my support system. He can't expect me to absorb all of his emotions for him! Not like last time. I can't do that again, Bill. I have my own emotions." Finally she looked me straight in the eye. "Right now I have no idea if my life's going to be part of his. Or what I want. Except that I want a break."

I was stunned that she'd already reached that point. I tried to take her a step back with my next question. "What happened last time, with Helen? I remember Chris being pretty stoic."

She patted her hand on the table a few times, thinking, before she said, "I can't talk about this with you, Bill."

"I'm not going to report back to him, Janet. I need to know how bad things are. It'll help me prepare him for whatever he needs to do next. You're afraid that what happened with Helen is happening now."

"Yes! We're going through this not once, but twice. Because Chris wanted it *twice*."

"He wanted to have Margaret but you didn't?"

"Bill," she said, then slumped back in her chair. She regarded me with a chilling anger. "Have you ever nurtured a child with your own body, your own milk and love? It was an incredible experience."

I nodded. Janet had me fixed in her sights, making sure I heard every word. "And then to lose that," she went on. "To see her dead in front of you. It's like having a chunk of your flesh ripped out of you. You're destroyed, and yet somehow, cruelly, still alive. Still walking around like a zombie, dead skin stuffed with cotton batting. But you keep going because that's what you do. Everyone around you and all the experts say the feeling of being alive will come back someday. So we did it. We went through the motions. Except, after a while, Chris couldn't do it. He was falling apart. He had to do something about it, to *fix* it. He insisted we try again. We couldn't let death beat us, he said. Another child was the only thing that'd save us. Eventually I went along. Because Chris and everyone else said I needed to. I needed to 'move on with my life,' 'get past it,' 'find closure,' all that *complete bullshit!*"

Janet's voice had reached a boil. She was sitting up, leaning forward. "And you know what? A little bit of the feeling did come back. Slowly. It surprised the hell out of me, Bill. I thought I'd hate going back to the clinic, but the good thing about being numb was I didn't really care. Dr. Sabell was in his expensive new facility. I guess the first sign I was starting to come back alive was that I hated taking the hormones. With Helen, I didn't mind because we were so focused on what we wanted. But this time I resented the hell out of Chris and Dr. Sabell, and I let them know it."

She paused, checking my reaction. I gave an understanding smile. Janet, normally, was one of the most patient people in the world.

"They made the usual jokes about women and hormones. I admit, acting like a bitch was the one luxury I enjoyed about the whole thing—the whole *fertilization* process. I felt like a damned lawn. Maybe it was just to avoid me, but Dr. Sabell excused me from the egg-extraction process. He said he had some of mine frozen from last time. He spent a lot of time working in the laboratory before Margaret was implanted. I went through a lot of miscarriages, but Chris insisted we keep trying, since we'd gone that far. Once she did finally implant, my feelings started to come back. It was like she kicked me awake. Margaret's birth—it was like a rebirth. The world came to life again."

"The fact that she was conceived in a glass, that didn't make a difference?"

"I was used to it by then." She gave an acrid laugh. "The fairy tale you grow up with is so simple. Girl meets boy, they fall in love, they have babies. Dr. Sabell gave 'Honey, let's make a baby' a whole new meaning."

I chuckled and said, "Nothing's ever as easy as it should be." I was thinking of all the boyfriends Janet had tossed back as not being "husband material."

She thought I meant something else. "Yeah," she said. "The first time was weird, but we were focused on the goal, not the process. The second time, I felt like I'd been abducted by alien scientists for some reproductive experiment. I called Dr. Sabell's clinic the mothership."

I laughed again. "I've talked to him a couple of times. His mind is definitely on another planet. I know that he targeted the cystic fibrosis gene. I also know about the music gene—"

Janet's hand went to her mouth. "Music gene? Are you saying that her talent—that Chris and George—"

"No, no," I lied quickly. "Just a speculation. The big question is what technique Sabell used to replace the cystic fibrosis gene."

"Chris handled all the arrangements with him." Janet's body was rigid. She was trying to comprehend what I'd just said.

"So you heard nothing about what happened, technically speaking, in Sabell's lab?"

"*Technically,* Bill, someone kidnapped Margy and she died. What does it matter now what Dr. Sabell did? Didn't you hear me when I said I wanted this *over?*"

"I want it over, too. With the right people in prison and the right people free."

"Do it, then! With Chris, not me. I didn't hire you. Don't ask me to relive this. Don't ask me to repeat *any* of it, ever again!"

The light went on in my head. "You're afraid Chris is going to want to have another child."

She gaped at me. Apparently I'd said something very stupid. She took in a deep breath. She was going to try to make me understand. "I know the progression, Bill. I've seen it from the first moment we knew she was gone. First he defies it. He tries to take control of the situation. He alternates between lashing out at other people and lashing in at himself. Someone must be punished. Then he realizes there is no control. He doesn't have it and neither does anyone else. That's when he starts to fall apart. His work goes to hell. His life goes to hell. He can't show his true feelings to others and he barely can to me. He's got no one to talk to. He's sinking. He's going under, Bill, and I can't let him go under. Even if I feel our marriage is cursed, even if I've just lost my daughter, I can't let Christopher drown. I become the caretaker, the nurturer. Chris grabs onto me like a life raft. Never mind about my own needs, my own wish to sink out of sight. He grabs on real tight."

Janet herself had recoiled, her body twisting in the chair and shrinking inside the robe, even as her arms traced arcs of sinking and saving in the air. I said, "Chris did react in a strange way to Margy's disappearance. Like he was worried about how it reflected on his competence more than anything else."

"I don't know if there's anything else there, Bill, other than worrying about how others see him." Her voice had gone low and quiet. "But I can tell you what happened next after Helen. Once he got his breath again, this little gleam came into his eye. Like he spotted land. Like he saw the future, a path to redemption. Another little girl. Not to replace Helen, but to show how much we loved her. To show we wouldn't let ourselves be defeated. Helen would be proud of us, he said. And . . ."

Janet faltered, her hands freezing in the air for a moment before she went on. "I felt the power of it. It was like he'd been touched by something beyond. I feel it to this day. Maybe the light of some little soul did reach out to him at that moment and enter into his eye, some angel took pity on us. I saw how that power was touching him and giving him this vision. I didn't have the feeling myself until later, when I was pregnant. Before that, all I knew was that Chris's vision was relieving his pain, saving him, saving our marriage. So I agreed to try again. That was the balm for him. His sense of hope came back. I was just glad no one was drowning anymore. See, that was where I made my mistake. He needed so badly to embark on this crusade to have another child that I didn't listen to my inner voice. I told myself my reservations were about being stunned and stung and afraid, that I'd get over it. Plus, now Chris was suddenly the strong one again, and I liked that. And so I went along. Put on so many fake smiles, my face hurt. I smiled at myself like an idiot in the mirror because I heard somewhere that the physical act of smiling, whether you mean it or not, improves your mood. Every time I did that, it was like biting down on a moldy lemon. All of that bile ran down into my stomach. No one knew I was absorbing it all myself. Even Penny—she sensed it, but I wouldn't tell her. I just said I was battling through."

"So if Chris gets in the grip of this vision again," I said, "you want to make sure you're out of its reach."

Janet folded her hands. She was clear-eyed now. "I won't sacrifice myself in order to carry on the Claypool line. This is terrible to say, but in some way I feel I'm finally free. Cursed forever, condemned for what we did to Margaret—but still, free."

"Cursed—you used that word before."

"Oh, Bill." She let out an enormous, collapsing breath. "It was my first instinct after Helen died. It was so clear to me that our union was cursed. That sounds irrational, but there's no other way to put it. I told myself it would eventually go away. But it didn't. It was like a fly buzzing around my head. It was superstitious, and at the same time I couldn't deny that it was *true*. I almost forgot about it once Margy was born. But now it's loud and clear again."

Everything that Janet had said made sense but this. It seemed unfair to read such a destiny into what was, after all, with Helen, an accident. "Where does that leave Margy?" I demanded. "On the one hand, you said she was a miracle. I believe that. Her personality, the way she bore her troubles, was incredible. It *inspires* me, Janet. That might be a corny thing to say, but I just said it. And you're trying to tell me she was a mistake, she was cursed from the beginning?"

"Both are true," she said, her eyes brimming. "In some terrible way, we asked for this. I can't talk about regrets—that's too small a word. I can't look back, only forward, or I'll shrivel up and die. But it's clear to me now that we shouldn't have tried again."

"Are you saying you're relieved she's gone?" It was a harsh question, but Janet seemed to be consigning Margy to some kind of permanent doom.

"Don't make me explain, Bill." Tears rolled out of her eyes. "It's so hard to talk about. Oh my God, I miss her. I loved her needs—her normal needs, the ones not connected to her illnesses. What a pleasure it was to change her diaper, or feed her, or button her shirt. I loved those little things so much. Now I even miss the trips to the doctor. I dream about her all the time. I see her, actually see her, coming around a corner, or tripping into the kitchen, or swinging on a swing. I can't even look at a playground, or a school, or a hospital. I detour blocks out of my way to avoid them. I have special routes I take, zigzagging through the city."

"I'm sorry, Janet. I don't mean to make you feel worse. I miss her, too. I didn't realize how incredible she was until she was gone." I reached out and took her hand. She was crying. Tears sprang to my eyes, too.

"It's all right," she said after a minute. "We're all reacting to the situation differently. We have to be true to ourselves. I found that out the hard way."

She wiped her eyes and got up to make some tea. I stayed and drank a cup with her. We shifted to the relatively easier subject of what might be happening to Chris at the police station. The detective and someone from the DA's office would speak to him and Mitch about the charges, giving each side a chance to press their advantage. Chris would be arraigned before a judge and would have to enter a plea. Bail would be set. Chris and his lawyer would arrange to post the bail. With any luck, he might be able to come home this afternoon.

She nodded. It was time for me to go. I asked if I should check in on her later to make sure everything was all right. She said she'd call me. I gave her my cell phone number. We hugged each other, and I left.

It was only as I walked down the steps to my car that I remembered the guy in the red pickup. I didn't have the heart to go back in and grill Janet all over again.

14

As much as my style mixed with Cole's like, say, lemon with milk, there was a certain comfort in going to him when things got bad. He had the answer for every situation. If ever you needed something taken care of, Uncle Cole was the man.

Even my mother admitted that. I'd been keeping her posted by email. After I relayed the news about Margaret, she'd written from a café in Crete asking if she ought to rush back for the service. I did her the favor, as she'd done for me when Helen died, of telling her she should not cut her trip short. Chris and Cole were at each other's throats, I said, and the whole scene would drive her crazy. She'd always felt sympathy and concern for Chris, watching the moldable young child being shaped in Cole's image. She advised me not to spurn Cole's help, but to believe only half of what he said. She meant it as a literal statistic.

My favorite way to approach Cole, the man who could not be surprised, was when I knew something he didn't. So when I told his secretary I had to see him, and she told me he was lunching at Bertolucci's, an old-style Italian restaurant in South City, I rushed right over.

There he sat with his cronies at a large round table in the dining room. Cole was a man among men, and never more so than at a table like this, one full of men who would command any normal dining party. He was regaling them with a story about a deal in Ireland several years ago, whose consummation, as he told it, hinged on his ability to drink dram after dram while losing neither the power of speech nor control of his bladder. The old nursery rhyme, which Cole himself loved to lead us in, came back to me: *Old King Cole was a merry old soul, and a merry old soul was he . . .*

Cole's face crumpled into a momentary expression of disapproval at my presence. He picked up his martini and excused himself from the table with a remark about his intrepid nephew trailing him like a bloodhound. We left the white tablecloths and heaping pasta plates of the dining room for a booth in the windowless bar. There I told Cole that Chris had been arrested.

He did not, of course, show surprise. But my assumption that he would take matters into his own hands proved wrong. He sat back on the banquette and took a sip of his drink, with a little smack of his lips, before responding. "I'm sorry for this. It's a travesty. The DA's office is out of control. I hope Chris is not in too bad shape?"

"He was oddly cheerful," I said.

"If there's one thing cops hate, it's not being taken seriously."

"Maybe they would take him seriously if they heard from the FBI. Now's the time to lay that card on the table."

Cole grunted. "Bill, I'm sorry if I gave you the impression that I run the bureau. They'll make their move when they're ready."

"You did promise me your files today on what they're investigating."

"It *is* Monday, isn't it? I've got quite a lot on my plate. We're waiting to hear back about our Jakarta proposal. It's only because of Wilson's superlative work that I can be enjoying myself here right now." He raised his glass again.

"And Chris's," I said.

"He laid the groundwork, certainly. But Leonard has carried it through."

Cole caught the look on my face. I was waiting for him to say that Chris had done something brilliant to cinch the deal. Instead he asked, "Has Chris been doing more recent work that I don't know about?"

"I have no idea."

"I see," Cole said, and left it at that, saving me from lying about Chris being in the office yesterday. "Again," he went on, "I appreciate how you're helping Chris. He's put himself beyond my reach. I have no choice but to respect that. He's testing his wings."

"Now's the time to step in before he falls."

"He's going through a rebellious phase, Bill. He needs to prove he can take care of himself. Good for him. I can't say I wasn't offended by his behavior at the memorial service—no, not offended, *outraged*—but he'll apologize, and we'll get over it."

I decided against trying to explain Chris's behavior at the service. I understood it but couldn't excuse it, and patching up their relationship wasn't my job. Finding out who caused Margaret's death was. "I saw George Sabell yesterday," I said. "You promised to tell me more about his patron, Austin Remly."

Cole's thick fingers dug the olive out of the glass. "I'm here for lunch with my friends and colleagues. Do you know what I've had to eat so far?" He bit off half the olive and displayed the other half to me. "This much."

"The clinic had reasons to kidnap Margy," I said. "They were afraid Chris and Janet would come after them for the mistakes

Sabell made with her. Sabell himself may not have been in on the abduction, but the clinic's security force could have done it and tried to make it look like a triad job. Is Remly the one in charge of security there?"

Cole had his eye on the bartender. As soon as I stopped speaking, he lifted a finger and called out, "Boodle's."

"Are you just going to sit here and let Chris go down for this?" I demanded.

Cole chuckled. "Many steps are to come before a trial, much less a conviction. It's good for him to fight for himself. He's the one who created this mess. Your generation flabbergasts me sometimes. It's not enough to have children, you have to have them when they're *convenient*. Not only that, the children must be precocious and adorable, yet eccentric, like those brats that smart-aleck fellow wrote about. Had a French name—Salinger, I think. I'd be happy not to meet another little Zooey for as long as I live. I hate those characters and their smugness, as if life's a parlor game of precious little turns of phrase. What happened to virtues like courage? Loyalty? Plain speaking?"

I gazed at Cole's empty glass and wondered what number martini he was on. He waved dismissively. "Never mind," he said. "I'm talking to the wrong guy. Listen, Harry Harvey will keep tabs on the case. Otherwise, I'm afraid Christopher is on his own."

That was more true than Cole knew. I was still reeling from finding out from Janet this morning that she was on the verge of deserting Chris. The creases in Cole's forehead wrinkled into a kind of smile. It occurred to me that if the case got into the papers in a big way, Chris's reputation would be ruined. The only possible employment he'd find would be with Claypool Construction Engineering.

"I'm not sure a triad-type gang did it," I said. "They would have made more of a show of grabbing Margy. Sabell's been looking into her death. He thinks it wasn't an accident. If gangsters killed her, they wouldn't use subtle means."

Cole slid out of the booth. I did the same. "It's been a pleasure talking with you, Bill."

He held out his hand. I shook it and held it. "What kind of deal did you make with Sabell? He admitted you were involved in Margy's conception."

The pit on his forehead turned angry, then he relented. "I merely paid some of Christopher's bills," Cole said, removing his hand from my grip. "Sabell charged astronomical fees. There was no need for Chris to know of my help. It would have embarrassed him."

"How closely does Austin Remly manage the clinic's security?"

Cole grunted. "You may be on to something there. Remly made his money on defense research contracts. He helped design the FBI's Carnivore software—what do they call it now? Totalitarian Information Awareness? Anyway, the clinic's his pet retirement project. Thinks he can live forever, I hear. I can't imagine he'd leave security to anyone other than himself. I know someone who knows him. I'll get you his number."

"How about getting it right now?"

The bartender himself brought Cole's martini. Cole turned to take it, lifted the glass in my direction, sipped off the brim, and went into the dining room without answering. Following him would do no good. He'd say the number was back at the office.

The CCE office was not far away. I drove back there, went up to the fourth floor, and told Cole's secretary that he wanted her to give me the name and number of his contact to Austin Remly.

She didn't recognize the name. "It'd be on his personal Rolodex."

"Can we check it?"

She smiled. "I'm sorry, I used an old-fashioned word. There's no physical Rolodex. It's on his PDA, which he took with him."

» » » » »

Clem was in her chair back at the office. She'd done research of her own on Austin Remly. His company specialized in cracking encryption software. "The Defense Department hires him to demonstrate how to crack the codes so that they can make better ones. He's got inside information on how the safekeepers design their encryption locks at the same time his business is to make the tools to pry them open. He also got in on this DARPA initiative, the Q Project, to track every single byte in cyberspace. Intercept, analyze, report."

"Yeah, Cole mentioned he worked on Carnivore, which they've renamed something else now."

"You've been with Cole all this time?"

"No. The arrest finally came." I gave Clem a short version of what had happened with Chris, then my conversations with Cole and Janet. "It sounds like Chris nearly cracked up after they lost Helen. I'm a little worried about what'll happen if Janet leaves him this time."

"He might feel the same way about her," Clem said.

"I don't think so. He's following the same pattern as the first time. He's looking for ways to counteract the loss. Every once in a while he realizes he has to just sit still with it—but he can't. He's lashing out at Claypool Construction right now. Cole admitted, by the way, that he was in contact with Sabell during the process of creating Margy. Says all he did was pay the bills."

"He must have taken his pound of flesh."

"You'd think so. But if Cole was pulling the strings, Margy would have been a boy, no question. Something Janet said surprised me, too. Sabell didn't extract any eggs from her. Supposedly he had frozen eggs from the first time."

"Fresh ones are a lot better," Clem said.

"We need to find out if Sabell's tinkered with the genes of his other clients. How's your fertility support group coming?"

Clem sighed. "We're in scheduling hell. These women are so busy, they don't have lives. One of them actually said we should have hot-synched our PDAs at the clinic. I've asked each of them separately about genetic engineering of their babies. None of them copped to it."

"Did you get anything more on Sabell?"

"One thing. I'm glad you came back when you did, because I set up a meeting with a group called GenVigil in"— she consulted her watch—"forty-five minutes. They're biotech watchdogs, a funny combination of religious folk and environmentalists. The Sabell Clinic is on their 'dangerous science' list. Want to come with me?"

I nodded. She paused, tossed her hair, and shifted her weight. She was back in a Western shirt today, with form-fitting jeans and the cowboy boots. The shift was mighty nice. She did it again and said, "Speaking of expenses—I've got all the receipts. What were you thinking of in terms of the pay schedule?"

"I got my check. Didn't you get yours?" I kept a straight face until Clem laughed. Then I said, "The fact is, I haven't billed Chris yet. According to the cops, he used most of his money on treatments for Margaret."

"Soooo—that means I'm working for free?"

"Not at all. I'll write you a check today."

"Thanks. There are a few, uh, *things* I need to take care of."

My brain scrambled to calculate whether the check would bounce back to me. I'd figure something out. Credit-card offers, primary funding source for the independent filmmaker, poured in every day. "Just write up your invoice, expenses included," I said. "Have you had any luck with Ulla and Wayne?"

"I think she's willing to point out where the abduction happened. It was unclear whether she'd go in person with us or just draw a map."

"I'll call Wayne again. Where do we meet these GenVigil people?"

"A little waterside park on Oyster Point. They didn't want us in their office. As if we might be spies or something."

I put on my old leather-collared hunting coat, Clem put on a tattered leather bombardier jacket, and we went out to the Scout. I'd never been to Oyster Point, a thumbnail of a park jutting into the bay alongside South San Francisco. Clem knew the place, though, and ticked off the names of biotech companies we passed on the way: Amgen, Cellegy, Exelixis. The park itself was a windswept bit of grass with a few widely spaced trees, a marina, a pier, and a snack bar. We bought ourselves hot dogs at the snack bar and loitered near the pier. A woman in her twenties, wearing a Gore-Tex jacket, approached us. Her name was Cynthia. A long plait of brown hair disappeared under the rolled hood of her jacket. Our hot dogs got a disapproving glance as she established that we were the ones she was meeting. We stuffed the rest of the dogs into our mouths and followed Cynthia to a bench where we were introduced to a man named Timothy.

"You mean *Father* Timothy," Clem said, extending her hand.

"Tim is fine," the man said, shaking Clem's hand, then mine. He was mid-fiftyish, in a tweed jacket and pressed slacks. His gray eyes crinkled with good-natured concern, while his long mouth was set in a confident but amiable line. "Would you like to walk?"

"Is that Genentech down there?" I said. I was looking south, across a small rock-lined cove, to a cluster of glass-and-concrete buildings stepping up a hill above the bay.

"Sure is," Clem answered, tucking a strand of hair behind her ear. The wind, whipping off the water, kept blowing her hair into her eyes.

"An appropriate destination," Tim said. He led the way along a broad walk, hands clasped behind his back. I fell into step beside him. Clem and Cynthia paired up behind us.

I got right to the point and asked Tim, "So what's George Sabell up to at his laboratory?"

Cynthia's voice cut in. "Why don't you tell us who you are and why you want to know?"

"We visited Sabell at his house yesterday," I retorted over my shoulder. "You're the ones who stand to benefit from this meeting."

Tim looked pensively out at the water. "The birth of a child used to be a marvelous mystery," he said. "A new and unknown person entered your life. A stranger who was instantly one of the family. We're in the process of draining the miracle of its mystery. *We* ourselves, through our technology, are the miracle now, and that's a dangerous thing. Like Icarus, we're intoxicated with our powers."

Tim was scoping us out. Diplomatically, under the guise of philosophy, but drawing out our views before he shared any intelligence, just as Sabell had done.

"My cousin and his wife took their chances in the genetic lottery the first time around," I said. "Their daughter died of cystic fibrosis. You can't blame them for asking science to improve the odds the second time."

"Ah, so it's a family affair," Tim said. "My sympathies to your cousin. However, this technology has the power to damage not just a few, but *every single* child in the future. To turn them into *creatures* manufactured, not begotten, according to the imperfect will and whims of the parent, scientist, or whoever controls the means of reproduction."

"You've hit the nail on the head in my cousin's case," I began.

"Everything's being turned into a commodity," Cynthia interrupted. "The trees. The earth. Animals. Us—'human resources' to be engineered. Our eggs and sperm are bought and sold on the market. Soon we'll be nothing more than products of the bioindustrial process. Under corporate control that is, not incidentally, primarily male."

"Kind of like the clergy," Clem said to Cynthia, "who also like to tell us what to do with our wombs. You two are sort of an odd couple, aren't you?"

I was relieved to see Cynthia's young, serious face break into a smile. "We learn a lot from each other. He believes life is sacred because God created it, I believe life is sacred because Mother Earth did. What's at stake right now is important enough that we can set aside our differences. The bottom line is, either you value human beings intrinsically, or you see them as a means to an end."

"So, Father," Clem pressed, "you don't mind if she worships trees and dances naked around pagan bonfires?"

His fingers fluttered in the air. "Dance away! I don't view God as being so small-minded."

"I'd think the cool thing about this new technology, for you, is that it allows for virgin births. If I remember my Bible, that's how Christ was born. Parthenogenesis."

I rolled my eyes at Clem. Tim turned to indulge her with a brief smile. "I hope your encounter with Scripture was not an unpleasant experience."

"I suppose it wasn't all the Bible's fault. It was the people who used it against me."

"I'm sorry. In the wrong hands, it can be dangerous."

"Yeah, people get to believing they've got absolute right on their side. Vigilante types," I said, watching Tim. Sabell had used the word, and it had occurred to me how close it was to GenVigil's name. The Father seemed fairly open-minded, but I wondered if it was an act and this meeting was all about getting inside information for some kind of raid against Sabell.

He touched my arm and turned to face me, his mild gray eyes boring into mine. "We are on a 'vigil,' a watch. Our mission is to make the public aware of what's going on in labs like Sabell's. We're completely opposed to violence. Do you understand?"

"How about making me aware of what's going in Sabell's lab?" I said, walking again. "We've seen your Web site. We agree that he's tinkering with embryonic genes. We need details."

"As do we," the Father said calmly. "But we can't betray our sources. How do we know you're not, in fact, working for the clinic?"

"Because I believe they killed my three-year-old cousin." I'd decided to tell them my story. If they proved to be fanatics, Remly's security force would have to deal with it. I told them about Margaret. Sabell had knocked out the cystic fibrosis mutation, but he'd done more, too, perhaps inserting exogenous DNA into her chromosomes. I needed to know what that more could be.

"If we tell you," Cynthia said, "will your cousin's family go public and expose what the clinic is doing?"

"That's up to them. It could be hard to keep it out of the papers in the long run."

"You mentioned that Sabell offered to treat Margaret after she was born. Did he say how?" Tim asked.

"Only that it was next-generation. I suppose he could have meant stem cell therapies."

"We've tracked a lot of communication between Sabell and researchers in the embryonic stem cell field, especially one named Krempe. The clinic's got access to plenty of embryos. We believe Sabell creates extra embryos for research he does in his lab up in the hills. Embryos the parents never know exist. Did you get a look at that lab?"

"No," I said, "he took us on a wild-goose chase in a labyrinth with a gravestone at the center. His gravestone."

"I imagine he sees himself as the master of life and death. A common wish, one shared by his patron. Goethe said it best: 'Men incapable of mastering themselves are all too ready masterfully to bend their neighbor's will to their own.' Austin Remly believes he can bend DNA to achieve a long, if not endless, life."

"And the Uterus Police think they can bend women to theirs," Clem interjected.

"Clem, you've already made your point," I said impatiently.

"It's all right," Tim said. "Cynthia and I have agreed to disagree on certain subjects. The fact is, abortion will become a mere footnote compared to what's brewing now. People aren't sure yet how they feel about genetic engineering. It hasn't delivered on its medical promises. We simply want to inform them what's being done. Human life is being treated like a science experiment. Dr. Sabell is brilliant, we acknowledge, but still not smart enough to know all the consequences of manipulating the human germ line."

"Not with my cousin—" I halted and put a finger to my lips. We were crossing the arc of the rock-lined cove. To our left, a family of ducks played in the water. But to our right, in a marsh of tall reeds, I caught a flash of glass or metal. Clem peered through the stalks with me. A thin rustling sounded a few yards away. I stepped closer. Someone grabbed my coat from behind, holding me back.

"That's sensitive habitat," Cynthia scolded. "Nothing but birds and animals in there."

"Birds and animals don't have cameras. Or guns," I said. "Was it one of your people?"

She checked with Tim and he shook his head. Clem turned away from the reeds and said to me, "Whatever, whoever, it was, they're gone."

I gave her a nod. She returned it. She'd be on watch. The four of us started along the path again, our steps more measured. "You were about to tell me about Sabell and Remly," I said. "We've got no background on the doctor. Where did he come from?"

"Isn't it obvious?" Cynthia said. "A petri dish."

Tim gave a brief chuckle, then said, "He enjoys his shroud of mystery. We've tracked down some former colleagues and verified a few facts. His mother died giving birth in some dark corner of Europe following World War II; his father's whereabouts were unknown. Young George went from orphanage to orphanage, foster home to foster home, a sort of tour of humanity. He did not like what he saw. Perhaps that's what convinced him the species was in need of dire improvement. He stowed away on a freighter to America and survived on the streets of Baltimore and D.C., living the life of a runaway. But he never lost an inner belief in his talents and intellect, and never ceased to stimulate them. He was an autodidact, learning English quickly, spending his days in the public library. At some point in his teens, when he was camping out in Rock Creek Park, a group of kids from an elite private school befriended him. He fascinated them; they helped him find food, shelter, and ultimately a scholarship to the school. The faculty viewed him as a prodigy. He went on to Johns Hopkins, where he stayed for several years, earning an M.D./Ph.D. But his troubled life kept catching up. He toiled in obscurity, conducting embryological and oocyte research. Again and again his relationships with his mentors blew up and Sabell had to move on. Using new names, he managed to charm his way into clinical positions, offering tragedy-laden explanations for taking on a new identity—tales of thugs from old Europe on his trail for some crime of his father's. His results dazzled the clinics. But he was never able to stay for long. Slowly he moved west: Kentucky, Chicago, Houston, Phoenix, and finally the Bay Area. Here he hooked up with Remly. The fit was perfect: Remly wanted the research to be secret and Sabell wanted his own lab, with no administration to answer to. He's been here for nine years now, probing, unfettered, the mysteries of human conception."

"What exactly is Remly looking for in this research?" I asked.

"Austin Remly aims to be the founder of, literally, a new breed. It's been called the GenRich, the GenElect, and so on. Remly's word for it is *genocracy:* a genetic aristocracy. He fought his way up from a roughneck background in Texas to win a scholarship to Carnegie Mellon, then after a few years at DIA, went on to make himself a fortune in computer cryptography. As he approached the age of sixty, he turned to bigger things. He has a visceral, almost pathological, hatred of royal families. Politically, he should love Bush the younger, but Remly despises him for his privilege, as well as for his views on embryo research. Remly's dream is to create a true genetic aristocracy, as opposed to the bogus royalty of bloodlines. A scientific aristocracy based on testably superior genes. Much like the old concept of eugenics, except now we are gaining the power to actually carry out such a program. Remly and Sabell have pulled themselves up from nothing. They understand each other. They also have something to prove."

"You said that Remly wanted to live forever."

"That's his ultimate goal. Stem cell research may yield ways to rejuvenate his tissues as they age. He recognizes those advances may come too late for him, so we believe he's embarked on a backup plan. We think Remly's having Sabell work on cloning him. Have you collected any evidence in that direction?"

"Sabell disparaged cloning. He thinks it's an atavistic impulse."

"Indeed," Tim said. "The puerile ego satisfaction of being mirrored, perfectly doubled."

"Didn't God create man in his image?" Clem asked.

Tim laughed gamely. "God has powers at his disposal which he does not put at ours. The fact is, we don't know ourselves well enough to go about making copies, much less design better versions, turning humans into a set of features that can be selected and deselected, like on a car. There's a subconscious idea that we'd somehow own our clone, but we don't know ourselves well enough to own even ourselves—not without God's grace."

"Or Gaia's," Cynthia injected. "We've been doing all the talking, Bill. Suppose you shed some light on Sabell now."

"Yeah, well, the cloning idea's got me thinking. Margaret did look a lot like her predecessor, Helen. But they weren't copies. Different hair color, different personalities, different medical conditions. That doesn't mean Sabell didn't test his cloning technique on Margaret. Correct me on the science here, but couldn't he have taken some of Helen's cells, swapped out a few genes, and then swapped the nucleus of one of those cells into Janet's egg? Then just give the egg a jolt and it starts growing."

"Yes and no," Cynthia answered. "Theoretically you can knock genes in or out of a somatic cell—say, a skin cell from Helen—but it's complicated. That also raises the question of how he would have obtained and preserved one of Helen's cells. If she had embryo-sisters in the deep freeze, he might have used them. Their cells would be easier to manipulate. That's not cloning, exactly, but close enough. He'd still do the nuclear transfer of the frozen embryo's DNA into the mother's egg and then try to get a viable fetus."

"Come to think of it, why even bother with the mother's egg?" I said. "Sabell extracted no new eggs to produce Margaret. He said he'd use her mother's previously frozen ones. But if he drew the nucleus, which had both parents' DNA, from an embryo-sister of Helen's, then any old host egg would do. Or rather, young host egg."

"You've got something there, Mr. Damen," Clem said.

"Possibly," Cynthia said. "It takes a boatload of eggs to conduct this kind of research. Rarest cell in the body. Human ones aren't easy to come by. They're worth ten, twenty thousand on the open market."

"Ex ovo omnia," Tim said. "From an egg, everything."

"Still, Sabell's known as the man with the magic hands when it comes to embryo and oocyte manipulation," Cynthia continued. "He's devised some legendary methods of oocyte culture and preservation. And I do mean legendary: No one's sure how they work, but they're dying to know. Rumor has it Sabell's going to sit in on a very exclusive symposium at Stanford on Thursday and Friday. He might spill some beans there."

"Remly's authorized that?" Clem asked.

"There's the rub," Tim said. "Remly wants him to keep his mouth shut, of course. But Sabell craves recognition—not from the public, but from a tiny elite who matter to him. He won't give away major secrets. Just a few tidbits to make them envious. It'll still make Remly unhappy."

"One more thing fits your scenario," Cynthia said to me. "You mentioned a variety of ailments from which Margaret suffered. They're not quite the same, but similar to, problems you see with cloned animals. The theory is they're connected to genetic imprinting, a complex patty-cake game where genes from the mother and the father are switched on and off in a certain order during the embryonic development process. The gametes play a role in this process. If the egg's not the mother's and there's no sperm from the father, the imprinting process goes awry. Nature elaborated it over the course of three billion years. I don't know why we think we should mess with it."

"What about the clinic's security force?" I asked. "I assume Remly controls it?"

Tim looked back at Cynthia, who gave a small shrug. "All we know about the security arrangements is that they're very strict," he said.

The path had emerged from the cove. We arrived at the green lawns and red buildings of the Genentech campus. It was mid-afternoon, but a group of employees were batting a volleyball back and forth over a net. We slowed our pace. Clem walked in half a circle, still on the lookout. I relaxed a little. No stalkers were in sight.

Clem stopped, facing Tim and Cynthia. "Nice place, huh? You guys can just stroll in and do some watchdogging. No fences or guards."

Tim smiled at her assumption. "Not on the lawn, at least. Listen, we don't tar the entire industry with the same brush. It's up to the investors in any one company to decide if their work's going to bear fruit. Our job is to pinpoint the few at the frontiers who are crossing the line. They tend to be privately funded, working in secret alleys and dark laboratory lairs, like the alchemists of old."

"Don't start with that, now," Clem objected. "Modern science has quite a different spirit. George Sabell might fit that bill, but I know plenty of scientists in the field. They're not Frankensteins."

"Not knowingly," Tim said, a flicker of apology crossing his face. "Look, whatever our differences, I think we can help each other. The scenario you've outlined hints at the clinic's weakest point. Sabell and Remly have different interests and different agendas. Their paths inevitably will diverge."

"That's when we strike," Cynthia said. "Margaret may be the bone that sticks in their throats. The time is coming sooner than we thought."

"So we've been helpful to you after all," I said.

She rewarded me with a smile. "We'll be in touch."

15

"Tell me I'm not crazy," I said to Clem.

"You're not crazy, Mr. Damen. Whatever was in those reeds was way bigger than a duck."

"Thank you." We were speeding across the Peninsula to Montoya County Park, where Margaret had been abducted. My cell phone had buzzed as we'd started to walk back to the Oyster Point parking lot. It was Wayne, with the unexpected news that Ulla was ready to show us where the incident had occurred. Clem and I dashed back to the Scout, sparing ourselves further homilies from Tim and Cynthia. They were all right, actually, though I wished they'd been more reticent about thrusting their belief systems at us.

"You think Sabell really used nuclear transfer technology on Margaret?" Clem asked.

"I've got to research this stuff. Nuclear transfer is when you suck the nucleus with its chromosomes out of one organism's cell and insert it into another's egg, which you stimulate to start dividing as if fertilized, right? The egg's reprogrammed with the donor organism's DNA. No one's done it before in humans."

"Oh yes they have. A Korean lab transferred a cumulus cell into an enucleated egg and got a ball of cells growing. Like most of the legit research in the field, it's all about stem cells, not reproduction. They're looking for the pluripotent cells in early embryos, cells that can differentiate into any kind of tissue."

"How come you know so damned much about this field, anyway?"

"I told you," she said, "I've had many incarnations. I was a blastocyst once myself."

"The entire universe was an infinitely hot and dense dot. Once."

"A blastocyst is probably the stage Helen's frozen embryo sisters would have been. Did a little bell go off in your head when Cynthia asked where Sabell would get cells from Helen?"

"A big bell. He got tissue from Margaret at her autopsy. I'm wondering if Helen had an autopsy, and where Sabell was when it happened."

Clem nodded, and my phone rang again. It was Wayne. "I'm taking the exit onto 280 right now," I told him. "We'll be in the convenience store parking lot where you said to wait in about ten minutes. Orange Scout, you can't miss it."

As before, meeting Ulla was fraught with cloak-and-dagger protocol that involved us waiting around to receive further instructions. I supposed Wayne had people watching the store to make sure no one else was with us. Clem and I sat in the parking lot for twenty minutes before Wayne called and permitted us to proceed along the frontage road to a cross street near the park. We waited there again until we were instructed to get out of the car, walk down one block, and duck through a hole in a wire fence. I kept him on the phone as we went down the street. Clem found the small gap in the fence and stretched it open. I went through, then held it open for her.

We were in the park now, at the edge of a steep, redwood-forested slope. Wayne told me to head due south, downhill. The soft earth gave way under our heels. We leaned back to keep our balance. It was easy to see how a little girl could disappear in here. The slope was cut into small ravines, one hidden from the other, the whole place made dark and silent by the towering canopy.

"Hold up," Wayne said through my phone. "There's someone by the fence."

I whispered to Clem to duck behind a tree. A minute went by, and I looked back up the hill. "I don't see anyone," I said to Wayne.

"He's moving on," Wayne said. "Young guy wearing a coat and cargo pants—getting a jet phone out of his pocket now. Dark cap. Watch for him."

"Son of a bitch," I said. "Sorry, Wayne, not you. I think I know who it is. Ignore him. We're coming down the hill."

As we neared the bottom, two blond heads flickered between the tree branches. "Go to your left," Wayne said through the phone.

We traversed the steep hill. Below, the two heads tracked in the same direction along a grassy field. "Hey, Wayne," I said into the phone, "look up, to your left."

Wayne glanced up and I waved to him. Clem and I ran the rest of the way down. I could only pray that Ulla didn't recognize me. I put up the collar of my coat and let my features relax into a bland putty. She hung back a few paces as Wayne greeted us. He didn't recognize "Sylvia" at first in her jeans and leather jacket.

Clem waved to Ulla and said, "Hello, it's me, how are you?"

Ulla came forward and they gave each other double-cheek kisses. I shook Wayne's hand. He introduced me to Ulla as "Dave." She knew she'd met me but couldn't place where. I gave her memory a push in the wrong direction, reciting a fake name and claiming we'd run into each other in Stern Grove. I had two kids of my own and was terribly sorry about Margaret.

Ulla replied with a demure thank-you. Her small, pale moon of a face seemed both harder and more delicate. Her blue eyes were cowled with suspicion and a lingering hurt.

Wayne was busy grinning at me, thinking he'd discovered my real name. I asked him, "What other names do you go by, Wayne?"

"Geert," he said. I tried to repeat the throat-clearing sound he'd just made. He told me to stick with Wayne. He'd gotten to like it. "Let's move," he said. "We don't want to be in this park any longer than we have to."

"Just show us where it happened," I said. "We'll take it from there."

We walked along the edge of the woods. The grassy field ended in a narrow horseshoe where the hillside curved to form a hollow. Ulla pointed to a swingset back in the other direction. "That's where we were when the man came and said he lost his dog. He brought us to this spot and said the dog went up into the woods."

I stepped back a few paces, took my digital camera from my pocket, and snapped pictures of the hollow, then the swingset. This corner of the park was deserted, as Ulla said it had been that Friday.

We went into the trees at the center of the hollow. The hill-side was less steep here. "I think this is about the path we took," Ulla said, picking her way through a line of Scotch broom that separated the field from the woods.

The underbrush in the hollow was thicker than on the more angled slopes. "I can see how you'd lose sight of someone in here," I said. "Where's the last spot you remember seeing Margaret?"

Ulla had stopped. Her face was melting into tears. "I don't know! That's the whole problem. I came with the police and it was the same thing. The bushes, the trees, they all look alike." The Swedish lilt grew stronger as she spoke. "My eye was looking for the dog, so I didn't notice where I was. The man went off that way"— she flung a hand to her right—"and I guess Margaret did, too. I ran up and down, through the bushes. I was blind, just looking for her desperately, and then—somewhere over there—I ran back down to the grass, calling for help."

"Can we go a little farther uphill?" I said. "Maybe you'll recognize something from before you started running."

She stared up the hill as if at an impenetrable mountain range. "No," she said. "I tried already. I'm sorry. I can't go back in."

I stepped closer, but Wayne elbowed his way between us. "You heard her, Dave. She's already made a big favor to you."

"How about the old man, then?" I said. "Tell us more about him."

Ulla wiped away a few tears. "He was in a wool coat. Dark, so he was hard to see in here. He wore a hat with a band around it—the kind the men in the old movies did. He had a bushy white mustache. His eyes were watery, pleading—he seemed so unhappy to lose his dog. Running shoes on his feet. I noticed them because they didn't go with the rest of his clothes."

Wayne took her shoulders and started to lead her down the hill. "Good luck, Dave," he called back up to us.

"Yeah. Thanks," I said. Clem called good-bye to Ulla, who gave a weak wave. We had a lot of territory to comb through.

"Are we going to find anything the police haven't?" Clem asked.

"We won't know unless we try," I said.

I was stopped by a scream from below. It was Ulla. She and Wayne had reached the swingset and, like a return of her original nightmare, two men in dark clothes were approaching from separate angles. I tried to bring their features into focus, but they were blurred. Again, stockings covered their faces, as if erasing their humanity. Wayne pushed Ulla, telling her to run. Ulla cringed, trying to make herself small. The men approached faster, trotting. Wayne shoved Ulla in our direction. She began to run. I tossed my phone to Clem, told her to dial 911, and moved down the hill in a crouch, using the bushes for cover. Wayne retreated from the swingset, gauging the point at which the two men would converge. They broke into a run, one coming at Wayne, the other at Ulla. Wayne sprinted in Ulla's direction but was intercepted by the man coming after him. The other man, who'd come from the woods where we'd descended, streaked for Ulla.

The great thing about learning a sport when you're young is that you can recall your skills instantly. I played safety on the football team until high school. The position was all about making tackles in the open field. Still hidden by the bushes, I scrambled closer to the edge of the grass. Ulla ran toward me. I waited until the second man was within ten yards, then bolted. I flew off my feet to hit the guy in the midsection with my left shoulder. His legs shot into the air and his body folded in two. He hit the ground hard on his back. An involuntary cry escaped his lungs. I pushed myself into a semi-sitting position and came down hard on him again with a fist to one stockinged eye, then the other. He screamed. I jumped off, gave him a kick in the ribs just to make sure, and took off after Ulla into the woods.

Another shout came from above. It was Clem. I raced past Ulla. A third man, who'd come from the top of the hollow, grappled with her. She lashed out with everything she had, kicks, elbows, fists. He ducked away and reached to his ankle for a weapon.

"Don't!" she shouted at him. "The cops are coming!"

I searched desperately for a weapon of my own. The best I could do was a branch, three feet long, two inches round, with a spray of leaves on the end. I charged up the hill as he pulled a knife from the sheath on his ankle. He backed up when he saw me coming from the new angle, putting me and Clem at equal distances from himself.

I waved my branch at him. A radio on his belt crackled. *"Get Snoose!"*

His eyes switched to Ulla, who was behind and below me. He circled down the hill away from me and Clem.

"Come up here, Ulla!" I cried. "Hurry!"

She ran to me. The guy with the knife cut a radius into his circle. I went to cut that radius off.

"Get Snoose!" the radio commanded again.

"You two go! Fast!" I ordered.

Clem grabbed Ulla by the hand and pulled her uphill. I jumped in front of the knife man. He slashed, surprising me with his quickness and how much ground he covered. Only my bit of wood saved me from being sliced.

"Make me do it again," he said in a dirty, guttural voice.

Sirens wailed. The deformed features under the stocking mask shifted like quicksand, not in my favor. He wanted to kill me now, regardless. But he was still gasping, gathering breath for the attack. I took the opening and jumped quickly to my left, finding protection behind a young redwood. As he approached, I slid away to the other side of the tree and sprinted down the hill. On the grass, I saw Wayne motionless near the swingset. His guy was coming for me now. I looked back up the hill. After hesitating, my guy decided to go after the two women. I spun back in that direction. The sirens grew louder.

I raced up the hill, hoping Clem and Ulla had found a way out of the park. I veered to my left, knowing the car was in that direction, but also taking a different line from the guy with the knife. Static from the men's radios crackled through the woods. I stopped to listen. The words were indistinct, but the tone suggested they'd lost visual contact with the two women. I kept going. The hill topped out in a vacant lot of fennel and mud puddles. I jumped onto the wire fence separating the lot from the street and prayed that I would find Clem and Ulla back at the Scout.

» » » » »

Clem and Ulla were there, but not in the situation I had hoped. Ulla cowered near the rear bumper. Clem was shoving a guy in light cargo pants into the street, away from my jeep. He blurted my name with relief. "Bill! Thank God you're all right."

"What the fuck are you doing here, Don?"

"Forget him, Bill," Clem said. "Unlock the car. We gotta go."

"It's the most amazing coincidence," Don began, then gaped at my chest. "Bill, you're hurt!"

I looked down. Under my open jacket, my denim shirt was torn and soaked with blood. I looked inside the collar. The cut was about three inches in length, across my left pec, but superficial, and no longer bleeding. I never felt it.

I unlocked the passenger door and told Ulla to get in. Don followed me like a dog. "Really, man, I was just cruising by—"

I grabbed him by the back of his collar and slammed his face into the rear passenger window. "Put him inside," I said to Clem.

She reached in to unlock the back door. Don tried to twist free and I slammed his face into the window again, smearing it with blood. I opened the door and shoved him inside. He moaned on the floor. I lifted his legs and pushed him the rest of the way in. Clem climbed in after him, sat on the back seat bench, and punched the heel of her cowboy boot into his groin.

"Jesus!" Don screamed. He turned on his side but didn't double up.

"Don't move or I'll crush them for real next time," Clem said.

I got behind the wheel, started the Scout up, and sped out of there. There'd been no sign of our pursuers, but still I zigzagged through the side streets before I found an entrance to Interstate 280.

"What about Geert?" Ulla sobbed. "Is he dead?"

"The police should be there by now. Geert had a couple more friends keeping watch on the perimeter, right?" Ulla nodded and I went on, "They're helping him, too, I hope. Right now we have to get you out of here."

"What are you doing to me?" Don squealed from the floor.

"Your turn is coming," I said.

Ulla, meanwhile, went into a fit of her own. "What have you done to us?!" she screamed at me.

"Don phoned in our position from the sidewalk," I said. "You've been following us since Oyster Point, haven't you, Don?"

"Bill, I'm on your side! I called the cops when I saw what was going down!" His voice was stuffy from the blood in his nostrils. "Who are those guys, anyway? I swear, I was just out—I come to this park all the time—and I happened to see you!"

Don's head was behind my seat. I couldn't see exactly what was happening, but judging from the position of Clem's left knee, her boot heel was poised to come down on his ear.

"Stop it!" Don screamed. "Okay—I swear, Bill—okay, yes, yes, I was tailing you. To demonstrate my surveillance skills. That's all. I had no idea about these commando guys!"

"You're lying," Clem said. She lifted her knee, ready to strike. "He tried to talk me and Ulla into getting in his car."

"I wanted to help!" Don was blubbering now. "I was just trying to impress Bill, man. I want to work for him."

"What about Antarctica?" Clem said, lowering the boot a little.

"It's on hold! I swear! I don't want your job, lady. I can be a contractor, a freelancer—whatever Bill wants!"

"I'm no lady," Clem snarled.

"Don, I can't hire you when you're obviously working for someone else," I said. "Who is it?"

Clem's boot tickled Don's ear. "GenVigil?" she demanded.

He nodded frantically.

"See, Bill?" Clem said. "I told you they're in deeper than they let on."

That was just barely plausible. I couldn't imagine the hoods hiring an amateur like him. "I need your home address," I said to Don.

He reeled it off, a street in the Marina. Clem repeated it.

"Get his phone," I said to Clem. "The address better be accurate."

Clem reached down. Don squirmed and squealed. She extracted his cell phone from a pocket and handed it to me. I hit REDIAL. It rang for a long time, then a standard automated voice said to leave a message.

"Your boy Don's with the police," I reported, "and he's spilling everything."

"You're going to get me killed!" Don wailed as I clicked off and passed the phone back to Clem.

"Oh, but Father Tim's pro-life," Clem said sweetly.

"Give me back my phone," he pleaded.

"Keep it," I instructed Clem. I intended to check out every number stored in it.

During our little talk with Don, I'd been exiting, then getting back on the freeway, watching for a tail. None was evident. To be safe, I took 19th Avenue when we hit the city, then side streets to the Great Highway along Ocean Beach. The breakers rolled in furious, white, foaming.

I pulled over at a deserted stretch of sidewalk near the Beach Chalet. "Get out," I ordered.

Clem pushed open the door and kicked at Don. He tumbled to the pavement.

"Bastards!" Don screamed. "I'm calling the cops! My blood's in your car!"

Clem dangled the phone by its antenna. "We've got your numbers."

Don receded in the rearview mirror, frantically waving his arms. I looked over to Ulla.

Her low lip trembled. "Who *are* you?"

Then it hit me. She'd heard Don call me Bill. If she hadn't figured it out yet, I wouldn't tell her. Not that it really mattered anymore.

"Who are *you,* Ulla?" I demanded. "Why do these guys want you so bad?"

"You can't think that I—!" She burst into tears. They went on for several convincing minutes. I glanced at Clem in the mirror. She rolled her eyes, but bought it, too.

"The guy with the knife had an accent," I said. "He sounded Dutch. Why is that?"

Ulla's face was in her hands. She shook her head that she didn't know.

"Why did they call you Snoose?" I pressed. She shook her head again. "No one's ever called you that before?"

"No!" she said through her fingers.

I asked, more gently, "Did you recognize anything about the men today?"

"No," she repeated. "Only, they were the same type as the gardener."

"We're going to a police station," I said. "Each of us will report what happened. We'll find out how Wayne—I mean, Geert—is. Then I'll take you home."

Ulla didn't reply. She wiped her hands on her pants and stared straight ahead. I began to think about the position I'd put her in and what harm may have come to Wayne. Maybe Cole had been right. Maybe I should have left this to the pros.

» » » » »

"That's going to be a handsome scar," Clem said.

"So I had to go under the knife before you admitted you like my looks," I replied. I was in my bathroom, wringing blood from a washcloth I'd used to clean up my chest. Small beads sprang anew from the cut after I wiped off the dried blood. The cut wasn't terribly deep. Clem held gauze pads in place while I taped them across my chest like small medals.

"Good as new," she said, then slapped me on the butt. She seemed to have gotten a charge out of our adventure in the park.

"You're an adrenaline junkie, aren't you?" I said.

"Everyone's still alive," she answered. "I'm hungry."

It was nearly six o'clock. We went down the long hallway to my kitchen. She sat me down and decided to whip up some grilled cheese sandwiches. I gingerly slid into a seat at the table. The pain from the cut had kicked in. I didn't feel so exhilarated.

Wayne was in the hospital with a broken arm and internal bleeding. After our interview with the police, Ulla had arranged a rendezvous with her other friends. She didn't trust me enough to have me drop her at her safe house. I'd been cautious in returning to my own place, circling the block several times before deciding it was safe to enter.

"Everyone's still alive," I said, "but it could easily be otherwise. There was something strange about the way it played out in the park."

"Yes. Having someone try to kill you is strange," she said, clattering pans in a cupboard. She found a cast-iron pan, put it on the stove, and went to the refrigerator.

"I'm talking about the ninja commando outfits. Same thing they wore on the boat shadowing us on Saturday. Like they're *trying* to play the bad guys."

"You're saying it was an acting job?"

"No, there aren't many actors that handy with a knife."

Clem contemplated a brick of Cheddar on the cutting board. "It *is* weird how all three guys used the same tailor. Would you like your fromage *avec du moisi* or *sans du moisi?*"

"Sans." The blue blotches of mold were visible from here. "The outfits are a real statement. They really don't want us doing what we're doing."

Clem nodded. The sandwiches sizzled in the pan. "You're sure the message was aimed at us, not at Ulla?"

"Ulla, too, to keep her quiet. But Don admitted he followed us."

"We could have gotten more out of him," Clem said.

"Yes. I wish you hadn't suggested GenVigil to him. He grabbed onto it too quickly."

"You're right. Sorry. It seemed likely at the time."

"That's okay. I want him to believe we buy his story. He's our best line to whoever's behind it, if we play him right. That means being nice to him. We're on the hook for assault and battery, if he presses charges. I might even have to pretend to hire him."

"Ugh," Clem said, scooping the sandwiches out with a spatula. She set one on a plate and put it in front of me. It was crisp, golden brown, and oozing yellow cheese. "Remly wouldn't hire a doofus like Don. I know he's your cousin and all, but is there any way Chris could have hired the thugs to scare Ulla out of testifying?"

"No way." I paused, feeling a slight pang at the idea of Chris playing Don off me. "I really don't think so. I think it's whoever did the original deed. Ulla's the only one who had close contact with the kidnappers."

"Until now. Eat your sandwich. Then you'll be ready to go visit Wayne."

"Eager for more action?"

"Mister, I put the *dame* into Damen Camerawork and Investigations."

I chuckled, which hurt, then bit into the sandwich, warm, gooey heaven.

» » » » »

I asked Clem to get the numbers off of Don's mobile. While she did that, I pored over the photographs I'd taken of the security men at the Sabell Clinic. I checked belts, shoes, hair, watches, any detail that might match with what I saw of the men who attacked this afternoon. None did.

I was at my computer in the living room, sharpening the digital images, while Clem sat on the green couch scouring data from Don's phone. Suddenly it went off, playing a ridiculous tune at high volume. Clem fumbled it onto the cushions as if it were a grenade.

"Go ahead and answer it," I said. I knew who it'd be. Don would have already warned his employer we had it.

Clem clicked it on but said nothing. I heard Don's squawk all the way from my desk. "Hello? Hello?" She handed the phone to me. Don railed at me for a few minutes about how he'd had to go to the emergency room, I'd broken his nose, and he had every reason to go to the police and have me arrested. I let him empty his tank. Finally he got around to offering to let me slide, on two conditions. One, that I return his phone. Two, I give him an assignment that provided him a chance to prove his trustworthiness and value. When finally he was quiet, I heard him breathing through his mouth. I allowed that I may have overreacted in a stressful situation and said I hoped his nose would be all right. Clem held her own nose. I promised Don his phone would be returned tonight to the address he'd given and that tomorrow the assignment would come. He immediately wanted me to spill all the details of the case to him. I was saved by the ringing of my own phone.

"Gotta go," I said. I clicked off, tossed Don's mobile to Clem, and picked up my own. It was Chris. I knew by the way he said my name that there was new trouble.

"Bill. I need your help."

"You're home? What happened at the Hall of Justice?"

"They arraigned me and all that crap. Bail was forty. It's just a crappy child-neglect charge. They're trying to pressure me to give up whoever's really behind it, as if I know. Some of the cops weren't so bad. I felt like half of them saw me as the murderer of my own child and the other half saw me as the victim."

"They're shooting in the dark. I'm glad you're free."

Don's phone went off again. Clem shut it down.

"Yeah," Chris went on. "So here's the thing. I get home and—Hold on." I heard a door close. "I get home and I have this *feeling*—like someone's just left the house. You know what I mean? For one thing, Janet has this glow in her cheeks. I saw it right off because it hasn't been there for so long. Her hair was sort of messed and she acted embarrassed—I mean, not apologetic, just really nice to me all of a sudden. I went to use the bathroom and I could smell this aftershave, Bill. Cheapshit aftershave like a guy looking for a date in, like, Hooters would wear. In my bathroom, Bill! I asked her point-blank if someone had been here and she said a UPS guy had delivered a package. I said, Where is it? She said it turned out to be the wrong address. You see what I mean?"

"I see what you mean. What do you want me to do?"

"Follow her tonight. She says she's going to her grief support group."

"Where's Penny?"

"That's the other thing. Penny went to stay with a friend in Sonoma. If Janet's so in need of support, why is Penny off in Sonoma?"

"Good point. What time is Janet leaving tonight?"

"The meeting's supposed to be at eight," Chris said, "but I'll call you if she gets ready to leave sooner."

I signed off with Chris, then relayed the news to Clem. She snorted when I mentioned the aftershave. "Yeah, like it'd be okey-dokey if he was wearing Hermès. Sounds like Janet's seeking comfort away from the bosom of her family."

"Yeah." It'd shock me if she was doing it so soon, but it might answer the question about the red pickup truck that had been turning into their driveway. "I know how she feels, but if she's hooking up with that guy in the Ranger—that's just wrong."

"Maybe, but what are you supposed to do about it?"

I thought for a minute. "Chris is my client. I want to know if this guy has something to do with Margaret's death. Beyond that, it's between Chris and Janet."

"You want me to go?"

"You've put in a long enough day. We'll wait until tomorrow to see Wayne. I might ask you to trade cars with me for the night, though. Janet will recognize the Scout. And, if you don't mind, take Don's phone back to him."

"Sure," she said, wrinkling her nose. "I'll insert it in the place where he's supposed to have balls."

16

Clem's Corvair was nicely tuned. It accelerated fast and purred softly as it idled. A reflection of Clem's better qualities, I thought.

I arrived in St. Francis Wood early, leaving plenty of time to wait up the street for Janet's car to exit the driveway. I putted along behind her to the light for Junipero Serra and managed to hit it as it turned green, still a safe distance behind her Volvo.

She took a left on 19th Avenue. From there, she made it easy. We cruised onto 280, then took the three-lane exit to Pacifica. We descended into the seaside town all the way to Linda Mar Boulevard, where she took a left. I hung back as Janet made another left, then a right. Two blocks later she pulled over and parked. I killed the lights while she got out of her car, then edged forward to see which house she entered. The red Ranger was parked in the driveway of a small, one-story, asphalt-shingled postwar job. I got a brief, backlit glimpse of the man who opened the door. His size and shape fit with the driver I'd seen in the pickup. He closed the door quickly.

I pulled over and scanned up and down the block. No one was out, so I walked on up to the driveway. I wrote down the Ranger's license plate number and the name on the mailbox: Pulgrove. The front yard was well-kept: The grass and the small hedge that ran under the living-room window were thick, green, and trimmed. A lozenge-shaped juniper tree grew by the walk, near the porch. I crouched low and ran to a spot behind the tree from which I could see into the living room.

The man walked to the window. I froze. He seemed to be looking right at me. His arm moved and the blinds lowered, then turned shut. There was a little space at the bottom, though, a half-inch opening between the blind and windowsill. I had to step into the hedge to reach the outside sill, where I could pull myself up to peer in. The skin on my chest, sliced open by the knife this afternoon, parted again. I watched for a few seconds, lowered myself from the window, and repeated the process.

I didn't see much, but I saw enough. They were together on the couch, not in a lascivious pose, but sitting close. Janet held a ruby glass by the stem. Pulgrove drank beer. I wasn't eager to stick around and see what happened next. If Clem was right that we all had fetishes, peeping on my cousin-in-law getting naked was one I could cross off the list.

Back at the Corvair, I called Chris. His voice was shaky and got shakier when I gave him the bad news. He asked me to return.

I drove back up to San Francisco thinking about Janet and the choices she'd made. She'd married Chris for the comfort and security he could provide. Pulgrove's little bungalow was a far cry from the Gothic mansion in St. Francis Wood. But Janet did not come from a privileged background, and she'd never quite fit in with Chris's family. Maybe her values had changed. Not for the worse, in my opinion, but that was irrelevant to the issue at hand. Which was Chris being hurt. And how long this had been going on. And whether it had anything to do with Margaret's abduction.

» » » » »

Chris did not come to the door. I pushed it open and found him in gloomy silence under the vault of his living room. The jauntiness of Sunday morning and the nonchalance about his arrest earlier today had vanished. He was slumped on the couch, wearing sweats, a cap pulled low on his forehead, his big feet in cross-trainers propped on the coffee table. A tumbler of scotch sat next to them. He stared at the hideous flower painting as if its falsity was finally dawning on him.

I took an armchair and said, "I'm sorry, Chris."

He didn't look at me. His voice was mechanical. "I wish I had some dynamite. I'd blow this place to hell."

"She might have met him at the support group. Maybe he lost a child, too."

"The group's only for mothers. What did he look like?"

"I didn't get a good shot. My guess, from his truck, is that he's a carpenter, electrician, something like that."

"The name's Pulgrove? I wonder where she met him." Chris reached for the scotch. "That'd be something, huh, to have my wife stolen by a nail-hammerer?"

We sat in silence. A clock ticked. Only a small table lamp was lit, casting ghostly shadows into the vaulted ceiling.

"Where did I go wrong, Bill?"

I took a deep breath. He was in a delicate state, but time was short. "I'm not sure. How's your legal situation looking?"

"Dandy," he said sarcastically. "We've identified the number one asshole. An assistant DA named Fitzpatrick. Some of the cops are on his side, too, but not all. What have you dug up lately?"

I told him about Ulla, playing down the incident in the park. "Did you ever meet Austin Remly?" I asked.

"Remly. Sabell. Sabell. Remly," he said wearily. "No, I didn't meet Remly. Just stick to the frigging facts, will you? It doesn't matter how Sabell screwed up on Margaret. Just tell me if he's the one who took her. I'll go up there and kill him."

"It's about motive. You're sure you never threatened to sue him?"

"I might have. Once. But then the whole thing would have been laid open. My father would have reamed me—well, that doesn't matter anymore."

"Have you talked to your father today?"

Chris seemed to have gone into a trance. Staring straight ahead, he said, "See, Janet wanted me to take charge. She was a wreck after losing Helen, and I was fired up about a new child. Only, it made sense to correct the cystic fibrosis, if it was within our power. Wouldn't I have been irresponsible, as a parent, if I didn't? Sabell said he'd developed new techniques."

"Exactly what, uh, specifications did you give Sabell?"

Chris pushed himself more upright in the chair. The bleariness, the self-pity, left his eyes. He spoke clearly. "You've never been a father, Bill. Try to put yourself in my shoes. You've just lost the most wonderful child in the world. The girl who made your life finally *make sense*. Of course you want her back. Not a replica of her. It was about *honoring* Helen, not duplicating her. Honoring her meant giving her sister all the advantages we could."

"Did Sabell use any genetic material from Helen in creating Margaret?"

"Jesus, no, what kind of freaky question is that? Sabell didn't believe in cloning and I never would have approved it. He said it was a matter of comparing genomes." Chris stared at me as if I was the freak.

"Was there an autopsy on Helen?"

"There must have been. It didn't find anything we didn't expect."

"Did Sabell request any tissue or organ donations?"

"No! Quit asking me that, Bill!" He became more animated, gesturing with his hands. "You need to understand me better. I always thought of you as the brother I never had. You were my pal when we were kids, my running mate. I knew all along you were different than me, but I cut you slack. You had all those weird ideas about what to put in our videos. I was okay with it, it entertained me. But you never saw what was going on with me. You kind of looked down on me, didn't you?"

"No, the opposite—you seemed like the perfect kid. The boy who did everything right. I had to tweak you now and then."

"Exactly!" he said, stabbing a finger at me. "I was the boy who did everything right. I followed the track laid out for me, like a railroad. Grades, sports, meeting the right people, wearing the right clothes. I followed the yellow brick road. I liked having my place in society, making money, contributing. Yet none of it ever seemed good enough for my father. I kept trying to prove whatever doubts he had about me were wrong. I secretly admired your freewheeling life—dressing however you wanted, having fun with cameras, making your own way—but see, I had *responsibilities*." Chris was full of backhanded insults tonight. "CCE is a frigging empire. When I was getting up toward thirty, marriage was the next station on the track. I met Janet and it seemed like we both wanted the same thing. It was a drag she couldn't get pregnant the natural way, but we found Sabell, had Helen, and—*bam!* That was when it happened."

"Cole finally treated you like an adult?"

"Christ, no. I'm talking about Helen. I couldn't wait to come home from work every night. I fell in love, Bill, in a way I never had before. It was like a *spell*. Sabell would say it's the genes at work. I don't care. It was magic." Chris sat back again, his eyes misting. "Everything was clicking. I was rising in the firm—Dad made me earn it, by the way—and I couldn't wait for the weekends to take Helen to the park. She was so delighted by the world. The merry-go-round, the pony rides, the buffalo. I'm not idealizing her—I mean, she was a fussbudget, too, she had to have things just so. She loved to fly kites. When she was four, Bill, we saw paragliders out at Fort Funston and she said that when she got big she was going to do that, too. That got her into birds. She kept her own little checklist of the ones she'd seen. Then airplanes, watching them come in off the Pacific. One night she noticed Venus. She was so excited when she figured out it was a star, not an airplane. I showed her Jupiter and Saturn and explained how planets were different than stars. You know what she asked me? She said, 'So Daddy, am I a planet or a star?' Because I used to point up to the night sky and say that she was a star, like the ones twinkling up in the heavens, and she'd come down to earth to live with us."

Chris wiped his eyes. "*Me,* Bill, the guy with no imagination—I thought of stuff like that. Because of her. For the first time, my life meant something. I knew what it all was for! Why I'd been such a good boy all those years. So when we lost her—see, that wasn't supposed to be in the cards for people like us. Suddenly I felt worthless. Every season of the year had some event to rub it in. Christmas, Easter, Fourth of July—Helen loved fireworks. And then the advice, especially from my family, about how it was time to move forward with my life. Everyone seemed to think it was their duty to tell me to find frigging *closure* after a certain deadline. Dad started talking about how maybe Janet wasn't right for me. That was the last thing I needed to hear: You already feel pretty unmanly when you've let your child die. Maybe he knew something about Janet I didn't. Or maybe he thought she wasn't from good stock."

"Janet seemed to feel like losing Helen was some kind of omen," I said.

Chris sniffed and ran his sleeve across his nose. "It was crazy. She decided our union was cursed. She was so up and down—unpredictable. You know how women are. I started thinking—it was like we got dealt a royal flush, and then found out there was a wild card and Death had five of a kind. And I said to myself, That's not right. Then it came to me. I could play another hand. Only this time, she wouldn't be at the mercy of nature. I had a kind of vision. It was kind of like Helen, after death, kept inspiring me."

"So you went back to Sabell," I said.

"I figured if death can go against the order of nature and kill our little girl before us, then I can go against the order of nature and bring her back. Not that I'd disrespect Helen's memory by trying to replace her, but we could have another one who was just as wonderful. That idea made me come back to life, too. I got re-engaged at the office and I learned karate. Things started clicking again."

"I remember the karate. I thought, Don't start a fight with that guy."

He made a grasping motion with his fist. "You have to take life into your own hands, Bill. Dad said that's what being a man was about. He told me the story of Prometheus, the Roman guy. Man didn't discover fire by luck, he had to reach out and take it from the gods. The gods struck back. Jupiter chained him to a rock and an eagle ate his liver every day, but it grew back at night."

"Early tissue engineering," I said.

"No, the point is, Prometheus knew the secret of how to overthrow Jupiter. That's the real reason the god feared him. Herakles came and unchained him, and Prometheus rose up again. See, Saturn had castrated his own father, Uranus, to gain power, and after that ate his own children to keep them under control. Jupiter escaped and overthrew his father, Saturn. That was how the world really worked, Dad said, and then he winked and said don't try it on him. Prometheus got the girl, too, some goddess named Io—a cow, Jupiter's old girlfriend. So that's what I believed at the time. Don't lie back and take it. Be the hero who unchains Prometheus. You're lucky, Bill. You seem to be able to sit back and let things happen for you."

"My work is more about observing than engineering. Then again, observing remakes the world, too, in a way."

"If you say so." To Chris, it was more nonsense from his "imaginative" cousin. "For myself, I had this vision of taking back what I'd lost. Sabell was gung-ho to try again. He gave us a break on the expense—a huge break, doing the work almost for free. When Margaret was born, I thought we'd succeeded. Caught lightning in a bottle again."

"Until you started getting the diagnoses. The diabetes, the seizures. Problems that hadn't existed in either of your family histories. There must be something you can tell me about how Sabell tried to treat them."

"He swore me to secrecy," Chris said. "But, you know, fuck him. Somehow or other, he had some of Margaret's stem cells. Like he knew from the start she'd have problems. He said the cells were omnipotent, or something. It's not illegal, right—if the police find out?"

I remembered Sabell's line again: *before the beginning*. "The FDA might want to talk to Sabell, if he used them as a therapy. Did it work?"

"At first. Her diabetes got better. Then, suddenly, it got a whole lot worse. I felt like he was just messing Margaret up more. He admitted he had no answer for it. That was when I told him it was over, he could have his syringes and infusion equipment back for good. He said to come to his house. He thought he'd get me up there and talk me out of it."

"It's a strange place. Was the poodle there—Gigi?"

"Yeah, she licked my hand. Sabell has this maze in back of his house—you saw it, right? He tried to get me to walk in it again, and I saw how his trap had closed in on me. He talked about how we were on this great adventure, prying nature's secrets from her womb. I lost it. I hit him in the solar plexus. It's my *wife's* womb, I yelled at him. I left him there, doubled over. That frigging dog came after me. Trotted behind me all the way back to my car, giving me this look. The next day, Mitch sent a letter telling Sabell to stay away. Yet Sabell kept begging us to let him see Margy, right up to the end."

"It's looking more and more like the clinic is mixed up with her disappearance. Someone's worried that I'm getting too close to the truth."

Chris shook the ice in his glass, staring at it as if a subliminal message would give him the answer. "Then go get them, Bill. You know all my secrets now."

"All of them?" I held his gaze. I couldn't afford to have any new surprises. "This is the time to tell me, Chris. Holding things back has slowed the investigation."

He drained the glass, getting only a few drops of melted ice. "Wringing me dry tonight, huh, Bill?"

"I'm asking for necessary information."

"Yeah, you're the big man now." Somehow I'd turned into the object of his rage. "Look, I admit it. Your way is better. Okay? I'm being punked by my wife. Nothing more pathetic than a jealous husband, is there? You made the right choice, with your junky old truck and your bachelor lifestyle. No worries, no responsibilities. So enjoy yourself. You deserve your reward. And I guess I deserve mine."

I was ready to leave, but something stopped me. Pity, maybe—and maybe this was a time for it. "No one's better or worse," I said. "I always liked that we were different, but still buddies."

He lifted his chin and appraised me, as if considering an offer from a car salesman. His blue eyes turned cool and empty. "I'm just about broke, Bill. Don't worry, I'll pay you, but now that I'm quitting CCE, I have no idea what I'll live on. See, our insurance stopped covering Margaret. They were sniffing around about what we'd done with Sabell. I had to cover the medical expenses myself. You'd think my father would help out, right? No way. He said it was throwing good money after bad. I guess he was right. The whole idea was cursed from the beginning, like Janet said."

Chris stared down at his shoes. He'd finally reached the point of admitting defeat, the point he'd worked for the last six years to avoid at any cost. Literally, any cost.

"There's this line from a Dylan song," I said. "'Just when you think you've lost everything, you find out you can lose a little more.'"

His fists clenched and his voice rose, as if to defy the thought. "And I keep losing! No wonder Janet would rather be with the pickup-truck guy. It never stops, Bill! I was going to be the President of Claypool Construction, father of a magical little girl. Now I'm President of Nothing, and I don't matter to anyone."

"Let's find out who killed Margy. Then we'll see what's next."

Chris froze and sat straight up. Then I heard it. The back door was opening. Then closing. Keys jingled in the kitchen. There was the rustle of a jacket being taken off. Then shoes on the floor: *clip, clip, clip . . .*

Janet was home.

» » » » »

"I should go," I said to Chris.

"Stay for a minute, Bill. Please," he said. He licked his lips.

"I'm not going to gang up on her, Chris."

"Just verify what you saw. Like you said, you're an observer."

The footsteps stopped. Janet had heard our voices. I sensed her in the dining room, listening. Chris called out her name.

"Hi, honey," she said. The steps resumed. She entered the living room.

"How was your group?" Chris said, artificial sweetener in his voice.

"All right." Janet's voice had the same pacifying sugar. Her eyes widened when she saw my chest. A streak of red had leaked through my shirt. "What happened, Bill?"

"Someone tried to kill me today. In the park. Three men. They tried to kill Ulla, too." I spoke harshly and watched Janet's reaction.

"That's terrible! What provoked it—I mean, who are these men?"

"Who do you think they are?"

"Well—I don't know! Didn't you say they're related to Chris's work?"

"I doubt that. They may have come from Sabell's clinic. Or the construction business, who knows?"

"Sabell?" Janet said.

"Did you go to him behind my back?" Chris asked suddenly, sharply. He didn't care about the attack in the park right now. His single focus was on Janet.

"No! I completely agreed with you about him, Christopher. I *never* wanted to go back to him. You know that."

Chris was coiled in his spot on the sofa, his jaw clenched. "What did you talk about in your group?"

"Mom stuff, like before," Janet replied. She glanced into the hallway. She wanted to escape upstairs.

"You meet in the city?" Chris asked. I wondered if he was leading her on in order to torment her, or to give her a chance to tell the truth.

"Usually," she said vaguely.

"Not in Pacifica?"

Janet's brow wrinkled. "Not usually," she said slowly.

"Been drinking?"

"A few of us had a glass of wine after."

"All women—no men?"

"I've told you that."

"How about men who drive Ranger pickup trucks?"

Janet glanced at me and I caught the flash of anger smoldering in her eyes. *"What?"* she said to Chris.

"What color is the truck, Janet? Can you tell me the color?"

She burst into tears. But they were not hurt tears. They were tears of helpless rage. "Why are you doing this to me?"

Chris stood up. "Is it *me* who's betraying *you,* Janet?"

Janet ran into the hallway and raced up the stairs.

"Tell me the truth!" Chris yelled after her. "One word of truth!" He started for the stairs.

"Chris!" I shouted.

He ignored me and bounded up the steps two at a time.

I went to the front door, but as I pulled it closed, I worried about what Chris was capable of. Leaving the door ajar, I moved down the walk and looked up at their bedroom window. It was dark. Chris's voice bellowed from inside, followed by some kind of pounding.

I went back inside and stood at the bottom of the stairs. His voice roared, no longer Chris's but the enraged bellow of a gored bull.

"You betraying slut!" he screamed. "Our daughter is dead and you're drinking wine with this asshole. You lie to me, telling me you're at your support group. With *mothers! Grieving!* And in reality you're living it up with this *cheap, shit, cowboy nobody?* That's *not* innocent!"

I didn't hear Janet's reply, though I could hear her faint sobs.

"I know who he is, Janet. I'll get him. *I know who he is!*"

Again Janet made some kind of reply. Again Chris bellowed. "No, I understand perfectly. You think I'm *stupid?* You're glad she's dead, aren't you? You were *celebrating,* weren't you?"

Footsteps pounded overhead. A door slammed thunderously, shaking the timbers. I mounted the stairs quietly and stood at the top landing, my ears ringing. The bedroom door was closed. I went down the hallway. The door to the room where Janet had been sleeping was closed. I hoped she'd locked it.

I slipped back downstairs. I made sure the front door lock was set, then closed it. This time I did not stop.

17

Wayne was proud of himself. His head, melon-like in the first place, was swollen and purpled by the punches he'd taken. His left arm was slung in a cast. Drips of Vicodin and morphine gave him a goofy smile and glassy eyes. Still, it was clear that every small movement brought pain.

He was in a bed at San Francisco General. Clem and I arrived first thing on Tuesday morning. He greeted her as Sylvia and me as Dave. He related, with a certain swagger, how he'd fought his attacker to a draw until a scream from Ulla distracted him. The man had knocked him unconscious and then, apparently, broken his arm with a kick.

Wayne's pride was a by-product of fundamental relief that he wasn't dead. I'd gotten a charge out of that same feeling when I woke up this morning. I needed it after I remembered that Chris and Janet's marriage was going down the tubes and I was still a long way from knowing who'd abducted Margaret.

If Wayne was forgiving about the fact that he'd become the object of an all-out assault, Ulla was not. She'd recalled my last name. "You are a friend of Christopher Claypool," Wayne announced with triumph.

"I've been hired by the family to determine what happened to Margaret," I said. "The only side I'm on is hers."

"You'd arrest Christopher if you had to?"

"I don't have the power to arrest anybody. But if he's the one, I'll turn him over to the police. Tell me about your attacker. Any hint of his identity?"

"He was a good fighter. I have some experience, but he had much more. I did well to delay him as long as I did." Wayne was trying to talk without moving his mouth, which made his accent sound more stilted. "I interviewed with the police. Did they not catch him?"

"The men were gone when they arrived."

A new emotion came over his face: fear. "Would they come for me again?"

"You're not the target," I said. "You were just in the way. They're after Ulla, or me, or both. I'll check with the hospital desk about security." It had been decent when we arrived. We had to give our full names and show IDs. Wayne was then asked if he wanted to see us, and a security guard had escorted us to his room.

Wayne nodded. "Be careful with yourself, Dave." He thought some more, then said, "He was very businesslike. If I may say, he handled it as a Dutchman would. There was nothing personal against me. He was doing a job. I said, 'Who are you? What do you want?' But he did not care to chat. He had an unmoving gaze as we fought."

"Anything you can tell me about his clothes, his smell?"

"I was unable to tear open the stocking mask. The material was quite strong, and I would recommend it to any woman who wears hose. I did notice a cut above his right eye, like a second eyebrow. A peculiar thing: He wore a scent, a cologne. And he was a smoker. American cigarettes, I believe. Together with the smoke in his clothes I thought, He has come from an expensive jazz club. Absurd, of course."

"Very observant of you. What was the scent?"

"Unfortunately, my observations brought no advantage. The scent was musky, but with a sweetness. As if he planned to seduce Ulla. He did not fight fair. He tried to put a knee into my privates. He made an unusual grunting sound—*orff! orff!*—and used a curious word—"

Wayne's eyes widened. If he'd been able to move, he would have sat up straight in bed. "Just now I realize why it was curious. I noted, in addition to what I have told you, a red stain on his pants. It was too shiny for blood. I speculated it was the favorite sauce of the Americans, ketchup. Along with the cigarettes, it caused me to assume he was one of your people. But the word he uttered, when I knocked him with a good punch, was *'Bliksem!'* "

"Bliksem?" Clem said.

"It means 'lightning' in Dutch. In Afrikaans, it's a strong curse word. It made no sense. I could not process it until this very moment."

I jotted the word in my notebook. "Good, Wayne. That's very good."

Wayne beamed. "What about your fellow?"

"The main thing I remember is a blade about six inches long," I said, "and a malodorous scent of sweat." I thought about it some more, making myself a camera, replaying the film. "He wore black, soft-soled walking shoes and a thick belt with a square buckle that formed the letter L."

"L for Loser," Wayne joked.

"I wonder how long they're going to keep up this men-in-black theme," Clem said.

"As long as they want to scare us. They'll switch to street clothes for their real business," I predicted.

"This was real business," Wayne said. "I assure you of that."

I met his eyes. "My guy would have stuck me a lot worse, if he could."

Wayne nodded solemnly. "I do not think Ulla will be staying for long."

"Will she be allowed to leave the country?" Clem asked.

Wayne replied only with an enigmatic smile. We thanked him and promised to look in on him again. He wished us luck and sent us off with some mangled advice: "Hang your shorts loose and keep your powders dry."

» » » » »

We repaired to the office, which was now known as Damen C & I. Clem had ordered up a door sign with the shorter name. It would cost less, she said, and create a greater air of mystery. I didn't need potential clients to be mystified about my line of work, but I let it go for now.

We'd picked up coffee from Scoby's. Clem squeaked in her swivel chair and I tilted back in a rickety wood chair she'd found, drinking my coffee while I filled her in about Chris and Janet last night.

"That reminds me," she said when I mentioned Chris's finances. She dug a neatly printed invoice out of her leather bag. I mentally calculated how much I'd have to transfer from a credit card to my business account. At least the fees were deductible.

Clem was using the Internet to track down the numbers we'd gotten off of Don's phone. I diverted her into looking up Pulgrove in Pacifica while I scanned Don's numbers.

"Don's got the number to Sabell's clinic," I said, "but not GenVigil. Not Chris's, either. When you're reverse-searching these numbers, look up the exchanges, too."

"The number we redialed in the Scout yesterday is just a generic mobile."

I punched that number into my own phone, just for fun. I got the same computer voice asking me to leave a message. Then I called my DP friend Andy, whom Don had given as a reference. He hazily recalled Don and the Antarctic project, but said that Don had been vague on the specifics. That sounded about par for Don. He was the kind of guy who bought every piece of gear he could possibly need before he had any reason to use it. Still, the fact that he managed to tail us yesterday meant he had at least one skill besides whining. I held my nose and called him next. He professed to be overjoyed to receive two assignments from me. I ordered up everything he could find on Sabell's clinic and lab, and also whatever he could unearth about a feud between Cole and Mike Gallegos, the DA.

In response to Clem's smirk, I said, "They're reasonably safe tasks. Better yet, we can check his facts. Best of all, if we keep him busy, he can't follow us around."

"Just be careful. Don's a sneaky one."

"He's the weak link that'll take us to his master."

"Or vice versa," Clem warned. "I found Pulgrove, by the way. First name is Steve. He's a cabinetmaker. Gets rave reviews for his craftsmanship and honesty from satisfied customers and a local business board."

"Sounds like Mr. Clean," I said.

"Those are the ones to watch out for," Clem said.

"Yeah. I hired a potential felon and it's working out all right."

"You have to know the criminal mind to solve the criminal mind."

"Who does your criminal mind like in this one?" I asked.

She squeaked in her chair for a minute, then said, "The Sabell Clinic has the best motive, and Remly has the means. But the cops are right—you can never rule out the parents. I don't know about Chris because I haven't met him. Janet's another sneaky one, though. Let's imagine Steve Pulgrove and Janet have been having an affair for a while. She tells him she'd leave Chris in a minute if it wasn't for Margaret. Steve rubs his chin and says, 'Hmm, so all I have to do is help this sick little girl into the grave?' He collects inside information about Ulla's patterns, skulks about the parks they frequent, learns their habits, then does the deed. Suddenly Janet's free. And guilt-free, if she doesn't know he did it. Not that I count her out as a co-conspirator."

"Where does Pulgrove get the commando types?"

"He could have been in the military. He's got buddies."

"Afrikaner buddies? We'll see. You know what we need to do? We need to talk to Austin Remly face-to-face. With his background, he's got to have connections to private military companies."

"Yep. Plenty of ex-apartheid-era guns for hire nowadays," Clem said.

"Cole supposedly has a contact that'll help us get to Remly. I've got to make a few calls, then I'll go see Cole. Remember how GenVigil mentioned they had a source inside the clinic? See if you can get Tim and Cynthia to tell us more."

"Yes, sir, Mr. Damen. I'm also going to try to talk to the three women I met at the clinic, even if I can't get them all together at once. I also found out Nurse Stacy's address. Come to think of it, she could be GenVigil's spy."

"Good for you. We can try to pin her down tonight after work."

"You mean when she's home? What's the fun in that?" Clem waggled her eyebrows.

I laughed. "You *are* evil."

» » » » »

I got back on the phone to Mitch Walchuk's office. His secretary put me right through. "I need an objective assessment of these charges against Chris," I said to Mitch. "He's not taking them very seriously."

"I know. I talked it over with his criminal lawyer last night. Here's our theory. The DA thinks Chris knows more about who took his daughter than he's saying, which of course is untrue. But Chris is the only one they can get at right now. The way it looks, Fitzpatrick will push it to the wall, maybe raise the stakes to homicide."

"Why not go after Janet, too?"

"She may be next. The threat had a visible effect on Chris."

"Hmm." I resisted saying that he might feel differently now. "Cole says Gallegos has it in for the family—especially Cole himself."

"I haven't been able to corroborate that. Fitzpatrick's the rabid dog right now."

"Cole does have a tendency to dramatize."

"Well, they did keep asking Chris about him. What kind of security men he employs, his relationship with Margaret, with Janet, and so on. Then again, they asked about everyone: Leonard Wilson, Janet and her family, George Sabell, Austin Remly, you . . . They're fishing, in my opinion."

"Who do you think's most likely?"

"Chris told me you're looking at the clinic," Mitch said. "Makes sense to me. For the moment, we're focused on the child-neglect charge and defending Chris's character. If they go for homicide, we'll want to hear everything you can tell us."

"Will do. Say, can someone in your office check on something for me? I'd like to know if Dr. Sabell is on record as attending the autopsy of Chris's first daughter, Helen."

Mitch said he would. I thanked him. It was nice to work with a cooperative person for a change. I'd almost forgotten what it felt like.

I dialed Chris on my way to the local FBI field office, near the Civic Center. I dreaded the conversation, wondering if on top of the charges he already faced, domestic assault would be added to the list. There was no answer at home or on his mobile.

The FBI administrative assistant who checked on Margaret's case came up empty. She offered to have an agent contact me. I gave her my card. The fact was, her results tallied with what the cops had told us yesterday after the attack in the park. I'd asked about the Feds, and one officer was nice enough to look it up. He said there was no record of FBI interest in the case.

No wonder Cole had put me off about showing his files. As I drove to his office, I called Dr. Tyrovsky. Her nurse took my message. I asked her to try to recall anything she could about Dr. Sabell's actions around the time of Helen's death.

Chris returned my call as I was getting checked through the gate to the Claypool Construction parking lot. I didn't tell him where I was.

"Janet flew the coop," he said as the guard waved me through. "Middle of the night, like a thief. I caught her. She was trying to talk real quiet on her cell phone while she packed. Said she was going to stay with Penny in Monterey."

Chris paused. I pulled the Scout into a parking space. "I said something kind of dumb," he went on. "I said, 'Great, that's how we lost Margaret in the first place.' Then she blew up at me. She said that Dad was my real family and had screwed up things between us all along. I told her I was done with him and CCE. She said, 'Oh no you're not. You'll go back. Claypool blood is thick as oil.' What a load of crap. I almost hit her. She was trying to push my buttons."

"Or convince herself she was doing the right thing." I didn't point out that Chris, in his more honest moments, had said the same things about himself. "She left after that?"

"She said she didn't feel safe in our house. She's so full of shit. She's not going to Monterey, she's going to Pacifica. I almost followed her, Bill. Then I thought, Fuck it. I know where the asshole lives."

"It's good you didn't go after her."

"Get this. She said she'd take out a restraining order if I didn't leave her alone. Bill, she's my wife! How did we come to this?"

I thought about how he'd acted last night. It may have destroyed any chance of repairing his marriage. But I couldn't honestly say I wouldn't have felt the same anger. "You need to respect her wishes," I said. "It's the only hope you have of getting her back."

He gave a derisive laugh. "I don't want her back. Good riddance. I'll need your affidavit, Bill, for the divorce papers. She'll get *nothing* from me. This Pulgrove guy, on the other hand—"

"Stay away from him, Chris. I'll handle this."

"*Don't* fricking tell me what to handle! I looked through our household accounts. The guy worked on our house. The old one, in Pacific Heights, after Helen died. I might have met him, I don't remember. Janet arranged it. Do you know what that means, Bill?"

"It means she's known him for six years."

"It means she's been *fucking* him for six years."

"Does your gut really tell you she's been fooling around for that long?"

Chris sputtered that his gut was not the organ in question. Then he blew up. "Quit doubting me, Bill! I got enough of that from my father. I don't need you giving it to me from the other end. Neither of you has any respect for what I think! There's a *pattern* in her behavior. Do you see the pattern?"

Momentarily struck speechless by the bizarre idea that Cole and I were ganging up on him, I could only sigh. The pattern was depressingly clear. With Janet gone, all of Chris's insecurities were rushing to the surface. "You're facing child-neglect charges," I said. "You've got to stay out of trouble."

"You find out more about this Pulgrove guy and you report it to me, Bill," Chris said in a savage voice worthy of his father. "*I* hired you. *I'll* decide what to do next."

"That's right. You take responsibility for yourself, Chris."

"*Frigging* right. I've got my Plan B. A man should always have a Plan B, Bill."

I didn't even ask.

» » » » »

I took a close look at the security personnel as I approached Cole's building. The armed guard in front was a crewcut man who scowled at everyone who approached, but gave a friendly greeting if you said hello. The man at the front desk was blondish, his hair close-trimmed, too. Nothing in their dark blue uniforms resembled what our attackers had worn.

The front desk man called up to Cole's secretary and was told Cole was in an urgent private conference. I took the phone and asked her to let him know it was me. She called back a minute later and told me to come up.

The secretary escorted me down a corridor, past the executive offices to a heavy inlaid wooden door marked PRIVATE. She knocked discreetly. Leonard Wilson opened the door. He shook my hand and ushered me into what I took to be an executive lounge. The carpeting was plush, the furniture a soothing dark red leather. The wood-paneled walls were decorated with large-format color photographs of Claypool Construction's projects. The lighting came from table lamps. An air of crisis hung in the room. Cole sat in an easy chair, wreathed in smoke. This was the one place, apparently, where he could legally light up his cigars. Wilson took the chair paired with Cole's. I was left standing. A wet bar occupied a nook in one wall, but neither man was drinking.

"Cozy," I said, looking around the room.

"Get a chair," Cole said gruffly.

I dragged a riveted leather chair to a spot facing the two men.

"Careful of the carpet!" Cole complained. I sat down. He held his cigar level with my eyes and said, "It's good of you to turn yourself in."

I replied with a non sequitur of my own. "Turn myself into what?"

Cole didn't show a hint of a smile. Wilson's hands were folded tightly in his lap. Cole thrust his cigar in my direction. "Enough crap, Bill! We're talking about millions of dollars now, not your penny-ante meddling in our family affairs. You'll pay the price for your role in this, nephew or not."

He was trying to coerce me into admitting something. I had no idea what. "I went to the FBI field office this morning," I said. "They're not involved in Margaret's case. At all."

"Are you calling me a liar, Bill?"

"What's got you so scared about me being on this case? Especially if I'm penny-ante. The Jakarta deal?"

He made an O with his mouth and blew a perfect hoop of smoke in my direction. Another one followed, forming for a moment the rings of a bull's eye. "What was Christopher doing here in the office on Sunday morning?"

I avoided the question with one of my own. "How hard did you pressure Chris on the Jakarta proposal on the weekend before last? Because that's what created the opportunity for Margaret to be taken. Chris working so hard."

"The opportunity was created by his incompetent, indolent wife." Cole's eyes never left me. I had the sensation of being pinned to a wall. "Sunday morning, Bill."

"I have no idea what Chris was doing."

"You weren't here with him?"

It dawned on me that Cole's security cameras had recorded our comings and goings. I didn't answer.

"Now who's the liar, Bill?" Cole said. "You'd better come clean about what Chris was doing and how you helped him."

"Helped him what?"

Wilson leaned forward. I'd sensed the tension building in him, an irate impatience at odds with his usual reserve. "It looks like Wong Fen Construction is going to get the Jakarta job," he said tersely. "And we know why."

I shook my head. "What does this have to do with Margaret?"

"I've spent a lot of time in Singapore, China, and the South Pacific over the last few years for our company. I've become acquainted with a lot of people in the business, including some who now work at Wong Fen." Wilson paused to make sure I was following. "The Jakarta client has let it be known to them that last-minute revisions to their proposal contained the same technical solutions as ours did, but at lower cost. Specifically, an air-filtering system every bit as effective as ours. Nearly identical, in fact."

"Our partner firm in Jakarta confirms what Leonard is saying," Cole added.

"I'm sorry about that," I said.

They waited for more. I waited, too. An inkling of what had happened was forming in my mind. I hoped I was wrong.

Finally Wilson burst out of his seat. I thought for a minute he was going to attack me. "The air-filtering system is proprietary information. There's only one place it could have come from!"

"Well, you should get after Wong Fen for stealing your technology," I said.

"It'll take years," Cole said. "I intend to get justice faster."

Wilson was pacing with the pure anger of a man who'd worked hard and been cheated out of victory. "Wong Fen didn't even want this project! It turns out they were only bidding on it to keep us busy while they pursued a bigger job in Shanghai. This is frosting on the cake for them—"

"Sit *down,* Leonard!" Cole commanded. "That's confidential!"

Wilson did not sit down. He stood behind his chair and focused his energy on gripping the top of the seat back, as if to strangle it. He'd tended to hang back before, do his job quietly. Now, with Chris gone, he was next in the line of succession, and acted like it. Winning the Jakarta contract could seal it for him.

Cole crossed his legs. "The official decision will not come until Friday. We may have a chance to revise our bid and still win the contract. But if we do, it will come at a cost of millions. So, Bill, if you want to avoid criminal prosecution, you'd better tell me what you and Chris did on Sunday."

"Criminal?" I scoffed.

"Industrial espionage. With a Chinese company. It has homeland security implications, if I choose to make it so. How would you like that?"

"You *would* do that to your own family, wouldn't you?"

"There's no limit to what I'd do to someone who betrays me."

Cole had worked my last nerve. My response was unedited but calm. "Maybe you should think about criminal prosecution yourself, Uncle."

Cole's brow worked itself into a full thunderhead. He jammed his cigar into the sand on the spittoon and bellowed, "Explain yourself!"

I undid the second button of my shirt to show Cole and Wilson the bandage. "The same guys who took Margaret attacked Ulla and me in Montoya County Park yesterday. We now know they're not triad-connected, because Wong Fen wasn't hot on the Jakarta job to begin with, right? More to the point, I got a good close look at these guys. They wore the same belt and the same shoes as the security men at George Sabell's lab." I wasn't sure what made me say the last sentence, which was a fabrication. It did appear to perk Cole's interest.

"It's time for you to tell me how mixed up with Sabell and Remly you are," I went on. "You've admitted you paid for the creation of Margaret. The only thing I don't know yet is your degree of involvement in her abduction."

Cole chilled his tone to equal mine. "Don't change the subject. How much money were you and Chris paid for the information?"

"You know that the DA would love to drag you into Margaret's case."

"*I* will detain you right now if you don't speak up."

"Better do it fast. My partner knows where I am."

"A lot of things can happen in an hour."

A finger of cold fear slid up my tailbone. The threat was real. I settled back in my seat. "Chris would never give away company secrets."

"We're tracing his electronic trail," Cole answered. "He broke into Leonard's computer to do the dirty work. A clumsy frame attempt. You were there, too. Own up, and I'll focus my attention on the primary miscreant."

I recalled Chris's wickedly elated mood on Sunday. I couldn't avoid the truth. I said, "You should be careful with Chris. Janet has left him. He's in a fragile state of mind."

"You're suggesting he's suicidal?"

"I'm suggesting he's in a great deal of anguish and he's expressing it in reckless ways."

Cole tapped his fingertips together. "Here's my offer, Bill. I let you leave this room. You go and convince Chris to come clean with me. If he comes to his senses, *and* is willing to suffer the consequences, *and* is sincerely remorseful—then we'll see."

I'd been focused on Cole, but now I became aware of the way Wilson's fingers were kneading the leather chair back. More than that, I became aware of the freshly stricken look on his face. He'd thought his new position was just about a done deal. Now it was dawning on him that Cole might take Chris back, in the end. Janet may have been right: The bond locking Cole and Chris together was more powerful than any other one in their lives.

I said, "I'll talk to him. If you give me a way to arrange to meet Austin Remly."

"Good boy. But I'll tell you, Bill, I'm proceeding as if Chris is not owning up. As if he is *not*. He needs to come to me very soon. On his hands and knees. Remember, you're at risk, too."

I stood and held my hand out. "The Remly contact."

Cole gave a sigh of exaggerated disgust. He extracted his PDA from his breast pocket, looked up a name and number, read them out to me quickly, and snapped the PDA shut.

I left. It was not until I inhaled the familiar oil and fumes of my Scout that I felt like I could breathe again. The visit had been worth the trouble, though. I had found out about the Jakarta disaster. I had a supposed contact to Remly. And, although I had nothing against Leonard Wilson so long as he wasn't involved in Margaret's death, I'd helped drive a small wedge between him and Cole. I drove back to the city convincing myself I'd fought my uncle to a draw. Of course, that might be the very illusion he intended to leave me with.

18

Some impulse, possibly a self-destructive one, caused me to veer over to the ocean side of the Peninsula after I left Claypool Construction Engineering. After my earlier talk with Chris, I'd decided the issue of Steve Pulgrove couldn't wait. I wanted to confront him about Janet and Margaret before Chris took it into his head to do so himself.

I dropped down Sharp Park Road into Pacifica. The day was slipping away. Already it was 2:45. On the way, I called Clem to let her know I had another stop to make. She said that I needed to get my butt back there because Don insisted on reporting to the office before the end of the day. I told her she'd have to deal with him, *nicely,* if I didn't get back in time.

"I'll be user-friendly," she grumbled.

I was pleasantly surprised to have the conversation interrupted by a call from the FBI agent who'd been given my note about Margaret's case. He confirmed that it was a local matter and the FBI was not investigating. I summarized the case for him. He was noncommittal, saying only to keep in touch if something new happened.

I parked around the corner from Steve Pulgrove's house, pulled on a hooded sweatshirt that would hide my face, and strolled up the block, hands jammed into the sweatshirt pockets. The blinds in the house were drawn. The driveway was empty. No sign of Janet's Volvo, either. I drove back to a pay phone in the shopping center on Linda Mar. Janet's mobile number gave me only voicemail. Then I tried Pulgrove's work number. He picked up.

"Steve, how's it going?" I said, buddy-buddy.

"All right. Uh—who's this?"

I exposed the handset to traffic and garbled a couple of syllables. "Hey, I was wondering if I could come by and talk to you about a little bathroom job. You going to be home soon?"

"Yeah, listen, not this afternoon. Maybe tomorrow. I'm not sure."

"You on-site right now? 'Cause I could come by. Where are you?"

"I'm in Half Moon Bay. I'll be finishing up soon. Look, it's a bad time. I'm—I'm booked. Let me give you a referral."

"Great," I said, and took down the name and number he recited.

Half Moon Bay. Finishing up. It could be an hour before he came home. I drove back to my parking place and walked around the corner to his house. I ducked behind the juniper tree near the porch, then slid along the hedge, testing the windows on the side of the house. Closed and locked. I jumped a red picket fence. The small backyard was neat, with beds of flowers and newly planted vegetables. A tall maple marked the back property line, a wood-slat fence the far side. In the little patch of grass sat a plastic yellow-and-orange tricycle. Mr. Pulgrove, it appeared, was a father.

The small concrete patio was shaded by a jasmine trellis. A glass sat on a metal tray beside a plastic chaise longue. The liquid residue looked fresh. I crouched and moved to the sliding glass door. A set of vertical blinds blocked my view inside. Gently, I pushed the handle. The door moved. I slid it open, quarter-inch by quarter-inch, creating enough space to slip in.

I waited, listening. Music played softly. Debussy.

Something brushed against the blinds. I moved back, still crouching on all fours, and waited.

"Mr. Kitters, you want to go outside?" a voice sang.

The cat meowed. The blinds whooshed open. I stood up. The cat hissed and puffed its fur at me. Janet shrieked. I leaped on her, clamping my hand over her mouth from behind. She kicked at me, trying to grab my hair. I pushed her farther inside and said, "It's only me."

She opened her mouth to bite my hand. I spun her around so that we faced each other. "Get out!" she screamed.

"Don't scream again, unless you want the police here asking questions about you and Steve," I said. "I'm sorry I startled you."

She swung at me. I never saw it coming. The inside of her fist smacked me full on the cheek. I staggered on one foot before regaining my balance. She strode to a telephone on the wall in the kitchen, separated from me now by a projecting counter.

"Go ahead and call Steve," I said. "I'd like to talk to him, too."

She stared at the receiver, then hung it up. "Why don't you use the front door like a civilized person?"

"I didn't expect you to be here. You said you were going to Monterey."

Her eyes smoldered as she moved to the counter, opposite me. An enamel cup, half full of coffee, sat between us. She picked it up casually, then threw the entire cup, overhand, at me. I dodged it, but got a faceful of cold coffee. "You spied on me! Creep!"

Wiping my face on the sleeve of my sweatshirt, I said, "Is that any creepier than what you're doing?"

"Don't you judge me, Bill. Don't you dare."

I got ready to duck again, but her fists were clamped tightly. "Can we sit down?" I said. "We've always gotten along well, Janet."

She tossed her head. "There's a stool under the counter."

I pulled out the stool, sat, and took a moment to look at the kitchen. "Steve's good at what he does," I said. "Nice cabinets. Takes a lot of care."

That much was true. The craftsmanship was excellent, although the greenish oak stain clashed with the rose walls, which clashed with the avocado stove.

"I'm glad you approve," she said sarcastically. "I can't believe Chris set you snooping on me. What the hell kind of trust is that?"

"The same kind that made you say you were going to your group, I guess."

"I *knew* Chris wouldn't understand. Okay, I admit I got comfort from talking to Steve. Talking, not sex. The idea repels me right now."

I looked down at the counter. "I'm honestly not concerned with what you are or aren't doing with Steve. It's only my business if it's connected to Margaret's death. I heard what you said to me the other day. It's not for me to tell you what you should do with your marriage or your life."

"You *do* judge me," she said. "Your whole family does."

"Don't get me confused with Cole," I said sharply.

"Steve is *totally* understanding. He's *there* for me in a way Chris hasn't been for years. No strings attached. I'm not promising him anything. I'm not saying I'll ever sleep with him again."

"Again?" She tried to shake it off, but I pressed. "No, tell me what that means. You slept with him last week?"

"No!"

I thought for a moment. "You had an affair with him the first time, didn't you? After Helen died. When he came to work on your house."

Her eyes were stony pellets circled by raccoon rings of sleeplessness. Her plum cheeks had turned into small, cold orbs.

"Look," I said, "I don't care about the sex. I don't care if the support group exists or not. That's between you and your conscience."

A spark lit in her eyes, an urge to prove the justice of her case. "We did sleep together this morning. Just slept. It was so nice to have a warm, comforting body next to me. Instead of an obsessed person. Chris is in a bad place right now, but even if he was the perfect, supportive, sensitive, strong husband—I can't be around him. Not now, maybe not ever again."

"Why do you say that?"

"He reminds me of the pain!" Her chin trembled with anger at being forced to explain. "I feel physically ill every time I look at him. The loss reflects back and forth between us, multiplying."

"I see," I said, trying not to. Her logic was brutal and unassailable, though I wanted to believe it was wrong.

She recognized my tacit acceptance and pressed her case, hoping to make at least one member of the family understand. "Early one morning last week, Chris's cell phone rang. I hate that thing, it's like the devil to me. I felt this panic that something had happened to my daughter—that she needed me. The call turned out to be from Jakarta. What got to me was that they needed him *right then,* needed him badly enough to call that early. Chris's work was a kind of refuge for him." Janet dabbed the corners of her eyes. "No one needs me anymore. God forbid a child ever does. I vowed at that moment never to fail a child again. Which means never having one again.

"That was only six days ago," she went on, "but it seems like forever. That was the moment I first thought—no, I *knew*—I had to get away. Start over. Chris says he needs me, but he'll discover that, actually, he doesn't. I *do* care for him, but . . . he'll pull through. He's got his family, and the company, who came before me, anyway. He can marry someone younger. Me, I'm out of options."

I wanted to tell her what Chris had said to me last night. That Helen, then Margaret, and Janet herself, had been what truly gave his life meaning. She would only think I was trying to talk her out of her feelings. I settled for a statement of fact: "I don't think Chris wants more children."

Janet gave me a canny smile, as if she saw through my subterfuge. "He might change his mind one day. I mean, that was why we coupled—to procreate, right? Procreate and carry on the Claypool line."

"Chris has left the company. Irrevocably."

She tilted her head. "I'll believe that if it's still true in five years. I don't mean to say Chris is some kind of ogre. I'm sure I did matter to him at one time. He used to say a wonderful thing to Helen, that she was a star sent down from heaven to be with us. So, what if that was true, but it turned out she was the wrong *kind* of star? You know, a Lucifer instead of an angel. Not that Helen herself was demonic, but maybe some power used her against us. Used her to ruin us. I know it sounds irrational. I can't help it. It feels *true*."

"There's no explanation for some things. Helen's death just happened. It was blind bad luck."

Janet gave the kind of nod that said I was missing her point. "You know how, when something terrible happens, people say, 'It was meant to be'? Or 'God only burdens you with what you can handle'? Well, my life, and Chris's life, are proof that that's a crock of shit. It's a placebo to make you shut up. Supposedly to help with your pain, but really it's for their own, so they don't have to bear, with you, what's unbearable. You may be right, Bill, that Helen's death was random and unexplainable, but you can't prove it. Your belief is based on just as much hard evidence as mine—zero. The one thing I've learned through all this is to listen to my instincts. I failed to do that with Chris's scheme to make our perfect in vitro baby. Helen felt like she came out of my womb, but Margaret was more like a girl in a glass. The conception process had so little to do with me. Call me irrational if you want, but to me it's this technology that's *super*natural."

"Okay, but it was a human being who deliberately caused her death."

"Maybe it was. Or maybe just vicious fate again. I can't linger on it. I loved Margaret unconditionally, Bill, yet at the same time, I shielded myself. I protected myself and prepared for another loss."

The tone of Janet's voice told me the matter was settled. Her eyes remained clear stone pellets. I glanced to my right, into the living room. A cluster of toy dump trucks and bulldozers were piled in a corner. "Steve's got children, too."

"A son. Part-time. Maybe I'll be with Steve someday, maybe I won't. Right now he's just a good friend and a good man who's helping me out." She looked at her watch. "And who'll be home any minute. It's time for you to go, Bill."

I stalled. "I'm sure it's comforting to have someone you can count on."

She looked at the left side of my face and couldn't prevent herself from a quick smile. "It's still red where I hit you."

I touched my cheekbone. "I deserved it, I suppose."

An engine roared in the driveway. Janet turned away, suddenly tense. Steve was home. I ducked down the hallway to my left and into the bathroom.

"Bill! You bastard!" Janet shouted after me.

I locked the door. "Out in a minute," I said.

And I was. The bathroom window was aluminum-framed, the type that slid sideways. I opened it and gave Steve a few seconds to get to the front door. The window slot was just big enough for me to wriggle out head first. Once the balance of my weight had shifted, I crashed into the azalea bush below in an undignified manner. That was all right. I wanted Janet and Steve to know I'd left. I ran in front of the kitchen window to make sure they saw me. Steve started for the door, but Janet grabbed his arm. I disappeared down the block.

A few moments later, I turned right back around. Running low, I tracked along the six-foot wood-slat fence separating Steve's house from his neighbor. No one had been in the neighbor's backyard earlier. I hoped it was empty as I opened a metal gate latch to enter it. A small trampoline sat in the middle of the yard, along with a couple of metal chairs, unoccupied. I took a run at the fence and boosted myself atop it, balancing for a moment before quietly lowering myself into the middle of Steve's newly planted vegetable garden. A scampering sound startled me. It was the cat, clawing its way into the maple tree. I moved on all fours myself to the concrete patio. The blinds were still down. The sliding door had never been closed. I lay hidden lengthwise along the wall and listened. The voices inside were loud. I'd started an argument.

"Why are you all of a sudden doubting me?" Janet cried. "I told you, he's not going to bust us!"

"He's working for your husband!" Steve roared back. "He's going to screw everything up!"

"What is there to screw up? You've known the rules all along."

"Don't get cold feet on me, baby," Steve said in a wilted voice. "I've waited a long time."

"No strings attached, remember? I appreciate your being here for me, but—"

"You're right, no strings attached, like I promised. It's just that—I never stopped thinking about you, Janet. Even when I got married and had my little boy, I fantasized it was with you. I held myself back from calling, but when I heard about Margaret, I had to—"

"Wait a minute," Janet interrupted. "You *knew* about Margaret? When we ran into each other at Tower Market, you already knew?"

"Well, I'd read in the newspaper . . ." Steve said defensively. "I figured you might need some comfort, someone who understood. Like the first time. I didn't ask for a whole lot in return. You know that."

"You *planned* that meeting at Tower, didn't you? And here I thought it was some wonderful serendipity. Fate bringing us together again."

"It doesn't matter! What matters is we're together."

"We're not together!" Janet cried. "I don't want *any* attachments in my life right now. Maybe not for a long time."

Car tires peeled out on the street. I heard Janet and Steve's footsteps.

"Son of a bitch!" Steve yelled. "I'm getting my gun!"

"No!" Janet commanded sharply.

I sprang back over the fence, through the neighbor's yard, and out to the sidewalk. Whoever peeled out had disappeared around the corner. As I emerged from behind Steve's truck, I saw the heaps strewn over his front lawn. Skirts, dresses, blouses, jeans, shoes, underwear, all flung angrily onto the grass. A light blue bathrobe confirmed my fear. Chris had loaded Janet's things into his Range Rover and dumped them here at Steve's house. A neighbor across the street stood on his porch, hands in pockets, gaping at the spectacle.

Steve was looking up and down the street. "He's gone," I said.

He whirled around and glared at me. "You did this!"

"No. I was trying to talk sense into him," I said.

Steve strode toward me, fists up. I reviewed his possible roles in the Claypool family drama: murderer, Lothario, knight in shining armor, pawn of Janet. The only thing I determined for sure was that he displayed his masculinity by walking with his legs apart, as if his underwear was bunched, and putting his dukes up.

Janet came out of the house carrying a plastic laundry basket. I saw the look on her face. I held my ground but kept my arms at my side. It was the best way I knew to win her over.

"Don't start anything, Steve," she said, setting the basket down. She started filling it with clothes.

I stuck out my right hand. "Bill Damen. Let's talk for a minute."

He regarded me with suspicion, unsure where to put his fists. He was about my size, six feet, with muscled arms and a hearty, uncomplicated face. His medium-length brown hair had been pressed close to his skull by sweat and a baseball cap. His eyes, behind wire-frame glasses, showed affront, not deceit.

He put his hands down without shaking mine. "About what?"

"I don't care about your love life. I don't care about Janet's.

I've got one question, then I'm out of here. All I need to know is where you were a week ago Friday."

"Bill!" Janet objected. "What kind of question is that?"

"The kind you ask of someone who says they're afraid of getting busted."

"Wait a minute, you heard that?" Janet said. "You eavesdropped?"

"You son of a bitch," Steve snarled, advancing on me again.

Again I didn't move. "You're going to need me. If it comes to a divorce with Chris, you'll need someone to confirm that the relationship between you two isn't sexual."

"Steve," Janet said wearily, relief showing on her face, "don't start a fight. I thought you were the one man I could count on. The one man with a cool head."

Steve nodded, taking his medicine. His jaw worked to corral his feelings. He was steamed that I knew he wasn't getting any and steamed to have to answer my question. His posture, hands on his hips, was that of a man whose truck has been rear-ended and now the miscreant was demanding compensation.

"Stupid asshole," he said. "Friday before last I was at my workshop in San Bruno, then doing an installation at a client's house in San Jose. Lots of people saw me at both places."

"Do you have any South African friends?" I asked.

"You said one question!" he barked. "Now get the hell off my property!"

I checked Janet. Her laundry basket full, she'd turned to go back inside. My remark about the divorce had made her reluctant to antagonize me. The fact was, I'd get nowhere near a divorce proceeding if I could help it.

"Tell me what you know," I said, once I'd caught her eye. "Steve appeared mighty conveniently after Margaret died. Once you were free of your obligations, Janet, he figured you'd hitch up with him."

"I'd never hurt that little girl!" he shouted, jabbing a finger at me.

"Steve!" Janet commanded again. "He'd never hurt her, Bill. Believe me."

"It doesn't connect to Margaret. Period," Steve said. "Janet was in distress after her loss and she realized her marriage wasn't right."

"What if it's because of *you* her marriage wasn't right?" I said. "So, Janet, it's decided? With Margaret out of the way, you're done with Chris?"

"That's right," Steve answered for her.

Enough doubt was in his voice that we both looked at her. She'd stepped into the front doorway. Her chin jutted, quivering slightly. Her eyes were cast down, gazing at her pile of clothes. I found myself thinking that she'd never looked so beautiful as she did now, suspended between lives, two or three men waiting on her, none of whom she was worried about pleasing.

"We'll see," she said.

Steve couldn't check his pleading tone. "The last thing I want to do is tie you down, baby."

I didn't need to hear more of this. I stuck my hand out again. "Nice talking to you, Steve." He took it by force of habit, then pulled away as if I had fish guts in my palm.

» » » » »

Chris knew he'd been a bad boy. I called him as I drove back to San Francisco. He didn't pick up. I left a message informing him just how bad he'd been. I'd have to try to take him unawares at his house tonight. For now, I returned to the office to rescue Clem from Don. Or vice versa.

"You bastard," she said when I came in. Don was gone.

"Everyone's calling me that today."

"He . . . would . . . not . . . stop . . . talking!" Clem was in her squeaky chair, shoes off. The office was warm and she'd peeled down to a sleeveless black shirt. The GenVigil Web site was on her computer screen.

"I said, 'Good job, son, Bill's going to write you a big fat check,'" she continued. "'But I'm real busy right now, so get the hell out of here.' And now you, Bill, are going to sit here and listen, just like I had to."

"Fine. But you're not going to believe who I just met."

"Damn you! Now I want to know. What happened?"

I told her about catching Janet at Steve's house, then about Chris's stunt, then about Steve himself. His alibi for the day Margaret was abducted was good, if it was true.

"I have a feeling it'll check out," I said. "Steve's gone to the bottom of my list of suspects. He may be the only honest man I've met in the past week. A real straight shooter. He can't hide his feelings."

"That won't hold Janet's interest for long," Clem remarked.

"You know her that well?"

She shrugged. "Wouldn't hold mine."

"I'll remember that," I said. "Maybe Cole's more your type. It turns out the FBI is not involved in the case in any way."

"Big shock. The question is what he's hiding."

"A lot, I'm sure. That's his M.O. He likes control—more than control, he likes omnipotence. But that wasn't even the big news today." I went on to tell her how Leonard Wilson had discovered that CCE's technology had found its way into the hands of its rivals. It seemed likely Chris had sold the information on Sunday. He needed money.

"He's acting out," Clem said. "One thing I don't get—why haven't you considered that Cole could be behind Margaret's abduction?"

"Oh, I have," I said. "But see, Cole lives by blood. Margaret, even with all her medical problems, was his blood. Besides, if he wanted to get her alone, all he had to do was offer to baby-sit."

"So you think all this business about the triad link to Jakarta is just an effort to leverage his granddaughter's death to gain some sort of competitive advantage?"

"That would be like him. He did threaten me today. Meant it, too. I warned him the police had their eye on him. That didn't faze him—he's blamed the whole thing on the prosecutors from the start. It was weird, though, when I threatened him. I felt detached from myself, almost like an out-of-body experience."

"Displaced Oedipal feelings, Mr. Damen. Cole functions as an overpowering father figure. He is your mother's brother. It's no wonder you censor your suspicions about him."

"Next you'll tell me I want to kill Cole and sleep with Regina."

"Just the kill Cole part. But who wouldn't?"

I put my face in my hands and shook my head. "Remind me never to introduce you to my mother. The two of you will hatch a hundred more crackpot theories together."

"Heavens no, keep me away from Mom."

I was relieved to see a kidding smile spread across Clem's face. Her role had not developed in the classic assistant format I had expected. In just under a week she'd become more like a partner. I didn't mind that, didn't mind it at all, so long as she remained a business partner. The thing not to focus on was the way her dark brows grew thick and wild above her Mediterranean eyes and the way her chest strained at the fabric of her tank top.

I said, "Wilson let slip that Wong Fen Construction was never that hot for the Jakarta project to begin with. That pretty much kills the triad theory, in my opinion. The blow dart was meant to throw me off. I suppose Cole might have had it put there, but we don't have a motive for him, unless he teamed up with Sabell, or Remly, or both, to get rid of Margaret. I just don't see how their interests coincide."

"For what it's worth, Don confirmed that the DA has got it in for Cole. He also gave me some information on the Sabell Clinic."

I waited for her to go on. All she did was stick out her tongue in a pantomime of dire thirst.

"Can I help you, ma'am?" I said.

"I've been in the office all afternoon. I'm suffocating."

"You need some air. Let's go down to the Ramp. We deserve a beer."

Clem rocked in her chair, imitating a squeaky dog wagging its tail. We put on our jackets and set off down Illinois Street. The spring air had warmed enough to lure the fog in. It lurked on the shoulders of Twin Peaks, as if the city's central ridge was holding the barricade against a teeming horde. The sun lit the edges of the clouds in a ragged halo.

We took a small table made of old dock planks. The water had a green, brackish look. I went inside and got us beers, chips, and salsa. Once Clem had taken in a little nourishment, she relayed Don's report. His contacts in the prosecutor's office supposedly said that Gallegos's vendetta dated to the last election, when Cole did everything in his power to smear Gallegos and help his opponent win the race. Clem said she planned to go down to the DA's office tomorrow and find out if Don was right.

"Good," I said. "What about the Sabell Clinic?"

"Most of what he said confirmed what we already know. In fact, it sounded suspiciously similar to what GenVigil said. I asked him how he got the information so fast. He said he had 'sources.' Same word GenVigil used."

"Same word a lot of people use. Did you talk to them?"

"I asked Cynthia point blank if she knew Don. She said no. I said it'd be nice if she'd introduce us to her source inside the clinic. She made it clear that's only going to happen as a quid pro quo for going public with the full Chris story. I told her that was up to Chris, not us."

"No way he wants to go public. Anyhow, is it all that shocking that there's a link between stem cell research and a fertility clinic? The clinic's got the embryos a lab needs to derive its stem cell lines."

"Eggs, too," Clem said. "It takes oodles of oocytes to do this kind of research. I'd like to know where Sabell gets them."

"We need to get inside that lab of his. Once we know exactly what he did with Margaret, we've got leverage to force him, and whoever else was in on it, to talk."

Clem crunched a few corn chips. "You're right, we don't have enough yet. We can threaten to report Sabell to the FDA, but unless Chris is willing to tell all, Sabell can cover up."

"Remember, Tim said Sabell's attending a symposium at Stanford on Thursday and Friday. That could be a time for us to get into his lab. Did you get to talk to those three women you met at the clinic?"

"One by phone, two by email," Clem said. "The one on the phone was interesting. She and her partner want to have a child together. Her female partner. Sabell says he can give them a girl who's got both their genes. She wasn't clear on exactly how it'd work—I'm sure Sabell prefers to keep her in the dark—but it would almost have to involve gene transfer, nuclear transfer, or both. Maybe mix together two pre-implantation embryos to make a chimera. Or derive oocytes and spermatids from stem cells created from each. Anyway, it all seems like too much for one man. He must have collaborators."

"What about the other two women?"

"Just regular breeders," Clem said. "I told you about the one whose previous fetuses had Down's. They've heard the clinic's the best, blah blah. They're working with Dr. Rosen, not Sabell."

"All right. What'd you find out about the numbers from Don's phone?"

"The clinic was the only one that matched with anything we have. I reverse-searched the local numbers. Of the ones that got hits on Google, I didn't find many film people. A fair number of lawyers, though. Ambulance-chaser types. I'll check with NYU tomorrow to see if Don actually did graduate from their film school."

I waved her off. "It doesn't matter. Let him keep playing his game with us. The main thing is to make him think we're not playing ours with him."

Clem grunted. "One of the numbers was a local chess club. At least he's got a hobby other than following you around."

I stretched. It was getting dark and chilly. I needed to eat dinner, then go to Chris's house and find out what shape he was in. Clem declined the invitation to join me for the meal. She waved the check I'd written her at me and said she needed to get to the ATM at her local bank.

» » » » »

It was after eight when I drove over to Chris's house. A few dim lights showed in the windows. I circled the block a couple of times to make sure the coast was clear, then parked down the street. I walked to the front door with trepidation. Every day there'd been a new horror behind it. Tonight, thumping music came from inside. I pictured Chris dancing around in his underwear, or partying with some old buddies who had no idea what was really going on.

I rang the bell and pounded on the door. No answer. I rang again and called both his phones. Still no answer. I went around the back, rolled Chris's deluxe gas barbecue underneath the kitchen window, and climbed up to look inside. The kitchen light was on. The sink was crowded with dirty dishes. An empty bottle of champagne sat on the counter, along with empty microwave food cartons. The lights in the living room were off. The party, apparently, was upstairs.

The window was locked. So I waited. It was tedious, and the position was not comfortable. After an hour went by, I made a circuit of the house, looking for other ways in. Nothing presented itself. I went back to my window. Thirty minutes later, Chris strolled into the kitchen to drop off another empty champagne bottle. I rapped on the window. He about jumped out of his bathrobe. When he saw me, he yelled at me to go away. I yelled back to let me in. This went on until I yelled, "Your father knows you sabotaged the Jakarta deal!"

Chris rolled the window open. "You idiot! Don't broadcast to the whole neighborhood!"

"We have to talk. Now."

He opened the back door. It was nice to sit at the kitchen table after standing for an hour and a half. "Word is that Wong Fen Construction has the inside track on Jakarta. They got their hands on some air-filtration systems that are supposedly proprietary to Claypool Construction. That allowed them to revise their proposal at the last minute and undercut CCE. Your father thinks you gave away the company jewels to Hong Kong on Sunday."

Chris swayed unsteadily, hands jammed into the robe pockets, and giggled. "Family jewels—did he say that?"

"Sit down, Chris. This is not a joke. He's going to bring charges against you. He doesn't care that you're his son."

Chris leaned heavily on a kitchen chair. "Can't blame the old fart."

"He still wants you back, Chris. On your hands and knees, of course, but he's hoping you'll return to the fold."

Chris burst into spittle-flying laughter. Either he was very drunk, or making a show, or both.

A woman's voice called from the stairs, playful and naughty. "Chriss-tooo-pher . . . where aaarrrre you?"

"I know that voice," I said.

Chris stumbled in the direction of the hallway. "Wait a minute."

It was too late. The woman came in through the dining room, her robe half-open, exposing a column of well-tanned skin. Her hair, dyed blond over dark, matted roots, stuck out in every direction. Her nose was pert and her mouth made for mischief. She let out a whoop of delight when she saw me, then tied the robe.

"Hello, Kiersty," I said. "Are you still Chris's secretary?"

"I'm his new boss. He's been a *good* bad boy."

Chris had his hands all over her, turning her back in the other direction. "Honey-bunny, I've got to talk to Bill for a minute. I'll be right up, okay?"

She shot me a humid look over her shoulder, as if I might be welcomed in on the action if I played my cards right. After Chris sent her padding back down the hallway, he joined me at the table. I raised my brows. He tried to act pissed at my intrusion but couldn't stop a big smile from drawing its way up his face.

"Plan B," I said.

He laughed. "Plan B, Bill! I'm telling you!"

"You work fast. Or was it in action before all this started?"

Chris's smile disappeared. "No way. I didn't cheat on Janet. Remember that. Kiersty was always on my side, though. She saw how Dad was using Wilson to put a burr under my saddle. We've always had this nice flirtation, made out at office parties a couple of times. I knew I could have her."

"She still works at CCE?"

"She's on leave. Kind of. I don't know why my father hasn't punished her for my sins yet."

"So, about those sins. Did you do it? Leak the company's proposal, with the air-filtration specs, to Wong Fen?"

"Did they win the contract already?"

"No, but Wilson got an inside tip."

"Maybe Wilson's lying. To cover his ass because he screwed up."

"The Jakarta partners confirmed his claim. I think you're the one who's lying, Chris. This is serious. Your father's coming after you."

"He can't touch me."

"Yes, he can!" I slammed the table to wake him up. "I hope you didn't get Kiersty involved in the leak."

"No!" he shouted, thumping his chest. "It was all me, Bill! But she would have helped if I'd asked. She's that loyal."

"Well, that's nice. So is she moving in, or this just a stop-and-pop?"

"It lasts as long as it lasts."

"Chris, what if Janet suddenly changes her mind?"

He grinned. "I'd love that. How I'd love it! 'Sorry, babe, missed your chance. Go help Mr. Red Ranger polish his lumber.'"

A giggle escaped from the dining room. I took a couple of quick steps and grabbed Kiersty, who was crouching near the door, by the elbow. She gave Chris a big-toothed grin and he returned it.

"You—you gave away the air-filterational system?" she blathered. "That is so awesome."

He high-fived her. "Kicked the old bull in the balls!"

"Up and down the street, daddy-o!"

I pushed myself up from the table. "I'm leaving. I just wanted to alert you, Chris. Be on the lookout. Do you know if your father uses some kind of private security force, besides the uniformed guards?"

Chris barely raised his face from nuzzling Kiersty. "Probably does. Probably old mob guys or something. I've never seen them."

That wasn't helpful. He'd say anything bad about Cole right now. I made for the back door. "I don't know how many more days you have left as a free man," I said. "I'll be back tomorrow."

Chris pushed Kiersty away and wheeled to face me. "Get off your high horse, Bill!" he burst, his tongue lolling in his mouth. "Admit it, you always thought I was a stick-in-the-mud. You're jealous, that's all. Not getting any yourself right now, are you?"

"That's true, Chris. You, on the other hand, have proven your manhood tonight," I said. I opened the door, then added something I shouldn't have. "By the way, Cole has known about Sabell all along."

Chris turned pale. He looked like he was about to vomit. I closed the door behind me and left.

19

Eager beavers bring out a mean streak in me. Who knew how long Don had been lurking in Scoby's Café when I got there for my morning coffee on Wednesday? The eight o'clock blur clouded my vision, and I didn't notice him until he pulled a chair up to my table. Low clouds streaming in from the ocean had turned the sky a solid gray, the air was pleasantly cool, and I was savoring the moment, wrapped in my hunting jacket, when the first warm bolt would hit my throat.

"How'd you like my report?" he said, all bright-eyed and bruise-faced.

I showed him my cup. "I have not had a chance to take even one sip of coffee yet, Don. If you do not wait for my coffee to do its job of civilizing my brain before you bother me, you might find your broken nose relocated to another part your body."

He touched the bandage on his nose, then looked away, his foot a nervous bobbin on the floor. I opened my newspaper to the sports section. Another pitcher had gone down with injuries during spring training. "Giants bullpen's got problems," I said. "No bulls, just calves."

Don looked at me blankly, then squinted at the paper. He opened and closed his mouth a couple of times, wisely settling on the shut position. I got some more coffee in me, checked the shooting and assist numbers for the Warriors' latest crop of young players, looked suddenly up at Don, and said, "How did you get your information on the Sabell Clinic so quickly?"

"Um . . . uh . . . I went and visited it, and also on the Internet found this group called GenVigil. Was it good information?"

"It was fine."

I watched him. He fiddled with a sugar packet. I kept watching. He shook the sugar packet in time with his nervous foot, until finally he couldn't stay quiet any longer. "What's my assignment for today?"

"Do you know who Austin Remly is?" He gave a tentative nod, and I said, "I want you to arrange for me to meet him. Me and Clem. We might let you come, if you do a good job." I'd called the contact Cole gave me yesterday but had gotten voicemail and, naturally, hadn't heard anything back.

"I'll get right on it," Don said.

I went back to my paper. Don didn't move. He said, "So, uh, when should I bill you? Heh-heh. Bill Bill."

I folded the paper, stood up, and said, "End of the month."

I left Don staring down at his sugar packet. Clem was in the office with a carton of yogurt and her own tall cardboard cup of coffee. Today she wore jeans, hiking shoes, and her bombardier jacket. I mentioned Don's new assignment and warned her he might show up again.

"Don't blame me if he knocks on the door and no one answers. I'm going to visit the DA's office to check up on his claim about Gallegos. I was also going to check out Stacy's house."

"Be careful."

Clem saluted. "Yes, sir, Mr. Damen, sir."

"That's better," I said. "In fact, hold on while I make a call or two. I might be able to come with you."

I dialed Mitch Walchuk first to find out if he'd had a chance to look into the records on Helen's autopsy. He apologized for not letting me know sooner, but he did have a paralegal obtain the report yesterday. Sabell's name did not appear. I thanked him, then dialed Dr. Tyrovsky's office. Her nurse answered, as usual. I said I'd like to speak to the doctor, and if she wasn't available, I'd come down in person.

Nadine Tyrovsky came on the line two minutes later. "I'm sorry I haven't gotten back to you yet, Bill. I only vaguely remember meeting Dr. Sabell. He may have come to visit Helen when she was sick in the hospital."

"This was when she was sick for the last time, right? Please think again. How many times did you see him?"

"I'm sorry I don't recall if I met him more than that one time. Look, I've got a patient crying in my exam room. We'll have to talk later."

"The hospital would have a record of Sabell performing any procedures, wouldn't it?"

"Chris can check up on that for you."

"What about other doctors who might have been involved?"

"They won't—Well, come to think of it, there was a nurse who was very good with Helen. Mark Baines. I think he still works there."

After I'd signed off with the doctor, I said to Clem, "I guess you're on your own. Call my mobile when you're heading for Stacy's house."

We left the building together. Clem pointed her Corvair south while I went across town to the hospital. I found the pediatrics floor and asked for the nurse, Mark Baines. The desk paged him. A man in his thirties responded. He was well-muscled, with short dark hair, a discreet silver earring, and stylish black shoes.

I asked if we could speak in private. He gave me a once-over, then turned on his heel. I followed him into an empty exam room. He closed the door and faced me with his arms folded. I wondered if someone had warned him about me. When I said I was there about Helen Claypool, he let out a short, relieved laugh.

"I'm sorry," he said. "I thought you were here about something else entirely. I do remember Helen. Very well. She was so brave. I remember her parents, too. Is it true? I heard they lost another little girl."

"Unfortunately, yes." I told him a little bit about Margaret, then said, "I'm representing her father, Chris. We're investigating Dr. George Sabell. I know that Sabell was here during Helen's last days."

"Oh, I remember him," Mark said, touching the back of his neck. "Weirdo. He said he came to say good-bye to Helen. He frightened her. It was like he knew too much about her in some creepily intimate way. I noticed she'd never look in his eyes. I have no idea what kind of medicine he practiced. Helen's parents and Dr. Tyrovsky accepted him being there, so I did, too."

"Did he just come that once?"

"He came every day, as she got worse. I don't know if he was authorized to read her chart, but he did. Hovered like a vulture. At least that's what it looked like to me. But Chris Claypool leaned on him a lot. They were always conferring, sort of secretively. They'd suddenly stop talking when I approached."

"So you have no idea what they were talking about?"

"Chris was just very upset. He was adamant about something with Dr. Sabell. Sabell seemed like the only person Chris could confide in. I never saw him treat Helen—not while she was still alive."

My heart leaped. “What about after she died?”

“I came in early that morning, specifically because of Helen. It turned out she’d passed just two hours before I got there. Her parents were leaving. I could see on their faces that it had happened. I tried to console them, then went to find Helen. Just to say my own little good-bye. I don’t normally do that, but like I said, she was special. She’d been taken to the morgue. Dr. Sabell was there, wearing a surgical mask and gown. He shouted at me to get out. I asked him what he was doing. He said he was doing a postmortem procedure at the request of the parents, and he’d have me fired if I mucked it up.”

“And you didn’t think to report it, or to call Chris?”

“We had a rush of new admissions that day. And I guess Sabell had scared me out of asking questions. I was brand new in the job at the time. He was a doctor and I was a nurse. He said he was authorized and sounded like he meant it. If I’d seen Chris and Janet again, I would have asked them. But I never did.”

“Did anyone say anything about Helen being an organ donor?”

“Not that I heard. I mean, she had cystic fibrosis. But I assumed that was what Dr. Sabell was doing. He had one of those little Eskimo coolers on the floor.”

“So how do I find out what Sabell did?”

“Hospital records. If her parents allow you to view them.”

“Thanks a lot, Mark,” I said. I stuck out my hand.

He shook it and said, “I really was sorry about Helen.”

“By the way,” I said, opening the door, “who did you think I was at first?”

“No one worth worrying about.” He flashed a mysterious smile. “Will you tell me what you find out about Dr. Sabell?”

“Oh yes,” I said. “You may get your day in court with him.”

Mark rubbed his hands together as if he looked forward to it. I thanked him again and left.

Somehow I had a feeling that even if I did get a look at the hospital records, they'd tell me nothing about Sabell's plunder. I got into the Scout and called Mitch Walchuk again. His office had obtained the autopsy report on Helen. Now I wanted to read it.

» » » » »

Clem was out when I got back to the office. A folded piece of paper was taped to our door. It was a note from Don. *Where are you? Got a hot tip. Call me!!!* The last two words were triple-underlined.

I locked the office door behind me, sat down at the desk, and opened the envelope I'd picked up from Mitch. HELEN MARY CLAYPOOL, the document inside was titled, AUTOPSY REPORT. Cause of death was listed as respiratory failure as a consequence of *Pseudomonas aeruginosa* pneumonia complicating cystic fibrosis. I flipped to the section with the internal examination of the genitourinary system. The weight of each kidney was noted. The bladder was described as empty, the vagina clear, the uterus of normal size and shape. At the end of the paragraph it was noted, without further comment, that the fallopian tubes and both ovaries had been removed. There was nothing about who took them or why. I checked the other organs. All of them were intact.

I punched Sabell's numbers in hard on my phone pad. His voicemail picked up, of course, and I left my message. The office phone rang a few a minutes later. I grabbed it, only to be greeted with Don's voice. He demanded to know if I'd gotten his note. I asked him what the hot tip was.

The cockiness had come back into his voice. "You know how you asked for a meeting with Remly? Well, check this out. Sabell's been summoned to his house this afternoon at three. Remly's cheesed off about Sabell appearing in some symposium tomorrow. You can get them both."

"What, I just ring Remly's doorbell and stroll in?"

"Hey, it's up to you how you get in, Bill. If you're half the man I think you are, you'll find a way. I've done my job, right?"

"Sure you have, Don. Let me know if you hear anything else."

He tried to quiz me about where my investigation was, but I cut him off, saying I needed to keep the line free for another call. To my surprise, the call actually came—and from George Sabell.

"I was about to call you myself, Bill," he said. "I've been wanting to talk to you about Margaret. The fact is, I'm a little nervous."

"I don't blame you," I said. "You've got a lot of things to explain. Shall we go to Remly's house together?"

"Remly's what?" Sabell sounded genuinely puzzled. Either he hadn't received the summons yet or Don was lying his pants off.

"You're meeting him at his house at three."

"No. Nor would I, if asked. I told you, I'm nervous."

"Nervous about the symposium tomorrow? Or about what you've done to *both* of Chris's daughters?"

Sabell was confused. "Uh, no, Austin isn't pleased about the symposium, but . . . let's not do this on the phone. It's too delicate."

"Yes, it is." I longed to tell him what I'd seen in Helen's autopsy report, but held back. I wanted to be watching his face when I hit him with it. "How about the Bullshead, down the road from your clinic? Meet me and Clem there at three-thirty."

"That's all right, I guess. I've always avoided the place."

"Just sit tight if we're late."

I hung up and waited impatiently for Clem to call. I was tempted to skip Remly's house and get straight to a confrontation with Sabell, but I needed to find out if Sabell was lying about the meeting.

Clem checked in a little before two from a pay phone outside the DA's office. Her plan was to visit Stacy Hatcher's house next.

"Forget Nurse Stacy," I ordered. "Get back here right away. We need to be in position at Austin Remly's estate before three o'clock."

» » » » »

We took Clem's Corvair, reasoning that if Remly's men were the ones who'd been after us, they knew the Scout. So pleased was she by what she'd learned at the office of the DA, she insisted on relating it before I gave her my news.

"I know this will come as a shock to you," Clem said as we sped down Interstate 280, "but Don's full of crap. I lurked in the hallway outside Mike Gallegos's office. When he walked by, I went right at him. I said I had solid information on Margaret's death, information that implicated Cole. I said I despised the guy and I knew Gallegos did, too. It was great. I exhaled it all without taking a breath, so he had to listen."

"He's not going to admit to hating Cole in public," I said.

"Exactly. He took me into his office. Closed the door. He said to turn over anything I had to the assistant DA, Fitzpatrick, but he wanted nothing to do with tainted evidence. I kept pushing, saying what a bastard Cole was. Gallegos wouldn't take the bait. He said, 'Sure, Cole financed my opponent, but hey, that's politics. It's not personal.' Gallegos barely knows Cole."

"Was he being honest?" I asked.

"Honest as a lawyer can be. The whole exchange lasted about two minutes. His reactions were quick, unrehearsed. Then he handed me over to an investigator. I had to come through on my end. I put a few ideas about Cole in the guy's head."

"How did he respond?"

Clem shrugged. "He wasn't surprised by anything I said."

"That tallies with what Mitch told me. He said it was Fitzpatrick who had the Claypool family in his sights. I suppose Don could have assumed the two prosecutors had the same agenda."

"Come on, Bill," Clem scoffed. "Don didn't get to Gallegos in person. He heard something in the office and inflated it to twenty times its real size."

"Sounds about right. We'll find out more when we get to Remly's. Don was the one who gave me the tip that Sabell would be there. One of the two is lying. But that's not the really big news, Clem."

She looked at me once, twice, then demanded, "What already?"

"Sabell took Helen's ovaries just after she died."

Clem's jaw worked but nothing came out. For once she was tongue-tied. When she did speak, it was almost a shout. "What a *freakazoid!*"

"No joke. What does he want with a six-year-old's ovaries? There are no eggs in them yet."

"Wrong. No *mature* eggs. Oodles of potential oocytes, though, which develop into eggs. A female fetus has millions of primordial follicles by the seventh month. It's a matter of waiting for them to ripen."

"Which doesn't happen until puberty." A new idea dawned on me, one I didn't really want to contemplate. "But if Sabell found a way to ripen them in the lab, he'd have a bounty of eggs for his research."

Clem's eyes went wide. "That's wrong. That's *so* wrong, if he didn't have permission from the family."

"But it can be done?"

"In principle. There was a woman in New York who had an ovary removed and frozen before she received chemotherapy for breast cancer. Six years later, doctors implanted strips of the thawed tissue under her abdominal skin, like a small string of beads. Her hormones, along with some fertility drugs, stimulated the ovary tissue into producing twenty eggs. The eggs were fertilized in vitro and an embryo was implanted in her uterus. It didn't take, but a similar procedure worked for a Belgian woman. She had a healthy baby girl."

"Those oocytes were from an adult woman's ovaries," I said. "This is a child."

"True. You'd need to concoct the right mixture of culture media and hormone stimulation to nurture them through the various stages. As far as I know, no one's taken human oocytes as immature as Helen's and coaxed them all the way along to metaphase II, haploid and ready for reproduction. It'd be a major breakthrough if Sabell succeeded. *Major.* You can get your oodles when you've got the whole ovary. So much easier than those painful extractions of eggs from live women."

"Metaphase II . . ." The next idea that came into my mind was more appalling than the last. "Do you know what that means? Helen could be Margaret's genetic mother."

Clem shook her head in disbelief. "Could, but—why? If I were him, I'd use them to produce new stem cell lines, maybe derive germ cells from those lines. That kind of work's well in progress. But it's true that if he was able to mature her oocytes all the way to metaphase II, he could use them for reproduction. The only problem is, they carry the cystic fibrosis mutation."

"Which he planned to knock out, anyway. Shit, this is too real."

I had the sensation of being out of my body again, as I had when confronting Cole. Suddenly the landscape around us seemed ludicrous. The little orbs of live oak dotting the hillsides, the too-green pastures, the popcorn puffs of cloud above the ridges—they seemed fabricated, something from a film set.

"Shit," I said again. The word was wholly inadequate. "I wonder if Chris knows anything about this. He keeps saying he's told me everything, then I turn around and find out about something new."

We coasted off the freeway and went winding up the local road to the clinic turnoff. "If we can get tissue from both girls, we can run a PCR test and compare their DNA," Clem said. "That might give us the answer."

"We need to get into Sabell's lab. Soon. He sounded scared on the phone. I don't know if it's because we're getting closer to exposing him, or because someone's threatening him, or what."

From the road leading to the clinic, we took a right on the small, unmarked lane that went up and over a wooded ridge. There was the iron arch, the wrought vines spelling out A. REMLY. It was no surprise to find his property more carefully secured than Sabell's. We pulled over and watched for a few minutes. The five-story ersatz Bavarian castle, with its wedding cake turrets and bays, stood half a mile away. Between us and it rolled a picturesque pastiche of fields, meadows, and fences, through which a willow-lined stream ran. Again I had the sensation that I was looking at a stage set.

I got out, opened my camera bag, and screwed on a long lens. A row of fir trees partially hid the mansion, but I still got a pretty good look at the front door and the gravel driveway. Sabell's black Saab was nowhere to be seen. Nothing aside from a small herd of Jersey cattle moved in the pasture this side of the creek. I went up to inspect the gate. A video lens and electronic lock were built craftily into the post, along with a more readily visible intercom. A fence of spiked metal pickets protected the property on either side. The gate had two sides that opened inward. I pushed at them. They parted a few inches. The gate was unlocked.

Clem rolled down her window. "Seems a little weird, huh?" she said.

I propped my elbows on the door. "I can believe Sabell was forgetful or didn't bother to get his gate fixed. Not Remly. Not a guy who's devoted his life to security."

"The question is, do we step into the trap?"

"Very carefully," I said.

I pushed the gate fully open and left it that way, in case we needed to get out fast, then got back in the passenger seat. Clem crawled through. The small, packed dirt road curved gracefully through the fields, making a gradual descent to the stream. There the road disappeared in a growth of willows and cattails, presumably to cross the creek via a bridge.

"Good ambush spot ahead," I said when we were thirty yards from the crossing.

Clem nodded. "I'll floor it."

"No, pull over. We can't see the bridge or who's waiting there. We'll go to the house on foot."

Clem cranked the wheel to the right to park the car off the road. I packed the camera back in the bag, then I checked my cell phone. The signal vacillated between weak and absent. The phone would offer no help.

Clem's head jerked up in alarm at something she saw in the rearview mirror. I turned. Two hundred yards behind us, another car was coming through the gate. "Sabell?" she said.

I shook my head. It could have been Remly, but what were the chances he drove an aging gray Honda Civic? I said, "We're out in the open already, so let's sprint for the house."

I slung the camera bag over my shoulder, and Clem and I jumped out, crossing the pasture at full tilt. We vaulted an old-fashioned split-rail fence and kept heading for the Black Forest monster in the distance. A bend in the creek was coming to meet us about sixty yards ahead. The herd of Jerseys stood between us and it.

A crack split the air. It sounded oddly small as it echoed off the hills, but left no doubt it had come from the bushes by the creek. We hit the dirt. Another report sounded. Two faceless figures, clad in black, emerged from the bushes. They pushed the branches aside, then brought their hands together to take aim again. The Jerseys collided with one another, cantering first in one direction, then the other.

"The cattle are our only source of cover," I said to Clem.

Clem and I ran, bent, for the confused herd. Two more reports sounded. We circled to the rear. The herd seemed to have decided on the bend in the creek as a destination. We ran with them. I empathized with their bewildered galumphing. There were more shots between the hoofbeats, then one of the Jerseys let out a bellow, stumbled, and fell. The herd swerved. Frightened lowing broke out. A calf turned abruptly and butted Clem in the chest. She flew backward, landing spread-eagled. I rushed to her, keeping my body between her and the cows and her and the shooters. She touched the back of her head, which had slammed into the ground.

"Stay down," I said. "Are you hurt?"

The last few cattle thundered by, in full gallop now. Clem struggled to get something from the right pocket of her jacket.

"Move out of the way," she gasped.

I rolled away and then saw what she had in her hand. She snapped the clip home, chambered the gun, and squeezed off two shots in the direction of the creek. The men had advanced cautiously on us. Now they froze.

"This way," I said. "Over the fence."

About fifty yards of pasture were between us and the black metal pickets. Across the fence were woods.

I pulled Clem to her feet. We stayed low and ran. Two more reports cracked across the valley. When we made the fence, I cupped my hands to make a step for Clem.

"Put down the gun first," I said.

She placed it on the grass and put a shoe in my hands. I launched her up toward the top of the fence. She grabbed the top bar and used her momentum to walk her feet up the pickets. Once she got the toes of her shoes wedged between the spiked heads, she teetered, then swung herself over to the other side. Gripping a crossbar, she lowered her body and dropped to the ground.

"You okay?" I said.

She pushed herself to her feet, gasping. "Yeah."

I handed the gun through the picket bars. She took aim. I grabbed the bars and scrambled up, spreading my legs for leverage. Clem fired a shot. When I got to the top of the fence, I propelled myself over, landing hard and rolling.

"Where are they?" I said, picking myself up.

"Taking cover," she said.

We set off into the woods, a mix of live oak, sycamore, and maple. Once we'd plunged far enough into the trees to be hidden from the pasture, I veered right. "Let's circle back," I said.

Clem nodded. We dodged our way through the tangle of deadfall and underbrush. She carried the pistol confidently at her side.

"Clem," I said, "what the hell is that?"

She peered at it. "Birth control. Nine-millimeter Beretta Cougar. One hundred percent effective. Legal, too."

"With your arrest record?"

"I've been observing your practice, Mr. Law-Abiding Citizen, and it's only by sheer luck and the grace of God that you don't have more arrests than me. No way I was coming unprepared, after what happened last time with Ulla."

"Yeah, well, you could kill someone with that thing," I said.

Her eyes narrowed. "If I'm a good enough shot." The grip fit all too easily into her hand. "I'm surprised you don't have one yourself."

"It's not a good idea for an unlicensed investigator to go around pulling triggers," I said. "In my experience, sidearms get you into more trouble than they get you out of."

"You can revise your experience as of today."

I had to admit that Clem's gun had come in handy. If I ever got my PI license, I might have to look into a firearm license, too.

We'd come over a quarter-mile north from the gate. After a few more minutes of working our way through the woods, I angled harder to the right. The trees opened and we found the small dirt road leading to the gate. Sticking to the woods' edge, we followed the road. The gate stood open. The Honda was not in sight. Nor were any men in black. Clem's yellow Corvair sat a couple hundred yards down the road.

We watched for several minutes. The landscape was still and empty. Even the birds had left the sky, scared away by the shots. I motioned Clem through the gate. We jogged down the road. As we came closer, something moved inside the Corvair. I pulled Clem to the ground. Through the back window we saw the motion again. The safety on Clem's Beretta clicked.

"You've got your weapons, I've got mine," I said, snapping open my camera bag.

I attached the long lens and zoomed in. Sitting in the driver's seat, peering through the passenger window at the field through which we'd run, was a dark head. I moved in closer but the head became no more distinct. It was covered by a stocking. I touched Clem and pointed back the way we came. We ran for the gate and pulled it closed behind us. Breathing hard, we jogged back up the road, over the ridge, and down to the main clinic road. Clem had put the gun back in her jacket.

The sound of tires on the gravel behind us startled me. As we spun to look, the gray Honda pulled up. The passenger window came down.

"Get in," a youngish woman's voice said.

It was Cynthia, reaching back to pop open the back door. Father Timothy was at the wheel. I glanced at Clem, who stuck her hands into her jacket pockets. As I climbed in after her, I saw by the motion of her arm that she'd closed her fingers around the pistol grip.

"What are you doing out here?" I demanded.

Cynthia turned, a miffed look in her blue-gray eyes. "We saw what happened back there on Remly's property. You're welcome for the help."

"Thank you," I said. "What are you doing out here?"

"They've been shot at," Tim said to Cynthia in a soothing tone. His eyes were fixed on the road. He drove fast, repeatedly checking the rearview mirror. To us, he said, "We were tipped off that Dr. Sabell was meeting Mr. Remly here today. We thought we might have a chance to intercept the doctor and discuss the paper he's scheduled to give at a symposium tomorrow."

"You will," I said. "You know the Bullshead Tavern? Take us there."

Tim nodded. I caught his eyes in the mirror. The look of genial concern, always present on his face, focused intensely on us now. Clem's hand relaxed and she withdrew it from her jacket.

"Thanks for saving our butts," I said. "Who gave you the tip?"

"It was emailed anonymously to the Web site," Cynthia said.

"And all you intercepted was us and the ninja squad?" Clem said.

Father Tim paused as we hit the main road. He checked behind us and, letting out a breath of relief, took a right. "We came through the gate and saw the, uh, ninja squad shooting at you. We turned around and drove up to the clinic. The receptionist said she would call the police."

"So Remly lured us both up here," I said. "Thought he'd kill two birds with one stone."

"An ugly expression," Cynthia said. "There's got to be an investigation. We should be able to close down the whole operation."

"If you can pin the attack on Remly," I said. "All we know for sure is that some guys in stocking masks were on his property. You and we both were sent by someone other than Remly. Do you know Don Masterson?"

Tim and Cynthia shook their heads simultaneously. It seemed sincere but could have been rehearsed.

Clem changed the subject. "What do you know about the in vitro maturation of human oocytes?"

Cynthia twisted in her seat. "What have you found out?"

"Nothing yet," I said. "We're wondering if Sabell has found a way to grow very young oocytes into fully developed eggs. No one's done it yet, right?"

"Not with human eggs," Cynthia said. "Cumulus-oocyte clusters have been matured in vitro to competence for nuclear transfer in animals."

"Well, there was that terrifying Dutch-Israeli experiment," Tim said. "Immature human ovaries harvested from four-month-old aborted fetuses. Primordial follicles grown all the way to the secondary stage. In vitro ovulation is the next step." He caught my eye in the mirror again and asked, "Is that what Sabell's doing?"

"Let's just say that it wouldn't shock me if he found a way to make it happen," I replied.

"If he did, he may talk about it tomorrow at the Stanford symposium," Tim said. "Only problem is, it's invitation-only."

"We'll get in," I said.

"You've got to tell us what you know!" Cynthia insisted.

"You can't reveal your sources and I can't reveal mine," I said coolly.

Cynthia looked at Tim. They didn't respond. The Bullshead came up on the right. Tim pulled in. I was glad to see Sabell's Saab in the dusty lot.

"One favor," Tim said. "We've never met the doctor before. Please don't tell him who we are."

"As long as you behave," I replied.

Dr. Sabell was sitting in a corner, huddled into a scarf wound around his neck and tucked into his jacket collar, not for protection from the cold so much as from the denizens of the bar. It was not busy at this time of the afternoon, but still there was a vociferous posse of bikers playing pool and a thumping game of liar's dice pounding the bar. Neil Young blasted from the stereo: *Hey, hey, my, my.*

Tim and Cynthia quailed from the scene nearly as much as Sabell. The doctor looked alarmed as they followed Clem and me to his table. I bent to shake his hand. "Who are those people with you?" he said.

"They helped us. We were attacked at Austin Remly's house."

"What?" Sabell shouted. "I can barely hear you."

"Hey, Zeke, turn up the music!" one of the pool players yelled to the bartender. "Some guy's shouting!"

"Sorry," I said to Sabell. "This is the only place I knew of near the clinic." He shrank a little more, looking small and vulnerable. I reminded myself that he was neither. He avoided Tim and Cynthia's gazes. I caught Tim's eye and nodded to a table next to Sabell's. I took a chair with Sabell.

Clem remained standing. "What'll you have?" she asked the group.

If she thought a drink would break the ice, she'd picked the wrong bunch. Cynthia requested spring water and Tim wanted iced tea. Sabell shook his head and cupped a mug of coffee as if someone might take it from him.

Sabell lifted his mug with both hands but grimaced when he drank. "You were attacked at Remly's?"

"Yes. Does that surprise you?"

"I don't know what to think." He glanced furtively at Tim and Cynthia. "Who are they?" he said again.

"Just friends," I said, and went on to describe the men who had attacked us on Remly's estate.

Sabell nodded grimly. "I've seen these men, too."

"At the lab?"

"No. On the road, as I'm driving. In parking lots. I think"—he glanced around again—"they were outside my house once. I catch a fleeting glimpse, then when I stop to look, they're gone. Like phantoms."

Clem squeezed by me. Somehow she'd managed to fit two beers, an iced tea, and a bottle of Calistoga between her hands. She passed them out. Tim and Cynthia pulled their chairs closer. Tim offered a toast.

"To the human race," he said. "And a human future."

Sabell remained hunched as we touched glasses. I was not in the mood for beer. I took a sip and put it down. The conclave was not going as I'd hoped. I wouldn't have brought Sabell and GenVigil together deliberately, but since it ended up this way, I'd hoped some revealing fireworks might result.

I lifted my glass again and said, "To Margaret. Her killer is known."

Again, four glasses touched. Clem stared at me expectantly. "Well, who is it?" I had no idea why I'd said it.

"Whoever Don Masterson's working for," I said.

Little reaction showed on the faces around the table. Sabell looked up. "This Don was in on it?"

"Do you know him?" I said.

Sabell shook his head and looked down again. Tim leaned forward. "Dr. Sabell, I'm curious what you're going to reveal at the symposium tomorrow."

Sabell's eyes bored into him. "Who wants to know?"

Tim got a twinkle in his eye. "'Pity this busy monster, man-unkind,'" he quoted, "'not. Progress is a comfortable disease.'"

Sabell glanced at me, then back to Tim. A smile broke over his face. "And here before you is a fine specimen of hypermagical ultraomnipotence! What a peculiar place to finally meet you, Pinhead."

"'Where all life die, death lives, and nature breeds,'" Tim said, "'Perverse, all monstrous, all prodigious things.'"

"'All beings so far have created something beyond themselves,'" Sabell countered. "'Do you want to be the ebb of this great flood and even go back to the beasts rather than overcome man?'"

"What the hell?" Clem said.

Sabell shook a finger at Tim. "He's my poetry correspondent. *Pinhead.* Wrong about everything, but clever nonetheless. He likes to quote from Milton's paean to Lucifer, bringer of light and knowledge."

Tim permitted himself a naughty grin. The debate with Sabell brought out his puckish side. "The angel who did everything wrong. Only one being ever created humans perfectly, my friend. Only one ever will. 'Lord, what an alchymist art thou, to transmute ill into good.'"

"An alchemist, maybe, but a poor parent," Sabell responded. "Jealous, controlling, unduly judgmental. You have your transmutations and I have mine. Only, I don't let dogma dictate which ones are acceptable. We're not in the Middle Ages anymore, Pinhead."

"Oh, but we are. Our tools are more elaborate, but the impulse, the motives behind our quest, are virtually unchanged. Stem cells are the latest version of the universal solvent."

Clem rolled her eyes at Tim, then looked at Sabell and asked, in a tone more curious than disapproving, "Are you a devil worshiper?"

Sabell folded his hands. "Clementine, you know very well that the elevation of the so-called Supreme Being was achieved at the price of suppressing too much previous knowledge. Authorities have always tried to deny us knowledge that is rightfully ours. Their strictures are a way to keep it for themselves."

Suddenly I understood who GenVigil's inside source was. It was not Nurse Stacy but Sabell himself, engaged in an Internet discussion with a man he knew only as Pinhead. We'd seen for ourselves how, once you got Sabell rolling, you couldn't shut him up. I wondered what his screen name was.

"Give us a glimpse of that knowledge," Tim said. "You've unlocked the power of the oocyte, haven't you? Found a way to shortcut the gene programming that occurs at each stage along the way to maturity."

Sabell shook his head and spoke with reverence. "What occurs in the oocyte's nucleus is a mystery beyond me. We can only feed it the right nutrients, give it the hormones it needs when it needs them, cut it loose from its nest of granulosa and cumulus cells. I hear it speak to me and I respond."

"I'll bet you can't wait to share your results with your colleagues," Cynthia said, straining to join in.

Sabell's eyes tightened. "They'll find out when they find out."

"So you did do it," Tim said slowly. Genuine awe came through in his tone. "Folliculogenesis. You coaxed the oocytes to resume meiosis."

"They're in metaphase II," Sabell said. "On the way to haploid cells. PGV dropped away."

The doctor was startled by the loudness of his own voice. The song that had been playing ended just as he spoke. Everyone in the tavern stared at him, until a guitar chord crashed through the speakers as the next song began. *Look out, Mama, there's a white boat comin' up the river . . .*

"Haploid," Clem said. "Only one set of chromosomes. Ready for reproduction, waiting to receive the other set from the sperm. You wouldn't leave them hanging like that. You must have tried. Was it via nuclear transfer or in vitro fertilization?"

Sabell looked down, like a father too humble to display the degree of pride he felt in his handiwork. "They're fully competent," was all he said.

"There's your oodles," Clem murmured. No one but me had an idea what she meant.

Timothy leaned back. "Wow. This opens up so much for you. You can derive stem cell lines at will. Create countless embryos for experimentation. I'm sure you're excited—perhaps frightened, too?"

"Why should I be? It only gives us more opportunities, more control."

Cynthia was squeezing her bottle of water so hard I was afraid it would explode. "Nature is not yours to control!"

Sabell drew back. "What's this? We're having a civilized conversation—"

"You're the barbarian!"

So the Powers That Be left me here to do the thinkin' . . .

I jerked my head at Tim. He touched Cynthia's arm and said, "We ought to go now and make our report to the police." They stood up together. Tim gave Sabell a glance of what appeared to be genuine remorse. "I apologize, Egghead. I'll see you online, I hope."

"Perhaps," Sabell said as Tim and Cynthia left. "Perhaps not."

Sabell turned to me looking wounded, betrayed. "What were they trying to do to me?!" The correspondence with Tim had meant something to him.

"There's a lot I don't know about them," I said. "You call him Pinhead?"

"When we first began our exchange, I made fun of him for wasting his time counting the number of angels who could dance on the head of a pin. He adopted the name himself. He's an endocrinologist with a religious bent, correct?"

Sabell had been so fully taken in online, so excited to talk about his ideas, I almost felt sorry for him. Almost. "All we know for sure is that someone sent them into the same ambush that we encountered at Remly's," I said. I didn't want to make Sabell more nervous about Tim and Cynthia than he already was. Tim's deception may have been for noble purposes, in his mind, but now I wasn't convinced he was innocent of anything, up to and including the abduction of Margaret in order to bring down Sabell's clinic.

Sabell still looked worried, so I said, "I'm sorry. I thought they could help us. You said on the phone that you were getting scared. I can understand why. The men in the black outfits have been following us, too. Do you have any idea who they work for?"

"No," he said. "I've been agonizing over it, and have made some delicate inquiries at the lab. I can't find any connection between these men and Austin. But now you've encountered them defending his estate."

"Has Remly threatened you?" Clem asked.

Sabell twisted his neck, as if trying to let the answer wriggle out. "Someone has. Overtly, Austin has only made clear his displeasure at my plan to speak at the symposium tomorrow. I'm not sure whether to go ahead with it."

I glanced at Clem and saw the flicker I was looking for. Sabell had pretty much admitted he'd developed a process to grow immature oocytes into competent eggs. I wanted to hear the details. "You should do the symposium," I said. "Can you put us on your list of guests?"

"I suppose," he said without enthusiasm. "It's quite beside the point. I've told you before, I want to help you with Margaret. I felt personally hurt by her death and I would like to bring justice for Christopher and Janet."

You'd also like to get us off your back, I thought. Sabell assumed we'd leave him alone once Margaret's killer was tracked down. What I said was, "Do you have new information for us?"

"I've been analyzing the samples I, er, obtained. I've also been researching juvenile diabetes. The official cause of death doesn't quite, erm, add up. I don't see how ketoacidosis alone would have killed her that quickly. Of course, one can never prove that."

"Keep going," Clem said. "Did the Ketamine do it?"

"The trace amounts were small, probably given to keep her quiet, not kill her." By now Sabell's eyes were shifting madly. "Really, I can't say any more."

"Because you think Austin Remly was behind it," I said. "To protect the clinic. To forestall legal action by Chris."

Sabell wet his lips. "His father frightens me, too."

"Chris's father? Austin's father?" I asked.

Sabell's mercury eyes became fixed, as if put in freeze-frame. He screened us away with his hands. "Stop it! This already distracts too much from my work. Please, do what you have to do. If you're successful, I'll give what I have to the police—anonymously."

I slid my chair over so that Sabell couldn't get up. "What did Cole want you to do with Margaret as you were creating her?"

Sabell edged back into the corner. He looked like he was about to have a panic attack. "That's my last question," I said.

"Last question," he repeated. "Cole wanted a male, and he wanted the moon. Genes for intelligence, risk-taking, aggressiveness—he said those were what his son lacked. Christopher was too obedient, in Cole's view. I laughed at him. I told him to come back in a hundred, maybe two hundred years. An SNP, a single gene associated with a single disease, was challenge enough. He was talking about traits that might have little genetic basis, or if they did, would involve large complexes of genes. It did give me the idea, however, to try out the sequence theoretically associated with absolute pitch. More as a lark than anything. I never expected it to integrate. Or be expressed."

"What did he say when Margaret was born?" Clem asked.

"I have never been excoriated as I was by that man. I told him, calmly, that yes, he did pay the bills, but that the parents' desires still took precedence over his. Then I severed my relationship with him." Sabell stood up, more decisive now. "I'm leaving."

We stood with him. I shook his hand. "There's just one more favor. We need a ride. Clem's car is still up on Remly's property."

The fear came back into his face. "You're joking!"

I smiled. "I meant a ride to the police station. No, we wouldn't go back up there by ourselves."

Sabell reluctantly agreed to that. As we went out to the parking lot, he mumbled something about my choice of the Bullshead and how we were lucky not to have been gored. Clem insisted on sitting in the backseat. I got in the front. Sabell, as he drove, was silent, preoccupied with something. I could tell that Clem, behind me, was quietly searching the back for evidence.

Finally Sabell came out with what was bothering him. "You know what I said about maturing oocytes and so on? That was fantasy. To impress Pinhead."

I gave him a long, hard look. He shifted uncomfortably. "Those were Helen's egg cells you were talking about," I said at last.

Sabell shook his head.

"Yes. The nurse who took care of Helen saw you in the morgue. The autopsy report says her ovaries were removed. You need to explain that to me."

The doctor struggled for words. "Chris was desperate. Before Helen had even died he pleaded with me to bring her back. *Pleaded.* I felt for him. I wanted to help this man in his pain, his bereavement. He was so angry."

"Did he tell you to take her ovaries?"

"I was *compelled* by his agony and his rage. His emotions pushed me to do things I would not normally do. To surpass myself. He pestered me daily. The cystic fibrosis mutation must be eliminated, he said. It was not enough to screen embryos for those that had only one copy. They would still be carriers. He wanted the gene stamped out entirely, both alleles—he wanted *revenge* on it. He drove me to the gene-replacement solution, which in turn required the use of stem cells."

"Which conveniently dovetailed with your own ambitions."

"He—at the time Helen was dying, he wanted it *eradicated.* The disease, the loss, everything." Now I was the one being pleaded with. "He didn't want to know the gory details. That's all right, few people do. He simply wanted his daughter back. I read between the lines. He was driven, and in turn I was driven. Yes, I admit, it became an opportunity. But I tell you, I never would have thought of it had he not been so inflamed, so insistent. I wish I never had. Believe me. I wish I'd left him to live with his pain."

Sabell pulled up in front of the police station and stopped the car with a jolt. "Me, too, Doc," I said.

Clem and I got out. "Thanks for the ride," she said. "See you again soon."

He grimaced. "I hope not."

» » » » »

In spite of our best efforts, we still ended up staring down the barrel of Austin Remly's shotgun. The police had received two reports about the incident on his property: one from Tim and Cynthia, and one from Remly himself. When we requested an escort to Remly's property to retrieve Clem's car, an officer agreed readily. He wasn't in the business of giving rides, he explained; he was only coming to ask Remly if he wanted to press charges against us for trespassing. At the gate to the property, he buzzed the intercom and posed the question to Remly.

"Nah," Remly said. "Just have them get it off my land."

The gate opened automatically. "There you go," the officer said.

"You're not going to take us to the car?" Clem asked.

"I told you I'm not in the business of giving rides," he said.

We got out and started walking. There were no signs of men in stocking masks, no sign of anyone, in fact, until we noticed the dust trail tracking its way from the house, along the far side of the creek, toward us.

We ran to the Corvair. Clem jumped into the front seat and put the key in the ignition.

"Wait!" I said. "Remember who the last guy in here was?"

We got out and began a thorough search—in the car, under the car, around the engine. The approaching vehicle became visible after it crossed the creek. A maroon Jaguar.

"Has to be Remly himself," I said. "Security guys don't drive Jaguars."

Clem's hand went into her jacket pocket. "Want to talk to him?"

"Why not?" I said. "I don't think he'll try anything. He knows the cop was just here. Be careful with that gun, though. You almost got us killed earlier."

"What?"

"I've been thinking about it. The attack this afternoon fit the pattern of the one in the park. If they'd really wanted us then, they would have brought guns. If they'd wanted us this time, they would have used rifles. The shots didn't come near us until we had the protection of the cattle. Those guys were trying to scare us, not kill us. If you'd hit one of them, their intent would have changed."

Clem shook her head. We stood in front of the Corvair while the Jaguar parked ten yards down the road. The driver took a moment before he got out. When he emerged, he did so quickly and with a shotgun.

"Come forward slowly," he said. "I have every right to shoot you, so be very careful."

Clem mimicked my voice. *"Why not?"*

"Arms out away from your body," the man said. "That means you, missy."

When we got within three yards, he lowered the shotgun to chest level and told us to stop. He was about six-four, wearing a crisp poplin jacket, wide-brim hat, and loafers. His skin was overly smooth, polished, pink. He had the hale look of a man who breathed only pure air and whose breakfast came out of vitamin jars and a blender.

"Your names," he said.

"Bill Damen and Clem Pirez," I answered.

"She owns the Corvair," he stated. "You trespassed on my property today, Bill and Clem."

"Well, we saw your men dressed in stocking masks and—"

"Those men trespassed, too!" he snapped. "I've reported it to the police. I want an explanation."

"It's hard to talk with a shotgun pointed at my face."

"Harder with your face blown off."

It occurred to me, a little late as it turned out, that Austin Remly might have enough connections to get the murder of two trespassers covered up. "We're looking into the death of Margaret Claypool. She was the daughter of a client of your clinic."

"Not my clinic. Not my problem."

"I see. There's not much more I can say. The men in the commando outfits were involved in her abduction and death. We were pursuing them."

"Commandos don't wear stockings on their heads." He lowered the shotgun to hip level. His accent, free-range Texan, came on stronger as he relaxed a fraction. "And it was foolish for two amateurs like you to be messing with them. Where's your sense?"

"Don Masterson sent us up here."

"I don't know any Don Masterson."

"Did you know Margaret? Chris? Cole Claypool?"

"I've heard the names. I provide money, you understand, but I don't run the clinic or the lab. I give my scientists their freedom.

That's how they make breakthroughs. They're good men. It's a good system. Now, you mentioned the name Cole. Tell me about him."

"He's my uncle," I said. "He's provided money to the clinic, too."

"So he claims. Your uncle, huh? A trustworthy man?"

"No, sir."

"I thought not."

"What does he want from you?" I asked.

"You tell me. You know him better than I do."

"He's got a beef with Dr. Sabell. Sabell handled Margaret's conception. Some say botched it. Cole's the type to hold a grudge."

"Uh-huh. That would explain his interest in the doctor."

"If you tell me more, I can help you more."

Remly laughed. "Oh, I've heard that one. My business is information security, son. You won't get anything out of me I don't want you to get out of me. Why don't you and the miss get in your car and get out. Just remember I've got your faces on my video camera, your voice on my intercom, and your fingerprints on my gate."

He kept the shotgun on us as we returned to the Corvair. We'd found nothing suspicious attached to the car. Still, I held my breath as Clem cranked the ignition.

The starter whined, then the engine caught. I exhaled. Clem made a three-point turn and we headed for the gate.

» » » » »

"Pinhead and Egghead," I said, tilting the wooden chair in our office back against the wall. "What a pair."

"Just another day in the life of Damen C and I." Clem blew a wisp of hair out of her face. "A long one. Was it my imagination, or did all those Jerseys in Remly's pasture look exactly alike?"

"I didn't have time to introduce myself to each one personally." I opened my cell phone to dial in for messages. Chris was still AWOL, but there was one from Cole demanding to know where his son was. The next message made me hoot out loud.

"Listen to this," I said to Clem. "Don wants to know how the 'operation' at Remly's house went!"

"Invite him over. I'll give him a personal re-enactment."

I shook my head as I hit his number. When he picked up, I imitated his way of speaking. "Don, you're the man! Thanks for the great tip. Yeah, it went really, really well. We talked to Sabell and we talked to Remly, both of them, just like you said. The case is pretty much wrapped up."

"That's—that's great," he stuttered. "Who's the doer?"

"You're absolutely right, we're out the door." I spoke loudly, as if I didn't quite hear him. "Sit tight, okay? I might have one more assignment for you. Keep your phone line free."

"Okay, Bill. Hey, congratula—"

I clicked off. Clem stared at me. "You've gone insane," she said.

"Don's like bubblegum. We can't get rid of him, so we might as well use him. Especially if he's dumb enough to believe we still trust him."

She looked at her watch. "It's five. If I leave now, I can still get to Stacy's house before she does."

"We've done enough for one day," I said. "Take the night off."

"Oh yeah? What are you doing next?"

"I want to go back to the park where Margaret was found. The police should have finished with it by now. Then I'm going to look for Chris."

Clem stood up, arching her brows to show she'd proved her point.

"Be careful, Clem. You're no help to me in jail."

"And you're no help to me dead," she said, slinging her bag over her shoulder. "You're wrong about this afternoon. Firing back was the right thing to do."

She closed the door behind her. The truth was, neither of us knew for sure. I called Cole at his office.

"Where's Chris?" he growled. No need for a hello.

"I wouldn't know. I've been on Austin Remly's property, getting shot at by the same guys who came after me and Ulla. I'm almost certain the security force at the clinic are the ones who took Margaret."

"If you say so. But don't count the triads out just yet. I suppose it could also be a group like Jemaah Islamiya, trying to keep us out of Indonesia."

"No. I know more about how she died now. It was someone closer."

"Then explain who sent us the warning note to stay out of Jakarta."

"Same people who put the blow dart in my car."

"Who's that?"

"I can't say."

"Why'd you bring it up, then?" he said, blasting irritation through the phone. "I've got much more urgent business. I *must* know what data Christopher delivered to Wong Fen. You failed to follow up on your promise yesterday, so I sent Leonard to Chris's house today. He got nowhere. And Chris doesn't answer his phone. You're in deep, Bill. Don't waste any more time."

"You know that Remly and Sabell did it. Why are you protecting them?"

"I don't give a shit about Remly and Sabell!" he shot back. "You don't get it, Bill. Margaret is dead; the issue is dead. Tens of millions of dollars are at stake, by the end of the week. That's less than two days away. Now, what part of this don't you understand?"

"Are you helping them? In order to cover up your own role in Margaret's conception?"

"You're going down with Christopher, Bill. I'm sorry to say that, but you've dug your own grave."

"I did go to Chris's, by the way, last night. He told me everything."

"And?"

"And—answer my question."

"I have! I paid for the procedure! I did Chris a *favor!*"

"But he crossed you up. Him and the doctor. So maybe it's not Sabell you're protecting. Maybe it's Remly. Maybe the two of you are out to get Sabell."

Cole inhaled a deep breath, as of infinite patience. "Are you going to make me go over to Chris's house myself? I'm warning you, the consequences will be severe in the extreme."

"No, I'll find him," I said, and hung up.

21

There was just enough light left to see the place where Margaret's body had been dumped. The fog had cleared a little ways offshore and the last rays of sun had disappeared behind it.

It was a place of no special place. I parked in the main lot and walked toward the grassy space where the family had been picnicking. Small footpaths entered the scrubby woods from various spots on the grass. A few shreds of yellow crime-scene tape still remained. In the center of a thick patch of blackberry bushes, head height, I saw the pressed-down spot where Margaret must have lain.

I continued past the bushes, still following the small path. Only a few mountain-bike tracks showed in its dust. It led through early-growth woods into an open area. The cypress and pine trees here had been taller once, but something had uprooted them. Their decapitated trunks, bristling with dead roots, projected from the ground at tortured angles. The branches had been cut and stacked in piles, the trunks severed into sections. A gravel service road took off from the area of dead trees toward the main paved road.

I returned to the blackberry patch. It was only about twelve feet square, but a small person could easily disappear among its tangled branches and prickles. This time of year, the leaves were bright green, the shoots fresh. They terminated in small white flowers and tiny hard buds.

I flashed on a day in Golden Gate Park with Chris and his family. It was last August, a day when the sun, shining warmly, alternated with fog breaking apart and re-forming overhead. Margaret had discovered a row of blackberry bushes along the margins of the grass. Chris and I picked the berries, plump and dark and ripe, with her. I remembered her delight at the fact that you could take them off a branch and put them straight in your mouth. Dark berry juice smeared her dimples, her chin, the cleft under her nose. We all felt her delight, as if we had not a worry in the world. Chris was relaxed for a change. We played ball on the grass. Margaret wanted to be "it" in a game of pickle. Janet's face glowed, and my girlfriend at the time, Jenny, liked being part of the family scene.

The blackberries took me back further, too, to the years when, late in the summer, I'd rent a house with a group of friends near the Russian River. We swam in the river, back when Fred MacMurray unofficially let people cross his ranch property to get to the banks and swim in the nude. We bicycled up the mountains, lolled on the beach at Goat Rock, grilled fresh-caught salmon for dinner—and picked the blackberries, turning them into pies and preserves or eating them raw.

All of it was gone now. Margaret. Jenny. Janet's glow, Chris's contentment. Fred MacMurray was gone, too. The unofficial parking area near the river was sealed off from the public.

I tucked my hand inside the sleeve of my jacket and pushed back the first line of bushes. The prickles grabbed at the fabric. I stepped into the thicket, one pace, then two, until I was looking down at the trampled spot where Margaret had been. She had probably not left much of a body impression: The real trampling had been done by the police looking for evidence.

The light was fading. I took a flashlight from my pocket and scanned the ground, making sure there was nothing they missed. Then I pushed my way out of the bushes and scoured the area around them with the beam. I thought, as I searched, about the family who'd found Margaret. How traumatic it must have been for the eight-year-old boy to discover his retriever dragging her little body out of the brambles. Their encounter with the unthinkable. There but for the grace of God . . .

Something glinted in the beam of my flashlight. I knelt and dug it out. A silver medallion with a picture of a horse. It was not new evidence: The little boy had described the medallions tumbling brightly from her pockets as the dog dragged her along. Still, I put it in my pocket, a little memory of Margaret.

My phone rang. It was Chris.

"Where are you?" he asked.

"I'm . . . at a park. Hobart."

"Where they dumped her." A long pause followed. His voice choked a little. "I haven't been there myself. I don't think I can."

He sounded like a different man than he had eighteen hours ago. His voice was broken now, infinitely weary.

"There's no need for you to," I said. "How are you doing?"

"Well, I . . ." There was another long pause. Finally, as if lifting each of the words from his mouth like a massive weight, he repeated the phrase that had drawn me into this hell in the first place.

"I'd appreciate it if you would come over."

» » » » »

Abandon hope, I said to myself as I pressed Chris's doorbell. His listless slump when he opened the door said that he did not expect to find hope again in this lifetime. He'd exchanged his bathrobe for a set of grubby sweats. He stood in the doorway, gaping at me, head drooping, knees bent, as if he'd been struck by dementia. His eyes were opaque, inanimate. A bolt of alarm ran through me. "Chris, have you taken pills?"

His head swung back and forth. *No.* I made a tour of the ground floor. No pills had been needed. Bottles were scattered through the living room, dining room, kitchen. It appeared that when Chris and Kiersty ran out of champagne, they'd moved on to wine, and beer, and scotch. The sink was a tossed salad of dirty dishes. Cartons and plates of food were stranded on the tables. Three champagne glasses sat on the counter, stems broken, heads lopped off. Chris and Kiersty had let it all hang out, all right.

Now the binge was over. Chris sat himself down on the couch. I took an easy chair. He stared vacantly. He was shriveled, defeated.

"When did Kiersty leave?" I asked.

He dragged his hands over his face. "I might have passed out. What day is it?"

"Wednesday. Seven at night."

"I'm sooo hung over." His tongue was thick and dry, his voice rough like a broken wheelbarrow scraping along the ground. "I was about to start drinking again to make the pain go away. That's when I called you."

"Good decision. I've been worried."

He watched me with the look of a man awaiting sentence—for his Jakarta betrayal, I assumed. When he spoke, he said, "Did you find anything at the park?"

I shrugged and thought of the little medallion in my jacket pocket. "Nothing new. Do you need some aspirin?"

"Probably should." His lips barely moved.

I went into the kitchen. After rummaging unsuccessfully, I took a glass of water out to Chris and told him I'd get the aspirin from upstairs. He nodded and brought the glass shakily to his lips. I mounted the stairs. The door to Margaret's room stared at me obstinately, accusingly. I opened it and flipped on the light. The room still looked untouched. I opened the chest drawer where she'd kept the medallions. She'd had them arranged in a special order in a sorting tray. Now I saw the tray had been upended, the medallions spilled. Ulla had said that the man masquerading as the gardener had forced her to give him the house keys and then gone inside. Chris had not mentioned anything being stolen. The man must have come in for toys for Margaret. Ulla had been sure she didn't have her blanket or horse medallions with her when they went to the park. The guy knew to get the medallions. He even knew to look in this particular drawer. It made my skin crawl to think about how her favorite toys had been used against her.

I pulled the door shut. A dark figure at the top of the stairs startled me. "Chris! I was just getting your aspirin."

"I got some from the bedroom. Did you find what you need in her room?"

"Yes."

He shuffled down the hallway without a word. I watched, then followed him. The door to the room where Janet had holed up was closed. Farther down the hall was a gabled alcove, a little pocket with a tall, hinged window. The alcove contained an upholstered chair, a toy chest, and a small telescope mounted on a tripod. Chris unlocked the window and pointed the telescope into the night sky. He got down on his knees and put his eye to the lens.

I sat in the upholstered chair. Chris moved the cylinder back and forth, zeroing in on a celestial object. "This was Helen's," he said. “We kept it, thinking Margy would want to use it someday. I’m the only one who does.”

The house was dark. A little ambient light outlined Chris’s shape in the room. The stars flickered outside the window. Chris slumped away from the telescope, back against the wall, knees up.

“I dreamed about her the other night,” he murmured.

“Helen?”

“Margaret. I was in the park, lying on the grass, looking at the clouds with her,” he said in a low, gravelly, mesmerized voice. “It was so real; she was right beside me. The grass was thick and green, with that good grassy smell. We picked out our favorite cloud shapes and said what they were. Everything she saw was either a duck or a horse. I kidded her: ‘Isn’t there *any* other kind of animal in the sky?’ And she didn’t answer. She was thinking about it, I guessed. Then I saw this cloud—it was silver and gray and yellow and blue all at once, with arms and legs and hair streaming in the wind. It was a little girl floating up there, with her arms outstretched. But I couldn’t reach her, she was too far away, floating up there.”

Tears trickled down his face. “I looked beside me and Margy was gone. I said, ‘Margy, why’d you go up there?’ She said, ‘I thought you wanted me to come up here, Daddy. I caused you too much trouble.’ I burst out crying, a flood. Then I woke up. My pillow was soaked.”

We went silent again in the shadow of the dream. I pictured the cloud-girl Chris had described, her hair the color of new wheat. It made me think of Chris when he was a boy, with his eager look and golden-boy gleam. He let out a long, tired sigh. “I gotta get it together, Bill. Kiersty maybe wasn’t the best idea, but . . .”

I nodded. “Did you see Leonard Wilson today?”

Chris dug his knuckles into his eyes, trying to wake himself up. “He came yesterday—today—whenever. We were in the bedroom when the doorbell rang. I opened my window and saw who it was and then, uh, yelled something obscene. He cursed me back and said I had to talk to him, I had to tell him what I gave Wong Fen. I, um, did a kind of obscene thing and said that was what I gave them and he could have the same."

"And then he left."

"Yeah, he left. Kiersty kind of danced in front of the window, too. I wish she hadn't done that."

"Now Cole knows you're bonking your secretary."

"Ahh, so what. He's going to fire her anyway. The thing with Wilson—it's between me and him. She was trying to help, I guess. Later on, she got this really worried look. She said I shouldn't let my father win. I said, 'What's he winning?' She said that if I walked away from the company, he won. I should go back, pretend to make up with him, worm my way back to the top, then stick it to him. I think she's scared of what Cole might do to me."

"I don't blame her," I said. "The Jakarta business is serious. He knows you used Wilson's computer on Sunday. He said he'll prosecute if you don't go to him and confess everything. I think he means it."

"I'm *sure* he means it."

"So why did you do it? Just to get back at Cole, or was money involved?"

"I didn't ask for and I didn't take a cent from them. I'm broke, I admit, but this one was on principle."

"This one—you've done it before?"

Chris exhaled a long breath. "He wouldn't give, or even loan, me money to take care of my own daughter, so I siphoned a little here and there. It was going to be mine in the long run, right?"

"Actually, your father did help out without telling you. He paid a lot of Sabell's bills when you were conceiving Margy. That's why Sabell told you he'd do most of the work gratis. Did you know that?"

"I didn't think Dad knew about Sabell until you told me," Chris said sullenly. "You're responsible for that bottle of scotch downstairs being empty, Bill."

"I'm sorry. I shouldn't have said it like I did."

Chris was coiling back into himself. His hands went to his head and his elbows pinched in at the chin. He squeezed his eyes shut. "You see? I can't even *fuck* right! He has to take charge of conceiving my children for me, too! He always told me that boys needed tests in order to enter manhood. Tests of courage, strength, obstacles to overcome to prove we can handle the world. He said I had to find my wings, learn how to grab the fire, but every time I do, he comes in the back way and takes control. He can't stop himself. He's sick."

"Yes, he is. I'm afraid he may have done more than reimburse Sabell. He may have taken a role in directing Margy's genetic design."

Chris curled further into himself, stricken. "No!" he wailed, then opened his elbows and said more calmly, "No. She would have been a boy. That's what he wanted, of course. The only way he'd finally accept Janet was when she produced a son. I didn't give in. I wanted another girl."

"Sabell said that you started talking about having another girl while Helen was still sick in the hospital."

"I might have. I don't remember." Chris's eyes had gone glassy. He didn't want to think about it. But I needed to know if Sabell's story this afternoon was true. I hadn't decided yet, with Chris in such a fragile state, whether to mention the removed ovaries.

"Did you insist that both alleles that could carry the cystic fibrosis mutation be replaced in the new embryo? That's the reason Sabell said he had to do the germ-line engineering."

"I guess I did go on a kind of crusade. I wanted to wipe it out from the family line forever. Maybe I went overboard."

Just a little. "Have you told me everything you know about Austin Remly?"

Chris shrugged. "I think so."

I recounted a short version of the ambush that had occurred on Remly's property today.

"Christ, Bill, you should have told me you got attacked again! Maybe we should leave this to the police."

His concern was touching. "We will, eventually. But I'm not stopping now." My tone came out harsher than I meant it to. "The question is whether these were Remly's men, or someone planted them on his property. What are the chances your father's hired a force like the one that's been after us?"

"We've used private military companies in other countries. To make sure a job gets done right, if you know what I mean. But I've never seen any guys like that around here."

I waited until Chris looked at me to say, "I'm afraid we can't rule out your father as a suspect in Margy's kidnapping and death."

He shook his head. "*Why?* He could have just offered to babysit her for a weekend. Not that he ever did. I mean, I hate the man's guts right now, Bill, but I don't buy it. His own flesh and blood? No way."

"Maybe he didn't see her that way. Maybe he saw her as Sabell's creature."

"That's a sick idea, Bill!" Chris spat. "Who would ever think that kind of thing? Sabell might have thought about her that way, or maybe Remly did, but not my father. You obviously don't understand him, Bill. He's a bastard, yes, but he doesn't act gratuitously. He's capable of almost anything, but only if it moves us—the family, the company, his personal fortune—forward. He doesn't waste time on anything else."

Chris fell abruptly silent. After a few moments, he said, in a subdued tone, "Then again, what do I know? It wasn't so long ago I thought the world was in the palm of my hand. Now look at me."

I did. The image of a carapace abandoned by its owner came to me. A smaller and more timid insect now made its home there, scuttling around inside the empty shell like an impostor.

"Do you know what I realized?" he said. "My entire life has been based on a false premise. The premise that I could step into my father's shoes someday. That I was a little Cole, a mirror, an extension of him. It never really mattered who *I* was. He was omnipotent. Naturally, I wanted to please him and *become* him."

"I vaguely remember that feeling about my dad," I said. "It didn't last too long."

"Maybe you're lucky. I mean—goddammit, I *still* don't know if I'm over it. I was supposed to be the next 'Mr. Claypool,' but every time I try to take the mantle, he undercuts me. Kiersty, last night, she had a, you know"—Chris pinched his fingers in front of his mouth—"blunt. After a few tokes, she said my shoulders were all hunched and I needed to loosen up. All of a sudden it hit me. I said, in that Butthead voice you get when you're high, 'Uh, it's because my dad's gonna come in here and kick my ass.' And I giggled, but it was true. No matter how much sex we had, how much booze I drank, I couldn't escape it. The feeling of cringing. Ducking the blow. Maybe you remember—I used to plan out my school clothes, my shirts and pants and socks, a full week ahead of time. Why? To be out in front. Unblameable."

"You always seemed pretty tough to me, Chris. Especially in our one-on-one basketball games."

"Right! Because I learned to hit first. You can't hit me if I'm already hitting you. That's why it's good to be on top, so you can deliver the blows. That's what I am. That's *all* I am."

"Come on, you always said you had the ideal childhood."

"What a delusion." He turned his head away and gave the telescope a swat. "Jupiter. The old striped bastard. That's what I was looking at."

We sat in a silence that felt like the vacuum of outer space. The stars burned in the night sky. I found myself thinking about their deceptive intimacy. How close and familiar they seemed, how cold and far away they actually were. Chris had been born under, way under, the sign of Jupiter.

He looked up at me with a kind of shine in his eyes. "Remember one weekend when I stayed over at your house? We were probably seven years old. I hung out with you and your parents watching a baseball game on a Saturday. It was so relaxed. Everyone kind of did their own thing. Your dad was reading, your mom was working on some papers, you and I played chess. The amazing thing to me was that no one was yelling at the TV. See, Dad howled at it, calling the players and officials filthy names. He had money riding on the football games. That weekend at your house was so different. It was like a little paradise—the slow pace of the game, the chatter of the crowd, just hanging out. For once it wasn't all about who *won*. Nothing with Dad was just for fun."

"Which meant he'd make sure you never won," I said. "You'd always come in second, which he told you wasn't good enough."

"Yeah. I vowed to be a different kind of father. I was actually relieved that Helen was a girl. I was kind of scared about having a boy."

"My dad was the opposite of yours," I said. "He let me do whatever, as if it didn't really matter how I turned out. I thought it must be nice to have a stable dad who got things *done*. Cole was scary—one day he was really nice, the next day an ogre. But still you knew he was there to protect you and watch out for you. I was afraid, like literally every week, that Dad would disappear and our family would fall apart. That's why I was so serious about camping. I figured I'd be out on the street one day, fending for myself. Mom and my sister wouldn't have time to worry about me."

"Then he went and did it when you were twelve. You guys did all right, didn't you? Your mom's a doctor. I know it's just a community hospital, but . . ."

"Oh, we were perfectly fine. Not quite like your family, though."

"Yeah, but your parents let you do what you wanted."

"Sort of. They always said, 'As long as you're happy.' But they said it in a certain way."

Chris's face turned glum. "I had no idea what would make me happy, until Janet and Helen came along. And then Margaret. Take away them, take away the company, and what's left of me? A bigshot looking to deliver a blow. That really is all I am. That asshole. Cole Claypool's son."

"Take some time, Chris. After we resolve the case, go away. Relax, don't even think about this stuff."

"The thing is," he said, "Dad always dared me to defy him. I thought I'd made myself cold enough, hard enough, gotten the killer instinct. But every time I try to break away—like at Margaret's memorial—I break myself instead. I've gone out on a limb and now I'm working really hard to saw it off."

I couldn't disagree. "I don't think you should go back to Claypool Construction. But you still have to respond to the Jakarta charges. Even if your father changes his mind, the board or Wilson could come after you."

"Wilson!" Chris's competitive edge came roaring back all at once. "Shit, I'm leaving the place wide open to him!"

This was not the reaction I'd hoped for. "Whatever you plan to do, you need to do it tomorrow. The contract will be awarded on Friday. For what it's worth, I think your father actually does want you back. You'd have to eat a lot of humble pie, and I personally wouldn't recommend being in business with him, but that's up to you. Maybe you'll decide that your place is with the company, but not doing it the Cole way. You could make a new name for the Claypool family, make it stand for something other than bullying."

"Maybe." Chris's fingers nervously drummed on the telescope. "I must be boring the crap out of you, Bill, with all this whining."

"I probably should get on home," I said. I hesitated, then decided Chris had a right to know. "There's one more thing. I hate to have to tell you."

Chris's head tilted, waiting. I took in a fortifying breath and said, "Did you give Dr. Sabell permission for any of Helen's organs to be removed or donated?"

"No. I already told you. Did you find out more about what he took?"

"We're talking about *Helen* now, not Margaret. Six years ago, when she died."

He shook his head, baffled. I said, "He removed Helen's ovaries when she was in the hospital morgue."

Chris's fingers slowly formed into fists. *"No!"* he bellowed. "My God, Bill! He did that? To her?"

"You're sure you gave no hint, even tacitly, that he could use her tissues, cells, gametes—anything?"

"Positive!" Chris screamed. He jumped up to his feet and paced the hallway. "No, no, no!"

"The nurse, Mark Baines, saw him performing an operation on Helen in the morgue. The coroner's report says her ovaries had been removed. It doesn't explain why. Sabell claims you put a lot of pressure on him to replace Helen."

"But what in God's name did he want with her ovaries?"

"It turns out that, even at that young age, a girl has most of the oocytes she'll have for life. He seems to have found a way to grow the oocytes into eggs. That would permit him to do the kind of reprogenetics he did on Margaret."

"That's—" Chris choked on his own words. His pacing became more frantic. *"Bill, that means I had sex with my own daughter!"*

"Don't jump to any conclusions. We don't have any evidence he used Helen's eggs. We need to compare Helen and Margaret's DNA."

"I'll kill the fucker!"

Chris clomped furiously down the stairs. I listened to make sure he wasn't leaving the house. I'd give him a few minutes to cool off, then go down. Yet another demon had been unleashed. His despair had disappeared, but so had his self-reflection. The outrage was back. That might be good, or it might be very, very bad.

I woke up tired Thursday morning. Getting shot at had taken a lot out of me, but the conversation with Chris had taken more. Just when he seemed to be coming to his senses and finding a balance between self-blame and self-aggrandizement, between loathing Cole and becoming Cole, I went and told him about Sabell stealing Helen's ovaries. That sent him into another spiral.

Clem had been busy last night, too. I met her at Scoby's at nine. It was a relief to be looking into her deep green eyes again, flecked with gold and mischief. Best of all, they were not asking me to explain her life, as Chris had his.

I recounted my evening with Chris. Clem caught on quickly. "'They fuck you up, your mum and dad,'" she quoted.

It was a Philip Larkin poem. "How does it end?" I asked. "Something about 'Don't you do it, too'?"

"'Man hands on misery to man,'" she said. "'It deepens like a coastal shelf. Get out as early as you can, and don't have any kids yourself.'"

"Touché," I said. "The weird thing about it is Chris believed for so many years that he had the ideal childhood."

"Total denial," Clem said. "Eventually it produces total rage. Not that I'm so *personally* enlightened, but I do know that as kids, we're so gullible, so open. Your parents are your universe. The parameters they lay down, you take as literally true, like the laws of physics, instead of one person's twisted subjective version."

"Which twisted subjective version did you get?"

"Oh, we're talking multiple delusions. Don't even ask. Chris is trying his damnedest to blame his father, is what it sounds like to me. Guilt is like water, it flows into every open channel. And you know what? I'll bet Cole went through exactly the same thing with *his* father."

"I never met my grandfather," I said, "but from what my mother told me, you're right. Chris is like two different people. Half the time he thinks he's king of the universe; the other half, he's a worthless worm. He doesn't know how to exist in between. The harder he tries to purge himself of his father, the more he turns into Cole. He needs an exorcism or something."

"He's his own doppelgänger. The one Chris is constantly haunted by the other." She took a long sip of coffee and said, "Want to hear what I did last night?"

"Shoot," I said.

Clem had finally paid her visit to Stacy Hatcher's house. Stacy surprised her by already being home from work. She was tired and her prickly defenses were no match for Clem's determination to get in the door. Stacy had fertility problems, as we'd guessed. Her husband was fixated on producing children. She took the job at the clinic looking for an answer. After several conventional attempts, she tried an experimental egg-transfer technique Sabell suggested. A series of miscarriages followed. Stacy felt like a guinea pig, which made her mad enough to threaten to sue him. In the end, she agreed to keep working, in her surly fashion, at the clinic until Sabell produced results. She said Austin Remly hardly ever came in. As for Sabell's lab at home, she said he'd never let the likes of her into his labyrinth. That was what he called it: the labyrinth. He talked about the twists of DNA as a maze. The succession of generations, the genetic shuffle, was an ever-branching garden of forking paths in which you could get lost.

"Not Sabell," I said. "He's the one plotting the labyrinth. The question is, who's the Minotaur?"

"I guess we know who the sacrificial virgins were," Clem said. "I felt sorry for Stacy. I see where her personality is coming from now. She's got pressure on one side from her husband, who she's afraid will leave her if she doesn't get pregnant. On the other side she's got Sabell making her feel like she's living in a petri dish."

"Chris's problem with his sperm bothers him, too. It makes him feel impotent on more than just the reproductive level."

"That boy needs to remember the stuff's for fun."

I raised my eyebrows. "I'm glad you think so."

She double-raised her eyebrows back at me. "After we went to the clinic, I picked up this book called *Why Sex Is Fun*."

"I didn't know you were in the remedial class."

"Listen to you, Mr. Fetishless. Supposedly the reason humans have such peculiar mating habits is due to occulted ovulation. Men are never sure when women are ovulating, so, unlike most animals, they want to have sex all the time. On the one hand, it's supposed to make a man stick closer to home instead of woofing off after other females in heat, because he doesn't know when his own is. On the other, it inhibits him from killing infants—like, for instance, gorillas will do—because he can never be sure which one's his."

"I'm still waiting for the fun part." I hadn't pegged Clem as the type to dabble in this stuff, but come to think of it, she'd mentioned going through a brainy phase.

Clem cocked her head. "Me, too, I guess. I got distracted by the infanticide idea. I thought about Margaret and about how the ancient Greeks exposed their infants. An early form of genetic culling. Then I got thinking about something that happened when I was a kid, about seven years old."

She took a drink of coffee. I asked her what had happened.

"My family spent a few years on a ranch," she said, her eyes focused somewhere beyond me. "We were caretakers. Five or six cats lived there. One of the females gave birth to a litter of kittens in this hidden place in the barn loft. I was the one who found them, making teeny, tiny, little mewing sounds, the mother licking them. I set the little family up with some blankets and went out there every day, bringing milk. I spent hours watching the new kittens roll around, vying for the teat, their cloudy eyes squinted and confused, awakening to the world. It was such a miracle to me that Mona—we called her that because she made these moaning sounds—was all fat and wobbly one day and the next had brought these incredible little fur bundles into the world. Every day they got more playful, better coordinated, more aware of what was around them. I didn't pick them up. I wanted to watch them grow without interference. I didn't let the rest of my family come up to see them, either. Then one morning, on my way out to the barn with my pan of milk, I heard this terrible wailing. It was Mona, wandering in the yard. Why wasn't she with her kittens? I climbed the ladder to the loft and pushed aside the bales of hay I'd used to hide them. All four kittens were dead, their throats ripped open like torn little stuffed animals. Blood and fur everywhere. I threw up. I went back down the ladder and into the house, crying, and asked my mother to get the rifle out of its locked case. I intended to shoot whatever had killed our kittens. A fox or coyote, I figured. My big brother was kind enough to explain that one of the male cats had done it. That's when I really burst into tears. Mom gave him a good whipping; she knew he'd said it to shock me, to demonstrate his own worldliness. I stayed in bed for two days, then I went looking for that tomcat. We had a hoe that we used to pin rattlesnakes so we could kill them. I was going to pin that tom."

"How did you know which one it was?"

"That was the problem. There were three. None of them had blood on his coat; the guilty party had licked it off. I grabbed each one by his front legs and looked into his eyes. I couldn't tell which cat had done it. No remorse, I guess. I perceived nature, and the whole world, differently from that moment on. We're animals. I don't know that I've really trusted anyone since that day."

"That's rough, Clem. Did it ruin your relationship with your brother?"

"Ruin?" She chortled. "It's easy to play the tough guy when your victim's a little girl three years younger than you. No, I didn't trust him, but I learned from him. He had access to the dark knowledge I would need to survive. He was the one who taught me about the rattlesnakes. I thought they were kind of cool, until I found out what would happen if one bit you. My brother and I killed every rattlesnake we found."

A strange feeling swelled in my chest. I felt bad for the little seven-year-old girl named Clem. I pictured her in denim bib overalls, her black curls full of ranch dust, and wished I could have been there for her.

"I'm sorry to go on and on, Bill. It just made me think—I wonder if the urge to commit infanticide really has disappeared in the human male. I wonder if Chris and Janet sensed in some intuitive way that Sabell didn't use their gametes to create Margaret."

I sat up straight. The thought was chilling, if unlikely. "We don't know what he used Helen's eggs for. Even if he used them for Margaret, they still contained both parents' DNA. Besides, Chris and Janet's grief is real."

"Sure," Clem said. "You may have blind spots about your family, though. From what you've told me, the thing Chris is most upset about is his failure as a father. And Janet's admitted it's a relief for her daughter's suffering to be over. Maybe what she really means is her own suffering. Now she's free to leave the marriage she wanted to escape six years ago."

"I thought it was just the males you worried about."

"The female may be less violent, but she's no less aggressive, and a lot better at hiding it. Don't let them fool you, Bill."

Her brow had taken on such a theatrically morbid look that I had to laugh. "Isn't there *anyone* you trust, Clem?"

She clicked her tongue. "Bugs," she said. "I find them simple, predictable, and I don't feel bad when I squash them."

» » » » »

Clem and I dressed up a little for the afternoon symposium at Stanford, where Dr. Sabell was scheduled to speak about his work. For me that meant dark pants instead of my usual jeans, a comfortable but not frayed white shirt, a suit jacket, and my work boots. Clem was in a loose, airy print skirt, red flowers on a black background, with black tights underneath and a dark sweater on top. I'd packed the sound and video gear we intended to use into a briefcase.

We left early so that we could stop in at the central police station to ask about the investigation into Margaret's abduction and death. Clem's interview with Gallegos had gotten us thinking it was worth another effort to find out how the authorities viewed the case.

"The way Chris was arrested the first time, in the middle of Cole's birthday party, makes me think someone was trying to make a point," I said. "I got the feeling down at the police station—Chris said this, too—that there was a split between those who sympathized with him and Janet for their loss, and those who saw them as likely suspects."

"I doubt anyone will want to reveal their true thoughts to Chris's cousin," Clem said, "but it can't hurt to ask."

We waited in a busy front room while the detectives working the case were paged. Families and girlfriends of suspects, along with the occasional lawyer, milled among the wooden benches, grumbling on cell phones. The walls were decorated with crime safety tips, "wanted" notices, honor citations, and photographs of officers on the force.

At last a clean-shaven young man in a coat and tie, hair combed back, came out for us. Clem and I expected him to turn and lead us back to his office. He just stood where he was.

"You must be Detective Ralston," I said, putting out my hand. "I'm Bill Damen. We'd like to talk to you about the Claypool case."

He gave a quick shake. "Yes. I know your name. You have new information?"

"Maybe. I'd like to compare notes with you."

His eyes did a little roll. "Sorry, I can't discuss it. If you have something worthwhile, I'll be happy to take a statement."

"We've been attacked twice in the past week by men wearing stocking masks."

"We have the reports. We're looking into the incidents. What else?"

"There's a good chance these guys work for Austin Remly and the Sabell Clinic."

"That was in the report."

I paused, gauging whether it was worth the trouble to push harder. Ralston chewed his lip impatiently. I said, "Can you at least tell me if the officers who arrested Chris Claypool a week ago Sunday are still on the case?"

This time the roll of his eyes was more obvious. "The arresting officers, like all officers, carry out assignments as needed. All right?"

"Thanks a *whole* lot," I said, turning away before I finished the sentence. Clem linked her arm sympathetically through mine.

We started through the waiting room. I jerked her to a stop in front of a photograph on the wall. I'd seen the photo before, only not with the legend OFFICER OF THE YEAR, 1997 written above it and the name written below. It was in an office at CCE that I'd seen the same officer, stout but erect, his uniform crisp. The name under the picture read RAYMOND WILSON.

» » » » »

I'd noted Leonard Wilson's number when I was in his office with Chris on Sunday. Now I dug it out of my wallet as we walked to the Scout.

"Leonard, this is Bill Damen," I said when he picked up. "I'd like to meet with you today."

"About what, Bill?"

"The Margaret Claypool case. That's my sole concern. It's not about Chris or Cole or Jakarta or anything else."

"I'm sorry, but I don't have anything to tell you."

"The thing is, I'm just leaving the police station. I noticed your father's picture on the wall. He's in the same precinct as the officers who arrested Chris the first time around."

"My father's involvement is zero," he said firmly.

"Can I give you my mobile number, just in case?" I reeled it off without waiting for an answer.

"All right. Now, if you'll pardon me, we're in crisis mode this week. As you know."

"Yeah. Chris can be a real dildo," I said. Clem covered her mouth to keep from laughing. The phrase had just popped out of my mouth, an effort to make Wilson more talkative.

"If you like small ones," Wilson said dryly and clicked off.

I shut my phone and started the Scout. "He claims to know nothing," I told Clem. "I'll try to get him again tonight."

"There sure are a lot of smart people around here who know nothing," Clem commented.

By now we were running late for Stanford. Sabell's panel did not begin until four, but I'd hoped to catch him before he went on. We had to hunt around for the right building, then hunt some more for a place to park the Scout. We went through one of a set of four glass doors into a lobby with polished floors. The event was taking place in Room 1A, a small auditorium right off the lobby. There wasn't the kind of buzz you'd expect around a symposium. Tim had meant it when he said it was exclusive.

An official with a badge and clipboard stood at the entrance to the auditorium. She didn't look like she was just there to say hello. I asked if we were in the right place for the embryo engineering symposium.

"Your names?"

"We're with Dr. George Sabell." I gave her our names. "He said he'd put us on the list."

She scanned her list. Our names weren't there. "It's invitation only," she said. "I'm sorry."

"If you'll let us in to find Dr. Sabell, he'll vouch for us."

She said that was impossible. I said I'd have to disturb him on his cell phone, which he wouldn't appreciate. She pressed her lips together and looked straight ahead, implacable in her official duty.

Clem remained planted in front of the door, staring down the guard. I went around the corner and punched in Sabell's number. He didn't answer, of course, but I spoke loudly about the guard's intransigence.

I came back around the corner, ready to have another go, when I saw a bulldog of a figure in a charcoal business suit striding toward the doors. He turned his head aside to send a stream of brown juice to the pavement, then came inside. I went to meet him.

"I didn't know you were interested in embryo engineering, Uncle."

Cole reared back, hands in the air, in a fake-hearty welcome of surprise. "Nephew! I was just thinking of you last night. I rented a fascinating DVD. *Kill Bill, Volume Two*. Great concept."

"Yeah. Shows how pissed off a person can get when you wipe out their family."

"Family values, Nephew. We've got to stick together." He changed tack and leaned toward me, speaking in a low, confidential voice. "What do you say we nail the bastards who did what they did to Margaret? I assume that's why you're here."

"In part. I'm also nailing down exactly whose DNA Sabell used in Margaret's conception."

"I'll tell you what, Bill. I'm willing to concede that Sabell is a plausible suspect. I admit that, at first, I didn't believe he'd destroy his own handiwork. But I've learned more about him. He's pissing in his pants that the truth about Margaret will become public. His mistakes, his liability—he might go after you and Christopher next. You should be careful."

"If Sabell's so nervous, what's he doing here today?"

"He's desperate to change the subject. They say he's going to reveal some fairly stunning aspects of his research. The big splash will drown out any revelations that might happen to come out about Margaret. Here's the rub: Remly paid for the work and wants to keep the lid on for now. Big blowup coming, Bill, *big* blowup. You watch."

I couldn't help smiling at Cole. His mouth had filled with tobacco spit. A dribble of brown juice slid over his lip. I nodded to a trash receptacle across the lobby. It sat where the lobby narrowed to a corridor, the same corridor into which Clem had melted, tying a scarf over her head, when Cole arrived.

Cole hotfooted it to the bin, and I followed. The official at the door pretended not to be eyeing us. Cole, as he straightened, glanced into the lobby. He was watching for someone.

"You did more than secretly pay Sabell's bills," I said, setting my briefcase on the floor to pin Cole close to the receptacle. "You told him how to design Margaret. You must have been pissed when she turned out to be a she."

"Son of a bitch." Cole wiped his mouth and cleared the anger from his face, as if it had been the tobacco annoying him. "I talked with George, of course. But it was Christopher's child. He made the decisions. I'd never take that away from him."

"Chris knows that you *did* try to take it away from him."

"Does he?" Cole's eyes suddenly sparkled, and I had no idea why. The very subject of Chris should have evoked the same anger Sabell did. Cole must have nabbed Chris. Either that or the worm had taken an unexpected turn.

Then I remembered Chris's tantrum at the end of last night, and I knew what it was. "Chris came back to the company." I said it as a statement.

Cole gave me a secret little smile and fished his cell phone from his pocket. As his thick finger poked at the buttons, I said, "Why aren't you in the office? Is Jakarta settled?"

Cole's smile got a little broader. He held up a finger and put the phone to his ear. "Hello," he said, "it's Cole Claypool."

I looked down the corridor. Clem saw me and picked up her pace. "Good," Cole was saying, "I'm right here."

I moved my briefcase so that it was between Clem and the trash bin. She rushed around the corner, hand outstretched to toss a wad of paper in the trash, and appeared to trip over the briefcase. I lunged forward to catch her. Our shoulders collided and she staggered into Cole, grabbing his jacket sleeve to keep her balance. Cole, in the process of sliding his cell phone back into his inside pocket, raised his arms. She knocked him backward.

"I'm so sorry!" she said, regaining her feet and brushing off his jacket.

"Idiot!" Cole blasted.

"I'm really sorry," Clem said, moving away.

"Oaf!" I called after her. She gave me a split-second glance that let me know she'd succeeded in her task.

"Who is she?" Cole demanded. "I know that face."

"No idea." The scarf had done its job. I changed the subject. "Anyway, it sounds like you've got the Jakarta situation under control."

"*Everything's* under control." Cole was still watching Clem disappear down the corridor. "Hey, you!" he barked after her. "Come here!"

I spoke more quickly. "I'm glad you're ready to acknowledge that Sabell and Remly are probably the ones behind Margaret's death."

"Of course," Cole said dismissively. He looked at me as if he'd just noticed I'd been talking. He recomposed himself and settled back into his Olympian manner. "You can leave it to me now, Bill. I'll reel them in for you."

"It's the security guys I'm worried about. I've gotten a good look at one of them. He's South African."

Cole gazed at me for an uncomfortably long while, the fissures on his face in motion like some kind of oracle about to decide my fate. "You're assuming they're the same guys," he said. "What if this whole masked-bogeymen business is a bait-and-switch?"

The words sent a shiver of doubt through my mind. It was clear the men were meant to scare us, but what if they had another purpose as well—to draw us away from the real action? It was also possible Cole's sole purpose was to sow that doubt.

Cole had turned to his left. A man was approaching. He was tall and slim, in a cream-colored turtleneck, Capri jacket, and crisp-pleated gabardine slacks. He moved in on us silently, in crepe-soled Italian leather slip-on shoes. I hadn't seen or heard the front door open.

"Austin," Cole said in the tone of a man relieved to see an old friend.

"I'm glad to see you, Mr. Claypool," Remly replied, his voice both suave and warm with Texas dust.

They shook hands. I got a better look at Remly now, had a chance to notice his slippery brown eyes and the trim efficiency of his movements and clothes. The edge of his hairline was so sharp it appeared painted on.

I stuck out my hand and said, "Nice to meet you again."

The slippery eyes turned sharp and skeptical. He offered a quick, limp hand, then turned to Cole and said, "Any sign of the man of the hour?"

Cole looked from Remly to me. "You know each other?"

"Oh yes," I said.

This troubled Cole. He took the reins back by saying to Remly, "Let's go outside where we can talk."

"Mr. Remly," I said, "you should consider the possibility that Margaret's death is closely connected to your clinic. You know all about GenVigil, of course. They may have kidnapped Margaret in order to turn her into a poster child against genetic engineering. They flubbed it and allowed her to die."

Cole could not prevent another puzzled wrinkle from crossing his forehead. He was not the only one capable of sowing confusion.

Remly was barely ruffled. "They'll be quieted soon," he said with cool certainty. I thought again of the ambush on his property and the fact that GenVigil had nearly stepped into it, too.

"And Cole," I went on, "you haven't even mentioned Janet. I'll bet you have no idea what she's been up to."

"I know exactly what she's been up to!" he snapped. He took Remly's shoulder and turned him toward the door. I started to follow, but Cole raised a thick hand in my direction. "Be a good boy and let the grown-ups talk now."

The two men exited but stayed near the doors, presumably to keep watch for Sabell, the "man of the hour." I went down the corridor behind the auditorium to find Clem. She'd made herself at home in a small lounge, where she was drinking coffee and talking to a trio of graduate students. I asked them where to find an exit other than the front door. They told me to keep going to the end of the corridor.

"Thanks for your help," Clem said to the students. She and I started down the corridor. "Got anything?" she asked me.

"Haven't tried yet," I said. "We need to move closer."

We went out a side door and found ourselves on a paved walk between buildings. I bent down, placed the briefcase on the walk, and snapped it open. Inside was the receiver for the tiny wireless microphone Clem had dropped in Cole's pocket. I put in a button earpiece, switched on the receiver, and listened.

"Too much static," I said.

Holding the receiver, I went to the corner of the building. Clem brought the briefcase. I turned left and walked along the front wall. The angle of the wall and a few maple trees shielded us from sight of the small concrete entrance pavilion. The voices came in more clearly now. "Got it," I said, and hit RECORD on the MP3 player attached to the receiver.

Clem watched my face as I listened. I nodded. The voices were muffled but just audible. We sat on the grass, our backs against the trunk of a tree.

" . . . can be of help to you," Cole was saying.

"What's your interest?" Remly said.

"My granddaughter has been killed. This deeply offends me. However, were the man I believe responsible to be brought to justice, some very private and rather embarrassing facts concerning my family would become fodder for the piranhas in the media. I want the man kept under control. Do you see why it's not only my interest but our common interest?"

"I see that we'd both like our doctor to shut his mouth. But I'm not convinced our reasons are compatible."

"Oh, they are. I give you the evidence I have. You use it to keep the doctor under your thumb for your purposes, I for mine."

The conversation stopped. I heard some rustling and shuffling, then voices of passersby.

"Who are these characters in the black outfits, shooting up my property?" Remly said.

"It seems clear," Cole said. "They were hired by Sabell. He's far too incompetent to execute an abduction himself."

"He doesn't have a great deal of common sense, that's true. I suppose he could be dumb enough to hire some crew like that. How do you propose to deal with them?"

"You have people. I have people. We'll deal with them."

There was a pause, and more shuffling. After some indistinct sounds, Remly said, "Let me sleep on it."

"Are you talking about a nap?"

Remly snorted. "You propose to get this rogue roped and tied in the next half hour?"

"You tell me. You're the one who's afraid he's going to let your cat out of the bag at his panel. Not that it's my business, but I'd think letting the profession know about a breakthrough would be good for your enterprise."

"My *enterprise* is not an enterprise, it's a vision. This technology is not for the common man. It's like plutonium. It must be safeguarded."

"I see. Why not just keep him locked up in his lab, then?"

"Your business is different than mine. Sabell is a genius. He's been something of a pariah in the field. Headstrong, difficult to work with. That's why I took a risk on him. As long as I control the purse strings, I control his research. But it must be done with a light touch. He's volatile. The relationship must continue to be mutually beneficial. I'm not going to strangle the golden goose."

"A man like that craves recognition."

"That, and he claims that if we don't show a few of our cards, our competitors could beat us to it and claim certain patents. I still believe what he really wants is what you just said: recognition of his brilliance. Acknowledgment. Not from the public. The only people he really cares about are his peers, the elite few. He also makes the point that we need to attract new talent to the clinic if our research is to reach full flower. It's a delicate balance for me."

"Ah, now I *do* see," Cole said. "He can't do all the work himself, of course. But it's more than just talent. At a limited gathering like this, insiders in the sector will have ears. Word will spread to just the right small circle of VCs. Is that it? Is he looking for more money?"

"His needs are bottomless. It's true that we'll require more capital at a certain point. But I guarantee you, the money is only a means for him. What drives him is ambition, fame. Not the media kind; I mean historical fame. Or infamy."

"What I'm hearing," Cole said, "is that your path and his path will diverge at some point. A breaking point."

"Inevitably. And I will deal with him at that time."

"Then we really are after the same thing. And I'd like to hear more about your, uh, vision. I could contribute on several levels."

"That's for another day," Remly said.

"What about this GenVigil bunch?"

"Troublemakers. They've published proprietary information about us on their Web site. I'm going to have them shut down but good," Remly said.

"There's nothing to what my nephew said about their possible involvement with Margaret?"

"Listen, those types of people have set off bombs near bioengineering facilities. Anything's possible. What about your daughter-in-law?"

"Janet? I'll give Bill some credit, I hadn't thought of that angle. I didn't trust Janet from the start."

There was some shuffling, then some static. "Look," Remly said. "Here comes our doctor. He'll try to avoid us. Don't—"

There was more static and more shuffling. They were on the move again. The time for Sabell's panel was approaching. I checked my watch, then looked to Clem.

She was staring at the trunk of the tree. Shock was registered on her face. Two feet above my head, stuck firmly into the bark, was a blowgun dart.

Clem and I crouched and scanned the lawn around us. Several yards away, on the sidewalk, jeans and bare legs walked by. Students. Otherwise, no one.

We stood up. "Did you hear anything?" I asked Clem.

She shook her head. The dart had been silent. She made a quick circuit of the area. I put the earpiece back in. Staccato bursts spat at me. Cole was out of range.

Clem returned, shaking her head. "No bushmen in sight."

"I want to get back in range. I have a feeling they're putting the screws to Sabell right now."

"I'm going to try to get in to hear his talk," Clem said. "The grad students said they can sneak me into an AV room behind the stage."

I picked up the briefcase in one hand and tucked the receiver under my other arm. Once we were inside, I tried the earpiece again. The hallways were more crowded than before. Clem ducked into the lounge, where one of her grad student friends was waiting. I kept moving up the corridor, my attention focused on my earphone. I bumped into a guy who was about three inches taller than me, with a chest about three inches wider.

"Sorry," I said, and moved to the side.

He mirrored my move. He was in his thirties, blond hair shaved close to his head. His features were rocklike, his sloping shoulders mountainous. He wore gray slacks and a coat and tie. There was no scar on his forehead, though, and only a faint scent of cologne. What caught my eye was his belt. It had the same letter L set inside the buckle as the guy who'd slashed me in the park. The boots were newly shined and polished.

I yanked the earpiece out. "What do you want?" I said loudly. People flowed around us, paying no attention.

"Mr. Remly needs privacy." I wasn't sure I'd know an Afrikaner accent if I heard one, but I guessed that was what it was.

"You work for Remly?" I asked, stupefied that he'd come out and say it.

He flashed a scalpel of a smile, looked at his fingernails, and said nothing. Everything began to happen at once. My cell phone buzzed in my pants pocket. The Afrikaner reached inside his jacket. I decided that going for something in my pocket, even if it was only a phone, was a bad idea. He froze, his hand in his jacket.

His hand came out empty. He pointed a finger at me. The words were implied. He spun and walked the other way. I dashed into the student lounge. Clem was about to leave. "Hold these for a minute," I said, putting the briefcase, receiver, and earpiece in her hands.

I hurried back down the hallway, pulling my cell phone from my pocket and switching it to camera function. The tall blond head of the Afrikaner was just visible on the far side of the lobby. I raced after him. When he got to the end of the corridor, I called out, *"Jou pielkop!"* I'd looked the phrase up on the Net after Wayne had told me about *bliksem*.

The color rushing to his face confirmed he spoke Afrikaans.

He opened the door to a stairwell and commanded, "*Varknaaier!* Come here!"

I snapped a photo, then reversed direction, back down the corridor. Clem was at the doorway to the lounge. "We're late," she snapped, and left.

I packed the receiver into the briefcase and headed for the lobby. As I walked, I hit the button on my phone to pick up the message.

"Bill. I thought you wanted to talk." *Click.*

It was Leonard Wilson. I called him back.

"Leonard," I said quickly, "I want to talk to you. I'm—"

I stopped. The Afrikaner had returned, neck muscles straining, clearly exercised by the syllables that had been, to me, nonsense.

I exited the lobby door. He followed. "I'm really sorry," I said into the phone. "Let me call you back in five minutes."

"Five," Wilson said tersely.

I turned around and went right back inside. The man stayed out, waiting for me. I backed through the lobby, the phone to my ear to make him think I was on the line. When I neared the corridor, I turned and ran for the side exit. I hit the door full tilt, burst outside, and sprinted for the Scout.

The Afrikaner was not in sight as I stabbed the key into the ignition. I dug my cell phone out of my pocket, tossed it on the passenger seat, and threw the Scout into reverse. Speeding through the Stanford campus, I picked up the phone again and hit REDIAL.

Wilson answered with an impatient, "Yes."

"I'd like to talk," I said. "Anywhere you want. Even the office."

"Not the office," he shot back.

A long silence followed. "Hello?" I said. I wasn't paying attention to the streets, just getting out as fast as I could. A dark blue

SUV appeared in my rearview mirror. No way the Afrikaner could have followed me, I thought.

Wilson took a breath. "Listen . . . I'm not sure I can trust you."

"The feeling's mutual." There was another long hesitation. I jumped in. "I don't know what to tell you. If you're taking a risk, I appreciate it. All I care about is who killed Margaret. I don't care about Jakarta or who ends up with whose job. As soon as the Margaret affair is settled, I'm done. I mean that."

Wilson was slow in answering. I waited him out, making random turns through the streets of Palo Alto. Finally he said, "I'm going to take the risk. I warn you, Bill: Do not betray me."

"I accept that." I checked my mirror and said, "Shit."

"What the hell is going on?"

The SUV was still behind me. I began to wish I'd chosen another word to test out in the driver's language. "Someone's following me. You wouldn't happen to know who it is, would you?"

"Are you kidding me?"

"It's a dark blue Blazer," I said. "You'll see it when we meet."

"No. We can't meet if someone's watching us. Let me think," Wilson said. "Okay. Here's what you do. Come down to the main police station. Park as close as you can—don't worry if it's illegal, we'll sort that out—and get inside. Tell them you want to see Ray Wilson, and that he's out back in the officers' lot. I'll be there in a Mercedes 220 convertible. If no one's watching us, we'll take a ride."

"You got it."

I put the phone away, shifted into gear, and took a left on Embarcadero Road. It was no shock to see the Blazer, in my rearview mirror, make the turn after me.

» » » » »

I parked at the station in front of a sign that was clear about the fact that my car, not being a police vehicle, would be towed. I gave my name at the front desk. An officer was summoned. The officer escorted me to a door that led to the parking lot in back. I found Wilson's Mercedes and got in.

"The Blazer?" he asked.

"Hung back when I pulled up to the station."

"Good." He started the car, put it in gear, and pulled out of the space.

"Nice car," I said. "What year?"

"It's a '64." He stopped at the driveway, checking the rearview mirror. I turned. A police car was behind us. The driver was Raymond Wilson.

"Nice of your father to back you up," I said.

"He'll make sure no one messes with us. He'll come down on you, too, Bill, if you're setting me up."

"I got a digital-phone picture of the guy who was following me. I'll email it to you and your father. What did you want to tell me?"

"You called me earlier today," Wilson said. "You thought my father was part of the Margaret Claypool investigation. He's not."

"All right. He might have heard a few things about it, though."

"He might have," Wilson said. "Of *course* he did. But he didn't pass them along to me—not until yesterday, when everything started to go to hell. He's straight as a redwood. I've done nothing with the information to advantage myself or the company. I wouldn't use my father that way."

"In contrast to the Claypool family."

"Yes. I'm concerned for the company. I've put in seven long years at CCE, and when I leave I want to do so with my reputation intact."

"You're leaving soon?" I asked. I had a pretty good idea why.

Wilson cruised a meandering path through the leafy streets. Just as I thought he wasn't going to answer my question, he said, "Several events have triggered my decision. Cole Claypool was the only one willing to go outside the old-boy network, bring me in, and open doors for me to advance. I knew the score, though, and never planned on staying forever. I never fully bought into him as my mentor and benefactor. He was using me for his own purposes. That was okay; I was using him for mine. I never wanted it to be anything more than business. The fact is, he treated me well. Let's face it, even if your goal is to do business in an honest way, you still have to know how the dirty tricks work."

"No better source for that than Cole. What you're telling me is that you were once willing to be his right-hand man, but no more."

"I want you to see where I'm coming from. I don't know how you really feel about your uncle. You act like sworn enemies, but you're still family. You could turn on a dime and sell me out."

"I've never been as cozy with Cole as you have," I said bluntly. "But now you're getting ready to jump the sinking CCE ship?"

Wilson shook a finger at me. "It's not sinking. I just may have pulled their Jakarta rocks out of the fire. My parting gift. It was always clear to me there was a limit to how far I could go, a ceiling. Not glass, but granite, hard as Half Dome."

"You're talking about Cole's forehead, right?"

Wilson laughed. "Right. Tell me another one."

"No, your turn. I want to hear the names Cole calls me."

Wilson returned a reserved smile. "No you don't." I kept nodding until finally he came out with one. "At the memorial service, he said something like, 'Amateur hour is in full swing.'"

"Eh. He says worse to my face."

Wilson shook his head. The tension in the car subsided a degree or two. He gave me a sidelong glance and said, "You've never liked me, have you? The rest of the family sure doesn't. Except Janet was decent to me. That was a surprise. But all the rest of you see in me is the lever Cole uses against his son. Not that I felt sorry for Chris. The guy was born on third base. A little competitive heat did him good. His curse is that he's stuck with Cole forever."

"I never quite understood why you stayed with my uncle for as long as you did."

"I didn't feel so great about it myself," Wilson admitted. "But he was my elevator to the top. He treated me like his protégé, like I had a shot at the highest position, depending on how he felt about Chris any given day. I figured he was blowing smoke, but he was still giving me the responsibilities. I learned a hell of a lot. If Chris and I went head to head, on a level playing field, I'd wipe him up. Yet and still, I've always known that there's nothing thicker than blood for Cole. Not even money."

"Just a couple of days ago, it looked like the top job might come through for you after all."

Wilson let out a long breath. "Cole made me big promises if I salvaged Jakarta. We'll find out tomorrow if I succeeded. I've rolled up my drawings and called it a day. Cole always said my one flaw was that I was too nice a guy. It was better to be feared than loved, he said. I never believed that. The fear always bounces back into your face."

"Is Chris physically back in his office, working?"

"The prodigal son has returned," Wilson pronounced mockingly. "He professes he's not worthy, he deserves only to be a hired servant. And he is welcomed with open arms."

"Talk about turning on a dime. I'm sure Cole will make him eat crow for several months."

"Sure, he'll eat out of the bad-dog dish for a while. But sooner or later, the ring will be put on his hand, the shoes on his feet, and the fatted calf killed for the feast."

"Even after the Kiersty thing? Or was she sent by Cole, too?"

Wilson checked me. "She plays all the angles."

I recalled Kiersty blathering about the "air-filterational" system. Her ignorance had been a front. She'd gotten Chris to admit what Cole suspected, then reported it back. "So she has her fun with Chris but remembers that Papa pays the bills?" I said.

"Close enough."

The sun sank toward the coastal hills. Traffic was heavy now. We spent more time sitting still than moving. I glanced back and saw that the police car had dropped away. Perhaps Wilson had given a signal.

"I hear Cole sent you over to reel Chris in yesterday," I said.

"It was an insulting errand," he said. "So distasteful. He was setting me and Chris up for a fight to the finish. If Chris didn't survive, maybe he didn't deserve the crown after all."

"Testing both of you."

"Exactly. He pushed me to do some underhanded things with Jakarta, too. Testing my loyalty. After all those years. A mistake for a man who keeps people around only as long as they're useful to him. That street runs two ways."

I felt better about Wilson's motives now. I hoped he felt better about mine. "So," I said, "what can you tell me about the police investigation?"

Wilson's caution returned. "Are you going to run right back to Chris with this information? He's *your* client."

"He is and isn't. Yes, he hired me. But . . . let's just say that I won't stop pushing even if he fires me. Or never pays me a cent. Margaret was my cousin. She deserves an answer. *I* want an answer."

Wilson nodded. "I want you to know, I have nothing against the little girl. You can't help what family you're born into."

"You wouldn't have, ah, encouraged your dad to suggest to those detectives that they get after Chris?"

Wilson laughed at that. "My pops would kick my butt if I tried a stunt like that. I'll admit I've enjoyed watching Chris twist in the wind, but as much as it'd tickle me to see him in prison, that's not why I'm doing this."

"Then why are you?" I asked.

"I've had my fill of the Claypool family and the Claypool business. I don't know who took that little girl, but I don't like having it on my conscience if I can help get them."

"Knowing what the police have found and what they're thinking would be a big help to me."

"I know it would," he said crisply. "They checked into some of the outsiders that Cole blamed—triads, gangs, and so on—but none of the leads took them anywhere. Experience told them to look first at the family. That made Chris the number one suspect. They tried to crack him by coming down hard with the first arrest, then filing the charges the following week."

"Why Chris? They didn't like the cut of his jib?"

Wilson snorted. "You start with those closest to the deceased. But yeah, it didn't hurt that he's a rich kid. Some of the guys get off on nailing a chump like him. Others felt bad for the fact that he lost his daughter."

"Was it just certain cops going after Chris, or prosecutors, too?"

"An assistant DA got it into his head that Mike Gallegos would approve of going aggressively after the Claypool family. Problem was, the evidence wasn't turning up to substantiate more than a severe child-neglect charge on Chris. So he pushed the police to look at others. Cole. You. Janet."

"They know about her boyfriend Steve?"

"Yes. That gives the two of them motive. The detectives are checking out Sabell and Remly, too."

"That's where I can help," I said. I sketched out what I knew about the clinic and my theory about covering up the damage they'd done to Margaret in vitro. "I found out just an hour ago that Cole's working on Remly to pin the blame on Dr. Sabell. I don't know if it's connected to the murder, or if it's just about keeping Sabell quiet. The three of them are a kind of jigsaw puzzle. I'm thinking that if I can nail down the process that led to Margaret's conception, the picture will become clear."

"If you know what goes on in Sabell's laboratory, then you're ahead of the police."

My cell phone buzzed. I picked it up, worried that Clem had run into the Afrikaner. She was fine. She'd gotten a ride to a coffee shop from one of the graduate students. I got the address and said I'd be there soon.

I put the phone away and watched Wilson for a minute. He gave me a curious look. "What is it?"

"What if it comes down to Cole?" I said. "What would that do to your future?"

"Let's not forget it could be Chris, too," he responded. "The acorn doesn't fall far from the tree. Be that as it may, I'm willing to take what comes. I've had it with the lies and the double-dealing. It's not how I want to live." Wilson hesitated, waiting for traffic to clear for a left turn. "My pops asked me last week if I was sure I was where I wanted to be in my life. I heard it in his voice: He's not proud of my role. I'm getting out as soon as it's practical, Bill, and if Cole goes down, it's because he set his own wings on fire. That's why I returned your call. My father can smooth the way for you to sit down with the detectives."

I nodded. "Thanks. I'll take you up on that. Give me one more day."

We'd circled back around to the police station. We made a few passes, checking for the Blazer. Its driver apparently had decided hanging around a police station was not wise.

Leonard Wilson dropped me back at the Scout. It was still in its space. The windshield was clean of tickets. We parted with a handshake and a nod.

» » » » »

Half an hour later, Clem climbed into the Scout. I breathed a big sigh of relief, but checked my rearview mirror every few seconds as we went back up to San Francisco. It was dark now, and every set of headlights seemed like one that could be following us.

"So, did Sabell drop the bomb?" I asked.

Clem shook her head, disappointed. "He looked about as happy as a wet cat out there. The panel talked about primordial follicles, culture media, hormone stimulation, and maturation kinetics. Sabell chirped in with a minor point now and then. Everyone looked at him for more, but he kept quiet, as if his jaw had been wired shut."

"So they got to him after all," I said. Clem gave me a questioning look. I'd forgotten that I hadn't had a chance to relay the conversation we'd eavesdropped on between Cole and Remly. I explained to her why each had his reasons to shut Sabell up.

"The other panelists talked about the advances they were making, puffing out their chests," Clem said. "It must have killed Sabell to bite his tongue when he's gone so far beyond them."

"I'm sure he was looking forward to his moment in the sun, having spent the past decade of his life in his dripping forest labyrinth."

"It's weird, isn't it?" Clem said. "How you can feel sorry for the guy, even though he's done some monstrous things. He has this strange kind of charisma. Anyway, what did you find out from Leonard Wilson?"

I told her what he had said.

"He's flying the Claypool nest?" Clem asked.

"Sometime soon. As warm and cuddly as Cole was with him, Wilson knew the score. He knew Cole's main purpose for him was to use him as a cudgel against Chris."

"It's nice to finally have the cops on our side," she said.

"I hope it's for real. I think it is." A sliver of doubt still lodged in my mind about whether Wilson's offer was another of Cole's manipulations. He could pull it off without Wilson realizing it.

"So Wilson flies when Chris returns. No accident."

"When he saw how Cole used every means at his command to bring Chris back, it drove home the truth. But still, I'm kind of flabbergasted at Chris. After all the things he said about Cole last night."

"Maybe he stared into the abyss he didn't know and decided the one he did know was preferable."

"That, and finding out Sabell got his hands on Helen's eggs. That sent him over the edge."

"It would me," Clem said.

We did our usual routine when we got to my flat, circling the block a few times to check for lurkers. I was nervous. If there was a moment when the thugs, and whoever controlled them, would decide to shut us up permanently, this was it. Clem admitted she felt a sense of impending disaster, too. The sky was clear but the wind off the ocean blew hard, making the windows rattle. Tree branches scratched and groaned against the glass.

I'd told Clem on our way up here that I'd cook dinner for us, but my refrigerator had converted from a food-storage unit to a mycological experiment. When Clem and I ate together, it seemed like beef was always on the menu. We stuck with this budding tradition and ordered barbecued ribs from Big Nate's. We spread the meat and the beans and the greens and the corn muffins on the table, and while we made a mess of ourselves, we tried to make sense of what we had on Margaret's case. Tomorrow was the day we'd try to seal it.

"Margaret's death has triggered this wave of flux," I said. "Janet leaves Chris; Chris leaves Cole, then comes back, leaves, comes back again; Sabell looks for recognition apart from Remly, while Remly plots with Cole to keep him quiet; GenVigil goes after the lab and Remly goes after them; and Leonard Wilson gets ready to jump ship from CCE."

"It reminds me of my good old days," Clem said. "Poker. We've got about five players still in the game. We're not sure what each one is holding."

"The problem is, until we can connect someone directly with the Afrikaner and his crew, it's all speculation. Maybe Ray Wilson will dig up something based on his photo."

"There's still only one way to win, Mr. Damen. Stay in the pot."

I grunted. "I'm using every bluff I can. I already got Remly thinking about GenVigil, Cole thinking about Janet, and Sabell thinking about Remly. Cole pretends to Remly that they're teaming up on Sabell, but I think Cole's really after Remly. And Remly's playing the same game with Cole."

"A web of misprision," Clem said. "You've certainly got *me* confused. There's just one man you left out. Your client."

"Don't worry, everyone's got him in the back of their mind. Except for Cole, now that Chris is back in the fold. If Cole knows he did it, he'll never tell. He'll use it as another weapon against Chris. We need our ace in the hole. Solid evidence of how Margaret was made. We can use it on Sabell, Remly, Cole, Chris, GenVigil. Someone *will* crack. I'm counting on the joker, Don, to help. Tip our hand to him and watch who takes advantage of it."

"Meanwhile, our ace is still stuck in the hole," Clem said. "Sabell's lab. If we don't find it there, Bill, you might have to consider turning what we've got over to Ray Wilson and saying, 'Good luck.'"

"Might." I surveyed the empty aluminum tins on the table. We'd scraped them clean.

Clem read my thoughts and said, "Another slaughtered dinner."

"You bring out the carnivore in me, Clementine."

"That's the nicest thing anyone ever said about me," she mock-cooed.

"I'll do the dishes," I said, tossing the empty tins into the trash. "There, they're done."

I went to the living room to send my phone-photo to Leonard Wilson and make my calls. I mostly wanted to plant seeds, so I didn't mind that no one picked up. Except for Chris. I wanted to know if he was on a new binge. Don, of course, had left messages bugging me about his next assignment. That'd wait until tomorrow.

It was only ten-thirty when I stretched my arms and yawned. It had been a long day. Clem was lounging on the sofa. "I should get on home," she said groggily.

"If you can stay awake a little longer, there are a few things I still need to wrap my brain around before we go to Sabell's house tomorrow. I'm not exactly clear on how all the different parts of his research fit together. Oocytes, embryos, stem cells, genetic modification . . ."

"I was trying to get it all straight, too," she said. "I talked to a friend who does embryology at UCSF last night. She explained it to me. I can't vouch for how accurate my version is, though."

"Give it a try," I said. "I've done a little research myself."

Clem drew her knees up, making space for me on the sofa. "The reason the audience this afternoon wanted to hear about Sabell's work is not because they want to clone human children. It's to use it to grow pluripotent embryonic cells—stem cells," Clem said.

"Stem cells come from embryos."

"ESCs, embryonic stem cells, do. There are other sources, like fetal stem cells and adult stem cells, but they've each got their problems. ESC are most promising, so let's stick with them. An embryo starts out as a new cell with two sets of chromosomes, one from Mom and one from Dad. That's a zygote: a fertilized egg. About thirty hours later the zygote divides to form two cells. After four days, a little ball of cells called a blastocyst forms. Inside the first ring of the ball is the inner-cell mass, the stems that can become any type of cell in the human body. They're pluripotent, and you want to keep them that way. So you remove a number of those stem cells and culture them in separate colonies on a supporting cell layer on tissue culture plates. The fantastic thing about human embryonic cells is that they're really good at staying alive in that state. They're self-renewing, practically immortal."

"Nice for them," I said. "Next you want to get them to differentiate, right? Direct them to turn into heart, muscle, liver, skin cells, and so on."

"Right," she said becoming increasingly energized. "They've even succeeded in getting human ESC to turn into oocytes. That could be a big next step. You need those oodles, both for the research and the fertility work. The Korean lab made their breakthrough partly because they had lots of eggs to work with. They took the nucleus of a somatic cell—a bodily cell, in this case a cumulus cell—and put it into an oocyte whose nucleus had been removed, then stimulated the reprogrammed oocyte to divide as if fertilized."

"Nuclear transfer. Cloning, in other words," I said.

"In that case, both the oocyte and the cumulus cell were from the same woman, so it would have been a clone of herself if they'd tried to implant it. That's not the point of the research, though. See, this is why people get cloning and stem cells so confused. So let's switch gears and talk about reproductive cloning. The big leap came with Dolly the sheep in 1997. Scottish researchers enucleated a normal sheep egg and inserted the nucleus from a mammary cell of another sheep. The mammaries—that's why they called her Dolly, by the way—of the unknown sheep had been sitting in a freezer for six years. They gave the egg with its new nucleus a little jolt and tricked it into dividing as if it was fertilized. A few days later the developing embryo was implanted in the uterus of a third sheep. Dolly was born as a clone of the unknown sheep. She was frisky from the start. She knew she was special, and demanded food from everyone who visited her."

"And now they've cloned horses, cows, goats, mice . . . There's that company in Sausalito, Genetic Savings and Clone, that's offering to clone your pets. I read about a calico cat who's a clone of her mother, and yet the pattern on her fur is totally different from her mother's."

"There's still room for individuality even between mammals with nearly identical DNA. The fact is, the environment in which a clone grows up, the whole circumstance of its birth and life, could produce an individual quite different than the original," Clem said. Her feet kept sliding a little farther down the couch, wedging themselves under my thighs.

"Different in bad ways, too," I said.

"True. No one's sure why. Normally, something called imprinting occurs, where maternal genes take control of certain developmental processes and paternal genes mark others. These imprints are set in eggs and sperm before fertilization. Since a clone is not created by conventional fertilization, it's possible that things go wrong because the imprinting process is not reset."

"As far as we know, Margaret was conventionally fertilized," I said. "Boy, does that sound weird."

"Yeah, but if nuclear transfer was used at some point in the process of creating her, the defects might have snuck in then."

"Like, what point? Why did people want to clone a sheep in the first place?"

"With animals, it's because they want to produce a line with certain characteristics. It might be for food, or to engineer in a human protein that'll produce a medicine. Stem cells are great for doing gene transfer. The problem is, unlike with human stem cells, scientists had a really hard time culturing animal stem cells. Nuclear transfer gives you another way to do genetic engineering, especially with larger species that don't reproduce quickly."

"Okay, so reproductive cloning is basically for animals. But with human stem cells, we're after something different. Something therapeutic."

"It's all about treatment of disease," Clem said. "Doctors like Sabell, using this stuff for reproduction, are outlaw exceptions. When you're creating stem cells for therapies, you never let the blastocysts develop beyond a few days. The only reason to clone the cells is to produce a cell line with a certain genetic profile. You do that so the cells will be compatible with the patient's DNA. Let's say my uncle has Parkinson's disease. You'd take a nucleus from a skin cell of his and implant it in a donated oocyte—which someone like Sabell now has oodles of. From that you grow ESCs with my uncle's genes. You direct the ES cell line to become brain cells so they can be implanted as treatment for his Parkinson's. Gene transfer is all about creating cell lines tailored to the individual patient."

"Otherwise his immune system would reject them, right? But with Margaret—she wasn't born yet when Sabell did the gene transfer."

"That's another way he may have crossed the line. I'm guessing he did germ-line modification, which means the changes he made to her genome were coded into her germ cells along with all the other cells. She would have passed along those changes to her children. Basically, gene targeting and nuclear transfer are two different ways of reprogramming DNA. Nuclear transfer does it wholesale. But with gene targeting you pick and choose which genes to knock in or out. Let's take the mutation involved in cystic fibrosis. It's been well defined. What you do is remove a certain number of stem cell colonies from your plate and, using a sort of enzyme scissors, break them up into small clumps of two to five cells. You put your clumps into a cuvette and add what's called the targeting vector. You've already created the targeting vector separately, using standard genetic engineering techniques. It's a non-mutated version of the cystic fibrosis gene, with things called homologous arms on either side of the gene's DNA sequence. The arms are identical to the sequences that precede and follow the gene in the stem cell's chromosome. Okay, so you put your stem cell clumps and your targeting vector together in a cuvette. You subject it to electroporation, which allows the targeting vector to get inside the stem cells and, you hope, swap in the new gene. Then you plate out the stem cells and subject them to an antibiotic. The targeting vector carries a marker, a protein resistant to the antibiotic, so the cells that took up the targeting vector and its new gene survive the antibiotic, while the ones that didn't die. You select those cell clumps that survive and culture them into colonies again. For standard gene therapy, you'd try to get your modified cells to integrate into a patient's existing diseased tissue, so that the healthy gene could produce healthy tissue."

"But with Margaret, we think he used them to create her from the start. That's why she never had the cystic fibrosis mutation."

"Uh-huh. We think. That's the big unknown." Clem's eyes were heavy-lidded. Her head tilted back on the arm of the sofa. Her feet had tucked themselves securely under my legs. "Sorry, sir," she said. "I'm hogging your couch."

"Make yourself at home. You ready for tomorrow?"

"Sabell's house?"

"Sabell's house," I said. I reviewed the plan with her. Sabell would be at the symposium in the afternoon. We intended to break into his lab and expose, as Clem liked to put it, the subtle tasks to which he'd been bent for so long in the solitary still nights of those woods. We'd search for evidence to back up our suspicions about Margaret's conception and look for tissue samples from both her and Helen.

Clem nodded, then her eyes started to flutter closed again. “I’m sorry, Mr. Damen. It’s been a long day. I shouldn’t have had that last rib.”

“Not to worry,” I said. I felt pretty wiped out myself. “You can sleep in my bed. I’ll stay out here.”

“No, just bring me a blanket.”

She scootched to the inside of the couch. Space was available for me to join her. The employer handbook clearly stated that this was a bad idea. I did it anyway. Her hands were folded under her cheek and her dark, wavy hair fell forward, half-covering her face. She smelled of sage and lavender. Her breath whispered on my face.

Her eyelids stuck together a little, then opened. Her lips parted in a brief, blithe smile. “Good night,” she said.

My eyes closed, too. I woke up an hour later. The lights in the room felt harsh. I switched them off, found a quilt for Clem, and spread it over her. She did not stir. I went down the hall to turn off the kitchen lights. Clem’s wallet, I noticed, had fallen out of her jacket. It lay half open on the floor. A small photo-booth snapshot came loose as I picked it up. When I opened the wallet to tuck the photo back in, my heart sank. In the picture, Clem had her arms around a very good-looking, sun-burnished, athletic woman. Just good friends, I thought. But I couldn’t help noticing the little flare in Clem’s lip, the same one she had whenever she said something flirtatious to me. Maybe it was better that way, if she wasn’t available. There was already enough danger in my life. I put the photo away, put the wallet back in her jacket, and went to bed.

24

Clem and I were all business in the morning. We got coffee and reviewed our files at my flat, getting ready for our visit to Sabell's house that afternoon. A little after noon, Clem reminded me that she wanted to hear for herself the conversation between Cole and Remly that we'd recorded yesterday. While she listened to it, I pulled a digital video disk from my files. I'd been meaning to review it for days. The disk was marked COLE BIRTHDAY. I slid it into my deck and watched it on my Avid editing suite.

The events seemed ages ago. Everyone was so happy and unworried, boisterous in their reunions, soaking up Cole's bounty. Everyone but Chris. I only had a few seconds of him. Even with his shoulders tense and his face drawn, he looked younger than now, just twelve days later. There were Chris's sisters, his great-aunt Henrietta, Regina in her lofty and detached state. There was Cole, lord of the realm. His manner of rule really was feudal: absolute, supremely assured of his superiority. There he was greeting me derisively as the "auteur." Then his mocking toast to Chris: "Afraid he'll never get his chance to step into the old man's shoes . . ."

There was Leonard Wilson, too, raising his glass without enthusiasm yet unable to suppress a secret smile. The moment I really wanted to see came at the end. We were seated at our tables. Cole, standing, tapped the microphone on the podium to give his opening remarks. He hadn't said more than a couple of words when he stopped. I'd kept the camera on him for another beat or two, then swiveled to catch the two cops striding through the crowd.

It was Cole's expression that I wanted to analyze. I went back to his last word before the interruption. Avid allowed you to stop time and dissect a moment into its constituent parts. The gestalt of all the parts working together gave the most complete picture, but now it was time to examine each one on its own. I went forward frame by frame, each frame one-thirtieth of a second, until I found the series recording the moment when Cole spotted the cops. His expression shifted from that of the charming, benevolent patriarch to that of a dismal, wrathful one. Then it recomposed itself, like the magnetic gas storms that rearrange Jupiter's surface, into a cooler look of bafflement and incipient outrage. My camera turned to follow focus on the approaching cops. They went past me, to the head table and Chris. For no reason—I was barely aware of it at the time—I shifted the camera back to Cole's face. In the following frame, before he had time to arrange the look of proper paternal concern on his face, was the microexpression I wanted to see: a strange pleasure at his son's arrest, a flash of grimaced satisfaction.

I showed the sequence to Clem. "The question is," I said, "is the satisfaction about the fact Chris *is* being arrested or that Cole's *not?*"

"What about both?" Clem said. "Imagine this: Chris is filled with anxiety over his worthiness to wear his father's boxers. In a fit of insecurity-driven decisiveness, he arranges for his daughter's death, in order to free himself from the financial burden of her medical care. But the moment it happens, Chris is overwhelmed with guilt. Then denial. If he were to lose it at the birthday party, it would prove his failure."

I thought back to Chris's words, actions, moods that night. I didn't buy Clem's theory, but I played along with it. "He's been afraid from the start that Margaret's disappearance meant he was a failure as a father. What if, in reality, it was about his fear of failure as a *son?* A son who'd lost the killer instinct, whose life was falling apart because of the expense of maintaining his daughter. Now, seeing the cops, Cole realizes that Chris *did* have the balls to carry it through."

"So," Clem said, "the question in these images is: Is Cole getting a perverse pleasure out of seeing his son fail—or out of seeing him succeed?"

"If Chris really did do it, then it's both. His success is his failure. He's taken the host of the beast and earned his place as the anointed one. Cole is pleased; but Chris realizes he may have lost himself completely. That's why he's had these wild swings of mood. He's spoken as little as possible to his father since the moment Margaret was taken."

"Bingo, Mr. Damen."

"I don't know, Clem. It's an interesting fantasy. I still think Remly or Sabell are the ones with the clearest motives."

"The fact is, there is no good motive for killing a child," she replied.

"That's true, too." I checked my watch. "Let's get ready. We need to leave soon."

We got to work. I'd turned off my cell phone because I got tired of Don calling every half hour. I turned it on now to make the last few necessary arrangements, and checked my messages. I almost fell out of my shoes. Austin Remly's voice was on the line. He said, "I apologize for giving you the short end at our meeting yesterday. I hope you understand. I trust I'll see you at the symposium today."

I called back and got a secretary who said Mr. Remly was not available. I left a message that I'd see him this afternoon if I could, but I had some other things to do.

Clem and I prepared for those other things. It wasn't until we were on the road, halfway to Sabell's, about to lose the cell phone signal, that I called Don. He was beside himself with impatience. His assignment, I said, was to find access to a lab that could run a genomic comparison between tissue samples from two young girls. Their names were Helen and Margaret.

"I can do that," Don said eagerly. "How are you getting the samples?"

"From the source," I said. "Tonight."

"What does that mean?"

"I can't tell you everything," I replied. I knew whoever he passed the information on to would figure it out.

"Have you narrowed down a suspect list?"

"Cole's in it deep with Sabell and Remly. The three of them conspired to kill Margaret. They hired the guys in stocking masks and made it look like a kidnapping gone awry."

"Wow," Don breathed. "That's terrible."

"Yeah, a real axis of evil."

"Okay, I'll be ready. Tonight." Don wanted to ask more but didn't dare.

"Tonight's the night," I said.

» » » » »

It was four-thirty as we wound our way up the last rutted dirt lane to Sabell's house, but dusk seemed to fall the instant we entered the forest hollow. The sky through the tangled branches seemed a distant, bleached blue, as far away as the stars.

I drove the Scout. There was no need to hide our presence, and it would handle the rough roads better if we had to take flight. Clem got out to push open Sabell's gate. He still had not fixed it. I was glad we could stay in the car and put off dealing with Gigi and her diabolically intelligent gaze until we reached the house. We did bring gifts for her: half a pound of raw hamburger, and if that didn't satisfy her hellish appetite, a can of pepper spray.

The Scout descended the long drive, in low gear, into the hollow where Sabell's house stood. The road flattened and widened just before the house. I jammed on the brakes.

"Why is he—" Clem began, then stopped.

Sabell's black Saab sat in the carport. I pulled up, blocking it in. We opened the doors very quietly. I watched where I put my foot, expecting Gigi's blood-pink jaws to close around it any moment. No music came from the house today. No sound at all. The ancient forest itself was silent, not even dripping. Only the crows cawed now and then, cold and insistent, from the distant treetops. They and the towering thousand-year-old redwoods watched us tread slowly through the rock garden to the door. Maybe because Gigi was absent, the trees seemed less ominous. They seemed detached, as if the doings of a few humans on the ground were barely worth notice.

I put my hand on the doorknob. Clem put hers into the pocket of her leather jacket, where she had the Beretta. The knob gave way to my twist. I opened the door inch by inch, looked in, and then stepped in.

The low hallway was dark. Clem and I stood close together, breathing, listening. No sound came to our ears. I reached into the bicycle messenger bag over my shoulder, took out a flashlight, and switched it on. We moved a few steps down the hall. The beam played over the contents of the first two hovel-like studies: books stacked at odd angles; papers, yellow at the edges, laced with old spiderwebs, the ink desiccated; random glass jars and vials, empty, greening; an ancient fax machine on a metal typewriter table. It all looked as it had before, yet the house felt derelict and uninhabited.

We moved down to the next room, a spare bedroom. Sabell's diplomas from Johns Hopkins were here, framed and dust-caked. A threadbare European quilt with a faded village scene hung over a metal-spring cot, balls of dust lapping at its hem. A set of small, painted wooden figures, a little family in the traditional dress of a European region unfamiliar to me, was crowded onto the rear of a bureau, forgotten, as if we'd stumbled into the room of a relative long dead. Four framed nineteenth-century illustrations were also stacked there. One showed the female genital tract, one the male. The other two were close-ups of a pair of ovaries and a pair of testes.

We proceeded into the main large room in the back of the house. The lights were off here, too. All was silent as we paced the room. I swept it with my flashlight. As we approached the kitchen, some deep-chested beast rumbled to life. We froze. Clem drew close, until we realized it was only the refrigerator.

"So where's our doctor?" she murmured softly.

"Wandering in his labyrinth?"

"Or his lab. Maybe he had some brilliant insight that was more important than the symposium."

We went to the center of the main room. I played the beam over the walls and ceiling. "The lab must be on the second floor. Can't be above this room, though. The ceiling's too high."

"So it's accessed from one of the other rooms."

We went back down the hall, closed the door to the bedroom, and turned on a light. We checked the room for any means of access to a floor above. The closet was stacked with old medical journals, beakers, hoses, antique-looking apparatuses. We moved on to the study across the hall. Working silently, we combed its nooks and crannies. Dust billowed into our lungs. We smothered our coughs, fearing Sabell was working above us. This room yielded nothing, either. We returned to the study closest to the front door. I opened a narrow broom-closet door. It contained an ironing board, broom, mop, and dustpan. It was hard to believe Sabell actually used them, yet they didn't have the same coat of dust as the rest of the room. I pushed at the plywood back wall of the closet. It gave way about half an inch.

"Take these," I said to Clem, handing her the ironing board and broom.

Now I saw the latch fastening the plywood to the side of the closet. I unhooked it and pushed at the false back. It swung open. My flashlight found a dangling string with a loop at the end. I pulled it and a light switched on. Behind the closet was a small landing. A set of steep, narrow wooden steps climbed from it to the upper floor.

We listened. After a few minutes and no stirring from above, I grasped a thin railing and climbed the stairs, my neck craned in expectation of Sabell's troll-like face suddenly looming at the top. But there was only light from below, and when my head broke the plane of the floor above, the laboratory.

I motioned for Clem to follow. A hooded work lamp, connected to a long extension cord, lay on the floor. I flicked it on. It cast eerie, underlit shadows over the large space. I found no overhead lighting. Instead, each area had its own local illumination. I pictured Sabell laboring on a stool at these benches, surrounded by pools of darkness, a single cone of light focused on the task at hand.

The room was like a giant attic. The floor was varnished wood and plywood sheets covered the rafters. In contrast to the rooms below, it was clean, without cobwebs or dust. The slightly sulfuric smell of reagents, mixed with chemical solvents, hung in the air. Two workbenches occupied the center of the room, outfitted with sinks at the ends, cupboards below, open shelves above, gas and vacuum nozzles at regular intervals. Near us, emitting a deep, throbbing hum, was a bank of freezers and incubators, along with a liquid nitrogen tank. Sabell must have installed an extra subpanel for the electricity needed by the machines. At the far end of the benches, in the dimness, appeared to be a desk and armoire.

Clem and I walked slowly among the benches, turning on work lamps as we went. The shelves were crowded with glass and plastic jars containing the reagents, buffers, and solvents needed to work his transformations. On the black countertops sat gel tanks connected to black and red insulated wires, PCR machines that looked like digital postal scales, vortexers, mixers, a microwave oven, racks lined with tubes, columns, and pipettes, plastic plates with wells for six, twelve, twenty-four, or ninety-six samples.

A nostalgic look came over Clem's face as she tapped a molecular cloning manual. "The Maniatis," she said, then went to a boxlike machine on the opposite counter. NUCLEOVISION, read the label. A computer station was set up next to it. "He's got all the toys," she went on. "You use the Nucleovision to image your gels. The genes you're looking for show up as dark bands, identified by molecular weight."

Clem paused to turn on a phase-contrast microscope sitting on a separate, lower table. My attention was drawn by a row of shelves set away from the others, with their own spotlight to illuminate them. I switched on the light and took in a sharp breath. The shelves were occupied by specimen jars, each with its own pink ovary preserved in formaldehyde like harvested fruit.

"You were wondering where the Minotaur was," Clem murmured.

"Have you seen any lab notebooks?" I asked.

"They're locked up, I imagine."

We gravitated to the rear of the room, where the desk sat. I turned on an old-fashioned floor lamp. "Looks like his living space back here," I said.

Next to the writing desk was a battered leather easy chair. Persian rugs covered the floor. Behind a freestanding screen was a single bed with a small side table, a sink, and a toilet. Sabell's pajamas were folded on the bed.

Clem opened the cherrywood armoire. A small collection of shirts, pants, and button sweaters hung from a rod. A metal safe sat on the bottom. She tried the handle. "Locked," she said.

"Look at this," I said.

The top drawer of the desk contained a notebook. I turned on the desk lamp and sat in the chair. Clem leaned over my shoulder. The entries appeared somewhat haphazard, scribbled, some of them with drawings. It wasn't an official lab book but a place for random thoughts. We leafed through it, pointing to entries that seemed particularly strange or telling. Some pages were nothing more than lists of what Sabell had eaten that week. He appeared to be trying to get a fondness for animal crackers under control. Others contained quotes, some from poets, some from scientists.

Origin of man now proved. Metaphysics must flourish. He who understands baboon would do more toward metaphysics than Locke. —*Darwin, M notebook*

A man has not truly lived until he has done the unthinkable. —*Borges*

Other entries had been scrawled quickly, like thoughts that jumped into his head and he jotted down for transfer to another journal.

I was born at once too late and too early. The days of myth are lost, days when the gods walked the earth, when life transmuted easily from one shape to another. Now we work our transformations in vitro, yet I will likely not live to see the greatest marvels our field will bring.

"That explains why he takes so many risks," I said. "His field is in its infancy. He can't wait to find out how it grows up."

"I'm glad someone's looking forward to it," Clem remarked.

Another entry read,

Children are like mirrors. They reflect back our own image. And what do we find? Our fears, desires, ego, desperate efforts to defy death—or something more noble?

Anything I destroy, I resurrect.

There were also pages of botanical drawings, the kind of thing Sabell might have done to keep his mind busy while pondering some facet of his research. They resembled the anatomical illustrations we'd seen downstairs, incredibly detailed line drawings of fruits, seeds, pods, ferns, showing a kind of obsession with life and its reproduction.

Other sketches were rougher, more schematic. They looked like efforts to work out a particular problem.

"Look at this one," Clem said. "It could almost be a diagram for Margaret. See, the embryo produces ES cells. This symbol indicates the cells are modified through homologous combination—

gene replacement. The name Krempe is next to them along with a date. That means Sabell used a technique developed by someone named Krempe—or had Krempe do it himself. That would make sense. I always thought all of this was too much for Sabell to do alone. Then you see this sequence." She pointed to a notation reading *GM ESC > NT*. "Modified stem cell nuclei are used for nuclear transfer into a new oocyte. Maybe an oocyte from Helen."

"The initials MW are in parentheses by the 'GM,'" I said. "The name Waldman appeared on an earlier page."

"So maybe Waldman helped him with the gene transfer."

"We're taking the notebook with us." I flipped through a few more pages. The last page had just one entry.

Keto + dehydr, 24 hrs > still not fatal. Keta > uncon > asp. undetected COD.

Clem stared at me. "A recipe . . .?"

"Yes, but I think he's reverse-engineering it. He's puzzling out how she died," I said slowly. "Remember, he told us to think about it? He's saying the hyperglycemia and ketoacidosis weren't enough to kill her in the twenty-four hours between her disappearance and death. The Ketamine was used not just to sedate her, but to help induce a diabetic coma. So was dehydration—the coroner mentioned she had a sunburn. Kidnappers usually keep their victims indoors, out of view. I'm not sure what 'asp' stands for."

"An undetected COD, whatever that is. A parcel? A bank deposit?"

"COD . . . Cause of death?"

"Undetected cause of death . . ."

"Like suffocation," I said. "'Asp' stands for asphyxiation. Could have been as simple as putting a plastic bag over her head once she was in a coma. Suffocation is always hard to detect, but if she was nearly gone anyway, the evidence could have been virtually invisible. Especially with no defensive marks and the diabetes and Ketamine being such strong candidates."

"Why not just do that in the first place?"

"They wanted to blame it on the diabetes. Or maybe in some sick way they thought they were being humane. Either way, they wanted the death to look like an accident brought about by kidnappers who didn't know her."

I looked at my watch. "We need to get out of here. Where do we look for the tissue samples—the freezers?"

"Start with the liquid nitrogen tank," she said.

We turned out the lamps and crossed to the other side of the lab. The liquid nitrogen tank resembled a white barrel with a blue cap. Clem pressed the RESET button on the control panel. It beeped and she opened the cap. Metal straws were hooked to the lip of the tank. Each hook had a tape label.

"'Embryos,'" I read on one label.

"Same here," Clem said. "Put on gloves."

We each pulled out a straw and carried it to a benchtop. Attached to the long straw were metal boxes. Liquid nitrogen poured from them, curling out like ghostly fingers. Even though we had gloves on, the boxes burned cold to the touch. Inside them were racks full of columns. Each column had a tape label with tiny writing. None of the names were familiar.

"What about Helen's ovary tissue?" I asked, my fingertips numb. "That's what we need the most."

Clem looked up. "Right. Uh, two places. The minus-eighty freezer. Or, if he was working with it recently, the incubator with the carbon dioxide tank attached."

That particular incubator was next to the hood, the enclosed glass bench under which Sabell worked with his cells. The hood was closed, its ultraviolet light casting a sterilizing twilight glow.

I opened the outer door, then inner door to the incubator and searched among the plates. One of them contained paper-thin, grayish slices of tissue, but Helen's name was not on it. I closed the incubator and went to the freezers. There was a plus-4 refrigerator, then a minus-20 freezer, and finally the minus-80. It was filled with rows of metal boxes, like small versions of an airline cart into which meals were slid. Inside the metal boxes were red boxes. I pulled out a stack of the large metal ones, slid the red boxes out from their slots, and quickly went through the racks inside each box.

"Claypool," Clem said, reading a column. "These are six years old."

"Embryos he created the same time he created Margaret," I said. "Keep that one. I'm still looking for a Helen sample."

We were jolted by a high, trilling shriek. Clem frantically slid the box she'd been looking through back onto its straw and returned the straw to the tank. She pressed the RESET button and locked down the blue cap.

"It's a telephone," I said, inspecting one label after the other. "Keep quiet, listen for his voice."

The phone stopped. Something in the room below us stirred. It made clicking sounds and then began to groan. Clem peeled off her gloves. "I really think we should go," she whispered.

I opened more red boxes. Finally I found it. A tube marked H CLAYPOOL. R OVUM. I held it up for Clem.

"You've got it, Bill," she said.

She put the freezer boxes away while I pulled a sheet of insulation material from my messenger bag. The insulation wouldn't keep the vials frozen, but at least it would keep them cold.

We switched off the lights and went to the top of the hidden stairway. The moaning sound below had ceased. I backed down the stairs, step by step, silently. Clem came down while I waited at the bottom. She drew the Beretta from her pocket. I turned off my flashlight. Slowly I pulled open the crude door that led back into the closet. The light in the study was still out. We were in complete darkness. I felt my way through the closet and into the room, where I stood still, listening. All at once it came to me what had made the sounds. The moan had been paper squeezing its way through the ancient fax machine.

I flicked on my flashlight. A piece of brown-edged fax paper, the old thermal type, lay curled on the floor. I straightened it.

GET OUT NOW, it said in big block letters.

"Do you recognize the writing?" Clem asked.

"No," I said. It was hard to believe the machine still worked. It seemed as if the note had materialized from the underworld.

Clem returned the broom and ironing board to their places. "Time to go," she said.

I put the sheet in my pocket. "Where's Sabell?"

"Someone must have given him a ride to the symposium," Clem said.

"Why would anyone come all the way up here when he's got his own car?"

"Maybe his car wouldn't start."

I shook my head. "Let's look out back."

"Mr. Damen, the fax message was not ambiguous."

"I want Sabell!"

I went down the hall, through the kitchen, and out the back door to the stone patio. True dusk was settling in. The air was thick and purple, the darkness tangible. I felt I could swim through it. Clem joined me reluctantly.

"We'll check the labyrinth. Quickly," I said.

"Watch out for Gigi," Clem warned.

I'd almost forgotten about her. Her absence was unsettling now.

I hadn't noticed, when Sabell led us into it the first time, how unobtrusive the entrance to the maze was. From the patio, it looked like nothing more than a small gap in a wall of ferns, their lower stalks ribboned with nettles to prevent jumping from one path to the next. You might think you were simply passing into another garden. Instead, you found yourself drawn in by the insidious beauty of the ferns and vines that formed the maze's walls, and then farther in, always with the sense that the thing you came to see was just around the next bend.

The maze felt familiar as we took our first few turns. Our previous visit with Sabell seemed a quaint stroll in the garden compared to what had come since. We crept along, thinking we might surprise him at any moment, wandering, pondering his mental labyrinths of dividing chromosomes and recombining genes. The vines were fragrant in the settling dusk. A moist scent exhaled from them and from the ferns. We turned and retraced our steps, turning again and again, but reached only dead ends.

We kept moving, going deeper, passing seemingly familiar spots, places I was sure we'd passed moments before. Every spot came to feel familiar, as if we were repeating circles on top of circles on top of circles. Yet every turn seemed to present a new point in the spiral, one we had not seen before, with a new mix of flora and a slightly altered height of the hedge.

We stopped again, our minds bending in on themselves.

"We're fully lost now," Clem informed me.

We let ourselves catch our breath. An inexplicable chill shuddered through both of us at the same moment. We looked at each other. Clem's mouth was set in a straight line. She did not want to speak her thoughts aloud.

"I'm ready to give up the stealth approach," I said. Clem gave a small nod, and I called, as loud as I could, "Dr. Sabell!"

As my words died in the forest, we heard the crackle of a footfall in the brush. We froze. Again there was a crackle, then three more in succession.

"Where is it?" Clem whispered.

"I can't tell if it's in the maze, or beyond," I whispered back.

We crept ahead again, slowly, if only because standing still was unbearable. Clem's hand was in her pocket again. I tried not to think as I forked through the paths, but to let my instincts guide me. That was the secret, I'd decided: Simply keep moving, instead of trying to solve the maze.

I imagined I heard the footsteps right behind us. I froze. They were only the rustle of my own coat. Clem and I listened.

The crackling sound came again. This time the noise was not from us.

I caught the motion from the corner of my eye. It was close by, perhaps only a few feet away, perhaps on the next path over. Clem drew the gun from her pocket. We stood unbearably still, waiting for the next move. The thing had disappeared, like a phantom.

Listening hard, I heard its breathing. Multiple breaths, as if it had several lungs. It did not move. We did not move. I felt I would jump out of my skin. I stared hard into the brush but saw only shades of green and brown, dark and darker.

In an instant, it made its move, with the crash of brush being knocked aside, bent, broken. Hooves thumped on the turf. A family of deer, a doe and two fawns from the glimpse I got, bolted. They'd been on the path just the other side of our fern wall.

"That was a severe pucker moment, Mr. Damen," Clem said, putting the gun away. I squeezed her arm and started moving again.

» » » » »

I didn't know how much time went by. It seemed many miles that we wandered, and yet the light remained, draining so slowly that the earth seemed to have stopped turning. Perhaps some light from the moon was dimly filtering through the trees now.

We came upon the small circular clearing quite suddenly. In the middle, stuck into the ground, was the white marble slab. GEORGE JOHAN SABELL. Below it, the blank space he'd yet to fulfill. He thought he'd had time.

Next to the stone, curled in a fetal position, was George Johan Sabell.

We bent to examine him. His face was as white as the skin of a shorn rabbit. A rivulet of blood, dried to a thick red color, trickled from the corner of his mouth. He wore his button-down wool sweater, flannel pajama pants, and a pair of slippers. His right hand was twisted at a grotesque angle, like a broken paw. I looked closer and saw the arm took an inexplicable bend: The ulna had been broken. So had the left ulna. Judging from the angle at which his left leg splayed, the fibula had been snapped, too, like a robin's neck in the jaws of a cat.

Wordlessly we bent closer. We scanned up and down his body and saw no visible signs of a weapon: no stab or bullet wound, no stun gun or electrical burns. All of it had been done by hand. Perhaps over a period of hours, during which each bone was broken and he was given the chance to experience the pain. Gigi, presumably, had suffered a similar fate.

I gave Sabell's arm a gentle push. Rigor mortis had not set in. I put two fingers to his carotid artery. To my shock, I felt a faint throb.

"He's not dead yet," I said, standing up. "But he will be if he's left out here much longer."

"No way we can move him. It really is time to go now, Bill."

Yes, it was. My cell phone was useless up here.

At that moment, a bolt of illumination shot through my eyes. It barely reached out here to the center of the maze and yet blinded me with alarm. The back-porch lights had been switched on. For an absurd moment, I felt as though Sabell had caught us. I grabbed Clem's hand. There was only one direction for us to go.

25

My logic was good, I thought. Once we were close to the house we could, from cover of the labyrinth, see who had switched on the lights.

Clem disagreed. Based on the fax warning, she believed we'd find only enemies at the house. I had to admit that I'd made a miscalculation. I'd assumed that Don's message would lead our suspect to grab Sabell after the symposium and bring him up here to try to nail us all together. But Sabell had never made it to the symposium. Ray Wilson was not due to arrive for another forty minutes. That meant whoever was in the house were people we wanted to avoid.

"We're sitting ducks in the labyrinth," I said to Clem. "I'm hoping they're inside, looking for the lab. We stop near the maze entrance and check out the patio. If the coast is clear, we slip around the side of the house, like we did before. We check the driveway; if someone's there, we retreat into the woods. If not, we either take the Scout or run down the driveway on foot. Either way, I want to know if who's there is who I think it is."

"It's foolhardy," Clem replied. Her hand slid into her jacket for the Beretta. "But that's what I like about you, Bill."

"We're dangerous together," I agreed.

We wended our way back through the labyrinth. The method of simply going, without trying to solve it rationally, had worked before. The light helped, giving us a fixed point to follow. Once we made it to the outer arc of the maze, we crouched behind the last green wall between ourselves and the floodlit patio.

Nothing moved. After watching for ten minutes, it seemed safe to assume the intruders were inside.

I put my mouth to Clem's ear. "Cover me."

She nodded. I slid over to the maze entrance and made my sprint. Within seconds, I was flattened by a brick wall that sprang out of nowhere. My back, then my head, hit the paving stones, hard. Everything went dark.

When I opened my eyes, I saw, through a small opening in the trees, the full, grinning disk of the moon. That's nice, I thought.

Then I heard the click of a hammer. The idea came to me that the leering moon would be the last thing I would see.

A blast ripped the air. A shape went spinning above me, then collapsed to the stones. Another shape emerged from the labyrinth.

"Don't," her voice ordered.

"Clem?" I said.

Her pistol was trained on the man-shaped heap a few feet away from me. One hand clutched at his hip, a dark stain oozing between his fingers. In the other was a gun, which he was attempting to aim at her.

Clem stood over him. She pointed the gun at his shoe. "I'll keep shooting until you don't have a foot to stand on."

Now I saw the man's face. It was the blond Afrikaner. The look of terror in his eyes was precious. I crawled on all fours to grab the gun from his hand. He dropped it in a flash, grabbed my arm with ferocious strength, and pulled me on top of him as a shield.

Clem still had clear aim at his foot. She fired. He screamed. I rammed my elbow into his face, then did it again. He went limp. I leaned over to pick up the gun he'd dropped and threw it into the maze.

"There's another one!" Clem screamed. She wheeled and fired at the corner of the house.

I glimpsed a figure in the shadows. "He's running!"

The shape disappeared around the side of the house. I went after him.

"No!" Clem shouted. But her footsteps were right behind me.

I fought my way around the side of the house, past the carport, in time to see the second man disappearing into the woods below the driveway. I whipped the strap of the messenger bag, which had been flopping at my side, over my head and left it beside the Scout. I told Clem to stay there, too.

The next thing I knew, she was following me into the woods.

It was darker in the trees than in the labyrinth. The redwood canopy obscured the light even of the full moon. The hill angled steeply. I was on a small cut etched into it, perhaps a game trail. I stopped, listened. The brush ahead of and below me rustled with movement. I traversed the slope, maintaining a high line from which I could attack.

"Bill?" It was Clem's voice. She was below me, too.

"Quiet," I ordered. Her voice gave away her position. The rustling sounds ahead of us became intermittent. That made me think our quarry was not merely escaping into the woods, but laying an ambush.

I started ahead again. Redwood columns loomed up on my left and right like silent sentinels. I stopped every few seconds to listen. The rustling sounds ahead of me were fewer and farther between. It was a game of cat and mouse now, and it was hard to know who was the hunter and who was the hunted. I wished again that Clem had stayed with the Scout.

Suddenly she shrieked, a gut-piercing sound. I scuttled downhill and hit a wider cut, an old logging road. The road, long out of use, was overgrown with brush and littered with deadfall. The hillside below dropped steeply into a ravine. I broke into a sprint, extending my arms to catch branches before they whipped me in the face. A redwood stump the size of a dinner table sent me sprawling. As I got back to my feet, a sharp, savory scent came to my nose. We'd entered a laurel dell, an area where the redwoods had been cut. The trees were smaller. A little more light filtered through.

Guttural grunts, then another shriek from Clem echoed through the wood. Plunging through the branches of a fallen laurel, I saw them, two dark shapes struggling on the small platform of the logging road. The man grappling with her had plenty of weight to throw around. One of his arms stretched to her head while the other fought for control of her right arm, which held the gun. He used his weight to swing her in a circle. From the way her head jerked, he must have had her by the hair. With a roar, he swung her in a wider arc, gave her arm a twist, and then pitched her over the ledge of the road. A black object flew from her hand.

Clem yelled and slid down into the ravine. I charged, covering the remaining fifteen yards in a few short seconds. The man was on his hands and knees, searching for the Beretta. I came into him feet first as he was rising and hit him in the shins. He cried out and vaulted over the top of me. The gun dropped. One of his knees hit me in the head, knocking me senseless for a second. He rolled and pivoted on all fours. I searched for the gun in the dimness. He lunged at me, mouth wide, like a wolf, clamping my wrist in his teeth. I screamed out in pain and swung my other fist into his ear. He howled. I rolled away and we both groped desperately for the gun. He rose up to let his full weight fall on me in a body slam. I tried to roll away, but he got enough to pin me. He grabbed at my hair and face, throwing his bulk on top of me.

That was when I felt the Beretta under my back. I went limp for a moment, afraid that too much struggle could cause it to fire.

His fingers poked at my eyes and nose, then went to my neck. I'd have to take my chances with the gun. As his hands closed around my throat, I swung both my palms, flat, hard into his ears. He roared, and with that opening I wriggled sideways from under his weight, scraping the gun along the dirt under me. He took a wild swing. It hit me in the back as I rolled to uncover the gun, feeling for its grip. The blow hurt, but I found the Beretta. I rolled the other direction to avoid the next blow. Lying sideways on the ground, I took aim.

"I'll shoot you!" I shouted.

He froze in a bent position, hands on knees, his clotted lungs gasping, staring at me with feral eyes.

"Don't move, Cole. I *will* pull the trigger."

"Idiot. Put that down."

"I thought it would be a Claypool. I didn't know which one."

"As if you're not one of us."

I snorted. "If only you could see yourself." His pinstriped suit was speckled with the soil and leaves of the forest, like a creature of the woods. His face, too, was mottled with dirt. Now that he knew who his opponent was, his body language switched over to one of command and superiority. But his eyes remained shifting and desperate.

"Sabell killed Margaret," he said. "I came here to prove it."

"Funny, that's what I told Don *I* was doing. Don was your plant from the start, wasn't he, as soon as Chris mentioned to you that I was looking for an assistant?"

Cole straightened casually, as if not worried the least about his situation. "I had to keep an eye on you and your meddling."

"Don's the one you used to tail me to the clinic. Then to Oyster Point, and the park where Ulla and I were attacked. He phoned in our position."

"Those men were hired by Sabell and Remly."

"You did your best to make me think that when Don sent me out to Remly's. And yesterday, when the Afrikaner blurted Remly's name. He'd never say the name of his real boss."

"I came here because Sabell killed—"

"No, no, no. You bullied Chris into causing Margaret's death. Then you had your Afrikaner take care of Sabell. Did it have to be so vicious, or was that purely for pleasure?"

"Sabell's dead?"

"Not quite. I hope you got what you wanted from him. He was on to you about Margaret. He was putting together the evidence on how she really died."

"He killed Margaret to cover up his mistake," Cole insisted. "Now look, Bill, a man back at the house has been shot. You can help me get him to a hospital, or you and your girlfriend can get hit with a murder charge."

The mention of Clem made my stomach clutch. He edged toward me. His voice was taunting. "She's down there, Bill. She needs you. Go to her."

I got to a kneeling position, the gun still on him, and said, "I won't tell you again."

He kept coming. "Stupid shit. You don't have the guts."

I swung the barrel a couple of feet to the side and squeezed the trigger. Nothing happened. Clem had relocked the safety during the chase. Cole's arm shot out with remarkable speed and grabbed the back of my neck. Too late I remembered his wrestling skill. He pushed me to the ground and fell on me with another bone-crunching body slam that knocked the gun from my hand. I spun onto my back as he tried to hook an arm around my upper thigh, then drove my neck up, smashing my forehead into Cole's nose. He yelled in agony, his hands instinctively clasping at the broken cartilage. I punched his soft midsection and rolled him off of me. He got to his knees. I dove for the Beretta. He fell on me, grabbing the bottom of my jacket, dragging me away from the gun with surprising power. I swung my fist in a wild backhand strike, giving only a glancing blow to his shoulder. He was on his feet and soon would be in a position to throw his full weight on top of me again. I pressed my palms to the ground and kicked backward like a horse, hitting him in the knees. He lost his grip on my coat. I scrambled ahead, groping for the dark gun in the leaves. I knew, as I found it, that he was charging me again. I threw myself to the side. He managed to hit my left arm, but for the most part went past me, faltering to the ground again.

I stood up and turned to face him, my thumb feeling for the safety.

Cole was back on his feet and about to charge when he saw the gun. "You stupid fuck!" he roared, blood dripping from his nose. "Listen to me!"

"The safety's off this time, Cole."

He advanced step by step. "You worm."

I backed up, both hands on the gun. My stomach churned, as much from the sick feeling that Clem was badly injured as anything else. I needed to get Cole out of the way so I could get to her. The trigger was a cold, hard sickle under my finger. I'd never shot a man before.

"Stop. Now," I ordered.

"Shit-eating coward."

He rushed me. I flashed on the image of him swinging Clem by the hair. The report shattered in my ears. Cole hit the ground hard, face first. He rolled, roaring in pain, clutching at his right thigh. That's what I'd aimed for, and I'd hit it. Not dead on, maybe, but enough to put him down, writhing and cursing me for all he was worth. The words, with all their sexual and excretory connotations, sounded ludicrous. I moved in front of him, keeping six or seven feet between us.

"Finished?" I said.

"Get me the fuck to a hospital!"

I hollered Clem's name into the ravine. A faint "Okay" came back. At least I hoped it was an "Okay."

"I'll get you to a hospital," I said to Cole. "Tell me exactly what you did, who you hired, and why."

He snarled at me again for a while. I decided to make sure he didn't still have a weapon somewhere.

"Empty your pockets," I said. "Jacket, then pants."

"I'm bleeding to death, imbecile!"

I fired into the ground a few inches from his foot. He barked in fright, then fumbled the items from his pockets, cursing the whole time, throwing them at random in my direction. His billfold came out, cell phone, handkerchief, cigar case, lighter, and a small tin. I picked up the tin.

"You will suffer for this, Bill. Long and hard. I found the microphone you planted yesterday."

"So you know you're on record." I held up the tin. "What's this?"

"Shut up! Get me help!"

I held it close, squinting at the label. "*Skruf.* It's a brand of Swedish chewing tobacco. S-n-u-s, they call it. How do you pronounce that word, Uncle?" He glared at me, snorting like a bull. "Is it like 'snooze'? Or maybe 'snuhss'?"

"Stop babbling!"

"I think it's pronounced 'snoose.' That's the code name you used for Ulla. Makes sense, her being Swedish."

He shook his head as if I was crazy.

"Your men used the name in the park, when they came after us. So the first thing I want is their names and the name of their firm. Or are they just freelance mercenaries?"

"I'm losing blood!"

"It's a bad feeling. Kind of like when you were feeding Margaret candy and her blood sugar went through the roof. Only different."

He moaned, clutching his thigh.

"Tell me about Margaret."

"Sabell killed her. Accidentally. You told me that yourself."

"Yes. Then I said Remly did it. Then GenVigil, then Janet, in order to flush you out."

He didn't respond.

"I'll leave you here to die, Cole."

"Sure you will. Murder. Even *you're* not dumb enough to do that."

I took a single bound toward him and planted the toe of my boot in the dirt just short of his right shin. He let out a howl in anticipation of the pain. "I'll follow through the next time. Like you did with Sabell."

"I've got more men," he gasped. "They'll find us."

"I've got more men, too," I said. "Maybe they've all met and they're having a party. I'll go find Clem and then come back. We've got all night."

He snickered. "She's dying, Bill. Poor little girlfriend."

The truth was, I was desperate to get to her. But I had to make Cole talk before he passed out. There was an outside chance he did have reinforcements, though the fact that he'd tried to make a stand here implied the opposite.

This time I followed through on the kick. Cole screamed. "What doesn't kill you makes me stronger," I said. "Isn't that one of your favorite sayings? I'll do it again."

His breath came in small choked bursts. He said, "The death was an accident."

"Bullshit. You knew all about her diabetes. You knew what to tell the phony gardener to get: her medallions and her blanket. You had the blame all arranged. The warning note. The men in black stocking masks. All part of the plan to pin her abduction on some sinister foreign force."

"The gardener will tell you. He was working for the triads."

"How would you know that, Cole? Because you *told* him he was working for the triads when you hired him. The blowgun dart was the wrong detail. If you really wanted to go the triad route, you should have cut off her ear. You were being humane, I suppose."

"It *was* humane! She was only half a human being! It was merciful!"

"I see. A mercy killing of your own granddaughter. As the paterfamilias, it's up to you to decide the executive outcome, isn't it?"

"Someone has to!" he bellowed. His rage was pushing aside his pain now. "Christopher was incapable. You're incapable. None of you, none of your generation knows how to take the reins!"

"But you do. So Chris wasn't in on it, after all." It dawned on me, now, why Cole had put such unreal pressure on Chris about Jakarta. It was so that he'd have no time to keep track of Margaret. Cole had spent at least a month setting up his son.

"Fine," I went on. "You acted alone. Why, Cole? Let's grant your premise that she'd have lived only a few years longer. That she put burdens on Chris and Janet, she was bankrupting them. They still loved her. What gave you the right?"

"Someone had to settle it!" he roared. "Chris was throwing away his life, his fortune! That woman was poisoning our family! It was a dead end!"

"Right. End of the Claypool line. Male line, that is, the only one you care about. You calculated right: Margaret's death drove Chris and Janet apart once and for all. Then you could get him back on the right track. Breeding the way you wanted him to. Grooming the line of succession. Only then would he be qualified to assume your mantle."

"You self-absorbed punk! You know nothing of what it takes to build a family, an empire. To leave your mark on the world. You self-righteously seal yourself away in your smug world. You'll die alone, William. Alone and penniless and broken. Because you don't know how to build. Only tear down."

"I haven't killed anyone. Yet."

"You ass. It was simple euthanasia. I took responsibility for what Chris should have done himself, but was too cowardly to do. I made the hard decisions, like I've made them all my life. And I've built something. Chris thinks he can waltz in and inherit it. All of you children are like that, with your sense of entitlement. What I did is nothing compared to the way he and Janet screwed around with the natural order of things."

"But you joined in. When you thought Sabell could give you the heir you wanted, you funded the screwing around full-throttle. You've probably been looking for a way to get back at Sabell ever since Margaret came out a girl."

"The man creates monsters."

"I see. You were doing a good deed, slaying the monster. But I wonder, if Sabell had engineered the boy you wanted—would you have helped Chris out with the medical bills? CCE has plenty of resources. Yet you wouldn't help with Margaret."

"You don't throw good money after bad. Any idiot knows that."

I looked at him in the darkness. My eyes had adjusted enough to make out his features, but they remained like a mask, pitiless, impenetrable. "I understand it now," I said. "I didn't believe it at first. Didn't believe you'd kill your own blood. But you did. You felt you had the right to terminate Margaret because you paid for her. You funded her creation."

His head lay back. He stared at the sky. "I'm going," he said.

"That's dramatic," I said. I *hoped* it was just theater. I wanted to make sure he lived to stand trial. It did seem likely that, at the very least, he would pass out soon. I wanted one more thing.

"Before you go," I said, "tell me who these thugs are that you hired."

His head lolled toward me. His lips stretched into something like a smile. "Anything I say is useless. You shot me. You tortured me. I only said what you wanted me to say."

"Of course you did. So now, one more item. Their names."

"Go to hell," he said wearily.

I was tempted to leave it there. But then I remembered the park. The blackberry bushes. Clem, somewhere in the bottom of the ravine. I took a big step in Cole's direction with my left foot, my right toe swinging for his bleeding thigh. I pulled up just short, kicking his elbow instead.

Cole's howling went on for a minute, then dwindled to a whimper. "Pieter Maritz," he said faintly, breathing hard. "Eeben Maritz. The firm . . . Lionheart Task Force."

"That's nice. Another father-son team. So the 'task force' did the dirty work while you stayed safely in your office. The kidnapping, then later smashing my windows, planting the dart, ambushing us in the park. Ulla was the one person who'd had direct contact with their men and you succeeded in scaring her out of the country. You thought I'd get scared off, too. Once you realized the foreign-gangster story wasn't going to work, you got busy trying to set up Sabell and Remly for the murder. You probably got the idea from me in the first place. You let me run with it. You counted on me getting the dirt on what Sabell did with Margaret. When that came out, suspicion would focus on Sabell. The uproar about how Margaret was born would drown out the investigation into how she died. I fell right into your plan. You kept the hired guns after me to make me think I was on the right track."

"There were so many times I could have had you killed, Bill," Cole said, his voice hoarse with regret. "So *many* times." The thought seemed to give him some comfort. But for that one small tactical error, his plan would have succeeded.

"Those family ties, they'll get you every time. It's too bad you didn't think of trying to pin it on Janet sooner. Because there was one thing that never made sense to me about how Margaret died. The candy. She was only three and a half, but she knew not to swallow the buttons in her button collection. She also knew to stay away from sugar. Only someone she trusted would have been able to talk her into eating as much candy as she did. That was the one time you had to get your own hands dirty. Grandpa came and told her it was all right to eat all the candy she wanted. Meanwhile, the Lionheart crew kept her out in the sun, without water, dehydrating her. But she wouldn't die. They dosed her with Ketamine and *still* she wouldn't die. That must have surprised you, a sick little girl holding on like that. Finally you gave in and snuffed out her last breath. The coroner went straight for the diabetes explanation, as you planned. But Sabell didn't."

Cole rallied himself enough to say, "It was diabetes. She died in a coma. You can't prove this fantasy of yours."

"The Lionheart Task Force will."

"They're good men. Loyal. They don't turn on their family."

"You thought the same about Leonard Wilson. You overestimate people's loyalty to you, Cole. When you're busy using them for your own ends—that street runs two ways."

"Leonard?" he said. Defeat was showing, at last, in his eyes.

"I'm going to find Clem now. Then I'll get help for you. Hang on a little while longer."

His courage returned. He raised his head an inch or two, so that the moon caught the glint of contempt in his eyes.

"You're dead," he whispered savagely.

I clicked the safety back on, tucked the gun in my pants, and looked down at my uncle a final time.

"I've never shot anyone before," I said to him. "It's not my style, and I can't say I enjoyed it. But I'm honored to have you be the first. It's the family way."

Somewhere in my heart, I knew it would take a lot more to kill Clem than a single shove from Cole. But the heart has its fears, and mine was pounding as I skidded down the slope of the ravine to find her, a metallic taste on my tongue. I slid on my butt, stopping every ten feet to call her name.

"Is that you, Bill?"

She was curled, about fifty yards down, at the base of a tree. Nothing could have made me happier than the sight of her bombardier jacket, except for the sight of her moving inside it. Her voice was soft. She seemed to be singing to herself.

I rushed to her, resisting the urge to grab her, cradle her. "Can you move all your limbs?"

"Everything checks out, Mr. Damen," she murmured, still a little dazed. "I couldn't hear all the words up there, but I got the gist. You done good."

I moved closer. Some blood was on her face. "Are you sure you're all right?"

"Watch it!" she barked, swiping at my hand. "It's just a few scratches."

I couldn't resist any more. I turned and gathered her up in my arms, her upper body across mine, her head on my chest. Her arms circled my back and clasped.

"Took you long enough," she said as we separated. We looked at each other. It was, if anything, darker down here than up on the road. Yet I could see her deep green eyes so clearly. We squeezed each other again. Above us, a bullhorn blared. Ray Wilson and his men had arrived.

» » » » »

Everyone but Margaret survived. Eeben Maritz, the young Afrikaner, landed in the ICU but was expected to recover. Had it not been for his son's condition, Maritz's father, Pieter, might have fled the country. But he stayed, and the members of the Lionheart Task Force who'd worked for Cole were taken into custody. Cole himself was confined to the ICU for a few days, during which time DA Mike Gallegos prepared the indictment for Margaret's murder. An indictment for the assault on George Sabell was presumed to be coming as well, if the Maritz pair cut a deal. Sabell was in a coma.

Don Masterson had a set of lesser charges to deal with. He left me pleading voicemail and email messages saying that it had been nothing personal, just business; I understood, right?

Right, Don.

Janet and Steve had fled to a resort in Baja after I'd barged in on them. She planned, after her return, to stay around just long enough to file divorce papers and give the police and DA what they needed from her. Then she would move to Oregon. Steve was trying to convince her to let him come along.

Clem escaped with a twisted ankle, a twisted knee, some bruises, and a lacework of scratches on her face. They would heal over time. I made her stay home and take it easy in the week that followed Cole's arrest.

She lasted until Wednesday morning, when I arrived in the office to find her in her squeaky chair, a tall cup of coffee in hand. She was going stir-crazy at home. If I didn't let her participate in the tasks of collation and documentation now ahead of us, she would sit and watch me do them, her chair creaking and chirping the whole time.

It was somber work, preparing the materials we would turn over to the authorities, then going down to make detailed statements for the police, DA, and coroner. We contacted Krempe and Waldman, the scientists whose names had appeared in Sabell's notebook. Neither knew precisely what Sabell was up to; they'd come into the lab to perform their step in the process and no more. Only Sabell had the whole picture of Margaret's genesis.

What we learned from the two scientists allowed us to put together that picture. Sabell had taken Helen's embryo sisters, the ones created at the same time she was, but frozen rather than implanted. He screened them for the cystic fibrosis mutation, culturing only the heterozygous embryos—which carried one copy of the mutation instead of two. From these embryos, with Krempe's help, he derived ESCs, embryonic stem cells.

ESCs grew well on plates and were amenable to genetic engineering. Since Chris had insisted on wiping out the mutation completely, Sabell still had to knock out the remaining copy in the ESCs through gene targeting. It was Waldman's turn now to come into the lab. He built a DNA construct carrying a healthy copy of the gene. Using recombinant DNA techniques, Sabell and Waldman replaced the remaining mutation with the healthy allele. While they were at it, they also inserted a sequence thought to be associated with perfect pitch. Sabell, using antibiotic-resistance genes as markers, selected and plated out a colony of modified ESCs that carried the perfect-pitch gene and no cystic fibrosis mutation.

Meanwhile, Sabell had cut Helen's ovary tissue into slices two hundred microns thick, the size needed to keep the immature follicles intact. His big breakthrough was to develop a process by which those follicles could be nurtured to produce full-fledged metaphase II eggs. He took a large number of the eggs he'd matured and enucleated each one—removed the nucleus, which contained Helen's unmodified genes. In its place, using nuclear transfer, he inserted a nucleus from a modified ES cell and stimulated the egg to start dividing. Chris's incest nightmare was true, in a sense, though not in the way he feared.

Having a large number of eggs to work with was crucial to Sabell's success. Most of the engineered eggs did not develop into embryos that could be implanted. Of those that did, many did not attach to Janet's uterus. But Sabell kept trying, Janet kept trying, and in time Margaret was born. Sabell brought Waldman back in to work on stem cell treatments for Margaret's diabetes. They were excited when, again with the help of the large number of oocytes available, they were able to culture healthy pancreatic cell lines. Waldman fled when he discovered Sabell planned to use them on a human subject with little prior testing. Stem cell therapy was still in its infancy. Sabell acknowledged he was in over his head, but he was desperate to save Margaret and, with her facing an early death, felt there was nothing to lose in trying.

Although we didn't tell Krempe and Waldman the entire story, they were appalled when they got an inkling of what Sabell had used their help to do. It was far outside the boundaries of accepted science in the field.

I didn't volunteer the whole story to Chris, either, and he didn't ask. When I went to meet with him a week after Cole's capture, I still had the image in my head of the broken man I'd seen at his house the previous Wednesday. I knew he'd returned to the company the very next day, but I was not prepared for his demeanor when I entered his office at Claypool Construction Engineering.

"Bill Damen," he said briskly, as if greeting a client. He stayed behind his desk, rising to give my hand a quick shake. "How the hell are you?"

"Not bad," I said. "How are *you?*"

"Never been better." His manner was all surface, professional, brisk. I felt as if I'd stepped into some kind of time warp in which Margaret was still alive and Chris was on his anointed path.

"Have you seen your father?" I asked.

"Nope," he said, flashing a quick, triumphant smile. He wore a three-button jacket, all three buttoned, over a stiff-collared blue shirt. His tie was knotted with authority, its blue and gold stripes diving neatly under the high lapels. I'd thought knowledge of what his father had done might destroy him. Instead, it seemed to have revitalized him.

"Talked to him?"

"Nope." There was a certain set to his jaw, a sort of impervious contentment. His emotions had been cauterized.

"But you know what he did?" I had to make sure. A shade of a nod said, yes, Chris knew. "Any thoughts?" I added.

He folded his hands and spoke as if addressing his board of directors. "The company will need a new president and CEO. I'm the natural choice. I expect to be installed in the next two to three weeks. Only the legal details remain."

"Congratulations." I felt numb, too, now. It was catching.

"Thanks for the good work."

I nodded, wondering if there was anything at all Chris was willing to talk to me about, or if he'd walled himself off entirely. "They say Sabell's starting to come out of his coma."

A cold look came into Chris's eyes as he said, "Sabell got just what he deserved." If Chris had been impervious before, now he seemed positively frozen. It appeared that Sabell, not his father, had become the primary object of his loathing.

"He may end up a vegetable," I said.

"We don't need to argue about it," Chris said, brushing his hands together, cleansing himself of the whole thing. "Did you hear—we won the Jakarta contract?"

"I hadn't heard. Congratulations." I didn't mention the Pyrrhic nature of the victory: His rival's sights had been on bigger fish all along. "Leonard Wilson must have done a good job."

Chris cocked his head. "I suppose he did. He deserves a reward. I'm putting him in charge while I'm out of town."

"Going to Jakarta?"

"No." A salacious smirk came to his lips as he said, "I'm taking a vacation. My lawyer, Mitch Walchuk"—he said it as if I'd never met the guy—"will handle the legal aspects of the transition while I'm getting some well-earned rest."

"Going alone?"

Again the smirk. "Kiersty's coming with me. Maybe 'rest' isn't the right word. It's just for fun, Bill—I'm not going to marry her. So don't worry. You two won't be related."

I forced a smile. "It's good of you to put Wilson in charge while you're gone," I said.

Chris bared a wolfish grin. "I'll fire his ass when I come back."

"Good luck, Chris," I said, rising to leave. I'd been a fool to think that Chris and I could recapture the bond we'd had in our youth, or that I'd been anything more than a bit player in his drama with Cole.

"Bill," he said sharply as I was leaving. "You forgot something."

I turned.

"Your invoice," he said. "With expenses."

"Of course. I'll mail it to you."

"Good seeing you, Bill," he said with forced heartiness. "Keep in touch."

I walked down the carpeted corridor to the elevator with a peculiar feeling of déjà vu. Chris's office was on the same floor as Cole's; I had the uncanny sensation of having just been to see the elder Claypool. Clem's words came back to me, what she'd said about clones and the uncanny nature of the doppelgänger. Chris swung between the poles of believing he was king of the universe and believing he was nothing. The two extremes were like shadow-twins. It dawned on me now that the same was true of father and son. Chris and Cole were each other's doppelgänger. A double, a dark twin. A clone, in a sense, or closer to it than Helen and Margaret ever had been.

» » » » »

By the end of the second week after Cole's capture, the landscape of the criminal indictments had taken shape. Don took a plea that would keep him out of my hair for a while. The Lionheart men came around, too, and cut their deals with Mike Gallegos. Austin Remly shut down Sabell's lab, pending further investigation. He told me that he'd been the one who faxed the warning to me at Sabell's house. He'd overheard Cole on his cell phone at the symposium, and had seen him leave with Eeben Maritz in a hurry.

Only Cole, the bull, the Minotaur, remained accused of first-degree murder. He recovered from his gunshot wound with remarkable alacrity. He limped around on a cane but had plenty of fight in him. He posted his million-dollar bail, took a formal leave of absence from the company, and mobilized his defenses. His strategy was to portray Margaret's death as a kind of accidental euthanasia and pin the ultimate blame on George Sabell. It seemed absurd, Mike Gallegos told me, but with the lawyers Cole could buy, nothing was guaranteed.

Gallegos had trouble putting in the last piece of the puzzle, the indictment for the brutal attack on George Sabell. Cole tried to pin it on me and Clem at first. He swore that he and Eeben had been at the symposium at the time of the attack, and a number of witnesses confirmed it. He only came to Sabell's, he claimed, because the doctor didn't show up at the symposium and he was worried that someone—Remly or I—had harmed him. Then, when the Lionheart crew flipped on Cole, he reversed himself and laid the attack on Eeben. Eeben, he said, had taken things into his own hands and sent another Lionheart man up to get information from Sabell. The theory made some sense, except for the fact that Eeben would not cop to it. Given that Gallegos had offered to fold in the Sabell attack as part of the deal on the murder charge, Eeben's obstinacy was hard to explain. So was an enigmatic phrase Cole had used, something about him bestowing a parting gift on Chris—in spite of his son's refusal to have contact with him—in addition to the "gift" of having freed him of Margaret. Sabell himself, when he was able to speak again, weakly, claimed to remember nothing of the attack or the day before it.

After Clem and I had wrapped up all the loose ends we could, we went down to the Ramp for a drink. Not exactly a celebration, given the morbid nature of the case, but an acknowledgment of the quiet closeness that had grown between us, a silent appreciation of the fact that we were still alive. A check from Chris had arrived by express mail the day before. I added a large bonus to the amount on the invoice Clem had presented me. We ordered some very good bourbon and toasted the fact that Damen C & I now had a decent pool of operating capital. When we ordered our second bourbon, Clem proposed a toast to her upcoming vacation. I was all for it, I said. She hinted that it might be quite long.

"That's all right," I said. "Your noisy chair will be waiting for you."

She looked down. "I've got some unfinished business to take care of."

That phrase induced a small gnawing in the pit of my stomach.

"This isn't good-bye," she said. "Trust me."

"Don't I always?" I said.

"No," she said flatly, then lit up with a smile. "But if you get a new case, call me right away."

When we parted that evening, it was with a kiss full on the lips. A break, I decided, was a good idea. Our relationship, whatever it was to become—all business, I reminded myself, all business—was still very young. In embryo, a fragile state of development where the wrong stimulus could do permanent harm. She'd proved willing to reveal certain slivers of herself when the moment was right. I'd wait for more of those moments. For the time being, I sat back and enjoyed the sense of potential.

» » » » »

I thought about Chris and his shattered family often in the weeks that followed, but I saw him only one more time in passing. Whatever business needed to be transacted between us was done by email. I attended a family event or two, at which I expected to see him. But no Chris. I wondered if he'd ever live down what he'd instigated with his daughter. The damage he'd done could never be fixed, and I was afraid that meant he'd already gone over to the "Cole side." But maybe he'd had time to think, on his vacation, time to realize that if he insisted on always being right, always unblameable, he'd never become his own person—that inevitably he would be sucked into the black hole of Cole's gravitational pull.

The last glimpse I had of him came one late afternoon at Stern Grove. I was at 19th Avenue and Sloat, shooting a short and rather silly fiction piece about a pair of adolescent sisters secretly living in the park, returning to the "wild." We were setting up a shot in which they decided to visit a mall down the road. I stood very close to the corner, pulling focus on the woods below, from which the sisters, their hair bestially tangled, would emerge.

The wind was blowing in off the ocean. The eucalyptus branches rubbed against one another in an eerie scratching sound, like an animal at the door. Some unnameable feeling made me turn at just that moment. The same moment that a metal-gray Range Rover careened, directly in front of me, around the corner, making a right turn. I had only a glimpse, but behind the wheel I was quite sure that I saw Chris's short blond hair and erect head, projecting forward like a Renaissance profile portrait, eyes hidden behind sunglasses, concentrating on the road as the Rover's engine roared with acceleration.

It was what I saw in the passenger seat that made the hair on the back of my neck stand up. It went by in a flash, so fast that I didn't register it immediately. But the after-image burned into my retina: the shaggy jet-black fur, the finely shaped muzzle, the mouth slightly open to expose blood-pink jaws. Most of all, the preternaturally intelligent gleam of the near-human eyes, striking into me like a tiny thread of lightning, a demonic spark playing midwife to yet more of what had come before.

Public Library of New London
New London, CT 06320
A2130 170684 6